KEEPERS OF THE HIDDEN WAYS

BOOK ONE

THE FIRE DUKE

KEEPERS OF THE HIDDEN WAYS

BOOK ONE

THE FIRE DUKE

JOEL ROSENBERG

An AvoNova Book

William Morrow and Company, Inc.
New York

KEEPERS OF THE HIDDEN WAYS, BOOK ONE: THE FIRE DUKE is an original publication of Avon Books. This work has never before appeared in book form. This work is a novel. Any similarity to actual persons or events is purely coincidental.

AVON BOOKS
A division of
The Hearst Corporation
1350 Avenue of the Americas
New York, New York 10019

Published by arrangement with the author
Library of Congress Catalog Card Number: 94-42586
ISBN: 0-688-14153-6

Printed in the U.S.A.

This one is for Dale

Acknowledgments

I'm grateful to the Usual Suspects—Peg Kerr Ihinger, Bruce Bethke, and Pat Wrede—for helping to point the way; to Harry Leonard, Victor Raymond, David Dyer-Bennet, Sharon Rosenberg, Dale Rosenberg, and Elise Matthesen for additional advice and encouragement en route; to Eleanor Wood, for making the trip pay for itself; and to Chris Miller, John Douglas, and Bob Mecoy for faith, patience, and enthusiasm at the beginning and through to the end. I'm also thankful for the copyediting of Carol Kennedy and the proofreading of Beth Friedman. Special thanks to Jerry Pournelle for giving me the key to Arnie Selmo, and for his consultation on the philosophy and practice of épée and foil fencing.

Much right is thanks to all of them; any mistakes belong entirely to me.

I'm particularly grateful to the people who lived in Northwood, North Dakota, in the late fifties and early sixties—every last one of them.

As always, I'm grateful to my wife, Felicia Herman, and my daughters, Judy and Rachel, for things that have both much and little to do with the work at hand.

PROLOGUE

In the House of Flame

Flame Melts Ice,
Wind Snuffs Flame,
Stone Blocks Wind,
Ice Cracks Stone,

(repeat four times, then:)

Sky Rules All,
Sky Rules All,
Sky Rules All,
Sky Rules All.

—Middle Dominion children's song,
sung in time to the bouncing of a ball

"Stasis," the Fire Duke said, pronouncing the word like a curse. "I have had my fill of stasis, and then some."

"Almost as much as you've had your fill of His Solidity, perhaps?" Rodic del Renald inclined his head. It wouldn't have been politic to observe that having his fill and then more was clearly a habit of the fat duke. A smattering of presumption went well with Rodic's profession and position, but only a smattering.

Besides, to be fair, the Fire Duke, Lord of Falias, wore his fat well. Maneuvering his vast bulk with a grace that still surprised the son of Renald, even after all the years of occasional service to His Warmth, the fat man rose to his feet and walked to the broad expanse of window, his hands clasped at his waist, as though he could hold any problem to him and crush *it.*

Which is perhaps true for any problem His Warmth can wrap his hands about, Rodic del Renald thought. Not that it would do any good here and now. Back before he had become duke, back when the future His Warmth was merely Anegir del Denegir, back when he was only the second son of the late His Warmth, he had been thought rather straightforward, for someone of his lineage.

That had changed, but perhaps not as much as His Warmth would have wished. There's only so much about yourself you can change.

"Not just the Stone Duke," the Fire Duke said, "but the Wind and the Ice, as well. And if the truth be known—"

As it is, in the long run, Rodic thought.

"—I'm less than fond of the Sky," he murmured. He smiled thinly, as though daring Rodic to acknowledge the treason.

"Then, my Duke," Rodic said, "by all means, complain endlessly about it. Tell me more, please, about how neither you nor any other of the Houses dare move too openly, too boldly against each other, for fear of bringing the wrath of the remaining ones down against the aggressor."

As though that was the only worry. Off to the east of the Dominion, Vandescard lay, perhaps waiting, perhaps not. One could never tell about humans who styled themselves the proper descendants of the Vanir. And one could never tell about the Old Ones in the North, or the younger, more vigorous cultures in the South.

We live, huddled among the bones of giants, Rodic decided, *like a bunch of aging men, waiting to become old enough to lay down their tools and die gracefully.*

And, yet, compared to the youngest of the Old Ones, the Dominion was still young and fresh.

There had once been more than a dozen Houses, and not merely the five remaining, inhabiting the ancient keeps of Falias, Gorias, Finias, and Murias, and the one so old it was known only as the Old Keep. One House had become powerful enough to take the Old Keep, and the title of the House of the Sky; only four others survived.

The rest were long gone, conquered and subsumed like the House of Trees, shattered and destroyed like the House Without A Name.

"Even the Sky," the Fire Duke said.

"If the Sky bothers you so badly, summon your son and heir back, and let him lead your soldiers against it."

As though that could happen. Venidir del Anegir and his Lady Mother were more or less a permanent fixture in the Old Keep, which apparently suited both of them and the Fire Duke well. Back when his elder brother died, even before he succeeded his father, His Warmth had seemed to have little use for his wife and his heir, and had long had them live as his emissaries to the Sky, returning to Falias but rarely.

It might bode well for the House of Flame to have its next duke so well connected with the Sky, or it might not; it was possible that too close a connection could trigger a revolt by the other three houses, fearful that they would be shattered or subsumed, too.

"You speak perhaps a trifle boldly," the Fire Duke said.

"I speak, perhaps, a trifle truthfully." Wondering if he had gone too far, Rodic sipped at a cold spun-glass flute of icy Prime Ingarian autumn wine. The berries, grown high on the surprisingly cool slopes of Flame Ingaria, were picked, shriveled, just before the first frost, and only the first pressing went into the Prime. After fifty years in a hidden wine cellar that could have been next to the duke's quarters or leagues of corridors away, the wine was sweet as wildflower honey, but with a rich berry taste that lingered on the tongue.

When the fat duke started fighting for control of his expression, Rodic knew that he had won, he had survived, yet again. The Art was not only his way of life, it was the key to life: someone as devious as the Fire Duke would not deal so straightforwardly with Rodic as to have him killed. No matter that, practically, it would be a matter of great simplicity for the duke to have Rodic killed here and now.

While there were undoubtedly abditories and adits and passages in the keep that the Duke of the House of Flame didn't know—the keeps had been built for the Old Ones, after all, and they hardly left behind a map!—His Warmth would hardly have picked as his private office a room without several secret entries under his control. Quite likely, a brace of soldiers hid behind the tapestry or perhaps in the ceiling, waiting and listening until a raised voice called for them. But probably only one such hiding place was available to His Warmth's servants. Knowledge of the Hidden Ways wasn't merely a convenience to the rulers of the Houses; at times it was a matter of life and death.

Politically, it would be the simplest thing in the world for the Flamebearer to order Rodic's death. After all, Rodic's use-name was his fullname: Rodic was only a second-generation noble. His two brothers were long dead in duels, and his sister married off to a Caprician knight minor.

There was no one to carry out a vendetta against nobility of any House, and certainly not against the Fire Duke.

But Rodic's father had long ago taught him that the Old Families respected impertinence at a level that cut below conscious thought, and that the only way to keep from having to constantly grovel before them was to refuse to, to constantly show an acceptable trace of disdain—but only an acceptable one.

Rodic didn't want to die the way his father had, not now. Another fifteen years, perhaps, and young Rodic del Rodic—with, by the Dominion, a true use-name!—would be established, perhaps even accepted as a cadet into the House of Flame. Or of Ice, if it came to that.

But *he* would not spend his life in what the true houses mockingly called the House of Steel, doing the dirty work of the nobility. That was for Rodic del Renald.

"You sent for me to complain about stasis, Your Warmth?" Rodic asked, then took another sip.

"No," the Fire Duke said, "I sent for you for two reasons. There's a small dispute with the Stone—I'd like you to represent me in it."

"A matter of honor?"

"No," the duke said. "Territory. A smallish part of a smallish holding. We have the records to prove it ours."

"I am, of course, honored." Rodic bowed his head. Not particularly. Money matters were of no interest to him; that's what he had a wife for, after all. "I'll have to examine the documents before I commit myself—"

"My word is not good enough?"

"Of course it is," Rodic said. "If you wish to face the House of Stone's representative yourself, Your Warmth. If you wish to steep yourself in the rightness of your cause, and then reinforce the strength and cunning of your arm with the appropriate rituals and herbs, why, then of course your word is good enough for me, and I'll proudly stand as your second, to bind up your wounds, if received, and help carry you from the field, dead or alive, should you fall."

He raised a finger. "But since I happen to know that Stanar del Brunden is representing the Stone Duke, and since I've received more cuts from his blade than I can count, I'll see your proof before I commit myself and my too, too tender flesh to your cause."

Perhaps he had gone too far. The Fire Duke's nostrils flared. "Have it as you will, this time. But don't think yourself essential, Rodic-of-the-second-generation. It's possible you could be replaced."

Rodic had to smile. There were few blades as good as he, and most of those were heavily tied to the Sky, not available to the lesser houses. "With whom would you replace me, Your Warmth? Thorian del Thorian, perhaps?"

It was intended as a jape, only. But the Fire Duke's face was too still, too emotionless, too suddenly. "That would hardly be possible, would it?" he said, the question clearly intended to sound rhetorical only. "There may come a time," the Fire Duke said, then stopped himself. "There will come a time, I hope, when I shall find you expendable, when I will represent my house myself."

No. The attempt to cover himself would not work. The Fire Duke knew something, and he had let it slip. But old nobility always tended to assume they were wiser than the new, and for once Rodic didn't resent it.

Thorian, he thought, as an attendant in fiery livery let him out of His Warmth's office, and down the unreasonably high-ceilinged corridor.

Thorian the Traitor.

Was it possible that Thorian was alive? And if so, where could he possibly be? Certainly not within the Dominion.

The duelmaster would have to be told.

Part One

HARDWOOD, NORTH DAKOTA

CHAPTER ONE

The Fencing Team

Torrie had long since shut off the tape player by the time they turned off I-29 at Thompson; there was only so much Van Halen he could stand. The floor of the car was littered—with McDonald's burger wrappers, still sticky and greasy in places; with empty Coke cans, drained and crumpled; and even with the Baggies that had contained the crudités that Maggie had insisted on buying at the SuperValu outside Minneapolis.

Being a veggie didn't make her a neat freak, Torrie Thorsen had decided. Or maybe it was just that Ian's bad habits were rubbing off on the two of them. Ian Silverstein wasn't really unclean, just messy; Ian would never hang up a damp towel on a rack or over a sink if a chair or a floor was handy.

"Hmmm . . . there's a gas station—hell, it's a real service station—in Hatton," Torrie said, winding down the window of the old Rambler so that he could hang his left elbow out. "We could stop off there and clean up a bit. Dump the trash out of the car, at least."

Maryanne Christensen partly hid a smile behind her hand, but Ian chuckled out loud.

"Mommie doesn't like a messy car?" Ian gave out a few more chortles.

"Give me a break," Torrie said, not that he really expected Ian to stop.

He was pleased to be wrong. "Peace," Ian said. "No offense intended."

Torrie looked into the rearview mirror, to see Ian holding up a hand. "But I tell you," Ian said, "you're all the same way. You, too, Maggie. You live your own life at school, but the moment you point your car—"

"I don't have a car," Maggie said.

"—the moment you point your *nose* homeward, you turn into Buck and Martha's baby girl—"

"My parents are Albert and Rachel."

"—Albert and Rachel's baby girl again. You stand up straight, you make a special effort to wash around the neck . . ." Ian scratched at where his sketchy beard met his collar. "Hell, I bet you even make your bed."

Maggie arched an eyebrow. "You don't?"

No, he didn't. The times that Maggie stayed over in Torrie's room, and Ian was kicked out to sleep on the St. Rock brothers' floor, Torrie had made Ian's bed. It looked nicer and somehow a bit less calculated that way.

Ian shrugged. "Well, to tell the truth, no—the way I figure it, if I'm going to be back in bed in sixteen hours, what's the point?"

"Well?"

"What is the point, Maryanne?"

"None," she said coldly, frowning. For some reason, Maggie hated her real name, and didn't like any of the reasonable shortened versions of it. Whenever Ian was irritated with her, he would seem to forget that. Which would only anger her.

None of that bothered Torrie, particularly. Things between him and Maggie were tentative these days; he didn't need Ian interfering. Not that Ian would interfere deliberately, probably. A steady girlfriend would be too much of a distraction from work and school, and while Torrie doubted that Ian really cared about school a whole lot, he went at it with even more energy and drive than he spent on the fencing strips.

Ian finally got around to apologizing. "Sorry, I meant to say, 'What's the point, *Maggie?*'—that better?"

"Sure." The frown melted into a real smile. "I still meant to say none. No point at all. None beyond, oh, a smidgen of neatness, a desire to make things look nice. So I still make my bed."

Giving a scornful toss of her head that flicked her short coal black hair from side to side, she folded her arms across her beige pullover sweater and leaned back against the pillow she had propped up against the door. She was into her short cycle these days, and would likely stay that way until the summer—Maggie didn't mind tying her hair back in a ponytail when fencing, but said she despised wearing a headband.

Torrie couldn't decide whether he liked her better in short hair or long. He had always preferred long hair, but something about Maggie's present almost boyish cut set off her button nose and stubborn chin particularly well.

Not that it would matter what Torrie wanted. Maggie might deign to share a bed every now and then, but she was hardly about to ask his permission before cutting her hair or picking out her clothes.

Which was really okay with Torrie. He wouldn't have thought the combination of an oversized beige chain-knit sweater and black tights to be sexy, but somehow or other it was. Tights? No, he had called them tights, but that was wrong. *Leggings*, Maggie had said. Leggings or stretch-pants or just pants, not tights. That was the trouble with women's clothes—funny names. A shirt was either a top or a blouse, but never a shirt. Tights were leggings. Ignorance was strength, maybe.

"What are you smiling about?" Maggie asked.

"Oh, nothing," Torrie said.

Maybe it was that the *leggings* showed off her legs well while the sweater announced that it concealed the rest of her. Or just maybe, Torrie thought, it was that it had been a full three weeks since he and Maggie had celebrated his Class A Épée win with a couple of icy bottles of Columbia Crest chardonnay—nobody said good wine couldn't be $6.95 a bottle—a quart of fresh strawberries, and a surprising quartet of condoms. It was getting pretty damn irritating, and Torrie was finding himself snapping at people without having any cause.

"Ian," Torrie said, "maybe you ought to think about taking up bed making."

"There a lot of money in it?"

"No, but maybe it'll hide the fact that you think sheets need to be changed every other semester or so."

"Well, there is that. Itches if you don't." Theatrically, Ian scratched at his crotch. "But I do make the time to change my underwear almost weekly, honest. And, hey, don't you think you're driving a bit fast?"

"If I *thought* I was driving too fast," Torrie said, "I'd slow down."

It was Maggie's turn to chuckle. After a moment, Ian joined in.

Torrie relaxed. He liked Ian—Ian Silverstein was quick with a joke or a smile, and his intensity at his studies was a good example for Torrie, who tended to slack off the books and spend too much time in the gym—but Torrie always had a little bit of worry at the back of his head about him. Ian was just too intense sometimes. Kind of funny that somebody with that kind of drive and fire had gravitated toward the foil, the most nonviolent form of fencing, but Ian was like that.

Torrie settled himself into his seat. He had deliberately saved the last driving stint for himself. The trouble is, what's normal is what you're used to, what you grow up with. City folks didn't understand how to drive out here.

The gently rolling countryside around Minneapolis had long given way to the flat plains of the east Dakotas: the road was as straight as a chalk line, and even though it was only one lane in each direction, Torrie didn't have a problem violating the posted fifty-five speed limit by a solid thirty miles an hour. You just pointed the car straight and set your foot on the gas until the car started to complain, then backed it off a little.

Through no coincidence, stop signs out in the country were larger than in the city, and you could see the big red octagon a mile away. Crossroads were the same—there was no point in slowing when you could see for yourself that there was nothing even approaching the intersection.

Occasionally, a car would *whoosh* by, going in the other direction, and even more rarely, a huge semi would approach, and Torrie would have to fight the wheel as the vortex of its passage tried to pull them from the straight path, but the drive was easy.

Here and now it was. During a snowstorm, it would have been suicidal to do this. Then, even at a reasonable speed, it was possible to find yourself in a ditch, your car quickly being buried. It had happened a few times to Mom, and even once to Dad.

But that was winter. This was spring, and the blue sky above was filled with big, puffy clouds, and driving as fast as he could was safe, it was reasonable; the only trouble with it was—

A siren blared, then gave a triple hoot; in the rearview mirror, Torrie could see the red light flashing on top of the car behind them. Well, somehow or other he had missed it. No sense in playing games now.

"Now we're gonna get it," Ian said. "Dammit, Torrie, I told you—"

"Shh." Torrie eased up on the gas and guided the car

over toward the side of the road. Not too far; the road was edged by a ditch. "Do me a favor?"

"Yes?" Maggie leaned back. "You want me to, like, unbutton my shirt a little and talk real breathy?"

"No. For one thing, you're wearing a sweater. Make it a little hard to unbutton your shirt, no?"

"There is that."

"What I was going to ask," Torrie went on, "is for the both of you tell me that you don't have anything on you that would be a . . . problem."

Ian had already opened a Pepsi. "Just one joint," he said, balancing it on his palm. "Figured that—"

"Don't figure. Just shut up and swallow. In case you haven't noticed, this whole country is in the middle of a drug witch-hunt, and I don't care to be burned at the stake." Torrie rolled down the window. "The law says they can take the car, you know."

"So I hear," Ian said, from around a mouthful. "Cost you all of eighty bucks to replace it, I bet."

"Just *do* it."

"I'm swallowing, I'm swallowing."

"Hey, Torrie!" The cop's voice was familiar, but it took a moment for Torrie to place it; then he swung the door open and leaped out of the car.

"Your Mom never tell you not to speed?" The cop crossed his arms over his thick chest, trying to look stern, although the grin on his face ruined the effect.

The cop was only a few years older than Torrie, and the broad, Nordic face under the shock of sandy hair was only about as familiar as Torrie's own. Torrie couldn't help smiling.

"Jeff fucking Bjerke," he said, giving the name just the right Norski pronunciation, complete to the raise in pitch at the end of the last syllable. The Bjerke family had been in North Dakota since the 1870s, and only the oldest of the old still spoke anything more than a few words of Norski, but, like most in this part of the state, they kept a trace of the old accent, more as a badge of pride than anything else. "How are you?"

Jeff's face was split in a broad smile. "If I'd known it was you," he said, "I—"

"Would have let it slide?"

"Nah. I'd have shot out a tire and seen how you'd handle a skid." Jeff gave a hitch to his Sam Browne belt. "I mean, I don't really care, but eighty-seven *is* a bit much for this stretch." He walked over to the car and peered in. "You going to introduce me to your friends? Or are you too good to hang around with the hoi polloi now that you've been a college boy for a couple years?"

Torrie had to laugh. "I seem to remember that you were supposed to graduate from Northwestern not so long ago. I didn't hear about you taking over for old John Honistead."

"Times are tough, a job's a job, and John retired in February," Jeff said, extending a hand in through the window to offer it to Maggie. "Jeff Bjerke," he said. "I used to beat the shit out of your friend when he was younger, until he started playing with pointed sticks."

"He still does, and he's gotten pretty good at it." Maggie laughed. "And I'm glad to meet you. I'm Maggie Christensen."

"Ian Silverstein," Ian said from the back seat, his voice still sounding a little funny. "Pleased to meet you."

Jeff grinned as he shook hands with Ian. "Hmmm . . . next time, just hold the joint out the window, break it up in your fingers. Easier." With a quick chuckle at Ian's pale expression, he let go of Ian's hand and straightened, clapping Torrie hard on the shoulder. "You back for all of spring break, or are you flying south?"

"Every minute," Torrie said. "I tried Orlando last time."

"Great. I'll see you around. Hmmm . . . the Dine-a-mite is doing dollar drafts tonight." A raised eyebrow made it a question; the set of his mouth made it a serious one.

"Maybe," Torrie said with a look at Ian that Ian met with a shrug and then a nod, and Maggie with a frown could have meant anything between indifference and dislike for the idea.

"Have to see what the folks want to do," Torrie went on.

Jeff nodded, and gripped his hand hard enough to hurt. "Damn it, boy, but it's been awhile. Good to see you. Give my best to your mom and dad, and to Hosea." He turned and walked back to the patrol car, and by the time Torrie had started up the Rambler, Jeff had pulled into a quick U-turn and was heading in the other direction.

"Nice man," Maggie said, as the old Rambler's starter motor whined for a moment before the engine caught.

With a quick glance at the mirror, Torrie pulled off the shoulder and onto the road. He nodded. "Yeah." He smiled. "Not that the deer think so."

"Excuse me?"

"He and his dad and my dad and my Uncle Hosea go deer hunting every fall, and they've yet to come home with any extra ear tags." Which probably had more to do with Uncle Hosea than anything else, but there was no need to go into that. Patience could—and did, often—serve as well as Uncle Hosea's tracking skills. Hunting hadn't taught Torrie patience, but it had taught him to wait.

"You'd murder Bambi?" Maggie asked, a strange tone beneath the joking lilt to her voice.

City people. "I've hunted a couple of times." Every season since he was fourteen, except for last year when he had come home from school with a flu bug.

Slouching in the back seat, Ian was chuckling quietly.

"Hunting is funny?" Maggie asked, a frown flickering across her lips.

"No," Ian said, still chuckling. "It's not that. We get stopped because Torrie's speeding, and what's the penalty? *I* have to eat a joint."

Torrie grinned. "Doesn't seem right, now does it?"

"Hey, life isn't fair. *I've* never been stopped by a cop for speeding and not gotten a ticket."

In deference to Jeff, Torrie settled the speedometer at seventy, then turned his head to eye Ian in the rearview mirror. "That's 'cause you're a city boy, and this is the country. Getting along with your neighbor, well, that's a lot more important out here than it is in the city. Now, if Jeff caught me driving drunk—or stoned—he would have landed on me with both feet, and to hell with friendship. But just *speeding?* Down a county road as straight and flat and wide and open as this? Hell, even if I screw up and lose it, the car only goes into a ditch, and it's my neck.

"Nah. He's not about to get me mad at him, or my mom and dad and Uncle Hosea irritated with him, not over that."

Torrie smiled at the thought, so amused by it he almost slipped by the turnoff onto the dirt road, marked only by the old elm tree opposite, standing all alone on the edge of the field. "Besides," he went on, "drinking age in North Dakota is twenty-one—if Jeff started to get all stuck on technicalities, we couldn't split a pitcher until next spring."

Maggie grinned. "I take it we don't have to worry about getting carded if we go to this Dine-a-mite—I hate that name—tonight."

Torrie smiled. "Depends. If some stranger is in, Ole would assume he's from the State Liquor Board—then he *would* card us, visibly as possible, if we were stupid enough to order beer, which we wouldn't. Now, if Orphie Selmo's there, nursing his weekly beer, Ole wouldn't bother carding us; he'd just serve us dark beer in coke glasses and throw in a straw—old Orphie's a pain in the ass, and would turn me in given half a chance, but his eyesight is horrible and he doesn't like to wear his glasses, and he doesn't notice much."

"All part of the system."

"Like I say, in small towns, getting along is more important than technicalities."

The Rambler jounced down the road toward the break in the trees ahead.

"We could go in through town," Torrie said, "and swing back out; the house is just at the east edge. Just about as fast."

"Lemme guess," Ian said. "But this is dustier and rusticker—"

"Rusticker?" Maggie raised an eyebrow.

"—and, therefore, more fun," Ian said.

"Well, yeah."

The house lay just beyond the windbreak of trees—one of the thicker windbreaks around, easily a hundred yards deep.

There was, Torrie decided, for more than the hundredth time, nothing all that special about the way it looked: it was a Big Old House in the Great Plains tradition: two full stories plus an attic, framed on one full side and part of another two by a screened porch that kept the bugs off in the summer and that Mom would be using as an outside freezer during most of the winter. It was whitewashed, but not freshly so. Mom and Dad could afford to have the house painted as often as they'd like, but putting on airs wasn't a good idea.

Off behind the house, the old dull-red barn stood, its huge door ajar to let in the light and air of the day. Now, *that* had been freshly painted—all that showed was that the Thorsens took care of their animals, and that was no secret.

A rusty old brown Studebaker stood on blocks in the

front yard, propped higher than looked quite natural. Torrie grinned: Uncle Hosea had another new toy. For somebody who hated to ride in an automobile, the old man had quite a way with fixing them.

Not that Torrie was surprised. Uncle Hosea was Uncle Hosea the way that Dad was Dad and Mom was Mom, and the things about the three of them that others found strange were as natural to Torrie as the comforting flatness of the plains around him.

He parked the car on the grass near the side door and shut the engine off, deliberating leaving the keys in the car and his door unlocked, even though it felt funny. The last time he had come home, Mom had had too much fun making fun of his city habits.

Maggie raised an eyebrow. "We come in the servants' entrance?"

"No such thing as a servants' entrance in the country; this is just the side door, and it's closest to our rooms."

The porch outside the side door was just a concrete block, with steps leading down to the grass; there wasn't room enough on the porch to put stuff without interfering with the door.

Torrie walked to the top of the steps and swung the screen door open, locking it ajar, then turned to the knob of the wooden door, loose in its collar, but locked tight.

In true country fashion, the front door of the house was never locked—what if somebody needed to get in?—but in a family quirk, the side and back doors often were.

Of course, as Uncle Hosea would explain, there was locked, and then there was locked.

Torrie banged his fist against the brass knocking plate set into the door frame. It was welded onto a section of stiff leaf spring that Uncle Hosea had cut from a junked car, then thinned down and bolted into a recess he had carved in the door frame: it gave the knocking plate just the right give in order to hit the doorpost behind it with a *thunk* that could be heard anywhere throughout the house. Hosea had nothing against doorbells, but the knocking plate was more elegant. It was loud enough to get the attention of anybody downstairs, but not loud enough to wake somebody sleeping upstairs.

Torrie knocked again, but there still was no answer.

Torrie closed his eyes for half a moment, leaning his knee against the door to hold it tightly in place. He put his shoulder against the frame of the door, adding weight until he could feel it barely give, as though loosely nailed, then pushed on the knob as he turned it slightly to the left. It always felt the same: smooth without being oily, the feel of precisely made parts fitted together perfectly.

The bolt let go with a slight click, more felt than heard, and then the door swung open with a satisfying squeal, and Torrie could relax.

The first time he had come home from school, he had gotten it wrong, and not only had Uncle Hosea had to spend the better part of the evening resetting the hidden lockwork, but all three of the adults had made more than a few comments at his expense over the next few days.

"Trouble with the door?" Ian asked, already loading suitcases onto the porch, while Maggie had a gear bag in either hand, the hilt of one of the cheaper practice sabers sticking out where the zipper had broken.

"Nah," Torrie said. "Just sticks a little." The hidden ways into the house were a family secret, and You Just Didn't Talk About Family Secrets With Anybody—good friend, lover, it didn't matter.

He stuck his head in the door and shouted, "We're *here*," for his parents' benefit, just in case they hadn't heard his knock. It wouldn't do to walk in suddenly on them. For a couple of old people, they went at it a whole lot, and it just didn't do for their son to either notice it or have to affect to ignore it. "Come on in," he said.

He wasn't worried about surprising Uncle Hosea; Uncle

Hosea couldn't be walked in on suddenly. *He* would probably have heard the clickety-clicking of the lockwork, or certainly the squeal of the door. Hell, Torrie wouldn't have been surprised if Uncle had recognized the rumble of the Rambler a mile away. If Uncle was home, which seemed unlikely at the moment. Ditto for Dad, and possibly—

"Torreeeeee!" sounded from upstairs, followed by a thunder of footsteps running across the hall and down the stairs.

"Hi, Mom," Torrie said, letting her throw her arms around him and give him a quick kiss on the cheek. There was no stopping his mother; he might as well get it over with.

Much of the stoic Norksi had been left out of Karin Roelke Thorsen, which perhaps was just as well: Torrie liked Mom the way she was.

She was dressed in her usual work outfit of an old, embarrassingly patched pair of Levi's and a plaid man's shirt, rolled up at the sleeves—like something out of the sixties, forgodsakes. Her blonde hair was pulled back in some sort of bun that went with the severe look of her glasses, but Mom was still Mom: she had touched up the edges of her cheekbones with just a bit of ruddy color.

"Hi, honey," she said, pulling away as she turned to Maggie and Ian, moving easily, gracefully, much more like a dancer than a stock investor. One slim hand removed her reading glasses, while another reached behind her head and tugged a small mahogany comb out, shaking her long, golden hair free.

"I'm Karin Thorsen," she said, extending a hand first to Ian—who held it a fraction of a second too long before letting it go. Torrie had forgotten just how good Mom looked—for a woman of her age, of course.

He didn't quite like the way Mom and Maggie eyed each other, Mom with a smile that reeked of suspicion, Maggie with a possessive glance at how close Torrie was standing to Mom.

Uncomfortable, he shifted half a step closer to Maggie, earning both of them a pursed-lipped smile from Mom. "And Mom, this is Maggie."

Mother's smile broadened. "And how nice to have you here, Maggie," she said, just a degree short of warmly. "We've heard, well, not enough about you." She turned back to Torrie. "I wasn't expecting you until later, or I'd have finished work for the day—I thought you weren't going to be up until *late* afternoon."

"We caught a tailwind," he said. Mom still hadn't learned how to behave in front of people, and Torrie had long since given up trying to teach her that you just didn't scold a son in front of his friends. She meant well, and that was enough, usually, and when it wasn't, there was nothing to be done about it.

"Well, your Dad and Hosea are out to the Hansens' working on Sven's tractor—supposedly just until after lunch, but you know how the two of them are about Sandy's fried chicken, and they'll likely be sitting around and belching there until when you were supposed to show up." She frowned for a moment.

That didn't make any sense. Why would Mom be worried about Dad and Uncle Hosea spending time out at the Hansen farm? People had been hurt fixing tractors, sure, but not Dad—he was conservative about machinery, and never seemed to quite trust it—or Uncle Hosea.

She caught his expression. "There's been a minor . . . problem out there. It looks like a wolf got one of their calves the other night. But mainly they went out to fix the tractor."

Torrie nodded, understanding why she wouldn't want to go into it, not in front of strangers, and had covered with a quick story about fixing the tractor.

Wolves were a protected species, and while farmers were

willing to live with having them around, should one or another lone wolf decide that it would prefer to raid livestock rather than hunt for, say, wild rabbits and prairie dogs, the only choices would be to put up with increasing losses—something a farmer wouldn't like; to have the Department of Natural Resources try to livetrap and remove the wolf—which they were too damn slow about doing, when they did it at all; or to have the wolf dealt with, informally but effectively.

Which also explained what Dad and Hosea were doing out there. Dad was fond of Sandy Hansen's fried chicken—so was Torrie; his mouth watered at the thought—but he was even more fond of the time that Sven had come along during a blizzard to pull Mom's stuck car out of a ditch. Dad liked doing favors for neighbors, but the Hansens were special.

Torrie shuddered. He didn't much like wolves. They figured too prominently in some of the scarier of the old stories that Uncle Hosea told.

"It's okay, Mom, really. We'll settle in, grab a shower, I'll show Ian and Maggie around."

"Can you?" She glanced at her watch and took a step back up the stairs. "I'm putting together an options order, and I *have* to get it in on time or I'm going to have to start all over again with the morning quotes—can I be a horrible hostess and let Torrie settle you in?" she asked, turning to Maggie and Ian. "I promise we'll have plenty of time later in the day to get to know each other—I'm not the one in this family who doesn't like to make promises—but this is a workday for me, and—"

"It's *okay*, Mom, *honest.*"

"That will be very nice," Maggie said.

"No problem, Mrs. Thorsen." Ian smiled.

Mom turned and walked up the stairs slowly enough for it not to be a retreat, and Torrie deliberately didn't watch

Ian watching the tightness of her jeans. There was something vaguely obscene about it.

Her door closed behind her; Torrie started up the stairs, the other two following in his wake.

The third stair creaked, just like it always did. Step on the left side, then quickly stomp on the left side of the fourth stair, and the fourth stair would swing up to reveal another of Uncle Hosea's abditories, this one containing an old Colt Military & Police .38 revolver and a roll of Charmin toilet paper.

Both of which were silly. Mom and Dad kept fully stocked on staples—it wasn't like they were a bunch of city folk or something. Torrie had never had call for the emergency roll of toilet paper any more than he had for the .38 revolver, but when his father had declared him a man at age fifteen, Uncle Hosea had shown him where all the family weapons were, and Dad had taught him to use each one to Dad's not-particularly-easy-to-earn satisfaction.

At least, Uncle Hosea had implied he'd shown Torrie where all the family weapons were. You could never quite believe everything he said, and he never quite told you everything.

Maggie cleared her throat. "Well?"

"Er . . . sorry. I wasn't listening. You were saying?"

"I said—I mean, I asked: and she makes a living doing this? Out here? In the middle of nowhere?" She smiled. "No offense intended, honest."

"None taken. And, well, yeah."

"And what was that about she isn't the one who doesn't like to make promises?"

Torrie pursed his lips. Nothing wrong with talking about it. "It's my Uncle Hosea. He doesn't like making promises. He'll do what he says he'll try to do just about a hundred times out of a hundred, but he won't promise." He shrugged. "It's just the way he is."

Mom's fingers were clickity-clickity-clicking on the keyboard in her office, down the hall to the right; Torrie led the other two down the hall to the left, past the closed doors to Uncle Hosea's room and his own.

"Maggie, you get the Guest Room," he said, dropping her bag inside, keeping his voice low enough not to bother Mom, although that was hardly necessary. When she was concentrating on a column of figures, it would take more than conversation to distract Mom.

"Ian, you've got the Sewing Room," he said, swinging the door open at the room at the end of the hall. "Nice southern exposure." They'd always called it the Sewing Room, although it was just another guest room, a bit smaller than the official Guest Room, but otherwise just as pleasant. The walls were painted in the same off-white with just a hint of peach for warmth, and the wooden floor was stained a warm light brown and coated with that high-tech plastic gunk that Uncle Hosea liked so much.

The battered oak dresser and matching vanity had been Mom's, back when she was girl, and they were due for a stripping and refinishing, but they were still serviceable.

Ian felt at the green plaid quilt covering the bed. "Your Mom?"

Torrie shook his head. "Actually, no. My grandmother—and you should find the bed comfortable; the mattress is a Posturepedic. Bathroom's at the end of the hall, and another one's just across from my Mom's office. Plenty of towels in the hall closet; help yourself."

The rooms were well set up for visitors; during the winter, on those two or three days when the risk of imminent blizzards made it too dangerous for the schools to let the farm kids take the bus home, the Thorsen house was capable of taking on a half a dozen overnight guests without any problem. That was always fun, staying up half the night with, say, the Thompson kids and the Gisselquists, listening to Uncle Hosea's stories about the Vestri and the Aesir, little Toby Thompson asking for the hundredth time for the story of Thor's encounter with Utgarda-Loki, or Honir's Run.

"A shower would be great." Ian stretched. "After all that sleeping on the drive up, I think I need a shower and then maybe a nap."

"And then maybe some rest, and a snooze?"

Ian grinned. "Yeah, and then maybe some relaxation and a siesta. So I'll be ready to rest after supper before it's time to go to sleep."

Torrie grinned back. "Good idea." It was good to see Ian kicking back a little; he probably could use a vacation more than anybody. Ian was just too intense most of the time.

Ian raised an eyebrow. "Er . . . if I get bored, is that fencing studio in the basement open for general use?"

Torrie forced his frown into a smile. That short rest had quickly become a possible workout. "Sure. Stairs lead down from the kitchen; light switch at the top of the stairs, on your left. Help yourself."

"Bath and nap first. Gotta keep the priorities straight." He was already unbuttoning his shirt.

Torrie was grinning as he closed the door and headed down the hall and down the stairs. Trust Ian to reduce even a vacation to a balance of priorities.

Torrie brought another load up the stairs, dropping his own backpack off in front of his room before bringing Maggie's small case to the Guest Room. He set the suitcase on the floor, over by the old rolltop desk. "You should be comfortable here," he said, quietly. "One of my favorite places."

Torrie liked the Guest Room. Back when he was a kid, when his own room got too messy to live in, he would often bring a book in here and stretch out on the double bed to read—at least, until Dad caught him at it, and made him go clean his room, or, more precisely, ordered him not to come out until it was clean. Dad would lock up the

Guest Room then, never having realized that Uncle Hosea had shown Torrie the secret door behind the bureau, the one that led from Torrie's room to the back of the Guest Room's closet. Torrie would take the small bent piece of wire from the top of his dresser, poke it through the almost invisible hole that looked even on close examination like a small gap in the joining of the paneling, then swing the door and the bureau out of his way, go through, and finish his book before cleaning his room.

"It's very nice," she said, leaning back against the door. Her smile was perhaps a touch too broad. "You didn't mention that your mother looked like a Playboy Playmate," she said. "I mean, the bit with the glasses and bun? Was I supposed to think she looks plain with her hair back?"

He had to smile. "She's a stock investor."

Maggie touched the tip of her tongue against the corner of her mouth. "My Dad has a stockbroker. He's a bald little guy with a potbelly and bad digestion."

Torrie shook his head. "No, not a broker. All brokers do is buy and sell stocks for other people, and try to get them to turn their portfolios over as fast as possible, like a blackjack dealer wanting you to play a dozen hands at once." He stooped to pick up his knapsack and Maggie's suitcase. "She's an investor—Mom picks the stocks out herself, and invests her own money. Well, hers and Dad's."

"Does she make a living at this, or does your father's farm bail her out?"

Torrie tilted his head to one side. "If you want to examine the family tax records, I think she's got all of them in the file cabinet in her office." Which was better than saying yes, or pointing out that of the farmland they owned, all except the five-acre family garden was rented out to the Norsteds.

It was family business, and private, although not secret.

The origin of the strange golden coins that were the source of the family fortune *was* a secret, and one that Torrie had often wondered about. But he would be told what he needed to know when he needed to know it. So Mom said, so Dad said, so Uncle Hosea said, and of all things, Torrie believed them.

Meanwhile . . .

Torrie slipped an arm around Maggie's back, and tugged at the hem of her sweater. She tilted her head up, and he kissed her, at first softly, and then hard, her tongue warm and wet in his mouth, his hand lifting the hem of her sweater and sliding inside the scooped neck of her shirt, down into the bra, cupping her breast. Her nipple was hard against his palm as her fingers toyed with his belt buckle for just a moment before pushing him gently away.

"Torrie! Your mother's just in the next room, and aren't your father and uncle around?"

He didn't remove his hand from her breast. "She won't hear anything while she's working, and if they're out this late, they won't be back until late afternoon, as you'd know if you'd ever tasted Sandy Hansen's fried chicken, or seen how she stacks it on a plate, and you're just stalling."

And besides, even if Mom heard something, she wouldn't have heard something.

He pressed her up against the door, and kissed at her ear and the side of the neck. She smelled of Ivory soap and lemon and roses, with just a slight overtone of sweat.

He hooked a finger inside her belt. "I'm a nice guy, and I'll take a no, but you've got to say no."

"And the idea of doing it with your mother down the hall turns you on in a way that I doubt *my* father the clinical psychologist would find particularly healthy," she said, as though he hadn't said anything.

"That wasn't a no."

She was fumbling in the back pocket of his jeans. "I see we don't have to go hunting for a condom."

"I used to be a Boy Scout."

She smiled as she unbuckled his belt. "You tear it open with your teeth this time."

"Fair is fair," Torrie said. Which, after all, sounded better than *About Fucking Time.*

CHAPTER TWO

Thorian and Hosea

Wearing only a jockstrap, a pair of cotton shorts, and the faded yellow Dartmouth T-shirt he had won on a bet, the padded mat cold beneath his hairy thighs, Ian Silverstein bent himself almost double, stretching his hamstrings until he thought they would snap.

Warming up was the secret of not hurting yourself with this stuff. Despite the reputation that fencing had—usually among people whose only exposure to it was sitting on their butts in front of the TV screen, watching Basil Rathbone pretend to lose to Errol Flynn (Rathbone was an Olympic-class fencer; Flynn, even sober, couldn't close his low line if his life depended on it)—fencing was about as dangerous as checkers, and much less so than baseball or basketball. A baseball player could catch a foul tip; a basketball player could collide with another jock or come down wrong on an ankle. Hell, a swimmer could wham into a pool wall, and any idiot who went out on a football field deserved what he got.

You had to keep your priorities straight, when all you could count on was yourself. The real danger in fencing was in hurting a muscle or tendon by not having warmed up properly. Ian Silverstein couldn't afford health insurance beyond the student infirmary, and he couldn't afford to spend a week recovering from a minor injury or most of a year getting over a major one, so he stretched himself until he felt like Reed Richards before he opened his gear bag.

Ian hadn't suspected that Torrie was lying about the basement *salle d'armes*, not really, but he was pleasantly surprised to find that Torrie wasn't even exaggerating: instead of the usual concrete floor, the basement was floored in wood, and well-lighted with overhead fluorescent panels, and fully equipped, from the regulation two-meter-by-fourteen playing strip to the racks of foils and épées and sabers and some strange practice swords that Ian didn't recognize, to the electronic timing system that seemed a bit smaller and a bit slicker than the one at school.

Must be nice to have money.

Three more years, kiddo, and we get to start finding out. No, make that three and a half. Finish up the B.A. this year, spend another summer teaching intermediate foil for D'arnot—with a nice, juicy ten percent bonus if he came out first in the citywide, twenty percent for a zone win—then three years of law school, and then after the money.

Be a lawyer, just like your Dad, eh?

Fuck, no.

He'd have more tens of thousands of dollars of student loans to pay off than Ian liked to think about, but he had a plan that wouldn't only pay it off but would help get back some of his own.

Ian knelt on the playing strip. Nice wood, lacquered evenly and marked like a skinny basketball court: a thick green stripe across the strip marked the center, and two thinner ones the en-garde lines, while two red lines—plus a third one that Ian wondered about—marked the warning lines for first the saber and épée and then foil. The retreat zone beyond either end was in darker wood, which Ian thought was hardly enough of a difference to be useful until he stepped on it: with every step on each board, it squealed, like chalk on a blackboard. That would give somebody plenty of time to slow down before whanging into a wall.

Ian didn't take a foil down from the racks—he would sooner have borrowed a toothbrush without asking. Instead, he unzipped his gear bag and pulled out his sneakers and his favorite practice foil.

Not quite as spiffy as his electronic sword, but the grip was identical, and the snap of the blade was even nicer, really. It was also a lot cheaper to replace if it got bunged up.

He left his mask, trousers, and plastron in the bag, but took out his glove. No need to burden himself with all that when there was nobody facing him.

He slipped on the glove and gripped the hilt of his foil loosely, then came to attention, heels together, right foot pointed down the fencing strip, left foot at right angles to it, palms turned outwards. Form is everything in foil. Learn to do it the right way, in proper form, and let speed and control come later; it will all fall into place.

He came on guard, then brought his foil up to sixte, his weight balanced on the balls of his feet, ready to lunge at the slightest—

He pushed with his left leg, the heel hard against the floor, and took a long step forward with his right foot, coming to his full extension, his wrist lifting to keep his point traveling along a line from his shoulder through his wrist, toward just inside where an imaginary opponent's armpit would be.

The ideal line. It was nice to be able to touch something that was ideal.

"Very nice, sir," sounded from behind him.

Even a year ago, Ian would have stumbled at the sound, but tournaments were full of unexpected sounds, and you had to learn to ignore them, or you'd be distracted by the slamming of a door and find somebody less twitchy scoring off you, and Ian gave up zero, zip, and no points without fighting for them.

So he lowered his point and turned slowly, smoothly.

It wasn't hard to figure that the fiftyish man was Torrie's father: he had the same frame, small-boned and of only slightly more than medium height, the same shock of light-brown-verging-on-blond hair, framing a face whose jaw was almost as square as the toes of his work boots. Overdeveloped thigh muscles bulged against the tightness of his jeans, and he wore a white pullover woven cotton shirt that looked like something out of Old Sturbridge Village, although Ian had seen the Deva catalog they came from, and similar shirts on Torrie.

Not that they could have been mistaken for brothers: years of sun and wind had carved lines into a sun-darkened face, and what should have been a straight nose had a slight quirk in it, as though it had been badly broken at one point. And there was a scar running down the right side of his face that looked something like the Heidelberg scar the ex-Nazi who coached the Dartmouth team probably touched up with red makeup.

Except that a Heidelberg scar was thin and white, expertly closed, with no sign of stitchery, and Torrie's dad's looked like he had a long white centipede stuck to his face.

It made his smile look threatening. "You would be Ian Silverstone?" he asked, his voice deeper but smoother than Ian would have thought.

"Yes, sir," Ian said, tucking his sword under his arm so he could remove his glove. "Ian Silverstein, sir. Torrie said it would be okay if I used the room." He gestured at the fencing strip.

"I am Thorian Thorsen," the older man said, taking Ian's hand. "I apologize for mispronouncing your name; I tend to translate names. And of course you may use the room, and be welcome; you are a guest in our home." His hand was hard with callus and muscle, and his grip was firm, but he wasn't into squeezing contests.

Ian figured he could live with that.

Thorsen tilted his head to one side. "You are a foil player exclusively? Or did I see a bit of saber in your recovery?"

Ian had to smile. "I hope not. I tried saber for a couple of months, but I'm better with a foil," he said, raising a hand in advance protest. "And I am a lot better at it than I am at épée, and a *lot* better at that than I am at that freestyle stuff Torrie does."

Was there a faint sense of disapproval in Thorsen's expression? Well, fuck him.

When that so-called father of mine kicked me out, the only thing I knew how to do to support myself was what Benjamin Silverstein called "that silly Robin Hood shit," and I have to be good at it. I'm good at foil, and—except for goddamn spring vacation, when the studio shuts down—there're always beginning foil students to teach, and I don't have the time to play around.

Fencing might be a sport, a hobby for some, but Ian didn't have hobbies. Goals and hobbies don't mix. Ian had taken up poker, rock climbing, and fencing for the same reason—to support his eating habit—and had dropped the one he enjoyed the most, rock climbing, when it was clear that it was going to take too much time and money to get good enough to support himself as a trainer or guide. He had taken to the foil quickly, and any idiot who didn't get emotionally involved with cards could make money in a poker game, if he picked it right.

Just a question of knowing your game.

"You don't like freestyle?" Thorsen asked.

"I wouldn't say that, sir." Ian shook his head. *I might think it, but I wouldn't say it.* "It's not that. It's just that my reflexes are all foil, and it's hard to turn them off and think in terms of épée targets, and forget about right-of-way and timing issues." That didn't go over well; the notion that non-foil fencers—advanced weapons fencers, they called themselves, too often with a sniff—forgot about timing wasn't an idea with a lot of appeal to non-foil fencers.

Even if it was true.

He tried another tack. "Besides, I think I may have scored twice off Torrie in a couple of dozen bouts, and that's frustrating." It was an exaggeration, but not as much of one as he would have wished. Torrie was one hell of a fencer. And under freestyle rules, where the goal was to touch your opponent anywhere, with either the point or edge, he was even better.

"I would imagine so." Thorsen cracked his knuckles. "Foil is fine. Would you mind sparring for a few minutes? It's been . . . some time since I've held a foil in my hands."

He was already heading for a gunmetal-gray cabinet at the far end of the room when Ian nodded.

After hearing the way Torrie talked about some of his parents' idiosyncrasies—and particularly after noticing how Torrie avoided talking about some of his parents' idiosyncrasies—Ian wouldn't have been surprised if Thorsen had pulled a suit of armor out of the cabinet; but all he extracted was a worn but remarkably ordinary set of fencing gear, the jacket old but serviceable, the glove of thinner leather than was common today, but not exceptional.

Thorsen pulled his shirt off, revealing a muscular set of pecs and delts, Ian decided, although any of the buffers who hung around the gym would have been working on the slight give in the abs, and would long since have shaved off the mat of light hair that covered Thorsen's chest and shoulders.

Then again, the bodybuilder types Ian knew weren't in their fifties, either. Not only was it unfair to judge Thorsen by the same standards he would use on men a generation younger, but Thorsen was a farmer, not a bodybuilder.

Ian reached for his own gear bag.

It might have been a while since Thorsen had done this, but clearly he hadn't forgotten how to dress; in just a few moments, Thorsen had his fencing shoes and plastron on, not having bothered to change his jeans for more formal fencing trousers.

He selected a foil from the rack, carefully examined the length and ritually tugged at the blunt point, then sliced it a couple of times through the air before coming to attention, then momentarily raising his foil in salute before pulling his mask down over his face.

Ian came to attention, saluted, pulled down his own mask, and stepped back.

"Let's begin," Thorsen said, dropping into a slightly off-looking guard, his point low.

Ian dropped into guard. If Thorsen fought anything like Torrie, he would be heavy on beating—although not the way that beginners were, not clumsy at all.

Thorsen closed immediately, his blade in sixte. Ian tried for the counter, but Thorsen beat his blade out of line and would have gotten the touch if Ian hadn't returned the beat as he retreated. Ian beat seconde—his favorite beat move; it swept the lines twice—but Thorsen simply disengaged, beat Ian's foil up, and lunged forward for a low touch to Ian's side, his foil whipping through the air as though it was weightless, a holograph of a foil.

Damn, but the older man had a powerful wrist.

"Good," Ian said. He couldn't see Thorsen's face behind the mesh mask, but he knew that the older man was smiling.

Let him. It was Ian's turn now.

They squared off again, but this time as they closed, Ian was ready for the beat against his blade; he dropped his point and extended it in a perfect disengage and lunge, and went right through Thorsen's defenses as though they weren't there, scoring a touch on the outer hip.

"That was good, as well," Thorsen said, punctuating the sentence with a grunt, stopping his point a scant inch or so from Ian's chest. "Your point."

After some preliminary feints and counterfeints, Ian made his second point with a deceptive lunge that started high and ended low, again touching the older man at the outer side of his waist. Thorsen countered Ian's lunge on the next point with a perfect time thrust that gave him a touch on Ian's chest while sliding Ian's blade safely out of line, but when he tried the same move against Ian's running attack on the next point, Ian used his longer reach and greater extension to touch Thorsen's shoulder a bare moment before Thorsen could touch him.

It was the same thing as with Torrie: Thorsen could force his mind to *think* in terms of right-of-way or first touch, but his reflexes betrayed him. His body just didn't think of a point as ending with the first touch, not if his opponent's point was in position to touch him after that. It was the problem that épée players always had when fencing with foils. Foil fencing was designed to simulate a deadly duel, where your objective was to kill your opponent or at least grievously wound him with a single blow: you scored by hitting in a limited area on your opponent, the triangle made up of both shoulders and the groin.

If you really were fighting, any real wound in that triangle would be serious, and in a premedical culture, most probably deadly.

Épée was a response to that, invented in a time when most duels were fought to the first blood, where any wound, no matter how minor, would end a duel: the whole body was the target, and most épée points were scored with a touch to the arm or leg.

Thorsen tried, but he couldn't help but fight épée style. On attacking, he would tend to follow a successful parry immediately with a riposte; he would avoid a running attack or any of the risky maneuvers that would speed his point to its target ahead of his enemy's—he fenced against the foil, not against the fencer.

But the old man was damned good, give him that—even with that edge, it was all Ian could do to get a five-three win.

"Nice bout," Thorsen said, pulling his mask back. His face was almost split in a grin. "Torrie said you were good with a foil, but he rather understated it—now, have you had enough, or would you care for a little freestyle?"

Put that way, Ian could hardly refuse. He slid his mask down.

"Have at you, sir!" he said.

What Torrie called freestyle—Ian had never heard the term applied to fencing before—was basically épée scoring with some quirky variations: the bout didn't stop with a touch, although the winner of a point was unable to score a point for at least two seconds following a touch; three touches on the arm ended the match prematurely.

It had swept through the fencing club on campus, particularly among the novice players trying to work their way up to intermediate: it was fun, and it encouraged a lot of beating of blades, and it involved a lot of jumping and swinging and dramatic moving, just like in the movies.

It was also contrary to almost every reflex a good foil fencer had: after an opening flurry of disengagement play with the tips of the foils, the old man left an opening that didn't quite turn out to be there, responded with a delicate croisé that simultaneously shoved Ian's blade down, out, and out of line while touching him in the middle of the belly, then easily parried Ian's free attack—Ian had learned from Torrie the value of attacking after a touch—until at least five seconds had passed.

An arm touch, a touch to Ian's exposed knee, another arm touch, and a final croisé ended the freestyle bout embarrassingly.

It had all gone quickly, but not quickly enough: Ian's

T-shirt was damp, and his eyes were stinging so badly from dripping sweat that he wished he had put on his headband.

God, what were you like twenty years ago, Mister? Ian thought to himself. *If this was what you're like, out of shape, out of practice, in your fifties, what kind of player were you at twenty?* Olympic class, certainly—and Ian was sure that there had never been a Thorian Thorsen on any U.S. Olympic fencing team. It was one of the reasons he was skeptical about Torrie's claims about his dad.

Not the main reason, though. Down deep, Ian really didn't believe in a father who didn't drink himself into a stupor and beat the shit out of you whenever some case went sour, or when the plumbing broke, or when he had a hangover. Like it was Ian's fault. Like it was Ian's fault that Mom had died of cancer.

But life isn't fair. That was one of Dad's favorite sayings, and he went out of his way to make it true.

Thorsen was smiling, but just not as broadly, as he pulled off his mask and glove and extended his hand.

"Well," he said. "It's good to see that I haven't totally lost the use of a sword. You must give me another chance at you with a foil, later."

Ian took a moment to catch his breath. "My pleasure, sir," he said, between pants.

Thorsen nodded. "You're quite good with foil, and very promising."

"Kind of you to say so," Ian said.

Thorsen's smile dropped, and so, it seemed, did the temperature in the room. "No. Just accurate," he said, then shook his head and held up a hand, "but no offense was intended, and I apologize for seeming to take some." His smile was back. "Have you eaten recently?"

"No, sir. And I haven't drunk about a gallon of cold water recently, either. As soon as I take another shower and become acceptable company, I'd like to find one."

Thorsen laughed. "My wife has seen sweaty men in gym shorts before; let us get you watered and fed first. Besides," he said, "you haven't met Hosea yet."

The others were gathered around the kitchen table, Torrie and Maggie avoiding looking at each other in a way that instantly told Ian that they'd been at it again—although where? Right down the hall from Karin Thorsen?

There was a glance from Thorsen to Karin—Ian couldn't help thinking of her by her first name; she was just too gorgeous—and back.

Now, now, he chided himself, *Zayda Sol wouldn't approve you thinking lecherous thoughts about your hostess.*

Which wasn't true, not really. And he wouldn't have cared if it was. His long-dead grandfather always emphasized that what went on between your ears was your own business, as long as you kept it there, and that what went on in your home was your own business.

It was only one step from that to it didn't matter how much you got drunk and beat the shit out of your son, as long as nobody else knew it.

"Sit, please. Hosea'll be back in a minute," she said, leaning over to pour a stream of steaming coffee into two more of the old china cups, each with its saucer. Company manners, Ian decided.

"Coffee?" she asked. "Or," a quick glance at the clock, "something stronger? We've got—"

Torrie shook his head. "Ian doesn't drink."

She arched an eyebrow; Ian forced a smile. "It's the secret of my popularity," he said. "Ian 'The Designated Driver' Silverstein they call me."

Her smile brightened the room. "Sounds like a Jewish mafioso."

He returned the smile, trying to seem casual. But it was one of his nevers, and Ian was not casual about his nevers:

Never drink alcohol, not even in cough syrup; if you never drink, you will never be a drunk.

Never raise your hand to somebody you love, because if you never do that, you will never hit them.

Never complain, because the world doesn't give a shit.

And never, ever stop looking for a chance to get some of your own back.

He hated the idea of practicing law, instead of doing something useful, of making his profession the manipulation of rules passed by a bunch of legislators during brief breaks between being bribed and fucking their secretaries. That's all that law was.

But even if the tool was corrupt, it was still a tool. There would be a new legal specialty in a few years, and if Ian had anything to say about it, it would be highly paid. Child abuse—that horrifyingly inadequate term for what it was like to live in the fear that you'd say something wrong, do something wrong, and set the bastard off—was not confined to the children of the poor. Ian Silverstein was a living witness to that.

It would be tricky, but he would do it—get some kids out of the homes of bastards like Benjamin Silverstein, and make the bastards pay, all in public embarrassment, and some in cold, hard cash.

In ten years, twenty at the outside, the phrase *Ian Silverstein's on the phone* would make any one of the bastards shit his pants.

And if that meant that Ian Silverstein had to spend years learning law and more years paying off loans, then so be it.

"Sit down, please. Torrie says you take yours black," she said, bringing him back to the present as she set a plate of cookies in front of an empty chair.

Ian levered himself into the chair, feeling like something that had come out of the barn in front of all these freshly washed people. Hell, Torrie and Maggie still had wet hair—had the two of them arranged to shower together?

He sipped the coffee. It was black all right, but brewed in the weak tradition that Torrie had warned him about.

Ian decided it made sense—for them: if you were determined to drink endless cups of coffee throughout the day, you had probably better make it weak, no matter how Norwegianly phlegmatic you thought yourself. Ian would rather have had one cup of coffee brewed strong and right, but he would rather have dropped his mask before saluting than insult his host and hostess by saying so.

She sat down across from Ian, between her husband and son, although for just a moment Ian thought she was going to take the chair next to his. "So," she said, "do you three have any plans for the next week?"

Torrie shrugged. "I figured we'd just kick back a bit. Do some fencing, maybe some riding; visit some people and show Ian and Maggie what a real North Dakota farm is like. I was thinking about working on the riding pen, but I see Uncle Hosea beat me to it."

"And probably did a better job than you would," his father said, idly.

The skin over Ian's temples grew tight. He recognized that tone of voice, that silky threat and promise in front of—

No. Torrie wasn't tensing up. He was just frowning, the way you did when you disagreed with somebody, not the way you did when you were wondering where and when the next slap was coming.

Ian lowered his hands below the table and clenched them together.

Easy, kiddo, he said to himself. *It's not the same with them.*

"Probably," Torrie said, his voice lowering the temperature in the room by a bare degree.

Thorsen raised a hand in protest. "My apologies. I didn't mean it the way it sounded." He grinned. "It's hardly rare for somebody to be less handy than Hosea, after all."

Torrie eyed him levelly. "No problem, Dad. And you're right—but I'll take over mucking out the stalls, and let Ian milk the bull." He looked over at Ian. "You did say that you didn't mind doing your fair share of chores." He eyed Ian steadily.

"Not one little bit. But that one didn't go over my head, honest." Ian grinned. "I don't know much about farming, but I don't believe you have a bull, and I'm darned sure I wouldn't want to try to milk it."

They all laughed at that, not stopping when the door squeaked open behind Ian.

"Hosea!" Torrie was already out of his chair.

Ian turned, and almost jumped out of his skin.

There was something Torrie hadn't told him about Uncle Hosea. Actually, there was a lot Torrie hadn't told him about Uncle Hosea, but the two things that sprang instantly to mind were that he was well over six feet tall and that his skin was as dark as good mahogany.

"Thorian," he said, declining Torrie's outstretched hand and wrapping his long arms around Torrie, "it is good to see you well." There was something strange about his voice, some thin and reedy note in it that strangely reminded Ian of the hoot of an owl, although he couldn't have said why. It was also ever so slightly slurred—but not drunk-slurred; it didn't set off any fear or anger in Ian.

He was tall and slender, almost as though he was a man of average build stretched a foot taller than he should have been, and the image persisted in his long face with high cheekbones and a long, pointed jaw.

His smile was small, but real, and his teeth were bone white behind thinner lips than Ian would have expected. He wore the local uniform of plaid shirt and jeans, the hems of the jeans tucked into a battered but clean pair of work boots, but somehow on him it seemed more like he was wearing a costume than clothes.

Torrie turned back to Ian and Maggie. "This is Uncle Hosea."

Ian was irritated. Torrie could at least have said something. The Thorsens had money, and there was nothing wrong with them having an old family retainer, and nothing whatsoever wrong with that old family retainer being black, but fucking Torrie could at least have *said* something.

While Ian was rising, Maggie was already on her feet and had taken his hand. "I'm Maggie," she said.

"Hosea Lincoln," he said, taking a limping step forward.

"Ian Silverstein," Ian said, taking his hand. Hosea's fingers were long and slender, like those one would expect on a classical pianist, and his grip was light without any sensation of being weak. His left hand, down by his side, was cupped sort of funny.

Slurred voice without drink; hand down by the side—it had taken Ian a while to figure it out: Hosea had, at some point, suffered from some sort of damage to the right side of his brain that had left his left side partially paralyzed.

"Shalom, Ian," Hosea said, his accent thick and pure, "Naim meod; ma shlom-cha?"

Of all the things Ian might have expected, to be greeted in perfectly accented Hebrew wasn't high on the list. He stuttered for a moment before pulling a stock phrase out of an old memory: "Ani lo midaber ivrit tov." Which was true; he didn't speak much Hebrew.

Torrie was grinning. "Hebrew, too?"

"Hebrew, too." The tall man's smile was barely visible as he turned back to Ian.

"I am pleased to meet you," Hosea said, the words sounding nonetheless sincere for the careful pronunciation and clear formality.

Karin was at the sink, letting the water run for a moment before pulling down a long tumbler and filling it. She set it down on the table in front of Hosea, who took a careful sip, then another, then carefully drained half the glass before setting it back down. There was something strange about the hand that gripped the glass, but Ian couldn't quite figure out what it was, and Hosea had folded his hands into his lap in a gesture that looked perfectly normal for him before Ian could figure it out.

"The stalls are clean, and the horses are well, although I would venture to guess that Jessie is not being ridden quite enough of late," Hosea said, the ends of his mouth barely turning upward.

Karin's face grew stern, although her eyes were shining. "I guess you're just going to have to ride her some, Torrie, and if you have to make your friends help, well, then, that's the price you'll have to pay."

Torrie laughed. "We'll live with it. I haven't seen her yet." He stood. "What say we look around the barn, and then around town—"

"Dinner at six."

"—and we can meet Jeff at the Dine-a-mite later on, after supper."

She frowned at that. "It's kind of a long walk."

"It's not that bad, but we'll drive."

"And ask Ole to drive you home when the bar closes?"

"Don't need to. Ian doesn't drink, remember?"

Ian raised his cup. "Sure I do. Gallons and gallons of coffee."

"Just like a real Norski."

Ian smiled, and nodded a silent thank-you when she offered him another cup of the weak brew.

Then it hit him. The palms of Hosea's hands weren't pinkish, or even lighter than the coffee-dark brown of his face and the rest of his skin. He was, as far as Ian could tell, uniformly brown all over.

Nothing wrong with that, but it was strange. The whole family was strange, from the mother who invested in stocks two thousand miles from Wall Street, to the master fencer father who seemed to have plenty of time to investigate wolf predations, to the tall, skinny, black so-called uncle.

Don't be such an asshole, he told himself. *You're just not used to a family that works.*

CHAPTER THREE

Wolves

Jeff Bjerke sat at a table in the corner and sipped his beer—even the Law could allow itself a beer, if nursed long enough, as long as he didn't do it often enough to start gossip—while over at the bar, under the Miller sign with the missing second *l*, the talk was about wolves, as it always was, these days.

The Dine-a-mite hadn't changed a bit since he was a kid and came in here for a pop after school: the tables in the battered booths up against one wall were still covered with the same patterned linoleum; the tiny window of the single swinging door into the kitchen was so dirty he couldn't tell if a light was on inside.

Shit, even the two men at the bar and the one standing behind it hadn't changed. Sure, Arnie was balder than he had been, and both Orphie's middle and glasses were thicker, and behind the bar, tall, skinny Ole Honistead didn't move as fast as he used to; but Jeff could have come in here a thousand times over the past twenty or so years and had the same tableau set out in front of him: The Three Graces, Arguing To Pass the Time.

"Now, Gunnar says that they got ten of his cows," Arnie Selmo said, tilting his feed cap back so he could tilt his beer back, then replacing the feed cap with the same movement, as though it really hid the bald spot on his head. "Doesn't sound like no lone wolf to me."

Jeff muffled a smile. Everybody had their secrets, and it rarely was his job to expose them—and never his pleasure. That was one of the things that old John Honistead had left him, along with the job: the responsibility. The badge, the car, the office and tiny holding cell in the basement of Town Hall—they were just tools, not the core of it.

Jeff was more of a department of justice than a town policeman. Cops worried about rules; justice had its own concerns.

Like: live and let live.

Not everybody felt that way. But most did. Enough did. Just as well. About ten years ago, a skinny little twelve-year-old girl who wouldn't give her name other than Kathy, running away from a stepfather of almost unbelievable cruelty, had stumbled into town, and been taken in by the Aarsteds—back then, the attitude on the farm was that there was always room for another mouth.

The story told around town was that she was a distant cousin of Bob's who had come to live with them, but she didn't look like an Aarsted, and probably nobody believed that, although almost nobody said anything. It wasn't the first time that a runaway had found sanctuary here, and it wasn't the last time—you just had to trust the likes of, say, a Bob Aarsted or Doc Sherve or Minnie Hansen or Michael Bjerke to do what was right.

There had been some talk by some of the more chatty housewives, but Aarsted had brought Kathy in for an exam and a quiet talk with Doc Sherve, and then Doc Sherve had had a quiet talk with the chatty, and it had shut off like a switch. Nobody messed with Doc Sherve any more than they did with Bob Aarsted.

Jeff didn't always like Bob Aarsted, but, then again, you didn't always have to like your father-in-law.

Orphie Selmo—a distant cousin of Arnie's, but it was hard to keep straight just what sort; there were almost as many Selmos as there were Olsens in the thin local phone book—grunted, and hooked his left hand in his suspenders, as though that could stop the tremor.

"Sure it's ten," he said. "Gunnar wouldn't think of using the wolves as an excuse to slaughter a bunch and sell them for cash to that Swede in Grand Forks, of course he wouldn't."

Arnie leaned over and grabbed a handful of peanuts. "Why bother? Gunnar hasn't turned a profit in five years. What you don't make, nobody can tax away from you." He jerked his head toward the window, and Selmo's Drugs across the street. "Take my word for it."

Orphie just sniffed. "Well, if you're too blind to figure it out for yourself, I won't show you."

Mixed metaphor, Jeff didn't say. It was hard enough being a college boy in a small farming town; no sense in making life more difficult for himself.

Arnie chuckled to himself. "Lot of things about wolves of late. Saw a book down in the drugstore, you wouldn't believe."

"About wolves?"

"Well, maybe, but I don't think so." He shook his head. "Cover of it had a lady in a leather outfit kneeling in front of a wolf, and the wolf was standing on his hind legs, like, she was getting ready to, well . . ."

"Like, well, *what*?"

"Like, well, something I can fondly recall paying a toothless whore in some village in Uijongbu to do every time I got into town, but I could never quite persuade Ephie wasn't sinful." He sighed, and sipped at his beer. "Though I do miss the old girl from time to time."

Jeff made a mental note to have a word with Neil Petersen. He didn't really care what books Petersen sold at the pharmacy, and knew that there was a thriving, if small, under-the-counter trade in titles that Reverend Oppegaard would preach a sermon on if he found out about, but it was supposed to be under-the-counter.

Arnie raised his glass. "To Dog Troop, 7th Regiment, First Cavalry (Dismounted)."

"Here we go again with Korea stories," Orphie said, with another sniff.

Behind the bar, Ole polished a glass with a towel, like a child rubbing a security blanket against his face. "Oh, Orphie, we've heard about Bastogne half a million times—"

" '—And I'll have you know I was in the third goddamn tank behind Creighton Abrams himself—' " Arnie said, mimicking Orphie's heavier accent.

"—and when young Dave's in, we'll listen to talk of what happened when it all fell in at Dac To. And we'll listen politely to how it was in Korea, too." He jerked his pointed chin at Orphie's glass. "You ready for another?"

"I don't see why not."

The bar went silent for a few moments, and Jeff glanced at his watch and thought about giving up waiting for Torrie and his friends, then decided to give them another fifteen minutes. Kathy was probably still over at the Aarsteds, and he hated coming home to a silent house. Time to start a kid or two, if only he could talk Kathy into it.

Ah, to hell with—

The door swung open, and Torrie and his two friends walked in. They seemed nice. This Maggie of his was cute, in a kind of skinny East Coast way. The tall dope-smoking Jew even had a pleasant smile, if a bit of an ugly one. Sort of looked like a young Abe Lincoln, before the beard really came in, maybe. Probably ought to grow a mustache.

"Two, er, root beers and a 7-Up," Torrie said, sliding into the booth next to Maggie, while the tall—while Ian sat down next to Jeff.

"7-Up?" Ole's brow furrowed.

"And two root beers."

Ole winked broadly. "Coming up." Orphie was so busy retelling the relief of Bastogne that he didn't notice that Ole poured the "root beer" out of the Grain Belt spigot.

It had been too long since Torrie was home, and he was developing city ways; it took him a moment to go and get the tray.

They sipped at their beers for a few minutes, while Jeff caught Torrie up on some of the latest gossip—the public parts. The Grand Forks bank had finally foreclosed on Johanson, and the auction would be next Saturday, and Doc Sherve had finally brought in a young doctor as a partner, and was talking retirement again. Florida, he said.

Finally, the discussion among the Three Graces worked its way around to the wolves again.

"I've got that new Kraut glass on my old Model 70."

"Yeah. Pre-64 Model 70 Winchester. We know, Arnie; it's a good gun."

"Yeah. And protected or not, I've half a mind to go chase them some night myself," Arnie said. "It's nothing—"

"Hah." Orphie said, punctuating it with a sniff. "What you've got is half a mind. Varmint hunting is one thing—"

Maggie leaned toward Torrie. "Varmint hunting?" she whispered. "As in, 'reach for yore iron, varmint'?"

She laughed. A pretty, easy, light laugh. Jeff envied Torrie that. That was something Kathy never did.

"Pest hunting," Torrie said. "Usually prairie dogs, but around here, it's woodchucks. A chuck can do a lot of damage to your fields, so farmers go to some trouble to get rid of them. A .22 shooting Stingers will drop them real well, but some people, like old Arnie, make it a hobby—they get rifles that shoot really well at long distances, and put expensive scopes on them."

"Sounds kind of bloodthirsty to me."

Torrie shrugged. "I've seen you stomp on a cockroach, and it wasn't going to take more than a nibble."

Ian licked his index finger and stroked the air in front of him. "Point Torrie. Maggie to serve."

Orphie was still holding forth. "—you going to shoot a *wolf* with one of them teenie-leetle .22-250 rounds? Sure enough, they'll plop a groundhog in his tracks, but they're too small for deer—and I wouldn't want to go after a wolf with anything that wouldn't knock a deer head over heels."

"So I'll borrow me a .30-06."

"So you'll borrow yourself a lot of trouble," Ole said, shaking his head. "What if you run into somebody else with the same idea?"

"You think I look like a wolf?"

"I don't think that heifer you bagged down South last season looked like a deer, either," Jeff said, loudly.

The tips of Arnie's ears grew red. "It was godawful misty, and I *swear*—"

Jeff held up a hand, and Ole copied him, silencing Arnie. "I know. It was an accident, and it could have happened to anyone. But that sort of thing can happen," Jeff said, "and I sure as hell wouldn't want to see anybody get hurt. Forgetting that it's illegal. You just let it be, Arnie," he said, turning to look pointedly at Torrie, "and see what happens."

Torrie gave a slight nod before he returned to his beer. "Sure. A lone wolf will probably just move on."

Orphie sniffed.

Jeff smiled.

Torrie nodded, again.

Thorian del Thorian awoke at the light touch, reaching for—

No. There was no danger. The dark shape leaning over the bed in the dark of his bedroom was only Orfindel. There was no need for the 9 mm Taurus pistol in the night stand—after all these years, firearms had become second nature to him—or the almost impossibly sharp silver-inlaid blade behind the headboard. It was only Orfindel.

Just Orfindel, he thought, with a silent inner laugh. Merely, Orfindel; trivially, an Old One, perhaps a Very Old One, had come into his room to awaken him, as though Orfindel was some peasant servitor to wait upon his pleasure.

Karin's body lay warm next to him, comforting in its warmth and presence. This woman of his could light up a dark room, and send night demons fleeing from his dreams. He touched two fingers to his lips, then gently, gently to the swell of her hip under the sheet.

"Yes?" he whispered. "What is it?"

"Young Thorian has just returned with his friends," Orfindel said, his voice low enough not to wake Karin. "He asks for a word with you."

"Very well, Hosea. Thank you; I'll join you in a moment." It was necessary, it had been agreed many years before, that Thorian would treat Orfindel as though he were a subordinate, and that he call him by the name the Old One had assumed, but he had made no bargain with or about his thoughts, and while most of his honor had long been driven away, leaving behind a need to overcompensate for it, Thorian del Thorian could still keep a bargain without paying any extra.

He dressed quickly, then gave his sleeping wife a quick kiss before exiting into the hallway; she barely stirred. Among Karin's many virtues was that she was a heavy sleeper.

Torrie and his two friends were downstairs in the den. They seemed acceptable, although perhaps a bit effete and citified. Thorian repressed a smile. In the twenty-odd years since he and Orfindel had made their escape through the Hidden Ways and out into the Next World, Thorian had become a proper peasant. At least eighteen generations of his family had lived in the Middle Dominion, and none of them had ever set a shod foot on plowed ground, much less a bare one.

But that was a long time ago, and far away.

Torrie had his serious face on, and Thorian could have guessed what it was all about. The wolves.

He looked over at Orfindel. They were just wolves, weren't they?

Orfindel couldn't really read minds, but sometimes it didn't matter. He nodded, but with some reservation in the cant of his shoulders, as though to say, *Not quite certainly, but as close as it is possible to be.*

"I was talking to Jeff Bjerke tonight," Torrie said. "He's been concerned about the wolf problem."

Thorian nodded. "He's hardly the only one. Sven was laying for one last night, and actually got a shot off. He showed me the prints today."

They went off to the south, which was probably just a coincidence.

It was like what Doc Sherve said, when talking about medical diagnosis: "When you hear hoofbeats, think horses, not zebras." Farmers everywhere had trouble with wolves. A whole chain of unlikely events would have had to have happened before it would even be possible that the source of the trouble was Sons of Fenris.

"Yes, but . . ." Torrie didn't want to come out with it.

Which was silly, if understandable.

Thorian smiled. "If you trust your friends enough to say this much in front of them, say the rest. He wants Hosea and me to go after them, yes?"

Torrie nodded. "Yes. He didn't want to come right out and say it, but . . ."

Orfindel smiled. "He wouldn't want to forswear himself, Torrie. If Jeff is asked, in court or elsewhere, if he gave us leave to kill a protected animal, he can answer honestly that he didn't." Orfindel was already shrugging into a thick down jacket. "And if we are not caught, then it never will have happened."

Might as well do it now as later. The moon was full, and Orfindel could follow a track through all but the blackest night—that ability hadn't left the Old One—although Thorian's eyes were merely human. As were his son's, and his son's guest's.

Thorian thought about raiding the emergency kits for nightgoggles, but decided against that. He really should buy another pair for everyday use, but he had never really wanted a set before.

Still, Thorian could see through a scope in the dark, and that should be enough.

Should he invite the guest? Local custom wasn't clear on this point, but what Thorian's upbringing would have compelled wasn't forbidden. "Thorian, Ian—would you like to come along?"

Torrie nodded. "Yes, sir."

The taller boy took a moment before answering. "Sure. I mean, I guess so. If I wouldn't be in the way, sir."

"You understand we'll be violating the law? I doubt there's danger of arrest or embarrassment, but there will be no shame in declining."

The girl frowned, as though she had expected to be invited. That was hardly her place, although one couldn't expect a Twentieth Century American Woman to understand that.

But it was not Thorian's place to explain it to her. Leave that to his son.

Ian smiled. "I haven't noticed a lot of people being picky about details about the law, not around here. I guess, uh, getting along is more important than the technicalities."

Well, it hardly surprised Thorian that Torrie would choose smart friends. He was a good son, and would choose wisely—this Ian had a good wrist, and a good head on his shoulders, it appeared.

"We'll go get the gear and the pickup ready; meet us outside in ten minutes," Thorian said.

He walked downstairs to the loading bench, and took two boxes of ammunition from the locked cabinet above it. He pulled open the boxes and looked at the long, slim rounds: .30-06 rifle rounds.

Strange: by local standards, the age made the cartridge a venerable weapon. Thorian had once had practice with swords older than that.

Hand loading of ammunition had become a hobby of his; it had been one of many things that he had learned from old Tom Roelke.

He wouldn't have admitted it, not even to Orfindel, but Thorian missed them, almost as much as he missed his homeland. But Tom and Eva were living well down in a retirement village near San Diego now, courtesy of the Thorsen gold. Thorian didn't begrudge one penny of it, not to the man and woman who had taken in him and Orfindel, knowing nothing about them save that they needed help. By Odin's Eye, back then Thorian couldn't speak the language, not any of them; Orfindel's Gift of Tongues wasn't bestowable here.

He eyed the silver tips. Yes, it was almost certain that they were faced with wolves, not Sons. But a wolf could fall to a silver bullet every bit as easily.

He thought for a moment about leaving Karin a note, but he had never gotten terribly good at writing, and, besides, she knew him well enough to know that he would be back. This was hardly the first time he had slipped off into the night; it would not be the last.

The others were waiting upstairs.

"We'll be late," Torrie said to the girl. "You'd best not wait up."

* * *

Maggie Christensen heard the quiet padding of feet behind her as she was pouring herself another cup of coffee. And fuming, albeit quietly.

Not wait up, eh? Well, if that was the way he was going to be, she would be waiting up.

It had always been that way, going as far back as she could remember.

She had Daddy to thank for it, probably. It was a family legend that back when she was about four—back when they still called her Maryanne—she had been riding in a car with her Aunt Maggie, Mom's sister, who was living with them at the time, and had announced, "I want to be an Aunt Maggie when I grow up."

Aunt Maggie had laughed and explained that first she would have to persuade her mother and father to have another kid, and then persuade the kid to grow up and have children, but even then she would be an Aunt Maryanne, not an Aunt Maggie.

"My Daddy," she had said, with a decided sniff, "says that when I grow up, I can be whatever I want," and from that day on, she insisted that everybody call her Maggie.

Scores of teachers had forgotten, only to be repeatedly reminded until they gave it up; and occasionally, on the playgrounds, boys would call out her other name, but she pretended never to hear it. Of course, that all had changed in ninth grade, when overnight—at least so she remembered—her braces came off, her skin cleared up, and her breasts and hips spunged out into woman-shape instead of girl-shape, and jeers had turned into stutters and leers.

All that was fine with her.

Maggie didn't want much. All she ever wanted was to have everything her way, but her way didn't mean "without effort." She didn't mind putting in work, and it didn't much matter to her what was the cost of getting what she wanted, even if that meant dating that geeky English professor who hated giving out As, because another B would bring her average down to 3.5; or going to half a dozen stores to find exactly the right shade of red to bring out the highlights in her hair without making it look dyed; or spending a few dozen hours in the gym with the other fencing club novices when it was clear that was the way to get between Torrie and his then-girlfriend; or spending hundreds more hours in the gym not because of Torrie, or even because she found that she was good at it, but because—to her surprise—she found that she liked it.

"Hel-lo," she heard from behind her. "I see you're up late."

She turned, completely unsurprised that Karin Thorsen was dressed in a shorty robe that clearly came from Victoria's Secret, with a lacy black teddy peeking through underneath. Granted, she was in good shape for a woman her age, but *really*.

"I hope I didn't wake you," Maggie said.

Karin shook her head, clearing a fringe of golden hair—it was golden, dammit, and not just blonde—from her eyes. "No," she said with a smile, "it's a family joke that I wake up when I want to." Her smile grew distant and perhaps a bit pensive. "Thorian used to have to wake me when I was breastfeeding Torrie," she said. "Even a crying baby didn't." She looked at Maggie for a moment, then shook her head, dismissing whatever private thought had run through her brain. "But sometimes I wake on my own. It seems that Thorian and Hosea are gone, and Torrie isn't in his—and Torrie's with them."

And maybe Torrie's bed hasn't been messed up at all. And maybe you were wondering if your baby boy was warming mine, eh? she thought.

"Ian's with them, too. Down at the bar—"

"The Dine-a-mite?"

"Yes. Jeff Burke—"

"Bjerke."

"Yes, he said something about a wolf killing some chickens or something, and about how convenient it would be if something were to happen to it. 'Who will rid me of this turbulent wolf?' " she said, more to see if Karin would recognize the quotation than anything else.

"Jeff would make a good king." Karin grinned. "And Torrie came home and woke Hosea, who woke Thorian, who immediately had to hare off to see what he could do, middle of the night or not, eh?"

Maggie couldn't help grinning along with her. "Something like that." She lifted the coffeepot. "Can I offer you a cup of your own coffee?"

Karin thought about it for a moment. "Please. But if we're going to wait up for the men, I'm going to go up and change into something a bit more suitable for sitting around and talking."

And which doesn't leave you feeling half-naked in front of another woman, eh?

Karin turned and left, less of a sway to her behind than usual.

Maggie smiled.

It didn't take Maggie long to find the cream—well, a half-used pint of half-and-half, which passed the sniff test that she wouldn't have used in front of Karin—but the sugar was harder to locate. The crystal sugar bowl with the glasses was empty, and by the time she found the right cabinet, unsealed the large plastic container, and—dipping a fingertip in it and to her tongue to be sure that it wasn't some huge quantity of salt—poured it in the sugar bowl and was going for a spoon, Karin was back, now wearing a loose set of black and yellow silk pajamas that would have looked unisex or sexless if they weren't belted tightly at the waist with a silken cord that didn't quite match the yellow.

She accepted the cup from Maggie, and sat down at the table, idly doodling on the table with a short-bitten fingernail. "Torrie doesn't talk much about school when he's home."

"Or about home when he's at school." Maggie sat down across from her. "He just drops a few hints every now and then."

"He's like that." Karin grinned. "Part of being the stoic Norski, I guess. I was wondering how long the two of you—"

Glass shattered in the living room, and the floor pounded to what sounded like dozens of footsteps, accompanied by a horrid chorus of snarls.

Maggie was frozen in surprise and fear, but Karin Thorsen had already leaped up from the table. Moving like a dancer, like she had practiced every step not just for efficiency but for grace, she took two quick steps toward the sink, then she reached up with her left hand and pulled a large butcher knife down from the rack over the counter, while with her right hand she seemed to fondle and then slap the cupboard over the sink. The side of the cupboard swung out on concealed hinges, revealing a stainless steel revolver suspended on a trio of pegs; Karin immediately snatched down the revolver.

She started her turn, but an obscene hairy shape leaped through the kitchen doorway and knocked her back.

She brought the gun down and fired.

The distant pistol shot brought Arnie Selmo out of the first sound sleep he'd had in a week.

After forty-two years married to the same woman, sleeping in the same bed, it was taking more than one year, six months, and two days to get used to sleeping alone, to doing everything alone.

Going to the grocery store was hard. When Ephie was alive, it hadn't bothered Arnie to shop; he had always liked going into Grand Forks with her every couple of weeks to stock up. But now shopping for one was no fun at all.

Nobody to banter with about the silly new products they kept introducing, as though somebody really needed some pill to turn the water in the toilet blue, or aloe—whatever that was—put into cloths to clean a baby's bottom. Nobody to sigh over how much a rib roast cost and to settle for a chuck, or, every once in a while, to say, "Ah, you only live once" and go for the rib.

Shopping was bad, and cleaning was bad—every dust bunny a reminder of Ephie—but sleeping was the worst. It would be so easy to help it along with a few pulls on the bottle of Four Roses he had always kept by his bed, but no: Arnie Selmo would take one nightcap, as he always had, but by God he would not drink himself drunk in Ephie's bed.

His dreams were the worst. It was the same dream every night: Ephie lay sleeping next to him, resting comfortably, not wracked in the pain that had turned her last days into the hell on earth that Arnie and Doc Sherve had finally helped her end. Each morning, Arnie would wake, still half in dream, and look at the open bathroom door and watch the sunlight splash onto the ancient six-sided tiles, and wait for Ephie to step out in that ancient, fuzzy blue bathrobe of hers—only to realize that it was the dream, again, and that he had survived to yet another morning without her.

So it was with something almost like glee that he came awake in the dark.

Another shot echoed through the night, accompanied by a scream.

There was a city-folk thing that Arnie had heard about. He wasn't really sure he believed it, but he'd heard that there some mugger stabbed a woman to death on a public street, with hundreds of folk hearing her screams, and that none of them did nothing about it. He'd heard that it had taken the killer more than ten minutes to do it, and nobody had done nothing. Had to be bullshit, but that was the story.

Half-awake, Arnie was already on his way to the gun case in the living room; he pulled his shotgun down with one hand while the other reached for a box of shells. Guns do not go off in the middle of the night, not without a reason. Screams do not echo in the night, not without a reason.

It was good to have a reason to do something.

He shoved his feet into his boots, not bothering with socks, and quickly set the shotgun and shells down so that he could tie the laces—he would do nobody any good tripping in the dark—then grabbed up the gun and shells, shrugged into a long coat.

He dashed out into the night, not bothering to close his door behind him.

Another shot—sounded like it was coming from the Thorsen place, and while they were certainly a strange enough family, they weren't the sort to be firing off guns in the middle of the night.

Across the street, the lights were on in Davy Hansen's place, and his door was swinging open. Davy's skinny chest was bare in the cold night air; he was wearing only jeans and work boots, as though this all had caught him on his way to bed.

Davy limped toward Arnie—he had left his right foot and most of that leg below the knee in a rice paddy in Vietnam—his rifle held muzzle-high in his hands, and it took Arnie a moment to realize why it made him envious. Davy was carrying an AR15, the civilian version of the rifle Davy had taken to war. Arnie's hands itched for the stock of his old Garand, and the shotgun couldn't cure the itch.

"Where?" Davy shouted.

"Thorsen's," Arnie said, breaking into a staggered trot that wouldn't keep him far ahead of the younger man, not for long, but which did let him stuff shells into the shotgun's tube.

The Thorsen place had been built on the very edge of town, into a thick windbreak; that left it screened on three sides, including the town side. A dirt path led behind the

Bjornsens', through the woods, breaking on the chest-high rough grasses that fringed the mowed lawn.

The grasses whipped at his hands and eyes, but Arnie pushed through—there were shouts and screams ahead.

And snarls.

He broke through the grass and stopped dead in his tracks.

In the doorway, Karin Thorsen, dressed in badly torn yellow and black pajamas, a long, bloody knife in her hand, was struggling with the largest wolf Arnie had ever seen, while three or four almost as large were crowding around, leaping and snarling and biting at her. A pistol lay on the porch; Arnie only noticed it when a skittering wolf's foot kicked at it, sending it tumbling to the lawn.

The big bay window on the porch had been smashed, and two more wolves were dragging a half-naked girl out through it, unmindful of the way the rough glass slashed at her legs. So was the girl—she had a knife in her hands, as well, and was flailing about with it, not having any more effect than Karin was.

Arnie couldn't fire in the direction of the women—not with a shotgun; with his old Garand he would have put a round within a palm's breadth of where he wanted it—but there were two wolves on the left side of the porch, waiting to get into the action. He pumped a round into the chamber, raised his shotgun to his shoulder, and fired.

It kicked hard, knocking him back, almost knocking him down.

It took him a moment to decide that it wasn't that he was old, but that he must have grabbed shells from the mixed box, the one where he kept odd shells from birdshot to deer slugs—this definitely was the kick of a deer slug.

He hadn't been aiming as closely as he would have if he'd thought he was shooting slugs, but still, the impact had bowled a wolf over. Another shot rang out, and then another, the high-pitched crack of Davy's rifle a tenor counterpoint to the boom of Arnie's shotgun.

None of it made sense. Karin was under attack by three wolves, but all that was happening was that she was being forced down the porch and onto the lawn—any one of them could have bit her in half in less time than it would take to sneeze. And while her knife kept rising and falling, and while even over the shouts and shots he could hear the meaty *thunk* of the blade hitting flesh, and while the blood gleamed satiny black in the moonlight, none of the wolves fell back, or even whimpered out in pain.

Arnie worked the pump and settled his sights on another wolf on the edge of the pack, and pulled, this time braced for the recoil of the deer slug.

It slammed hard into his arthritic shoulder; he winced as he pumped it again.

I'm getting too old for this, he thought. *Jesus, let me be young again for five minutes.*

That was all he needed, then the good Lord could take him—just five minutes with the strength and eye of youth.

Two bunches of wolves were carrying the two women away, and there was nothing he could do about it. But at least he could kill some of the wolves and make it easier for somebody else to do what was important. Arnie wasn't too proud for that.

But—but he had fired twice, and Davy had fired at least another half dozen shots, but where were the dead wolves?

Arnie knew he'd hit the first one square in the chest, but it wasn't lying on the ground. It had gotten up, and was stalking toward him, legs stiff, jaws wide to reveal ugly teeth.

Smoothly, he pumped the gun again and settled the sights on its chest, then squeezed the trigger gently, tenderly enough that in the back of his mind he could almost see his old drill sergeant smiling, although that had to be a false memory, because Sergeant Homer Abnernathy wouldn't have smiled at his own mother, even if the bastard had had one.

The recoil knocked him back, harder than before, and the slug knocked the wolf down. A fifty-caliber deer slug should have broken enough bone and torn enough flesh to keep it down, but the animal slowly rose to its feet, and broke into a trot toward him.

Somewhere over to his right another high-pitched crack told Arnie that somebody else was shooting, and there was a twin boom over to his left that said that the Larson brothers had joined the game, and that was good. Maybe they'd have better luck than he was having.

The wolf wiggled its haunches almost comically, then, its rear feet firmly set into the ground, pushed, launching itself into the air toward Arnie, its jaws wide, ready to bite, to tear, to kill.

There was no time to pump the shotgun again, and, besides, it wasn't doing any good.

To hell with it, then. Arnie dropped the shotgun to one side. One hand fumbled for a moment at where, almost half a century before, his bayonet would have hung in its scabbard, but all his fingers clutched was air.

To hell with that, too, then. To hell with all of it.

Corporal Arnold J. Selmo, Dog Troop, 7th Regiment, First Cavalry, drew himself up straight. A corporal in Dog Troop, 7th Regiment, First Cavalry, didn't need a horse; the First Cavalry had gone to Korea as infantry. A corporal in Dog Troop didn't need a rifle. A corporal in Dog Troop didn't need a knife. All he needed was his hands, and an enemy's throat, and by God he *had* hands.

Arnie Selmo reached out, praying not that he could push the wolf away, but that he could, at least for a moment, fasten his fingers around its throat.

And if he couldn't get his fingers close enough, Lord Jesus, at least his teeth.

CHAPTER FOUR

Hidden Ways

White-knuckled, Ian clung to the shoulder straps for his life as the Ford Bronco swung wide onto the dirt road toward the Thorsen house. Beside him in the back seat, he could feel Torrie's fear. Hell, he could almost smell it.

Thorsen drove like a madman, or maybe like somebody who thought that an extra-hard stomp on the accelerator, a more-violent-than-necessary turn of the wheel could make the car move faster.

The only one in the car who seemed calm was Hosea, who sat in the righthand front seat calmly, seemingly unworried and unruffled.

They turned down the road toward the house.

Thorsen skidded the car to a stop amid a scene of carnage.

Under the electric lights, bodies were scattered on the grass. Blood was slick and glossy on the grass, while fragments of bone shone too brightly, and yellowy worms of intestine lay motionless.

It perhaps would have been kinder if they were dead, but two were groaning.

A thick-waisted heavy-bearded man in a puffy-looking

down coat was leaning over one of the wounded; the open black bag at his side on the ground proclaimed him a doctor.

Jeff Bjerke was at the car door as they opened it. His right arm hung down by his side, as though useless, and he didn't seem to notice that he had a revolver in his fist.

"Doc Sherve says that Arnie'll live, but Ole Hansen's dead, and both the Larson boys," he said, his voice unnaturally calm, and in shocking contrast to the tears running down his cheeks and into his beard. "Davy Hansen's tracking the wolves; they fled almost due south. I told him not to, but everybody knows you can't tell Davy shit. He took along a roll of my yellow crime scene tape—said he'll blaze a trail with it for you."

His hand gripped Thorsen's shoulder. "I'd feel damn silly telling anybody else this, but I have the feeling you know that the wolves took your wife—and your son's girlfriend. And that bullets don't even seem to slow them down."

Thorsen took a step toward where the doctor was working over the old man that Ian decided had to be Arnie Selmo.

"No," Bjerke said. "No time for it. The staties'll be all over us within an hour. If there's anything you need to do, you'd better do it now. Doc and I'll cover for you, but—"

"I must talk to . . ."

Bjerke grabbed Thorsen's shoulder and spun him around, bringing the pistol up until it pointed at Thorsen's face, his knuckles white as his pale face. "Don't you fucking *dare*," he said. "Don't you even fucking think about it. You deal with your guilt some other time, Mister Thorsen, you confess it to your minister or you dissolve it in a bottle of whiskey. Some other time. For right now, you remember that your neighbors died trying to save them.

You won't waste it, you fucker," he said, each word curiously without heat. He let his arms fall down by his sides.

Thorsen didn't say anything for a moment. "There's much that you don't know."

"I probably know more than your own kid does—you think the only thing old John Honistead passed on was this badge?" Jeff Bjerke looked Thorian in the eye. "Get to it." He stalked away, calling out orders to a team of stretcher-bearers.

"I will." Thorsen turned to Hosea. "You know what they want. I need you to come with me."

Hosea shook his head slowly. "Not this way, Thorian. There's another route—"

"You know what they'll do if we don't follow," he said, his voice flat.

"No, I do not know what they will do. I know what their actions . . . threaten, yes. Not all keep their promises, overt or covert."

"No. If we don't follow—I'll follow them, even if you won't."

Hosea rubbed two fingertips against the bridge of his nose. "Then do what you must, as surely I will."

Without a word, Thorsen turned and ran for the house.

Ian placed himself in front of Torrie. "Will you tell me what's going on?"

Torrie shook his head. "I . . . don't know." It was hard to make out his expression in the light, what little there was streaming out through the open door to the house.

Old Hosea's voice was thinner than usual. "Yes, you do, young Thorian. You've heard the stories—some of them. And some of them even were stories."

"And some of them were true? About the wars of the Aesir and Vanir? Dvalin and Silvertop? The Vestri and the Tuatha? The Tuarin? All of it?"

"True enough, although somewhat outdated. There are few of the Aesir, and probably are no more Vanir as such;

the Aesir always were ready to war on anyone when they were younger."

"And the Tuatha?"

"What there is left of them." The tall man nodded. "And very much the Tuatha."

"The Brisingamen—"

"Broken and dispersed, the jewels hidden." Hosea tapped a long finger against his temple. "Even from me."

"About the New World and Newer?"

"Yes, and the Ways between them, bent ninety degrees out of space. Yes." Hosea gestured off toward the south. "Your father and I came through some years ago, some miles that way, in a spot that the Lakota used to hold sacred, through an adit that does not exist here; it needs to be held open from the New World. Which it surely is, as a trap. Intended to trap him at least." His smile was distant. "Not that that will stop your father, will it?"

"No." Torrie closed his eyes for a moment. "Because the Sons are cold and cruel, because if the bait doesn't draw the prey, then there's no reason for them not to eat the bait." He opened his eyes. "Yes," he said. "It won't stop either of us. 'The blood of heroes,' eh?"

Hosea nodded slowly. "Oh, Torrie, you've always had that, eh?"

"Thorian," the elder Thorsen called to his son from the doorway. Torrie caught the first of the tossed two large leather rucksacks and threw it into the car, then the second.

"One more moment." Thorsen disappeared back into the house.

It was only then that Ian realized that Thorsen had had a sword belt buckled around his waist. Even with jeans and plaid shirt, on him it looked natural.

Torrie's face was pale as he turned to Ian. "I'm sorry about all this, but—" He shrugged. "No time for explanations—Dad will leave without me if I don't keep up. I . . . if things work out right, and you get the chance, tell Maggie I'm sorry, if I don't get the chance. If I'd thought—" he caught himself.

"Thorian," Hosea said quietly, "remember everything I've taught you. Some of it may serve you well." He touched two long fingers to Torrie's forehead for just a moment, then took a shuffling step forward to gather Torrie in his arms. "As some may not. Take care of yourself."

Thorsen appeared in the doorway, a pair of rifles tucked under one arm, and two sheathed swords in belts clutched in his hands.

"Once again, Hosea," he said. "I ask that you accompany me. I have a sword here for you."

Hosea shook his head as he released Torrie. "I can't. It would be not only dangerous, Thorian, but pointless."

Silently, Thorsen turned and walked toward the car.

Torrie quickly clasped hands with Ian for a moment before running toward the car. He managed to get the door open and himself into the front seat just as his father started the engine and gunned the car into motion.

And then they were gone.

Ian stood, stunned. None of it made sense. Not the carnage on the lawn, as bad as anything he had seen the summer he had supplemented teaching fees with work as an ER orderly. Not the talk of wolves carrying away Karin and Maggie, not—none of it.

Hosea was watching him. "Come with me into the house," he said, long fingers plucking gently at Ian's shirt. Ian followed him inside, and then down the stairs into the basement, their footsteps too loud in the silence.

Hosea reached out and pulled a string; fluorescent light flared in the light panels above. He crossed his thin arms over his thin chest, and leaned back against a workbench. "The young one was correct; it will be a trap. They didn't attack while I was here, because here the Sons would have no power over me. So they would lure me to where they do."

"I don't understand any of this."

Hosea nodded. "True enough. And you have every right to, friend Ian, but not the time. All you need to know is this: if we're very fortunate, we can rescue your friends, our friends, within a few hours, and then return safely. If we are less fortunate, we may yet be of service, although the way will be longer and more difficult." Fingers worked at a knot on the paneled wall, and a square section of paneling swung out, revealing a leather knapsack and a pile of brown cloth that Ian thought was a blanket until Hosea pulled it out. It was a cloak of some sort.

Hosea set it on the floor, and worked at another spot on the panel, this time revealing a pair of recurved bows and a quiver thick with arrows. He pulled one out; its razor tip shone silver under the fluorescent light. "The Sons can't stand silver," he said. "Some of the others have trouble with steel." He pursed his lips for a moment. "And that which is properly tempered in the right blood can kill anything."

Ian cocked his head to one side. "So why no silver bullet?" It was crazy. He had no business asking questions, as though the old man was sane. What the situation called for was to head for the door and walk away from the crazy old black man and all his friends. Let the authorities handle it.

The old man gestured toward the end of the workroom, where a reloading press stood under a covering of plastic sheeting. "I trust Thorian has taken some with him. We swaged them ourselves—silver around steel. They will be useful if he catches the Sons before they make their way to the Old Way. But not in Tir Na Nog; the guns wouldn't work, or they would work too well."

"So you want me to go hunting wolves with you with nothing more than a bow?"

"No." Hosea walked to the wall and pulled a sword

down from the rack. "I . . . invite you to accompany me, and keep them off me while I hunt them. If we're fortunate enough to locate them quickly."

He presented it hilt first. Technically, it was a basket-hilted saber: the narrow, silvery blade was sharpened back from the needle tip on both sides, as though it was intended to cut as well as stab, but it felt stiff and light like a rapier or épée. The blade was straight, its surface uninscribed, the pommel a simple silver cap purely functional, no decoration.

It was a fighting weapon—not a practice saber, intended to score points with a quick flick: It was not a cavalry saber; it was intended to be used against somebody else with a sword, not to hew down peasants or Indians from horseback.

Ian gave it a few trial sweeps through the air. It moved with the stiffness of an épée, not the lightness of foil. The hilt was cord-wound over something that had just the right give; it almost seemed to grip Ian's hand back.

It felt embarrassingly right in his hand.

"And if not?" he asked. "What if I don't want to accompany you?"

"I don't know. I will seek them, I will see what I can still do." Hosea shook his head. "But there is one end for all, eventually: the fortunate, the unfortunate, the quick, and the slow."

"And you want me to leave with you now? How? To go where? With what?"

There was a long pause. "There will either be plenty of time for that, or we have far too little." Hosea kneeled at the fencing strip, and pushed one hand down on it, then set his cupped fingertips to the surface as though he was pulling on an invisible doorknob.

The whole side of the fencing strip swung up, like an absurdly long door opening in the floor, until it balanced neatly on its side.

Beneath it there was mostly dirt, except for what looked at first glance like a hole.

But it wasn't. A hole wasn't of the purest nonreflective black.

Straightening, Hosea took a paintbrush from the nearby table and returned to poke its tip down into the black circle.

He pulled the stick out. The end of the brush was gone, cut so cleanly that the tips of the fibers shone.

"Be careful not to touch it, unless you wish to step through," Hosea said, tying the end of a ball of string to a hook on the underside of the fencing strip. "It is a way in, but not out."

A small, silvery knife that Ian hadn't seen before was in Hosea's hands; he cut off a length of string, ran one end through an overhead eyelet, and tied the ends together. He rummaged through a box of vials on the workbench before he came up with a glass bottle, stoppered with glass. He carefully, gingerly removed the stopper and touched it to the string next to the eyelet. The string immediately began to smoke.

Hosea frowned, and touched it again, apparently satisfied when the smoke thickened. "That should do it," he said, restoppering and replacing the bottle. "That will give you just a few moments before it swings shut," he said. "You'll find a spare rucksack and a belt and scabbard for that sword in the closet behind the door," he said. "Follow me, if you choose. There's no shame if you're unwilling to. You've made no commitment, and you weren't born to it, the way young Thorian was." His smile broadened and he started to step off the edge.

"Best to decide quickly." The words hung in the air.

Hosea disappeared into the blackness, and Ian was alone.

* * *

Ian knew what Benjamin Silverstein would have said, would have wanted Ian to say.

Go off to rescue somebody, a silvery sword in his hand?

Don't be silly, boy. It's just more of that Errol Flynn shit, and it's about time you grew up. Get through school and into law school, and be a lawyer like your father. That's fine; I'll pay for that—but no more talk of this nonsense about becoming some sort of advocate for a bunch of juvenile delinquents. You find something worthwhile to do.

No, he had said, finally. No. I'll do it my way. I don't want to be some sort of corporate lawyer. I want to work for abused kids, I want to drag their parents into court and hold them accountable, make those bastards pay for it.

And he should have added: like I wish somebody had done with you years ago, you bastard, and I swear to God if you ever raise your hand to me again, I'll run you through.

But he hadn't.

Still, you didn't say no to Benjamin Silverstein. And when Benjamin Silverstein took a step forward to slap you into submission, again, you didn't set the point of a sword against his chest, a point you had ground from the button at the tip of a foil, turning a practice weapon into something very real.

Ian's hand clenched on the hilt of the silvery sword the way it had on the foil, that day. Benjamin Silverstein was a bear of a man, and strong as a bull, but it was over: he was not going to beat Ian anymore.

Get *out,* Benjamin Silverstein had said. Fill that backpack of yours with your clothes and get out. You've been eighteen years old for more than a month, and I don't have to put up with your shit anymore, boy. If you're not out of my house in five minutes, I call the cops.

* * *

Benjamin Silverstein wouldn't have approved. Don't be stupid, boy, he would have said. Just more of that silly Robin Hood shit.

In the final analysis, that was enough for Ian. More than enough. He took the rucksack from the closet and slipped the straps over his shoulders. Another cloak lay folded on the shelf above it; that, too, went over a shoulder. He belted the scabbard around his waist, but didn't slip the sword into it. It felt too right in his hand.

"Fuck you, Dad," he said.

Smiling, Ian stepped into the darkness.

Part Two

The New World

CHAPTER FIVE

The Sons of the Wolf

The road lay flat and straight like a taut ribbon under the swollen moon as far as the eye could see, but all it would take would be one deer lunging out from a windbreak, its eyes shining back the headlights, and the Bronco could be rolling in the ditch.

Still, Dad pressed down more heavily on the accelerator. "I haven't spoken to you of strategy," he said quietly, his eyes never leaving the road, his face, lit only by the light of the dashboard, a horrid green.

"There's a lot you haven't said. You taught me better than to ask."

"I did, at that. We're getting closer. Get me a set of the nightgoggles, and do the same for yourself."

Torrie unhooked himself from the seat belt. Two of the leather emergency bags were in the back, behind the seat. Each was heavy, intended to be thrown in the back of a car, or carried a short distance and then some of the contents buried.

He knew their contents the way he knew the abditory where they had been hidden: two mini Maglites, along with spare batteries that were changed twice a year; two pounds of jerky, and as much of the waxy chocolate that wouldn't melt; a physician's kit, complete with pharmacopoeia that ran from broad-spectrum antibiotics to morphine, Vistaril, and Demerol; a long Gerber hunting knife and a Swiss Army knife and a SOG Paratool, each with blades better sharpened than they had been at the factory; a fire-starting kit; a coil of climbing rope; several dozen latex condoms, capable of carrying small amounts of water or of keeping wooden matches dry as well as for more traditional uses; copies of each of their four passports, copies that would stand the closest scrutiny; a roll of duct tape; water-purification tablets and filters; a box of Tampax; a dozen gold Krugerrands and ten thousand dollars in twenties; a fiberfill sleeping bag, squeezed into the smallest stuff sack it could fit—it used to be down, when Torrie was a kid, but fiberfill had gotten better, and the emergency bags had been updated; a food-getting kit, including fishing hooks and line, barbs for a fishing spear, and a black Ruger Mark I, along with a brick of Stingers; dry socks, and stretchy polypropylene turtlenecks and drawstring trousers, capable of fitting Dad, albeit a bit tightly, or Torrie or Mother, albeit loosely in different places; large squares of Mylar sheeting that could be used as a ground cloth or pitched as a lean-to; a Zeiss monocular; and a set of military nightgoggles.

He pulled out two metal cases and set them on the seat, opening first one, then the other. In each, in a foam compartment to protect it against shock, lay a pair of goggles, each with its battery pack.

Torrie pulled out one and pushed the test button, gratified when it went green, then turned the goggles on and handed the set to Dad, who clumsily pulled it down over his eyes. Dad did something with a switch on the dashboard, and the interior of the Bronco went dark; a moment later, the headlights went out.

Torrie already had the other set of goggles out and on his head. Like much else in the emergency kits, the goggles were expensive, but Dad and Mother had never been ones to pinch pennies over such things. The idea was that in case of any emergency, be it nuclear war or a tornado, they should be able to reach for the hidden catch at the top of the frame to the front door, then slide the wall panel aside as they grabbed an emergency bag on their way to the car, and be able to survive, perhaps even survive with a bit of comfort. There were additional kits in the trunks of each car, but their contents were more restricted; they were always kept in the cars, and had to be able to stand up to a Canadian border crossing or, theoretically at least, a police search.

He turned the goggles on, and the world sprang into shades of blue and black, like watching an old-fashioned black-and-white TV.

But now the moon cast enough light for him to see as far as he cared to, although he had no peripheral vision. Practiced reflexes returned; Torrie automatically began to scan from side to side.

"I'd better load up." The boxes of ammo were on the floor, and he couldn't load the rifles without detaching himself.

"You'd best, at that." Dad glanced over at him as he removed his seat belt, but didn't say anything else.

"You left too much unsaid," Torrie finally said. "I don't even know where to start asking you questions. Are all the stories Uncle Hosea told true?"

"All of them?" Dad shook his head. "No. I doubt it. But many of them, certainly. Most of the ones about the Aesir and the Vanir, yes, they were largely true. The Tuatha? Some of them still live." His smile was a private one. "As Hosea ought to know."

"And the Vestri? Are there really dwarves?"

"Certainly," Dad said. "Although they . . . look somewhat different than they did in your picture books."

"Why did you never tell me about this? About any of it?"

"I . . . had my reasons." Dad's mouth twisted. "I wanted you kept away from it. And I dislike being thought to be a liar. Even your mother doesn't—didn't—believe half of it, and she has had better reason than most to believe in it."

Or maybe Mother wanted me growing up normal, and not out looking for Hidden Ways to Tir Na Nog, Torrie thought.

As long as it was just the stuff of tales that Uncle Hosea told, it was safe.

But when the Sons of the Wolf stepped out of story and onto your back porch, it was all different, but not strange, not surprising. That was the shock: that there was no shock, that he was cruising down a county road heading for a confrontation with the Sons of the Wolf, and he wasn't burdened by any doubt.

"Like the gold?" Torrie asked.

"Like the gold. Stolen from the Fire Duke when Orfindel and I escaped. Melted down, and carefully sold off in small lots." He smiled. "The foundation of the family fortune, although your Mother has increased it some. Rather more than some," he said, correcting himself with a smile.

Torrie picked up a box of cartridges. In the eerie green light, he could barely make out the label. It read Winchester Super-X, in .30-06; the rifles were old Garands. He had grabbed the right boxes. Just as well.

After setting one rifle to safe, Torrie opened the box and pulled out one of the cartridges. It felt swollen, huge.

Torrie mainly fired .22s; most of his time with a rifle was spent under the tutelage of Dad or Uncle Hosea at the range, although in his senior year in high school, he'd gone through a phase of almost compulsive rabbit hunting that only ended when Mother had sworn that she would turn vegetarian before she would cook or eat another rabbit stew, fricassee, or stir-fry.

But .22s were teeny little cartridges, and each of the huge .30-06 rounds was the size of Torrie's middle finger.

And each was tipped with a homemade silver bullet.

"Stripper clips underneath," Dad said.

There was something suitable about giving the Sons of the Wolf the finger.

"So tell me about strategy." Torrie quickly lined up the stripper clip, and pushed the eight cartridges into the Garand—making damn sure it was on safe before he let the bolt slide closed—then turned to slip it into the rifle rack behind their heads. He started on the second rifle, cursing at the way his fingers shook when he tried to pull the bolt back.

Dad was silent for a long moment, although muscles played at the side of his jaw. "We may not be able to take them, not here and now. They'll have assumed we have what's needed to deal with them, so they'll have your mother and your woman secured, they'll threaten them if we don't surrender. If you can, work yourself into a position where you can shoot any who get near to either of them, while I distract them from the front.

"But if not, if that doesn't work, we may get the chance to kill a few first, but that may be all; we won't be able to do more than to trim the pack for them and save their leader the trouble. We may not be able to rescue the women, not here and now."

"So what do we *do?*"

Dad shook his head. "In the long run, I don't know. For the moment, it's clear: we fight if we can and then, if necessary, we surrender. They'll guard me closely, but they may well take you less seriously—you wait for a chance to make a break and then you take it. If I see one, I'll drop the word 'vague' into a sentence—or *posfe*, in the Old Tongue. When I do, you move. Don't stop to think; just go."

"And then?" Torrie slipped the second rifle into the rack, and started loading stripper clips. Dad didn't think things through as well as he should have; all this ammo should have been stored on stripper clips.

"And then use your judgment, young Thorian del Thorian," Dad said. His face broke into a smile for just a moment. "There's too much to tell you, and too little time to tell it in. Be careful in your prayers, for you may be heard; remember that the Tuatha and the other Old Ones can take on many forms, but most are bothered by cold steel; fight with your head as well as your arm."

"Always brush between meals."

"Ah." Dad smiled. "And I was going to say that you should try to keep your sense of humor about you, for it may stand you in good stead." The smile vanished. "You're good enough with a sword that you should be able to take on most, but not all. What else? If you can escape, keep your true name to yourself unless you need to use it. There are those who will be beholden to you in Orfindel's name, but don't use the name lightly. It has power, too, but there's danger in it. Some might think you know too much, although others would help you just for the naming."

Torrie found himself mimicking a gesture that he had seen his dad make: he formed his right hand into a fist, and struck it against his palm.

Dad shook his head. "No, Asa-Thor is long dead; Hosea once saw his bones."

An old dirt road on an earthen berm cut across the fields ahead, leading from the pavement to where a stand of trees loomed, large and threatening. Deep in the woods, something glowed, but what it was, Torrie couldn't say.

"There's a path," Dad said, "that cuts across the road, about, oh, twenty yards in. I'll slow the car there; you get out and head down it. The goggles will give you some benefit," he said, reaching into his pocket and producing a blackened revolver, "but silence will give you more."

Reflexively, Torrie thumbed the release and opened the cylinder. The bases of nine bullets shone back at him. Little .22s.

"Silver," Dad said, handing him a small box. "And in

here, too. You'll need a head shot to drop one quickly with this, but the gun's fairly quiet. Not silent, by any means, but quieter than the Rugers in the emergency kits."

"And what are you going to do?"

"I'll drive further in, and then get out and stalk my way in from the west." He shrugged. "Or, perhaps, just confront them and wait for you. Depends on how well they have the road watched."

Torrie closed the cylinder and tucked the gun into the pocket of his jacket.

"Don't forget your sword," Dad said.

Torrie looped the belt over one shoulder, then reached for the topmost Garand.

Dad reached up and flicked the dome light switch as he slowed the car. "Now."

Rifle in one hand, his other free, Torrie threw the door open and leaped out the door into the artificial brightness of the night.

He staggered for a moment, then dropped into the field beside the road, his free hand batting brush out of the way to protect his goggles.

The car rumbled on down the road.

His head half obscured in the brush, Torrie froze in place. He had learned that on a deer stand, and learned it better from Dad and Uncle Hosea than others would. They had insisted on a ground stand, despite the fact that deer would rarely look up into a tree.

But a ground stand worked, too, if you had carefully washed traces of your scent from your body and clothing, and if the wind blew the right way, if you could hold still.

Torrie could hold still, and he did, even though the cold wind in his face would have drawn tears from his eyes if they weren't covered by the goggles.

He could hear his heartbeat, and started counting. If a watchman waited just behind the tree line, he might have seen something, or nothing.

There was something wrong with him, Torrie decided. He should be shuddering in sympathy with whatever had happened to Mother and Maggie, or trembling in fear, but he wasn't. It was as though everything Dad and Uncle Hosea had taught him was a preamble to this moment, and he was just going through practiced motions.

In the light of the goggles, the dirt road was almost painfully bright out in the open, and darker but still visible where the trees shaded it from the overhead moon. But bright or dark, the road was empty, and—

There! To the left of that large oak next to the other side of the road, something had moved, and then it moved again.

Beneath the level of the road, Torrie reached into his pocket and gripped the butt of his revolver tightly in his hand.

Moving swiftly but gracefully, the wolf stepped out onto the road and took a hesitant step toward Torrie, not venturing beyond the line of shadow. Walking stiff-legged, back and forth, it sniffed the air a couple of times, then took a step toward the lighted part of the road, then a step back.

It didn't like the moonlight, apparently.

It was a huge beast, easily half again the size of the Petersons' St. Bernard, and while its jaws were open to reveal long teeth, it was still somehow beautiful.

It was also on watch.

Torrie waited, motionless. He could do none of the others any good as long as the wolf waited there, and simply doing something for the sake of doing something wasn't allowed when you were on a stand.

The wolf took a step down the road, and then broke into a trot, snuffling as it came, heading for a spot across the road from where Torrie crouched, motionless.

He drew the gun slowly, trying to prevent any sound of fabric on fabric, and brought it up at the end of an outstretched hand, his thumb carefully pulling back the hammer until it locked with a click that he only felt, but couldn't hear.

It was then that he heard the *wshhhh* of something moving through the air behind him, and turned just in time to catch a blow across the face that sent his goggles spinning off into the night and sparks flying around the inside of his brain.

Blinded, in pain, he brought the pistol up and pulled the trigger, rewarded by the quiet crack of the .22 and a grunt of pain.

Something large and foul-smelling knocked him down, and fingers clawed at his chest, but he managed to keep hold of the gun and plant the barrel squarely into whatever it was before pulling the trigger again.

He barely felt the recoil, but whatever it was let out a low groan, and fell away from him in the dark; Torrie's eyes could focus enough to see whatever it was stagger a few paces away to fall on the plowed ground.

Torrie turned, quickly, as the wolf sprang, and fired once, blindly, the little .22 spitting fire into the darkness, while on the ground next to him, a fully loaded Garand lay.

For a moment, he thought that he had missed: the wolf landed in a crouch as though to spring again.

But then, its bright left eye went all flat and dull in the moonlight, while the other eye, the right eye, was a dark pit, and it flopped to the ground, limp, as though its muscles had turned to Jell-O.

Torrie turned to look at the other wolf.

But . . . it wasn't a wolf, not anymore; it had been changing as it attacked him, and now a naked woman lay on her side on the plowed ground, dead eyes staring unblinkingly up at the moon overhead, her too-white torso mottled by a cicatrix of scars across her belly, and two small holes in her left breast.

The wind changed, and it brought Torrie the stink of her fouling herself in death.

He looked over at the other of the Sons, still a wolf, and remembered something that Uncle Hosea had said about the Sons, about how they were the children of Fenris's mating with a wolf bitch, and how Fenris himself was the product of the Trickster mating with a witch, and how even the Oldest couldn't tell whether one was a wolf pretending to be a human or a human pretending to be a wolf, and here, at least, it seemed that it was true.

It was strange. The first time he had shot a deer he had felt strange, a combination of exhilaration and guilt. It was just as well he had gotten it with a heart shot, as his hands had trembled so hard he could barely put his rifle on safe, and would probably have dropped it if Uncle Hosea hadn't been there to lay a steadying hand on his shoulder.

But this didn't mean anything. There were just two bags of shit and muscle and bone, one sprawled on the road, one lying on the ploughed ground, and they didn't mean anything to him.

That thought made him feel unclean, and the thought that he was wasting time while Mother and Maggie and Dad were all in danger made him feel worse. He shook himself, once, then spent precious seconds finding his nightgoggles and seeing that they still, thankfully, worked. He settled the loop of his swordbelt around his shoulder, then reloaded and pocketed the pistol before picking up the Garand.

He started down the road at a trot, and turned off down the trail, walking as quickly and quietly as he could.

Growls and voices sounded from around the bend ahead; Torrie slowed his pace, carefully scanning back and forth for any watchman. That was the trouble with the nightgoggles: while they gave him better night vision than any animal, the field of vision was too limited. On his workbench at home, Dad had a Starlight scope and a heavy Soviet night-vision device that he had bought; Torrie would almost have preferred that to the nightgoggles.

Too-bright light knifed through the leaves ahead, sending overly bright beams splashing into the forest. Torrie slowed to a step-watch-and-step, forcing himself to keep his finger off the trigger of the Garand.

He crept into a dark patch and dropped first to one knee, then to his belly, and crawled forward on the cold dirt until he reached the base of a huge oak.

Carefully, slowly, he brought his head around until he could see out into the clearing.

The Bronco was parked, its engine silent, but the headlights were on, shining on a small cairn of stones in the center of the clearing.

There was nobody there.

Dad had been there; both of the survival kits had been torn open, and their contents scattered around the clearing, as though in a tantrum, but there was no sign of him, nor of Mother or Maggie.

Or of the Sons.

An oval of ground in front of the cairn was a solid black, even in the light of the Bronco's headlights as amplified by the nightgoggles, but save for that, the clearing held nothing strange.

They were all gone, and he was too far away in the dark to spot any footprints, to try to pick up a trail.

Torrie raised the nightgoggles to his forehead.

Even in the naked light of the headlights, the oval of darkness was still black as black could be. And the clearing was still empty.

Torrie waited. There wasn't much he could do, and what little he could do made even less sense, but it was the only thing that made any sense at all. He could run around blindly, shouting pointlessly, or he could wait.

If anybody was watching for him, they had probably already seen him, but if not . . . if not, the best thing he could do would be to remain motionless.

He froze in place, and waited.

That had always been the hard thing in hunting, and the most important lesson. It had been impossible for him at fourteen, and Uncle Hosea had sworn that he wouldn't take Torrie into the woods again in season if he continued to twitch.

So Uncle Hosea, in his usual way, had turned it into a game, in which they'd go for a walk in the woods, and at the command "Freeze," Torrie would do just that, to be rewarded with a treat of some sort—a new buckle for his belt; a matching set of silver buttons sewn onto his favorite shirt; another story of the Aesir and Vanir; later, the installation of a new carburetor in his car—when he did it well.

Most importantly, he would be rewarded with a smile from Uncle Hosea. That was no less precious for being common.

He hoped Uncle Hosea was still smiling back at the house as he froze in place, forcing himself not to move, not even to breathe deeply. No twitch, no headshake, nothing. It was, as Uncle Hosea said many important things were, both simple and difficult: the secret to not moving was simply not to move.

He counted his heartbeats until he reached a thousand, then started all over again. The moon rose slowly, and shadows moved.

That was something else he had learned on a deer stand: that the woods were never silent.

Off in the distance, an occasional car whooshed down the county road, but none turned off onto the dirt road; he would have heard that, easily. A vague, distant reek of skunk was in the air, but that was easily a mile off, and not offensive; Torrie had always found a distant skunk smell kind of pleasant, actually.

Above his head, a scrabbling in a nearby tree told of some squirrel on a nocturnal errand, but he couldn't hear any other animals in this patch of woods.

He tried not to think about where the others were and how they were. Uncle Hosea had told him stories about the world being honeycombed with Hidden Ways, and maybe they weren't just stories, but . . .

He had waited at least half an hour when he finally rose to his feet. He was alone.

Cradling his Garand in his arms, Torrie straightened. It hurt, but that was nothing unusual—it always hurt when you started to move again after freezing.

He stalked carefully toward the cairn. The leather emergency bags had both been ripped to shreds, as had every item in them, from the sleeping bags to the bottles of pills out of the medical kits. His first instinct was to put it to senseless vandalism, but that didn't feel right.

He stalked over to the Bronco. The upholstery had been shredded, as well, and the glove compartment lay open, its contents scattered, as though whoever had done it was searching for something, something small.

Torrie thumbed his flashlight on. There were stains here and there, and the interior was wet, but that was likely from when whoever it was had dumped out the plastic water bottle. The cab smelled of window-washer fluid.

Nothing looked like fresh blood, and nothing smelled of death.

Good.

He shined his flashlight on the ground. It was soft outside the driver's side of the cab, and Dad's work boots had made a solid imprint in the damp ground. He had stepped down—not with his rifle; that lay on the ground on the other side of the Bronco—and walked toward the cairn. Four-toed animal prints inside his footprints told of Sons following him; other prints to the side could have been made before or after.

Dad had left the road a few feet in front of the car, and Torrie lost the prints in the low grasses, but they pointed toward the cairn. Torrie followed.

Still, nothing. He shone his flashlight ahead; the oval patch of darkness seemed to be a hole, although he couldn't see into it; his Mini Maglite wasn't powerful enough.

There was a quiet rustle behind him. He set his finger on the trigger of the Garand and took a step forward. Another step, and he would clear the front of the Bronco; he could duck to one side, and take up a defensive position, all it would take—

"Easy does it, Torrie," a familiar voice said.

Torrie turned to see Davy Hansen limping out of the tree line, one palm held up, fingers spread; his chest bare in the cold air; his AR15 held muzzle-high with his other hand.

Torrie had never much liked Davy Hansen. Davy kept mainly to himself, supplementing his disability check with odd repair jobs, and sometimes seemed to resent Uncle Hosea's ability to do the same work he could, only better, and faster, and as a favor instead of for pay. Torrie had always figured that as long as Davy had all the work he was willing to handle, he had no grounds for complaint, and should keep the occasional dropped comment to himself, but he'd never seen any point in discussing that opinion with Davy.

Davy nodded toward the hole. "They went in through there, all of them, and then the tunnel started to shimmer for a moment, but just for a moment."

"You just watched them?" Torrie asked, regretting it the moment the words were out of his mouth.

Davy only smiled. "Yeah, I just watched them. I watched a wolf change into a man to stand next to your mother and hold a knife to her throat until your father surrendered, and I watched while that wolf-man bound the wrists of all three of them and handed them down into that hole. All I did was watch." He shrugged. " 'Course, back at the house, I tried to shoot the fucking things, but all that did was annoy them. Winchester hollow points don't seem to do it—you got any silver bullets?" he asked with a sarcastic smile.

"Lots," Torrie said.

That took Davy aback for a moment, but then he nodded. "Figures," he said. Davy Hansen was too much the stoic Norski to show surprise if he could help it.

"Them?" Torrie asked. "Were they . . . ?"

"Okay? Peachy keen, kid. All three of them. The women were scratched up some, and your Dad took a punch to the gut when he didn't move quite fast enough to suit one of them, but they all looked fine when they were lowered down." He shrugged. "I didn't see any point in making some sort of pointless gesture." Davy smiled, as though over a private joke. "I've already done that enough for one life, maybe two."

Torrie set the Garand on safe, then set it down on the Bronco, the barrel pointed away from Davy. "This is loaded with silver bullets." Moving slowly, carefully, he pulled the revolver out of his pocket and set it down on the hood, following it with his nightgoggles. "This, too. Some scattered around on the ground."

"I don't like handguns." Reluctantly, Davy set down his rifle and picked up the Garand, reflexively pulling back the bolt, even though that ejected one of the cartridges, sending it tumbling to the ground. He locked the bolt open, stooped to pick up the cartridge, and replaced it in the rifle, letting the bolt close on a loaded chamber. "Then again, with this on me, I don't need a handgun." He shrugged. "Somebody from town'll be along, I expect; you want I should hold it?"

"Yeah. On the other hand, I don't want you to freeze." Torrie set his scabbard and sword down on the hood before he shrugged out of his jacket. It should fit Davy, albeit only loosely.

Loosely was good enough. He tossed the jacket to Davy,

then slung the swordbelt over his shoulder and went to the rear of the Bronco.

There was a Coleman lantern in the car's emergency kit, and a spare rucksack; in a moment, he had the lantern brightly hissing, and in its white light stooped to pick up scattered items from the ground.

The two plastic packets containing the stacks of twenties had been opened, then tossed aside, but the Krugerrands were gone. One of the medical kits had been torn apart, but the other lay undisturbed. Both of the sleeping bags had been shredded, as though by razors, but the Mylar sheeting had been left alone. The pistols were gone, but he found two of the slim magazines under the slashed leather bag that had carried all of the stuff.

It probably made sense, but Torrie couldn't make any sense of it. He would have been surprised at how calm he was being, except that his hands shook as he loaded the backpack, then stood for a moment, idly opening and closing the pliers of his SOG Paratool.

"The one searching threw the pistols into the woods," Davy said. "I can find them come morning."

"You'll keep watch on this place," Torrie said more than asked, as he picked up the revolver from the hood of the car. He reloaded it, then tucked it into the back of his belt.

Davy nodded, once. Just once. "We'll handle it."

Torrie handed him both packets of bills. "In case of need—" At Davy's glare, he held up a hand. "It won't do any good where I'm going," he said, "or they would have taken it."

"I don't need your fucking money, Thorsen," Davy Hansen said. "But I'll watch it, too."

There was a story that Uncle Hosea used to tell, about the time that one of the Tuatha had tried to trap Honir with a doorway that disappeared behind him.

Torrie hoped that he would acquit himself as well as

Honir had, but doubted it. The Sons were probably waiting down the tunnel for him.

But what else could he do? Wait here? Davy could handle the waiting. Anybody could wait.

He walked to the edge of the tunnel and shone the lantern down into the blackness. The tunnel went straight down about fifteen feet or so, and then led off to the south. Divots cut into the side of the wall would provide a way to climb down to the tunnel floor.

Davy tossed him the end of a rope, a bowline already tied into it, leaving a loop that Torrie could step in. He looked up; the other end had been looped under the Bronco's front axle, and Davy stood, the Garand slung over one shoulder, holding the coil of rope.

"Ready to belay," he said.

Torrie tightened the backpack's waist strap, and felt at the hilt of his sword.

No sense in waiting any longer. He could trust the carved handholds and footholds, but Torrie would rather trust a neighbor any day.

He sat down on the edge of the hole and set his right foot into the loop.

"On belay," Davy said.

Slowly, gradually, Torrie transferred his weight to his foot, and slowly Davy began to let the rope give.

Lantern in one hand, the other clinging to the rope, Torrie was slowly lowered into the dark.

"Semper fi, kid," were the last words he heard from above.

Just as he stepped out of the loop and onto the hard stone floor, the rope gave way, falling in a tangle to the floor. Reflexively, Torrie reached out and grabbed an end.

The Thorsens didn't do things by half; the rope they kept in the back of the Bronco was a rock-climbing rope, certified to hold an absurd amount of weight. Its tough fibers could take hundreds of hours of abrasion against rock, and they would give even the sharpest knife a hard time.

But the end had been sliced through, neatly, as though by a single stroke.

Torrie tried to shine the light of the lantern up, but all he could see was darkness, and what appeared to be solid rock far above.

He thought about calling to Davy, but decided against that. Sounds could echo a long distance down the tunnel.

Well, there was no point in waiting here, not with the tunnel leading away. If he had to, he could try to climb out using the handholds, but there was no rush, not now.

He drew his sword—it made him feel better—and started off down the tunnel at a slow walk.

It was shaped sort of like an egg, wide side down, in cross section; the ceiling, a few feet above where he could reach, came to a tight curve up top, while the floor was gently curved, almost forcing him to walk down the middle of it. The walls were stone, roughly cut, although no trace of tools had been left. He reached out a finger; they were warm to the touch, but not hot.

Ahead, the tunnel bent left in an arc that was gentle at first, but became more severe as it went on. It led into a series of sharp cornered turns, each section of tunnel no more than ten or twelve feet long, the wall at each turn cut roughly but sharply into an archway some few feet over his head.

For the longest time—later, he was never sure quite how long—Torrie could hear nothing except the quiet hissing of the Coleman lantern and the quiet thrumming of his own heart.

Gradually he became aware that a very gentle, cool breeze was blowing in his direction, although he couldn't quite figure out how. The tunnel, after all, dead-ended back where Torrie had been lowered. Did this mean that it was now open back there? Or what?

He quickened his pace to a fast walk, hoping that would keep him ahead of anything that might be following, as he went through turn after turn, through archway after archway.

Finally, an archway ahead opened on blackness. Torrie stopped for a moment, and thought he could hear some hiss in the distance, although perhaps it was just the lantern. He walked back a few feet, carefully set the lantern down, then walked back, stopping at the archway to listen.

Yes, far off was a rustling, a hissing, perhaps like that of running water, but when he peered around the corner, there was no light in front of him, just the vague grayness of the path, lit by the lantern behind him, seemingly ending in blackness to either side.

He retrieved the lantern and walked through.

And for a moment, his head began to spin; he almost fell.

The stone path ahead was surrounded by nothing, save where the flat stone wall behind Torrie rose far above his head, far further than the light of the lantern could show. Gently, carefully, he looked over the edge and could see nothing except a gray rock face stretching far below. The path itself, while just as roughly carved from stone as the floor of the tunnel had been, didn't seem to have any side to it: it just ended, and gingerly proddings with Torrie's sword tip didn't find anything hidden in the blackness underneath it.

There was still that distant sound of running water, but he couldn't for the life of him say whether it came from above or below or in front of him; the only thing he was sure of was that it didn't come from behind him.

The path through the air stretched out ahead in the darkness, and there was nothing to do but follow it.

The rock face quickly vanished behind him, swallowed

by the gloom. He started to count his steps, and got to six hundred seventy-eight before he noticed that the gloom ahead was broken by grayness that became another rock face as he approached.

Eight hundred three, and he could make out an archway ahead of him, identical, as far as he could tell, to the one behind him.

He stopped counting, but another hundred hurried steps brought him to the archway, and through, and into a small room—where beady eyes shone back at him out of the dark, and before he could think to move or do something, his sword and lantern had been snatched from his nerveless fingers, and rough, strong hands seized his hands and shoulders.

He struggled helplessly, pointlessly, while the largest wolf he had ever seen, easily three feet at the shoulder, stepped out of the darkness and stopped in front of him. In another time, he would have thought of it as a magnificent beast, with its thick mane all in black and white and gray, but this wasn't another time. But, still, he couldn't take his eyes off it as it leaned back, as though sitting on its hind legs, and then lifted its front paws off the ground.

And changed.

The long muzzle receded, some hairs receding into flesh, others changing in length, while the forepaws melted into long fingers, tipped with yellowed but pointed fingernails. The chest, crisscrossed seemingly randomly with scars, was covered with a mat of dark black hair.

The Son's thin lips were split in a triumphant smile, but it was the eyes that held Torrie, that made him feel like a mouse facing a snake. "Greetings, Thorian son of Thorian," the Son said, his voice raspy and harsh. "Your friends await you, ahead and above."

CHAPTER SIX

Tir Na Nog

Afterward, Ian was never quite sure how long they walked through the dark tunnel, their way revealed only by an accompanying sourceless light that left behind no shadow and lit only their immediate surroundings. Perhaps a dozen feet in front of him and as many behind him, the dark rock merged with darkness. The effect was of walking on a treadmill, perhaps, of his feet pushing the tunnel away behind him, never really making any progress, no matter how far he walked.

And he had no idea how far that was. After some time, it occurred to him that he could have simply counted footsteps and multiplied by three or so to get a general idea of how many feet it was, and then divided by about five thousand to get the mileage.

But what would be the point? The tunnel seemed to stretch out indefinitely behind and ahead of him.

Hosea kept up a steady pace, a determined smile on his dark face, but refused to answer Ian's questions or to respond to anything he said, other than to put a long finger to his thin lips and shake his head when Ian tried to talk.

Ian didn't see what the need for silence was, but probably that was the point.

Ian hadn't been aware that there had been any mining in North Dakota, although it was clever of Hosea and Thorsen to have situated their house above a mining tunnel.

No, that didn't make any sense; he was trying to apply reason to a situation that was beyond reason. Mineshafts, no matter where they were, simply didn't have a one-way entrance that could nip off the end of your finger as easily as it could a brush. You didn't need to travel by a mineshaft in order to chase down a gang—bunch? band? party? pack? That was it: pack—you didn't need to travel by mineshaft in order to chase down a pack of wolves. And mines weren't lit by some sort of directionless light that stayed with you.

He tried not to think. Gripping the hilt of the sword at his waist was more comforting than thought could be. Not thinking was easy. It was like the time he had his appendix out, and then was sent back to his dorm with a bottle of Demerol and Vistaril pills to keep him company. Torrie had helped him down to the TV room, and set him up in front of the TV, and there he had sat. Time had changed in its nature. It was no longer linear, but instantaneous: he was sitting in an overstuffed armchair, he had always been sitting there, and he always would, that's how it had felt.

It was much easier to float through life than to think about it, much easier then to sit in an overstuffed armchair, as it was here and now to just keep walking, as though he could do it forever without tiring, without suffering from hunger or thirst.

He became aware with something akin to a shock that the tunnel was slanting up, and that it had been slanting up for some time now, although it was only his sense of balance that told him so; his ankles didn't complain, the way they would on a long hike uphill, and he wasn't at all winded, even though Hosea hadn't for a moment slowed his pace.

And finally the tunnel ended, up ahead: it turned at more than a ninety-degree angle, pointing straight up, topped by stone about ten feet above Ian's head.

Handholds and footholds were carved into the hard stone walls; Ian followed Hosea up, wincing for a moment as bright sunlight streamed down from above.

He was alone in the upshaft; Ian quickly pulled himself up and through—and into bright green loveliness.

Far upslope, the jagged gray top of the mountain was capped with snow that seemed, at least from this distance, to be of pure white. But here—at the base? halfway up? Ian couldn't tell—the meadow was rimmed by tall pines and capped by a sky of darker blue than any Ian had seen before. Beneath the noon sun—how long *had* they been walking?—soft grasses rose knee-high, their green expanse spotted by wildflowers of dark red and pale, wan yellow. The wind brought Ian a dark comfortable reek of rotting humus, lightened by hints of flowery perfumes and the warm tang of sunbaked grasses.

High above, a black bird, its wings spread wide, wheeled across the sky, orbiting above the meadow several times before it flew off toward the mountaintop.

Hosea was already replacing a thin slab of rock over the hole they had come through.

"Os hast dju veerisht?" he asked, although given the normal slurring of his voice Ian wasn't at all sure what he meant to say, much less what he actually said. Something about how he was feeling?

"Eh?"

"My apologies, young Silverstein," Hosea said. " 'Are you unwell?' I asked."

Not in any language I've ever heard. But he didn't say that. "I'll live."

"I would hope so. You may sheathe your sword, if it please you," Hosea went on. "We . . . took a wrong turn."

"We didn't take any turns."

Hosea just smiled, his teeth too white. "You might see it that way. Others might say we're turned ninety degrees away from everything you've ever seen. It depends on your perspective, I suppose."

The situation called for some sort of witty comment. "Somehow, Toto, I don't think we're in Kansas anymore," he said.

Hosea's brow furrowed. "Toto—oh. *The Wizard of Oz,*" he said with a smile. "Yes. I watched it with young Thorian, just recently." His smile was secretive, as though over some private joke. "When one gets to be my age, it's hard to keep everything straight," he said. "I would venture to guess that makes me Glinda, or am I the Cowardly Lion? I can hardly be the Scarecrow, as I have a brain, even if it does not work as well as it once did." He tapped a finger against his temple. "Damaged, don't you know."

"Where *are* we?"

Hosea frowned. "Well, we're not in the High Wastes, which is where we should be. Where we would be, if we'd taken the right turns." His upraised hand forestalled Ian's objection. "Yes, yes, you saw no turns. Had the binding not been breached, even Thorian would not have seen the entrance the Sons used." Hosea looked up the slope. "Well, we're in a meadow, and above us is the peak of Mount Æskja, which means we're in western Vandescard. There was a time when I could have told you to the . . . inch, to the inch where this exit was, but . . ." He sighed, and lifted his pack to his shoulders, carefully draping his cloak over it. "Well, shall we?"

"Vandescard?"

"A country. A part of, oh, call it Tir Na Nog, if you'd like: the New World, the Young Land, if you please. The final home of the Sidhe, the Aesir, the Vanir, and the rest of the Old Races."

* * *

Ian swallowed, hard. It was too much. Bit by bit, he had swallowed the strange uncle who practically bristled with secrets, the wolf attack in which Karin Thorsen and Maggie had been captured, not killed; he had been hurried down to the basement and into a one-way door to strangeness.

But enough. Aesir, Vanir, Old Races—never mind how crazy that sounded, because the best, the safest possibility was that Hosea was insane and some of that insanity had infected Ian.

He took a step back. "Look, Hosea, I . . . I'm not sure this is really a good idea."

"Which? Your friends in danger, or our attempt to aid them?"

"No, I mean this chasing off after . . ." He gestured.

"What's done is done. What is yet to be—"

"—is yet to be. Business is business, and let boys be boys." Ian raised a hand, fingers spread, to forestall Hosea. "I want out; I want to go home."

Hosea's face grew somber. "Even if I were to tell you that it's only you that can stand between them and disaster? That if you cannot find the way to be what you are, your friends and much else are lost?"

"Right." Ian snorted. "Yeah, you see a big red S on my chest?" Ignoring the other's look of puzzlement he went on. "Am I some sort of superman, is that what you're saying?"

Hosea shook his head. "I . . . don't do that sort of thing, not anymore. Once . . ." He let his voice trail off, and shook his head sadly. "But this is not once, this is now." He straightened, and smiled sadly. "As you decide: but if you are not going to accompany me, if you are not going to follow through with this, then we shall have to make other arrangements—"

If you're not going to follow through—

* * *

Benjamin Silverstein snickered as he handled the half-finished Model T, then set it down—carefully; he always handled the goddamn models carefully—and flicked a finger at the tiny pieces on Ian's desktop. "Looks pretty shitty, doesn't it, kid?" he said. "I bought you this thing almost a year ago, and this is as far as you've gotten? When I was your age, I was scrounging for real canvas for sails—and let me tell you, putting together Old Ironsides is one hell of a lot harder than one of these dinky little fifty-piece puzzles. Just can't follow through on anything, can you? If you're not going to follow through, what good are you?"

There were a lot of things Ian could have said. He could have talked about how making plastic models was his dad's hobby, not his; he could have said that what he had wanted when he had suggested that he might like a model of some sort for his tenth birthday was to have something to do with his dad, not something to be crapped on for not doing.

But you didn't talk back to Ben Silverstein. "I'm sorry, Daddy," he said. "I'll try to do better next time. Really I will."

Ben Silverstein snorted. "See that you do."

"If you are not going to accompany me, if you are not going to follow through with this, then we will have to make other arrangements—"

"Fuck you, Hosea," Ian said, with more heat than he intended.

Hosea looked down at Ian's waist. Ian followed his gaze down to where Ian's hand clasped the hilt of his sword, and for the life of him he didn't remember putting it there. He spread his fingers and took his hand away, letting it drop to one side. "Sorry, sorry," he said. "It's—you just sounded like somebody else for a moment."

Hosea accepted, then dismissed, it with a nod and a shrug. "You have my apologies, Ian," he said, gently, perhaps too gently: an adult dealing with a child's temper tantrum. "No offense was intended. If you wish to go back, likely we can find a way at Harbard's Crossing, when we come down the other side of the mountain," he said, looking up for a moment toward the empty sky.

"Harbard's Crossing?"

"A village, and the place of Harbard's Ferry—on the river the Aesir used to call Gilfi, and the Vandestish call Tennes."

Ian jerked his thumb at the stone that capped the tunnel they had come through. "And why not that way?"

Hosea smiled. "Lift it."

Ian dropped to his knees, slid his fingers under the cold stone, then lifted. It was heavier than it looked: it took all his strength to get it past forty-five degrees, and flipping it over onto its back, its damp dark underside facing the sky, revealed—

Dirt. Soil, broken only by a network of grass roots that looked like it had been there a long time.

"You'd best see for yourself," Hosea said, producing a folding shovel from his rucksack. He extended the telescoping handle, then snapped the blade forward and into place, then set it against the dirt. A booted foot pushed the shovel deep into the soil; Hosea levered a dirt clod out, threads of roots trailing from the blade.

There was no tunnel, nothing besides dirt and a writhing section of earthworm where Hosea dug.

Self-control was something he'd had to learn when his father beat the crap out of him given the slightest provocation; it was something he'd needed when he was thrown out of what had been his home with no notice, no time to make arrangements, no friends he could trust with this, because he could never have friends over, never knowing when something or nothing would send *him* into one of his fits.

This wasn't the worst. When his father had thrown him

out, Ian had stopped himself on the sidewalk, his pitiful few possessions packed in a backpack, sixteen dollars in his pocket—the rest of his money was in Ben's bank account ". . . for safety—you've never been responsible with money," and his stash, less than a couple hundred that he had squirreled away and, yes, stolen from Ben Silverstein's pants when he passed out, was in the garage, hidden at the bottom of the woodpile. It had been safe there; Ben had never carried a log to the fireplace or built a fire himself when he had a son to do it.

That was worse than this. He was all alone then.

But the same mantra applied. "I'll panic later," he said, as he had calmed himself and said then.

It was easier now. Then he had been a frightened kid, standing in the actinic glare of a mercury vapor streetlight, surrounded by darkness, without a plan, by himself. Compared to that, this was easy.

Now, at least, there was somebody else with him, and while he didn't entirely trust Hosea, Ian liked the older man. "I'll panic later," Ian said, more to himself than to anybody else. It was half of his mantra. The other half: "For now I'll just handle it."

"I'll just handle it." Ian dug his fingers into the ground, coming away with only dirt. "Exit only, eh?"

"Yes." Hosea waved his hand around. "There likely is another exit close by, but I don't know it, and it's likely as much bound as the ones in your world."

"Bound?"

Hosea pursed his lips. "I'd say spellbound, but that would imply a spellbinder, and there's none who would be able to say about that. Exits to Hidden Ways tend to . . . not to hide themselves, but there is something about them that tends to cause others to ignore them."

"Eh?"

Hosea paused for a moment. "The French call it *jamais vu*—the sense of never before having seen something familiar. Have you ever noticed something—a store, a tree, a hole in the ground—for the first time, even though you've passed it a hundred, a thousand, a hundred thousand times without knowing?"

Ian nodded. There had been a March day, when he had dropped his books and notebooks beside his desk, thrown on a T-shirt, a pair of walking shorts, and his old climbing boots, and then gone out for a walk, lest any more studying and working and sleeping and studying and working and sleeping drive him absolutely bugfuck.

Three steps out of the building it hit him. He must have walked under the old oak tree outside Sprague Hall thousands of times, but for the life of him he couldn't remember it even being there.

But there it stood, easily a hundred years old, gnarled limbs reaching protectively over the sidewalk, leaving him with the sensation of a father hunching over his child in a hailstorm. He had reached out and stroked its rough bark for just a moment before walking on.

"Yeah," Ian said. "I've felt it. An oak tree, once."

"Well, think of the time before when you saw it."

"Eh?"

"Think of the time before the time you noticed it. It was there, mind you, but it didn't make any impression on you until you noticed it." Hosea shrugged. "Entrances to the Hidden Ways are like that, most of the time."

"And what happens when somebody builds a house in front of one and tries to put a sidewalk over it?"

Hosea shook his head. "He won't. An architect who went out to the site would find himself planning around it, avoiding building on top of it. And if he didn't, somebody else would. You can ask any builder who has been in the trade long enough; some time or another, often for very good reasons that he just can't quite remember later, a set of plans has to be changed."

He rose to his feet and offered Ian his hand. "Enough talk. Let us go."

Ian accepted his help, and then brushed his pants off. "What do we do now?"

"Now?" Hosea asked. "Now is very simple: we walk. And then we walk some more. If we make Harbard's Crossing quickly enough, we may yet intercept our friends, or if not, surely we will be able to find some word of them." He looked at the sky again. "I doubt that their capture will be a secret, or their destination, from every . . . thing. So let's walk."

Ian nodded. "I can do that." He looked over at the stone and smiled.

Hosea returned the smile. "I'm pleased that something amuses you. What might it be?"

"Oh, I was just wishing we could take that stone along with us. The next time Maggie asks me what rock I crawled out from under, I could show it to her."

CHAPTER SEVEN

In the House of the Fire Duke

Were the truth to be known—although he was always resolved to do his best to prevent that from happening—Jamed del Bruno preferred to report to the Fire Duke with ill news rather than pleasant.

It was not merely that he disliked His Warmth—although he did; he found the title "His Warmth" to be an offensive oxymoron—it was that the Fire Duke was always much more conscious of his obligations to those beneath him under stress than otherwise. His Warmth was, Jamed del Bruno had long decided, a cruel man more playing at than living the part of the Duke of the House of Fire, and was much more likely to play his part well when adversity reminded him of his obligations than otherwise.

As he made his way down the broad steps of the amphitheater toward His Warmth's loge, two long-stemmed glasses of blood-red Tenemid and the note he had just been handed held high on a silver salver, Jamed del Bruno wished for bad news for his master, although, as always, he was careful to keep no trace of expression whatsoever on his smooth face, just as he had made no comment when it was Lady Everlea rather than Lord Sensever who arrived to command His Solidity's champion at the duel. It was a vague insult on the part of His Solidity, implying as it did that this dispute was a matter simply of money, not honor—something His Solidity implied ought to be left to women to handle, rather than noblemen.

He made his way down past the seats of the middle class, where a burly rancher, just a generation up from cowherd, argued passionately with a smoker; their wives, each in her garish finest, watched the nobility below.

Disdaining the seat that was barely large enough to contain his bulk, the fat duke stood next to the railing, overlooking the dueling floor below, his bulk at least partly concealed in a cowled cape that fell from neck to ankles. To his right, Lady Everlea stood, tilting a glass of pale, straw-colored wine to her full red lips, the plain onyx ring that proclaimed her allegiance to the House of Stone in open display on her ring finger. Her golden hair, gathered into a complex Ingarian knot, so closely matched the braiding about her bodice and the hems of her long sleeves that Jamed del Bruno wondered if, perhaps, the black silken gown was garnished with her own hair. That would have been a young girl's affectation, he decided, and definitely out of place for a woman of her age.

What was her age? Her skin had the smooth and creamy softness of a young girl's, with no trace of wrinkles at the corners of her blue eyes or firm mouth, but something in the way that she held herself spoke of a more advanced age. It was always possible, of course, that she had a strand of the Old Races in her heritage, and they always concealed their age well.

"Ah, Your Warmth, I see your refreshment arrives," she said, her voice half a tone lower and more musical than Jamed del Bruno would have expected. "And perhaps some news, as well."

The expression on His Warmth's face could have been a smile, but perhaps not. "Perhaps not," he said, taking both glasses from the salver and politely offering Lady Everlea her choice. She set her now empty glass on Jamed del Bruno's tray while considering which one of the proffered glasses to accept, as though it mattered in an idle sort of way, not as though the tradition arose from the Poisoning of Orfi.

"A fine wine," she said. "Although His Gelidity apparently has a higher opinion of its value than Her Ladyship does."

"I have noticed," His Warmth said.

Lady Everlea barely raised an eyebrow, and Jamed del Bruno kept his face impassive. His Warmth was constantly confounding his servants by handling financial matters himself—and directly, at that!—rather than relying on his Lady Wife—difficult to do, with her and the Heir, Venidir del Anegir, effectively banished to the House of the Sky—or some of the ladies from the major families of the House of Fire.

Below, the two swordsmen had entered the amphitheater. Under the watchful eyes of the crowd and the more watchful eyes of their assistants, the two men stripped down to shoes and shortened trousers, and launched into their stretching and warming exercises.

Standing on the tiled floor below, Rodic del Renald and Stanar del Brunden could have been two waxy Vandescardian marionettes cast from the same mold: each was long-limbed and well muscled in a wiry sort of way; each carried an assortment of scars from hairline to ankles, light on the face and lower belly, heavy on the sword arm; each studiously ignored the other as they went through their preparatory exercises.

Jamed del Bruno waited patiently until, finally, Lady Everlea selected a wineglass and waited until His Warmth politely raised his glass to his livery lips and drank before tasting her wine.

"You seem to be in no hurry to read your note, Your Warmth," she said.

"True enough." His Warmth smiled. "Simply a matter of trust; I trust that Jamed del Bruno will have carefully heated the envelope in the kitchen's oven, then read the contents before reinscribing the seal. I would trust him to bring the letter to me immediately, not stopping to decant two glasses of a fine wine, were the news of great import." He sipped at his glass. "Ah. Note the pleasant overtones of vanilla and berries, with just enough sweetness to make the tannin palatable. Pleasant, for such a young wine."

"Young, Your Warmth? I've never heard of anyone decanting a Tenemid that's less than a couple score of years old."

His Warmth shrugged. "And this is from the 1156th year Under the Sky, more than twice that age. But still young; it's all a matter of proportion." His smile was of some private joke.

Jamed del Bruno kept his face emotionless as he waited, the letter still on the salver. His Warmth was quite right, and quite wrong; Jamed del Bruno habitually opened any message he could, and had a deft enough hand with his small metal probe to be able to counterfeit any wax impression in a matter of moments. But this time he hadn't. There simply hadn't been time to do that and prepare the wine for His Warmth and Her Ladyship, and Jamed del Bruno always did his duty first.

The two swordsmen below had completed their preparations, and quite quietly moved to positions of attention, waiting until the hubbub in the audience ended.

His Warmth bowed Lady Everlea toward her seat, and took his overlarge one next to her. "May I wish you fortune, Lady?" he asked, formally.

"Of course, Your Warmth. As I wish you fortune," she said, her eyes twinkling. "Although you will forgive me, in this instance, if the fortune I wish you is not good fortune."

"Of course, Lady." His Warmth sipped his wine.

One of the swordsmen took a step forward. "I am Stanar del Brunen, Master Swordsman in the hire of the House of Stone. I represent that the field formally known as The Remnants of Findell's Heath is properly the property of the House of Stone, through persistent use over five generations, and swear with blade and blood to prove it so."

He stepped back, and the other man took his place. "I am Rodic del Renald, Master Swordsman, employed by the House of Fire. I claim that old maps, recently recovered from a dusty case of papers, prove that the boundary between the Houses falls with The Remnants of Findell's Heath firmly and provably on the side of Fire, not Stone, and swear with blade and blood to bring said field back to the Fire."

The two faced each other, brought their swords up in a mirrored salute, and turned toward the Duke's loge.

His Warmth turned to Lady Everlea. "If you will . . . ?"

She nodded. "Of course, My Lord." Gracefully, smoothly, she rose to her feet and gestured to the two swordsmen to begin.

Jamed del Bruno waited patiently, wondering whether he was being kept waiting in order to permit him to watch the bout without explicitly being granted the privilege—once he delivered the message, he would have to be about his duties unless His Warmth ordered him to stay—or simply for the sake of keeping him waiting. His Warmth was certainly capable of either, or both, but Jamed del Bruno was certain that His Warmth never did anything, from dropping a hint to bedding a serving girl, without carefully considering the consequences and implications.

If it was a favor, His Warmth could have saved himself the bother. While Jamed del Bruno accepted as an intellectual proposition that it was the sword that kept the Middle Dominion free of domination by the younger and larger nations surrounding it on three sides, and had no difficulty at all believing that the so-called House of Steel, as the prime exponent of the way of the sword, was the key player in that, perhaps as important as the House of the Sky, he simply found swordfights boring.

Below, the two swordsmen—Jamed del Bruno found it hard to tell which was which—had faced off and extended their weapons, each with his free hand on his hip while the tip of his blade toyed with the other, circling in what seemed more dance than combat, at least to Jamed del Bruno's untrained eye.

And then one sword tip snaked out, barely touching the opponent's arm, and the victorious swordsman retreated a few steps, parrying or countering or whatever swordsmen did to keep an opponent's blade away from his chest as he did.

The blades clicked and clacked against each other for a few moments, until Lady Everlea stood once more, and the two swordsmen disengaged, saluted each other, and turned toward her.

"Rodic del Renald," she said, "your blood has been shed, and you have been unable to shed your opponent's. Do you now concede the falsity of your claim or will you press onward?"

Rodic del Renald looked toward His Warmth, no trace of pain or fear on his face.

The Fire Duke shook his head. "I thank you for your service, son of Renald," he said, "but it appears that the House of Stone has the right of this matter, and to shed more of your blood would be foolish."

"I concede my error, Lady," Rodic said. "The field is properly property of the House of Stone, not of Flame."

The two swordsmen saluted first the Duke, then the crowd, then each other, and it was all over. Each handed his sword to an attendant, and while a chirurgeon dressed Rodic del Renald's injury, his former opponent walked over and accepted Rodic del Renald's congratulations with a handshake and a clapped hand to Rodic's shoulder, the two of them chatting casually all the while.

His Warmth didn't smile as he gestured to Jamed del Bruno, then opened the envelope, glancing quickly at the piece of paper within.

"Ah," he said, turning to the lantern on the table and touching a corner of the paper to the flame.

It disappeared in a flash, leaving behind nothing but a wave of heat and a light scattering of ash. His Warmth brushed at the sleeve of his tunic.

"I would not care to gamble with you, Your Warmth," Lady Everlea said. "You meet adversity with the same equanimity with which you greet success. I assume the letter spoke of some success."

His Warmth's smile was genial. "Assumptions are always interesting." He turned to Jamed del Bruno. "Send: Well done."

Jamed del Bruno nodded and bowed, and left, Lady Everlea's empty glass balanced effortlessly on his silver salver. He heard the smile in His Warmth's voice as the Duke addressed the emissary of the House of Stone. "Perhaps it will be different, when next our houses contend. I believe I have a new champion."

"Oh? May one inquire as to who that might be?"

Jamed del Bruno didn't hear the answer.

CHAPTER EIGHT

Captives

The pack leader's smile was wolfish, understandably. Torrie would have liked to have taken a pliers and pulled out each of the pointed teeth, one by one, but it didn't look like he'd have much of a chance, at least not now.

Patience, he told himself. Dad and Uncle Hosea had gone to some trouble to teach him how to develop what Dad called the "patience muscles." This was different from holding a crouch for hours on a deer stand, but the principle was the same: you wait until it's time to make your move, and now wasn't the time.

"It's a pleasure to greet you here, Thorian del Thorian the Younger, as it has been to greet your father, and your mother and your woman," he said, gesturing Torrie toward a bench by the fire.

Torrie wasn't sure how he understood the language, but it wasn't English, and it wasn't the little Norski he had learned in elementary school, or the French that he had tried to pick up in college. He had always admired Uncle Hosea's gift with languages—it seemed that Uncle Hosea couldn't hear a language without understanding it—and had thought that it would be a wonderful thing.

But it wasn't, and not just because he was a prisoner who had been dragged through a tunnel, then marched at spearpoint up and down hills from noon to past sunset; it wasn't wonderful because it was so natural, as though he had always been able to speak Middle Bersmål.

"I don't believe your tongue was cut out, although to arrange that would not be difficult," the Son said. "It's considered polite to respond to a greeting."

"Oh," Torrie said.

The Son was large and hairier than most, his face and body covered with salt-and-pepper hair thickly enough to almost give the impression of him being clothed, if Torrie didn't look down to where his somehow strangely pink penis peeked out from the dark fur. The impression was further enhanced by the jewelry that the Son wore: a golden chain from which a small amber amulet depended. The amulet was a teardrop, and embedded in it was what appeared to be the last joint of some thick finger.

His little finger sported two familiar-looking golden rings: Mom's and Dad's wedding rings.

"Please to sit," he said.

"I'd rather stand."

"And I would rather you to sit, and I would much rather to come, you and I, to an understanding now than later, son of Thorian," the Son said. "Will it be necessary to beat you? Or are you one of those . . . stoics who choose to laugh under the iron?"

Torrie drew himself up straight. To hell with you, he thought. "*Da Nivlehim vast dju, hundbretten,*" he said.

The Son laughed. "In another time, in another place, I'd enjoy to make you pay for that in pain and in blood. But my contract is to bring Thorian del Thorian to His Warmth without overly damaging him—and I shall—"

"*Du skal ikke selge skinnet før bjømen er skuut,*" Torrie said. It was an old Norski saying, and while few in Hardwood still spoke Norski, a few phrases circulated in collective usage. Like, this one: Don't sell the skin until after you've shot the bear.

The Son's hairy brow furrowed for a moment, as though working out a puzzle. "Ah. But I have already to *skut* the *bjorn*," he said. "Thorian del Thorian is in my hands. In fact, I now have two of them. And while that gives me to have a spare Thorian, it would be a shame to spend that casually." His smile disappeared. "On the other hand, that peasant girl of yours is not necessary, nor is your mother. Need I to bite off one of their fingers to persuade you to accept what hospitality I have to offer? Or will you simply to *sit*?"

There would be a time to confront the Son, Torrie promised himself, but this wasn't it. He didn't know the situation; he didn't know where Mom, Dad, or Maggie was, and he didn't have any business assuming the Son was bluffing.

Torrie sat.

The . . . den, Torrie decided it was, the den had been dug into a hillside. The tunnel in led up a short slope, then across and down. It had been neatly shored with timbers, now gray from creosote and age, worn smooth over the passing of many years. Not at all the sort of old construction he would have expected from a pack of Sons of the Wolf.

"Good boy," the leader said. "I'm called Herolf," he said. "They call you Thorian, like your father?"

Name, rank, and serial number wouldn't do it. "Thorian," he said. "You can call me Thorian."

The Son nodded. "Very well. I wanted to chat with you for a moment, privately, to explain your situation to you so that we can reach to an understanding. I'd thought about chaining you and your father, but anyone who can escape from one of the Cities, carrying an Old One who had been . . . held with chains that should hold anything, forever, well, I would expect that such a man should shortly be able to escape from any physical restraints I were to impose.

"Which is where your mother and your woman are to come in, and yourself, for that matter." He tilted his head to the side for a moment. "If either of you is to misbehave, if either of you tries to escape, I'll have one of the women thrown into a mating den with a bitch in heat, and leave her there to amuse the waiting suitors—and I assure you they will be able to amuse themselves with her for longer than she is likely to live. And if she survives, I'll have her throat torn out. Understood?"

Torrie nodded. "Understood."

The other three were waiting for him in a small room at the end of a small tunnel, secured by a barred, round wooden door set into a circular framework. The framework was probably largely buried in the walls of the tunnel. It looked strange, sort of like an oak airlock.

When the Son guarding the door slid aside the bar so that the door could pivot on its central pole, the bar slid easily into a socket in the tunnel, all the way to a lip that caught on the edge of the socket.

The small room was amply lit by their own Coleman lantern, hissing quietly as it hung from one of a dozen hooks on the ceiling perhaps three feet above his head. Beyond it stood a passage to another unlit room, although Torrie was sure that wasn't an easy way out, if it even *was* a way out.

Torrie was unceremoniously shoved inside, and the door shut behind him.

"Torrie," Mom said, rising from where she crouched next to Dad. "Thank God you're okay."

Maggie, dressed in nothing more than a torn and dirty nightshirt whose printing used to read "Somebody went to Puerto Rico, and All I Got Was This Lousy T-shirt" was slumped up against the wall; her eyes didn't even seem to see him.

She looked okay, if a bit battered, and the same went for Mom, whose oversized pajamas were if anything dirtier and more torn than Maggie's clothes, but Dad lay on his side on a blanket, his face a mass of bruises, his left arm in a splint and sling.

He looked at Torrie with his one open eye and grinned, revealing a missing canine. "I'm glad you're well, Torrie," he said.

Dad, it seemed, hadn't meekly gone along with whatever the Sons ordered; he had at least put up some resistance, Torrie decided, loathing his own passivity. But what good did it do? They were all in the same pit.

He crouched next to Maggie. What could he say to her? He had invited her to come home with him because it would be a pleasant week off—and because he didn't like to sleep alone—and because, more than a little, he didn't often get a chance to show off Mom and Dad and Uncle Hosea, and he was constantly pleased with how terrific the three of them were.

But no. Not for this. This was something out of the stories that Uncle Hosea used to tell, and while in the back of his mind he had always wondered if there was something in the stories that could reach out and touch him, he never—

She would have to hate him for this, and he couldn't blame her.

"Maggie, I'm—"

Her upper lip curled. "Shut up," she said, loudly, just the quiet side of a shout. "You just leave me alone."

"Maggie—" He reached out for her, and surprisingly, she grabbed hold of the front of his shirt and yanked him off his feet, holding him close, her breath warm in his ear.

He could barely hear her whisper. "We're both safer if you don't give a damn what happens to me, and vice versa.

So I hate you for getting me into this, and after you try to win me back, and can't, you resent me for it." As she spoke, her arms held him tight.

He opened his mouth, and then closed it, and took her in his arms, putting his lips next to her ear. "I'm sorry I got—"

Her fingers were warm against his mouth. She shook her head, and put her lips, once again, to his ear. "My Daddy would shake his head and say 'I raised you better than this' if I started blaming the victim." She held him close for a moment, then gently pushed him away.

Her voice said, "You bastard, how could you get me in this kind of trouble? How could you think of putting me in this kind of danger?"

But her eyes said, *It'll be okay.*

Torrie had spent a futile hour—two hours? maybe three?—exploring every inch of their tiny pair of rooms, with no luck at all. There was a duct at the juncture of wall and ceiling in each room—in the other room, it was in the corner under the large stone thundermug—and fresh air flowed in through it, but the ducts were made of stone, and nothing larger than a rat could make its way through them, and even then it would have to break through the grating that covered the duct.

And he wasn't a rat. Torrie decided that the room was probably a meatlocker, which helped to explain the barred door—there would be some way of locking the door outside, as well, and given that the Sons didn't want their food eaten by rats, it was necessary to seal it in tight.

He would have discussed his conclusion with the others, but by mutual consent, talk was kept to a minimum. If Maggie and Mom and Dad were sure they could be overheard, then they could be overheard, and there was no sense in trying to weave some sort of plan only to give it away to the wolves.

What he wanted was a high-capacity autoloading rifle with a few dozen full magazines.

But he didn't have that; he didn't have anything much. The Sons had searched him, and while they hadn't taken his wallet or his keys, they had taken his Paratool and everything else in his pockets. Uncle Hosea always carried a double-edged razor blade—carefully wrapped in wax paper—in his wallet, just in case he found he needed to trim something with a really sharp edge, but Torrie had never acquired the habit.

So what he had was a Coleman lantern and a small flask of kerosene for it. That spoke of Molotov cocktail, which would do less than a lot of good with a Son of the Wolf.

He would have to wait. The right thing to do, the reasonable thing to do, would be to roll himself up in a blanket or two and try to get some sleep, the way that Dad was doing, and that Mom at least pretended to do, although Maggie just sat, slumped on her blankets.

Wood thunked on wood outside. "Stand back from the door," a harsh voice said in Bersmål.

The door pivoted open, revealing two large, hairy Sons and a short, stocky, ugly man, dressed in boots and what looked more like a wraparound canvas sarong and tunic than anything else. His face seemed almost alien under the neatly trimmed, straight black hair and neatly combed beard—too little forehead, the ridges above the eyes too heavy.

With both hands, the short man carried a platter piled high with slightly wilted-looking apples and carrots surrounding an uncorked clay bottle that appeared to contain at least a gallon. He set the platter down on the hard floor, and then, under the watchful eyes of the Sons guarding it—him?—walked silently out of the room without saying anything.

The door shut behind them.

Wincing, Dad forced himself to sit up. "I hadn't thought I'd see one of the Vestri again," he said.

Mom shook her head. "Vestri?"

"Dwarf," he said, slapping his good hand against the wall next to him. "Sons don't build, not this well, and while they live underground, they don't tend to do much digging; I should have guessed they'd have Vestri serfs."

Maggie cocked her head to one side. "It looked like a Neanderthal to me."

Torrie frowned at that.

"Yeah, right," she said, sarcastically, "don't listen to anything I have to say. I can't know anything; I'm just a girl, right?" She pursed her lips together for just a moment. "But take away the clothing, and the neat haircut and beard, and what does it look like to you?"

Torrie was about to say something to the effect of how silly that sounded when he saw his father nodding. "I made the . . . opposite guess years ago, when I saw a picture in one of Torrie's schoolbooks. Your Neanderthals look awfully like unschooled Vestri," Dad said. He stretched, painfully. "We had best divide the food, and then blow out the lantern. The fuel will not last forever, and they're unlikely to replace it for us." He took a sip from the clay bottle. "Fresh water," he said.

Torrie had been planning on not sleeping, but there wasn't anything else to do in the dark, after he had eaten enough to quell hunger pains and drunk enough to ease his thirst.

What he wanted to do was hold Maggie in the dark, but if the door suddenly opened, that wouldn't square with the idea of them not getting along.

But what of it? He couldn't make a break, even if the Sons decided that punishing Maggie for it was pointless—they would still have Mom.

Planning was pointless. All he could do was drive himself crazy. The right thing to do was what Uncle Hosea always said: when you don't know what else to do, eat a meal if you're hungry and sleep even if you're not sleepy.

He never knew quite when he slipped from lying silently in the quiet darkness into a sleep that was even quieter, and every bit as dark.

CHAPTER NINE

Town Council

The unofficial town council of Hardwood, North Dakota, was already in session in its usual meeting place, Doc Sherve's living room, when Betsy Sherve led Jeff and Arnie Selmo in, Jeff constantly having to restrain himself from offering to help Arnie on his crutches. Arnie had his pride.

Betsy excused herself with a silent smile and a reassuring nod, closing the door behind her.

"Evening, Jeff." Michael Bjerke raised his head from his coffee and coffeecake. He glanced pointedly at Arnie, then raised his eyebrows and pursed his lips.

Jeff shook his head, then shrugged. By all rights, Arnie shouldn't still be in the hospital in Grand Forks—he should be as dead as the Larson boys. But Arnie had insisted on coming home the way he had insisted on surviving the first few hours, today smilingly claiming that the intermittent questioning from a curious state trooper was starting to break him down, and had further insisted that Jeff bring him to the next meeting "over at Doc's."

Arnie exchanged handshakes with Doc and Reverend Oppegaard, both of whom rose to greet him, then walked to stand in front of the old maple rocker next to the overstuffed armchair where old Minnie Hansen sat, her reading glasses perched precariously at the end of her nose, seemingly absorbed in her needlepoint. Jeff always thought that a gray-haired old woman who habitually did needlepoint ought to dress the part, but Minnie was in her usual uniform of work shirt and jeans. The only time Jeff had seen her in a dress was at church.

Jeff nodded to Bob Aarsted, his father-in-law, although there was no need for small talk between the two of them; Jeff and Kathy had just had supper at the Aarsteds' less than an hour before, and everything that needed to be said had been said then.

Aarsted and Michael Bjerke could have been cast as a Norski Laurel and Hardy, from the looks of them—Aarsted was all thick and round, while Bjerke was tall and saturnine, although they both sported the identical brush cut, complete with balding patch in the middle of their blond-going-to-gray hair.

"Sit down, Arnie," Bob Aarsted said. "Make yourself comfortable—you look like death warmed over."

"And not all that much warmed over, either," Mike Bjerke said.

"I came here to say something, and then I'll leave and let the lot of you talk," Arnie Selmo said, his voice more air than sound. "I . . . don't know a lot or a little about what happened, but Davy says that young Torrie said that a silver bullet will kill these wolf-things, and I've heard Davy Hansen called a lot of things over the years, but never a liar, and if there's anybody who doesn't respect the Thorsens, why, you just let me know.

"Now . . . Torrie showed Davy where the tunnel comes out, even though Davy said that it disappeared in front of his eyes.

"Well, he's marked where it disappeared from, and he and I are going to sit on that tunnel, like a wolf waiting for a gopher, except that we'll be waiting for wolves." He pulled a stack of bills, wrapped with a rubber band, from his pocket. "Davy collected these there; I don't need no charity, anymore'n he does, so I'm turning it over to you."

"That's fine, Arnie. But is that all you're here for?" Doc Sherve shook his head, as though to add: *I doubt it.*

Arnie scowled. "I didn't say that was all. The two of us aren't enough. We need at least two more, and I'd rather have six more—pairs would work better. I'll take Orphie, and the midnight to eight shift. I don't sleep that well at night, anyways." His eyes went vague and distant for a moment, then he shook himself. "We'll need somebody to partner with Davy, and I want two more pairs," he said, his voice somehow that of a man younger than he was. "Arrange it."

After all these years—even Jeff didn't know how far back the unofficial meetings went—it wasn't necessary to take a vote. From Minnie's nod and Doc's sigh, from the way Dave Oppegaard sat back and crossed his arms over his chest, and Bjerke and Aarsted each *tsk*ed, it was clear that there was a consensus.

Doc Sherve spoke for them all, as usual. "You want two pairs of men, at least, to report to you, say, at eight tomorrow morning. With guns?"

Arnie shook his head. "No. Without guns. We've got Thorsen's Garands, and I'm going to bring Orphie's BAR—and that's what we'll use, if we have to. And there's going to be talk—I don't want kids coming around, night or day."

Bob Aarsted grunted. "I don't see a problem doing it for a few days. But, hell, what if this goes on for weeks and nothing happens? We had enough trouble getting a crossing guard across Main Street on school days. It'll be hard to keep that manned, particularly with two men per shift."

"Think about it, Bob," Jeff spoke up. "We've got a hole

that werewolves pop out of and people we know disappear into—you want to leave that unguarded?"

"Well, now that you mention it, no, not particularly."

Jeff frowned. "We could cut a road into the woods, and then back a cement truck up to it, and fill the damn thing up, but—forgetting that we hope our neighbors climb out of there—are you willing to bet that cement would stop werewolves?"

"I don't see why not."

"Yeah," Arnie said, "and you didn't see me shoot two, three of them with deer slugs and watch the bastards shake it off, either. I want that hole guarded."

"You've got it." Doc Sherve nodded. "They'll be there. Hell, I'll take a shift, if I have to."

"You do that." Slowly, painfully, Arnie levered himself to his feet. "I'll go have some coffee with Betsy, and let the rest of you talk."

"Werewolves, demons, and magic." Bob Aarsted shook his head. "If there were only two of you swearing to it, I think I'd be calling for a shrink, and not a meeting." He looked at the door Arnie had closed behind himself when leaving.

"Well . . ." Doc Sherve said from around the stem of his pipe, "if you've got any doubts, we can ask Jeff to dig up the bodies we buried." He puffed a few times, then took a long draw, and blew it out. "I don't think the . . . woman got hair on her palms from playing with herself." Doc tilted his head to one side. "I'd thought about taking pictures, but . . ."

"Well, I said *if*." Bob Aarsted shrugged, dismissing the issue. Bob Aarsted prided himself on being a phlegmatic Norski, although the Aarsteds had been in Hardwood for at least four generations before him, and not one of them had been known to set foot back in the old country.

"How's it going, Jeff?" Reverend—Dave—Oppegaard

asked. Well into his seventies, the minister still had a booming baritone voice; Jeff not only remembered it from childhood but remembered his father waxing nostalgic about how it hadn't changed since *his* childhood. It was hard to think of him as Dave, even though that's what he insisted on being called when he replaced his collar with a cable-knit sweater. With his large arms and broad chest, he looked more like a fisherman, but Jeff's mind always saw him standing in the pulpit.

"Well enough, Dave," he said.

"No." Oppegaard frowned. "I didn't mean 'how are you?'—I meant, how is it *going*?"

"Oh." Jeff poured himself a cup of hot coffee from the carafe on the table before he took his seat, sitting down more heavily than he had intended. It had been a long couple of days. "It's pretty much settled, at least as far as the staties are concerned. Ole and the Larson boys were killed in a car accident, which the local authorities—that's me—had mostly cleaned up by the time they were able to send out a unit. Rumors that they were out hunting wolves when that happened are just rumors. Accidents happen, and the deputy medical examiner's"—Doc Sherve raised his coffee cup in a sarcastic toast—"certification will be just fine. On another, unrelated matter, a couple of stray dogs were shot outside of the Thorsens' barn, trying to get at the chickens." He shook his head. "Damn." There were no nicer people in town than Jeff and Bobby Larson, and while he wouldn't call Ole a nice man, he had been a good neighbor.

Jeff was trying to sound casual about it, although he was anything but. The carnage on the Thorsen lawn was the worst thing he had ever seen, ever since the time, a few summers ago, that he was working with old John Honistead, and they had to go out to the Olsen farm, and found Dan Olsen with half his head blown away by the shotgun still held in his hands.

Oppegaard shook his head. "I still can't quite believe it. We always knew there was something strange about Hosea, but—wolves that can't be killed? Silver bullets? Disappearing tunnels? And where is he, and that friend of Torrie's? The last thing anybody saw was them walking into the Thorsen house." He snorted. "Not exactly the sort of thing we learned how to deal with in seminary, even back, shortly before the Earth cooled, when I was a student." He sat back and rapped his knuckles against his knee. "I . . . don't know that we should keep quiet about this. I don't know that I can."

Aarsted shook his head. "What are you thinking of doing—calling Father Swenson in from Grand Forks to perform an exorcism?"

"I'm thinking about it." Oppegaard's lips were white. "Don't think that hasn't occurred to me." He shook his head. "But it's not that. This whole . . . thing could blow up in our faces. We could handle the Thorsens' disappearance—but there are those two friends of Torrie's. They've disappeared too."

"Ian. Ian Silverstein and Maryanne Christensen." Jeff nodded. "Nice folks; I had some beers with them over at the Dine-a-mite the other night. Ian isn't a problem; he doesn't have a family. It's likely to be a long time before anybody comes looking for him."

"Oh?" Mike Bjerke made a face. "I thought Jewish families were supposed to be close."

"Oh?" Bob Aarsted raised an eyebrow. "And how many Jews do you know real well?"

"Well, there's my dentist, in Grand Forks. Nice fella."

"I was worried about that, too, Mike." Jeff said to Bjerke, ignoring the by-play between Bjerke and his father-in-law. "There's exceptions to everything. Oh, there may be a distant cousin or something like that, but the closest living relative is his father, and they haven't spoken for some years. Father sounds like a real bastard, but he's not a problem. Maryanne is—she comes from St. Louis, and her parents are probably used to hearing from her every couple of weeks. Figure a month, maximum, before they're concerned." He shrugged. "If they *un*disappear by then, we should be okay. If they never do, we have to come up with some sort of explanation."

"Her poor parents . . ."

"*Så meget vil jeg si til hans fordel at han er i grunnen et godt menneske*," Minnie Hansen murmured to herself, then reverted to English, "but what silliness." She made a face. "I suppose they would be reassured if you told them what really happened, that the last time anybody saw her, a pack of werewolves were dropping her down a tunnel that now only goes down a few feet." She sniffed.

"Be that as it may." Doc Sherve pursed his thin lips. "I don't see what the problem is. At some point, somebody comes to investigate. The kids took off in Torrie's car, after a week of vacation; the two Thorsens and Hosea left in the Thorsen car for a long-planned driving trip, down through Mexico, we think, and nobody's heard from any of them since." His smile was forced. "I doubt anybody's going to guess the truth." He puffed on his pipe, then reached over to the coffee table and turned the little electrostatic air cleaner up higher. Its whining filled the silence, interrupted by Doc's pipe puffing.

Mike Bjerke cleared his throat. "I'm more worried about the Larsons." He pulled at his long chin. "I had a talk with Olav and Ruth," he said. "They're hurting, and they want some explanations that they're just not going to get."

"I'll speak to them, if necessary," Minnie said, her high voice with the Scandinavian lilt that all of the pretelevision generation had. "I taught both of them in school, and they'll still listen to me."

"What are you going to say?" Doc Sherve asked, passing a tired hand through his thinning hair. Doc had been tired for all of Jeff's life. Even in the years when he had a partner, he still was on call half the nights, and most of those, four seasons a year, were interrupted by something, be it a birth or an injury.

"I'm going to say to them just what I'm going to say to you, again," she said firmly. "That's why people believe me—because unlike some people," she said with a sniff in the direction of Dave Oppegaard, "I don't tailor the sermon to the congregation. I'll tell them everything I know, and that no good would come from making it public. I'll say to them: do you want to turn this town into a circus? Do you want reporters from the *National Enquisitor*—"

"*Enquirer*," Doc put in. The two of them had been genially correcting each other for more than a generation.

"—nosing about? Do you want teevee camera crews spread out across the Thorsens' yard, interviewing everybody right and left about a werewolf attack? Do you want Thorian Thorsen's background investigated, and then questions asked about how he could live among us so long without anybody talking about it? Do you want every secret this town holds to be investigated and held up for public scrutiny?" Her eyes locked on Jeff's for a moment, then swung past.

No, he didn't want every secret made public. Years ago, he and Bob Aarsted had quietly gone to Chicago to try to track down Kathy's stepfather, but the bastard had long since disappeared. If he was still alive, Jeff didn't want him knowing where Kathy was.

You can't save the world, old John Honistead had said, when he had turned the badge over to Jeff, but you can preserve the peace of this part of it.

That was hardly the only secret, either. Nobody spoke about it, but everybody in the room knew what Ethel Holmstedt had done to that asshole she married, and nobody in the room was willing for that to come to light, either. Dick Holmstedt had officially died when he had fallen from his seat on the combine and into the threshing blades, and that was the way that was going to stand.

There were other secrets, as well.

"We take care of our own, here," she said. "And if our men die protecting our own, well, they've done that before." She drew herself up proudly. "My husband died on Makin Island, and my oldest son in the retreat from Chosin Reservoir, and right now I have a grandson sitting on a helicopter carrier off the coast of Somalia." She looked down at her needlepoint, and with a muttered syllable or two began to pick out the stitches she had just put in. "My great-grandfather Gerhardsen," she said quietly, "took his young wife from her home in Trondheim and settled in New Ulm in eighteen hundred and fifty-three. He lived through the massacre in eighteen sixty-two, and moved here a year later, and died of the flu in the winter of sixty-eight; my great-grandmother's journal says he caught it dragging home a deer he had shot, to feed the family—to take care of his own. We take care of our own," she said. "My husband and my son did that when they marched off to war, and Doctor Sherve, you and I and Eddie Flagstad did that back when we changed Johnny Thompson's birthday to give him a higher draft number."

Doc Sherve leaned forward as though to say something, but her glare silenced him. "And," she went on, "did Davy Hansen ever complain about that? Even when only part of him came back from that horrible Vietnam place?" She shook her finger at the lot of them, and for a moment she was the teacher and Jeff her student again.

"We take care of our own," she said, with quiet faith, and looked back to her knitting. "You do what you have to, all of it."

"Yes, Minnie," Doc said, and after a moment, Dave Oppegaard nodded.

Jeff sipped his coffee.

CHAPTER TEN

Mount Æskja and a Bergenisse

Mountain climbing turned out, at least here and now, to be an anticlimax, Ian had decided. It mostly consisted of walking, upslope. Far above, the peak was covered with snow and ringed by clouds, but here all they had to do was follow a path.

The idea, Hosea explained, was to take the path that led part way up and around the mountain, and then down. They certainly could have simply walked down the mountain and skirted it, but since they were already more than halfway up, this would be faster.

He didn't know how many miles he walked or how far it was to their destination—Hosea wasn't helpful on that, or much of anything else while they walked—and Ian couldn't make a good guess. Ten miles? Thirty, maybe? How tall was this mountain, anyway, and how high would they have to go?

It wasn't all bad. At one point, as the path dipped down the side of the mountain, it became a well-worn stone-inlaid trail, half as old as time. Raspberry brambles grew high alongside an impenetrable thorny jungle edged with tiny berries of such a dark red as to seem almost purple.

Hosea stopped for a moment, and carefully selected one of the largest; he popped it into his mouth and smiled.

Ian did the same. It was more tart and less juicy than he was used to, but there was wild rich sweetness that he had never quite tasted before. Following Hosea's example, Ian gathered them by the fistful and relieved his hunger and most of his thirst, getting only a dozen or so scratches for his effort.

Hosea produced a pair of quart-sized Ziploc bags from his rucksack, and handed one to Ian. It took only a few minutes to fill both of the bags, not even beginning to dent the supply of berries, and another moment to inflate the bags to protect the fruit, and stow them away in the top of their rucksacks.

The brambles tapered off as they climbed; the stony soil, finally, was broken by only a few stubborn plants and by the path. The path had seen better centuries, Ian decided. He kept away from the crumbling edge, and every once in a while had to leap a thankfully small gap in the path, being sure to land well beyond the cracks.

"Is one permitted to ask why such a difficult route has a built-in path?"

Hosea shrugged. "It's old, but one of the Old Ones, known as Fenderel, used to live in a cave near the top, living on honey and melted snow. He . . . was generally thought to be wise enough that many walked up to consult with him." Hosea shrugged. "Eventually, the people in the village at the base of the mountain built a toll road up the side of the mountain. And then, not to be outdone—or to compete for the pilgrim traffic; it's hard to tell—the people in the village at the base of the mountain on the other side did the same."

Ian looked up the slope, toward the icy peak. "Is he still there?"

Hosea shook his head and smiled. "No. There was too

much traffic, and he had retired to the mountain for privacy, after all. One day he was gone."

"Whatever happened to him?"

"He left." Hosea shrugged. "I don't know everything." His smile was friendly, but distant. "Not anymore."

Ian had gotten so involved with what was in front of his face, and with not looking down at the way pebbles and rocks kicked over the side would skip down the mountainside, that they were well around the side of the mountain before he looked down and out.

Far below, a thick, twisting silver-gray river cut across a landscape all quilted in the dark, rich greens of the forests and earthy yellows of the grain fields. A strand of puffy cloud floated halfway down the mountain, it seemed, casting part of the valley into shadow.

The air was clearer than Ian was used to; he could make out individual people, as a gang of what must have been farmworkers—no, *peasants*—moved through the green rows below, weeding or picking or something.

"There's Harbard's Crossing," Hosea said, pointing.

The river twisted around a small peninsula where a few low buildings stood, one of them right at the river's edge. A twin to it stood on the opposite shore. As Ian watched, a barge was unloading on the far side, a team of something, probably oxen, pulling a cart onto the road, and toward where the road disappeared in the trees.

Ian nodded. "By nightfall?"

Hosea shook his head. "Tomorrow's nightfall, perhaps. The day after, more likely. The road is not as easy as we might wish, and the landing farther than it seems." He looked up at the blue sky. "The day gets no younger, and neither do I."

By the time the sun set, turning the western horizon all rosy and golden, Ian had long decided that Hosea was right; the road was longer and harder than he would have thought. It twisted like a snake that had swallowed a Slinky as it wound its way down the mountain's face. Ian decided that the builders must have had some religious prejudice against straight lines.

They made a rough camp beside a small cirque lake, no more than fifty yards across, fed on one side by a trickle of stream that emptied on the other. There was no sand on its shore: just rock, and clear water.

Ian already had the Sierra cup out of his pack, but Hosea held up a finger, then knelt down by the stream and cupped his hand, bringing it up to his lips. He smiled and nodded.

Ian dipped his cup. The water was so cold it made his teeth hurt, and it tasted vaguely of pine. By the time Ian had had his fill, Hosea had gotten a small fire started in a charred depression in the bare rock, and was busily harvesting fallen wood from upslope for it.

A quick supper consisted of a couple of sticks of surprisingly tender beef jerky from their packs and the remaining raspberries, both washed down with gallons of cold water.

Hosea seated himself tailor-fashion across the fire from Ian, his face lit almost demonically in the flickering firelight. "I'll take the watch, young Ian. I have little need of sleep, and you have much need of it."

No argument there, at least on the latter. Ian spread out his plastic groundcloth on the stone, took off his shoes and slid into his sleeping bag, the ground hard underneath him. As he pillowed his head on his arms, his last thought was that he was going to have trouble falling aslee—

A scream brought Ian awake in the gray predawn light.

The night had been horrible, filled with light sleep punctuated by constant wakings, seemingly every few seconds. Every scritching in the trees had had him almost leaping out of his sleeping bag, and every change in the night breezes had woken him, too. Even the time he could sleep was just a set of nightmares, of Torrie and Maggie and Torrie's mom being hung on hooks, flayed alive in front of his eyes. He would wake in a cold sweat, jerk up to a sitting position, then force himself to lie back down, sweaty and cold in his sleeping bag. When you're on your own, you learn to take what sleep you can; Ian could force himself to fall asleep, if not to stay sleeping.

So it took him a moment to realize that this scream wasn't from a dream, but from something or someone else.

He leaped out of his blankets in the predawn light to see Hosea stagger back from something, some *thing* Ian couldn't recognize in the gray light before dawn. It was the size of a huge man, and vaguely man-shaped, but it was covered with a mat of what could have been thick locks of greasy hair or horribly long, greasy wattles of leathery flesh.

It shook its massive head to clear the wattles from its eyes, and lunged for Hosea again, thick arms reaching out for Hosea's face or head.

I'm no hero, Ian thought. The only thing to do was to run, maybe grabbing his things, better not. Only an idiot would stoop to pick up a sword by the hilt, fling the scabbard aside with a quick swing, then charge on whateverthehellitwas, sword in front of him, shouting at the top of his lungs.

Ian's shouts were incoherent, even to his own ears, as he stumbled toward his gear, ignoring the way cracks and ridges in the hard stone surface cut through his socks and into his foot, then scooped up his sword and scabbard, flinging the scabbard aside with a quick swing, bringing the sword back into line, into an ideal line, as he ran at the creature.

With a deep growl, it threw Hosea aside as though he was a rag doll, then turned toward Ian.

He had no chance. He would have to run away, and

hope that he could run faster than it, that Hosea wasn't badly hurt enough, hoping—

He lunged, in perfect extension, realizing at the last moment that his fencer's reflexes had betrayed him, that he would barely touch the beast's chest with his sword tip, that instead of being run through it could merely stop and bat his sword aside with one of those massive arms, and then it would be upon him.

But his muscles and nerves followed the familiar path, and as the sword tip touched the creature's chest, clouds of smoke erupted from the point of contact, as though the thing was a huge, smoke-filled weather balloon that had been pricked.

It screamed, and raised a hand above the sword, ready to slap it aside, but Ian had already remised, and executed as gorgeous a thrust as he ever had in a real match, this time bringing the tip of his blade into the monster's lower belly, again rewarded by a smoke spume.

This was too much for whatever it was; clutching its massive hands to its belly, it fled down the road, leaping off into the thick brush a few yards in.

Crashing sounds diminished in the distance.

Hosea had propped himself up on his rucksack, one hand cupped tightly over the dark stain spreading across the right side of his waist. His trousers were bloody and torn in several places, and there were scratches all over his face and what Ian could see of his chest.

Ian knelt next to him, fumbling with the strings of Hosea's rucksack. "Is there a first aid kit here?"

"No time," Hosea said. "It's not the cuts; they can hurt me, but will do no more than that. It's the poison—its saliva is poison, and it always licks its claws before it attacks."

Well, Hosea knew more about this thing than Ian did. "What was that?"

"A wicht, perhaps that's the best name for it, or a bergenisse. A bergenisse. They used to be all over the mountains in Vandescard, but I had been given to understand that the last one had long since died, at least here." The foam of spittle at the corner of his mouth was red.

Hosea's fingers spasmed over the wound on his hip. "And it burns, it burns."

"What can I *do?*" Ian asked, desperate.

"Harbard's Ferry—Harbard's wife is a healer, and he has some of the skill himself." Hosea tried to rise to his feet, but his knees started to shake and to wobble; Ian got one of Hosea's arms around Ian's shoulders and helped him to his feet.

"I shall walk as far as I can," Hosea said. "I may well be able to walk far enough."

With that, his eyes rolled up, his eyelids rolled down, and he dropped to the hard stone limp and lifeless, only a slow pulse at the base of his throat and the slight flow of oozing blood at his hip indicating that he was alive.

Ian knelt next to him. He would have to bind the wounds first.

Ian had to keep it simple.

Step.

Step.

Step.

Step.

Step.

Step.

Step.

Step.

Rest for three breaths.

Ian stood for a moment, not lowering the poles of the travois he dragged behind him. He had to keep it simple, not think about anything beyond the next eight steps, and the next three breaths he would take while he stopped.

Breath One. As he got more tired, the world had narrowed, from the broad and lovely expanse of the mountainside and valley below to the six or so feet of path in front of him, all the rest gone. But tunnel vision was vision, and all he needed to do was keep pulling.

Let it out and take:

Breath Two: How long had he been walking? He couldn't even guess. The only thing he could tell was that his palms were rubbed bloody from the poles, that his back felt like somebody had stabbed him in it several times, and that there was six feet of decent road in front of him.

Release and try:

Breath Three: Just keep your eye on the road.

Step.

Step.

Step.

Step.

Step.

Step.

Step.

Step.

Rest for three breaths.

He couldn't tell if Hosea was still breathing as he lay on the blankets that Ian had converted into the bed of the travois, and he could only hope that the two rucksacks had stayed tied to it. His sword—he couldn't bear the thought of being separated from it, not after what it had done to the bergenisse, whatever that was—hung at his side.

Third breath; exhale, and pull.

There was no point in counting; there was no point in not counting. Yes, there was a point in counting, he reminded himself. Without those eight steps, Ian would have spent all day waiting to catch his breath.

The trick, he decided, was to lower his expectations. He would expect to hurt, to ache, he would understand that his lungs would burn with a distant fire that grew always close. He would expect to be cold and rained upon, and it didn't matter.He would expect that his forehead would turn red and blister in the noon sun, and that there would be no respite for the pain, for the tendons burning like wires in his shoulders, for the blistering and peeling skin of his forehead, and that there would be no end of pain for his hands.

Step.

Step.

Step.

Step.

Step.

Step.

Step.

Step.

Rest for three breaths.

The poles of the travois were sticky under his hands; some surely from the sap, some from his own blood.

Not good, Ian, he thought. Not good at all. He should let down the travois for just a moment, and see to his sore, bleeding hands, to lie down or sit down for just a moment, to rest his aching feet.

But he knew that if, even for just a second, even just once, he were to let go of the poles, he would never be able to pick them up again. He was Ian Silverstein, dammit—a human, made of flesh and blood, and this was too much to ask of flesh and blood. It was always too much.

He ought to set the travois down and go back and check on Hosea. Really, if the old man was dead, then Ian could rest, for at least a while.

Step.

Step.

Step.

Step.

Step.

Step.

Step.

Step.

Rest for three breaths. Now, was that eight steps or only seven he had taken?

Step.

Step.

One to be sure it was eight, and another to stop himself from cheating.

And again:

Step.

Step.

Step.

Step.

Step.

Step.

Step.

Step.

Rest for three breaths.

It occurred to him that the road had stopped twisting a way back, and that he was walking on smoothed cobblestones, interlaced with a thick moss. How far had he come? How much farther was it?

"Havadh er derein isti vejen?"—*What's the matter?* a rough voice asked.

Ian looked up, too exhausted to be pleased, or even surprised, that he had understood the Middle Bersmål with the idiosyncratic emphasis, much more like something out of Old Bersmål, or some language even older.

What do you think *is the matter, asshole?* he thought. But he didn't say that.

A man stood in front of him, wearing only breeches and boots, his lined face wreathed with white beard and white hair, both the hair and beard streaked with gray and black and dirt in places. His face was wrinkled like old leather, the creases dark even against his sun-darkened skin.

Ian would have guessed his age at about seventy, but he stood like a strong young man; under a mat of snowy hair, the muscles of his torso were firm like a bodybuilder's, although a bodybuilder's chest wasn't crisscrossed with old scars like this old man's was.

"Havat' defeiler engroden?" he asked.

"Not I," Ian answered in the same language. "I am only fatigued. My companion is the one who has been hurt. He was savaged by a horrible thing—a bergenisse, he did call it." Ian didn't remember letting go of the travois, but his bloody hands were now free, and in front of him, gesturing.

"Can it be?" The old man was already kneeling by the travois. "By the hairy balls of—Orfindel!" he said, laying a hand on Hosea's shoulder, and shaking Hosea's limp form gently. "Orfindel, can you hear me?" He took Hosea in his arms and stood, showing no effort at all. "Come. I am the ferryman, called Harbard, sometimes known as Harbard the Old. My wife, Frida, is a healer, and Orfindel has need of one."

Ian's tunnel vision was narrowing, but he followed Harbard for about five steps before he fainted.

CHAPTER ELEVEN

The Middle Dominion

"Move faster, ye," Herolf said, turning around for a moment to glare at the four humans, then turning back. "We have another four or five days to travel until we reach the edge of Dominion territory and I can turn you over to the House of Fire, and I'd sooner it be four than five, and just as soon it be three, were ye to ask me."

Torrie was surprised that the four of them were allowed to walk unfettered, but he didn't feel like looking a gift horse in the mouth. Could they have forgotten to do it? That didn't make sense. They even were allowed to space out a bit as they walked in the middle of the party, preceded by half a dozen Sons, followed by twice as many.

No, it wasn't out of carelessness. A Son could easily outsprint the best of them. But that was just in the short run, and that gave Torrie an idea. Uncle Hosea once said that humans were the best, most stubborn runners, that a healthy man or woman could run any other creature on the planet into the ground. It was a hunter's thing—but maybe it would work for the prey, too?

Okay, he thought, assuming I can break away, how could he manage to take the others with him? Or maybe not all the others—if Herolf only had one Thorian del Thorian in hand, what could he afford to do to him?

Nothing, probably. And with Torrie free, maybe Torrie could do something useful. He remembered stories Uncle Hosea used to tell about the Vestri, and particularly Dvalin's Folk, and about how important the status of guest was to them. If he could find one of their burrows—and did Uncle Hosea say where the Vestri were to be found? Torrie couldn't remember. Torrie hadn't asked him a lot about the geography of the mythical countries that Uncle Hosea's stories flowed from; he hadn't been planning to have to fucking walk through them, either.

Ahead, the road followed the ridges toward the mountains rising off at the horizon, while to the west and below, the river Gilfi twisted all silvery through the valley.

Ten miles away? Fifteen, maybe? Fifty? It was hard to tell. It didn't seem to be getting any closer.

The worst of it was the way Dad acted. It was as though the Sons had taken all the spine out of him.

He would flinch every time one of the Sons walked by, throwing his arm out defensively, as though for protection, no trace of threat in his manner.

The Sons despised that, both wolf and bitch. So did Torrie, although he didn't say anything. What would he say? Show a little spine, Dad? Act like you're a man instead of a coward?

But Torrie didn't believe it for a moment.

Ahead of the procession, another road T-ed into the main one, leading off across a raised berm, toward a village no more than a mile away.

"Herolf?" Torrie walked briskly, up toward where the leader of the Sons trotted more back and forth in impatience than forward and backward. "Herolf? Can I ask you something?"

The large head, golden fur trimmed with black, turned toward him, and the wolf cocked its head to one side.

A hairy bitch in human form, her face covered with a light brown fuzz, stopped rubbing the scar that was where her left middle nipple ought to be, and growled at Herolf, spreading her hands and growling some more when he answered in a way that Torrie was sure was sarcastic.

She turned back to Torrie. "It would depend. If it's 'how much longer is it until we get there,' I get to eat two of your fingers." Her smile showed teeth that were ample for the job. "So lie to him, please."

Torrie shook his head. "It is about shoes. My mom and Maggie have but slippers," he said. "Good soles on them, but there is a village there, I see—would it be possible to get them proper shoes? Humans don't have thick soles on our feet the way Sons do, and—"

Herolf cut him off with a growl, then growled at the bitch.

" 'What would you plan to use for money to pay a cobbler?' he asks," she said.

Torrie swallowed. "I had thought to use some of the gold that you seized from my pack and that of my father."

He had never heard a wolf laugh before, and Torrie was sure that the answer was not only going to be no, but to be offensively so, when the bitch turned to him and snarled, "Have it as you will." She dipped two long-nailed fingers into her pouch, and dropped a Krugerrand into his palm. The gold coin was, as always, heavier than he thought it should be.

"Four for guard duty," she called out in Bersmål; the snarls that followed were probably a translation.

Dad flinched, cowering away, as one of the Sons brushed too close to him. Mom reached over and patted his shoulder, while Maggie ignored the lot of them.

"I've gotten Herolf to agree to let us go into the village and get a cobbler to, er, cobble together a pair of shoes for each of you."

Thanks, Maggie mouthed.

"Thank you, Torrie," Mother said.

Dad didn't meet his eyes.

The four guards turned out to be two Sons in wolf form, and a pair of bitches in human form.

"Torrie," Dad said, "just be careful. I'm . . . vaguely concerned," he said with a slight wink.

Torrie forced himself to keep his face calm and emotionless. The word "vague" or the Bersmål equivalent, *posfe*, was supposed to be the code word for him to run, but Dad hadn't used the word, not exactly, but something close to it, and the emphasis and wink made it clear that it wasn't accidental.

A chill washed up and down Torrie's back; it was all he could do not to shiver. Dad wasn't a coward; but he was pretending to be one. Let the Sons think him cowed, and they'd be less careful around him, until it was time to move. Torrie could have kicked himself for thinking Dad a coward. He knew better; he ought to have known better.

So when Dad threw an arm around Torrie, pulling him close and hugging him, saying, "Be careful," Torrie wasn't in the least surprised that his free hand unbuttoned a button over Torrie's belly, and quickly slipped what felt like two small scabbards inside.

Torrie pushed Dad away and drew himself up straight, as though disdainfully, but mainly to pull closed the opening in his shirt. "I don't need any of your words, you who flinch from the Sons."

Torrie's bodyguards snickered. One of the bitches turned to the other and muttered something low.

"It'll be soon," Torrie said, as though to the Sons.

Dad nodded once, so slightly that if Torrie hadn't been watching for it, he wouldn't have noticed.

The village was known as the Village of Mer's Woods. Not terribly creative, all and all, given that the village was in a clearing at the edge of a hunting preserve owned by the Margrave Mer, but there was no reason to think the Vandestish terribly creative, after all.

As he followed Maggie and Mom into the dark cobbler's shop, none of their bodyguards preceded them, but two followed them into the small, dark, dank room.

There was no other door, unless the vaguely door-shaped tapestry hanging from the rear wall hid one. It was gorgeous, though: a long, skinny waterfall in a wooded setting, splashing down into a green meadow, its head and foot wreathed with spray. Very, very pretty.

The rest of the walls were covered with cubbyholes filled with scraps of leather and wood and tiny bits of round metal, presumably eyelets for laced-up footwear. Over the much-battered workbench under the mottled-glass window, there was a rack of tools of all sizes, some of which—mainly the knives—Torrie had no problem in identifying, others of which he had no way of identifying.

"Enh." The lead bitch snarled. She pointedly looked at the rack of tools, then reached out a long, hairy arm and snagged something that looked like a scalpel on a foot-long stick. "Go on, if ye want it. Cut me good, trying to escape, see how much good it'll do ye and yers."

"No," Torrie said, swallowing.

Mom pursed her lips for a moment, but then shook her head. Maggie just stared off into the distance.

There was a tingling that sounded more like glass crystals than bells, and a dwarf—no, a Vestri, Torrie reminded himself—pushed through the waterfall that now clearly consisted of thousands of loose, painted strands hanging from above where the doorframe would have been.

"Bindur, at yer shervish," the dwarf said in a thick Bersmål rendered almost unintelligible by his lisp. He looked from Torrie to the women to the Sons, and gave the slightest of shrugs, as though to say it was none of his business. "Do ye noble lords and ladies have need of me poor services?"

There was a perfect opening: the lead bitch was paying attention to Bindur, and the Son in wolven form had lowered his massive head and was sniffing around the legs of some of the tables, as though getting ready to mark his position.

But the moment went by, and was gone. Torrie explained that they needed good shoes or boots for the women, and flashed the Kruggerrand as a demonstration of his ability to pay.

Maggie was soon sitting in a bench, her slipper off. The dwarf kneeling over her had taken a peculiarly marked wooden board down from the wall, and was holding it up to her foot, making several sets of markings on the board with a piece of white chalk. His second set of measurements came from Mom's feet.

He nodded. "I can have those ready tomorrow if you'd like." He rubbed his hands together. "Now, we ought to decide on a price . . ."

Torrie pulled out the gold coin, again. "We need them now, and this is your price. All of it."

The dwarf's massive head tilted slightly to one side. "Well, well, I could modify a couple of boots I was making on speculation, you see, on speculation, but then the price—"

Torrie picked up the Krugerrand.

"—will be amply paid by your gold, amply paid, young lord. Sit ye down, sit, sit, and it will be just a matter of moments."

This wasn't exactly a normal sort of situation, but even under bad circumstances Torrie always enjoyed seeing somebody who was good at it work with his hands. Within just minutes, the dwarf had taken down two pairs of boots and with a small, pointed knife, removed the stitching that held sole to foxing; he carved on each sole, in one case simply making it slimmer, in the other case making it shorter and slimmer.

It was just a few moments, but the Sons were starting to get impatient. "We need to move today," the bitch said. "Herolf is generous with our time, but even he would not be overgenerous."

Torrie knelt down in front of Maggie, and checked the lacing on the calf-high boots. "In a moment," he said, turning back to Maggie. "You're going to have to pull this tighter," he said, grabbing hold of her wrists and gently pulling her forward. "When I say now," he said quietly, slipping a scabbarded knife into her hand, "you go all out—you pull hard, eh?"

Dad had probably wanted him to give the knife to Mom, but Maggie was the fencer, not Mom, and while the knives Dad had passed him weren't épées, they were the closest thing he had to that, just as Maggie was the closest thing to a knife-fighter.

It was supposed to be scary, Torrie decided, but there was something about it, something strange, a feeling like this is what he had been born for, been trained for, for all of his years.

He might not be able to do it right all the time, but nobody could: but it was the right thing for him to be doing.

He slipped the scabbard from his remaining knife, and used his thumb to pin the hilt against the palm of his hand, letting the length of the blade lie along his arm, parallel to it.

"Look." He gestured with that arm, and when the bitch followed his gesture, he spun the knife around in his hand and slashed back, low, catching her across the belly.

She let out a bark, and then a howling scream that trailed off into a bubbling moan.

Torrie wasn't waiting. He had already lunged at the Son next to her, the one in wolf form, ducking under outstretched claws to slip the knife in between his ribs. The flesh parted easily, too easily, as though it was Jell-O, not hard muscle under tough skin.

The two Sons on guard were already dashing in. Torrie barely nicked the one in humanoid form, but tripped him as he lunged past, and turned to face the other. There was nothing to do but hope that Maggie was able to handle the injured one, because the wolven Son flattened himself against the floor and sprang.

Timing, Father used to say, was everything: Torrie ducked to the right—the only direction open—transferred the knife to his left hand, and planted it firmly in the Son's throat, twisting as he withdrew it.

He turned. Mother had flattened herself against the wall, but Maggie was covered with a Son's blood from her chest to her feet, and while her face was white, her jaw was set.

"Quickly," he said. "We've got to run, to get out of here." Torrie turned to the dwarf: "Does this shop have a back way out?"

"Hurry, hurry," the dwarf said, urging the three of them toward the rear of the shop, down a narrow hall and into a storeroom that ended in a thick, barred door. The dwarf slid the bar aside and yanked the door open. "Go left down the alley, and then right at the end of it, and run for your lives, run, run, run."

As Torrie opened the door, he heard a click behind him. The three of them were alone in the storeroom; the dwarf had disappeared.

He stepped out into the alley, and froze. The mouth of the alley was filled with a dozen swordsmen, each with a drawn blade, each wearing black livery edged in crimson orange, decorated at the chest with a flame design. Behind them, holding the reins to their similarly liveried horses, a quartet of Vestri waited patiently.

"Well done," said the largest swordsman, sweeping his black crimson-edged cloak aside as he bowed. "It is just as well that we had the Sons . . . forget to tell you that we were to accept delivery here and now, or you likely would have escaped several days ago, and quite probably gotten yourself killed for the trouble."

The troop parted, to reveal Dad, his arms bound before him, a swordpoint at his cheek forcing him to tilt his head to one side, and even that wasn't enough: a thin trickle of blood ran down his unflinching cheek, dripping off his jaw and splashing on his already dirty shirt.

"His Warmth would like to see you all in person, and alive," the leader said. "I trust that can be arranged?"

Behind him, the Sons growled.

"I really would advise surrender," the leader said. "But have it your way—" He nodded to another swordsman near Dad, who pulled back his blade, ready to—

"Wait." Torrie put up his hands.

"Very good." The leader smiled.

CHAPTER TWELVE

Harbard and Frida

Ian woke, lying on his side, a warm, damp cloth on his forehead and the smell of roasting beef filling his nostrils, making his mouth water. There was a distant taste of sweetness at the back of his tongue, powerful, but not cloying.

He waited for the pain to hit. After the way he had exhausted himself, every muscle in his body was going to ache; dragging the travois halfway down the mountain had ripped the palms of his hands raw, and no doubt the blisters on his feet had all burst. This was just a pain-free moment as he emerged from the respite of sleep, and in an instant the agony would be back, redoubled by comparison with this island of no-pain.

But the pain didn't hit, and after a few moments he opened his eyes, feeling kind of foolish.

Under a thin brown wool blanket, Ian lay on a sleeping frame a few inches above a slab-wood floor; a skin, stretched tightly across the frame, gave the surface enough give to be comfortable. A few feet in front of him, a small fire burned in a huge stone hearth. A roast of some sort turned slowly on a spit, although it was hard to guess what the motive power was, as one end of the spit simply lay on the crotch of an upthrust Y-brace, and the other end was sunk into the wall.

It was getting either dark or light outside; a low sun cast a buttery light through the window, turning swords and spears hung on the wall opposite all golden.

He turned over. He was in a largish room, maybe twenty feet by thirty. The walls were all rough-hewn wood, as though the building was really just a log cabin, but the spaces between the slabs appeared to have been caulked with mortar. A large sleeping frame stood in one corner, glossy furs neatly folded on a shelf above it, while the far side of the room was unmistakably the kitchen, dominated by a huge cast-iron woodstove topped with four dull flat iron burners.

But what really struck Ian about the room was how full it was. What appeared to be a large dresser and two bureaus, each intricately carved and decorated, stood over by the sleeping frame. Above one an oval wood-framed mirror hung on the wall. There were a dozen wooden foot-lockers of various sizes spread around the room, some stacked on each other. Easily ninety percent of the walls were covered with shelves, and the shelves were covered with all sort of things: small wooden carvings; crystals large and small; beakers and tankards of wood, silver, and leather; what appeared to be shards of glass and whole painted eggs.

It reminded Ian of his visits to Zayda Sol. The old man had never thrown away a souvenir in his life, and kept his shelves filled with little bells and small crystal carvings. This was like that, except more so—most of these things looked like souvenirs.

There were some exceptions. Next to the thick door, above where the crossbeam would have rested if the door were shut, a spear hung horizontally, supported on a trio of brass hooks that had been shaped to appear to be hands, and below it hung a horn bow and a quiver full of long arrows; to the side was a sword similar to Ian's—and at that thought, his hands, as of their own volition, sought the hilt of it, finding it on the rough-hewn floor next to his bed.

Ian swung his legs out of bed and got to his feet, the world spinning about him for just a moment; he tried to regain his balance as he stood, wearing nothing but a pair of jeans. The floor was cold beneath his feet, but, amazingly, his feet didn't hurt. He hopped on one foot for a moment, bringing the other one up.

There was no sign of the blisters he knew he had. Not on his feet, and not on the palms of his hands. They weren't scarred over—it was as though the whole trip down the mountain had been a dream.

It would have made more sense if this whole thing had been a dream, but he wasn't used to waking up from dreams in some strange log cabin, a sword—not a foil, but a blooded sword—at his side.

But it was, and he was well. How long had he slept? Weeks, apparently—months? Years?

He was trying to figure out what to do next—should he belt his sword about himself and walk around, check things out? Should he call out? If so, what should he call out, and in what language?

Should I holler something out in English, or in this Bersmål that I seem to have picked up without studying it, and that I can even slip into ofrivillig?

It was all very strange.

He had just decided to at least take a look out the door when the door swung open ahead of a woman carrying a huge load of firewood. Ian started—the door had opened by itself, and then it shut, quietly, closing the darkening night out.

"Let me help you with that," he said in English, then switched to Bersmål and repeated himself when she didn't immediately answer.

"No, no, no," she answered in Bersmål, quietly, her voice lower and more airy than he had thought it would be. "You are to be resting; I can manage by myself."

Her hair was long and definitely white, but straight and glossy; it hung down to her shoulders, parted neatly in the middle, the bangs cut short. Her long legs were bare down to sandals; she wore only that and a less than knee-length blue cotton shift, belted with a particularly nice silver buckle, tight around a slim waist, showing full breasts that would have looked overlarge if her shoulders weren't just a touch broad.

She reminded him of a woman bodybuilder—not the overmuscled types who looked like men with small breasts, but the Rachel McLish style: rounded, well-developed muscles that were still very much feminine.

The muscles that played under the shift must have been in awfully good shape; she was carrying at least fifty pounds of wood without any apparent effort. When she leaned over to dump it unceremoniously in the woodbin beside the stove, the only thing that strained was the cloth of her shift, and he found himself hoping it would give.

She turned as she straightened, every movement like a step in a dance, and clapped her hands several times to clear them of dust and dirt. "Good morning to you," she said in Bersmål. "I see that you've slept all the way through another night?"

"Er, I would . . . guess so."

"But you seem to have healed well. I'm so glad." Her smile took his breath away.

Ian found it difficult to guess her age. The white hair suggested age, but of course there were women and men who went prematurely gray. Her complexion was smooth—only the vaguest hint of laugh lines around her eyes as she smiled—but not the rosy glow of an eighteen-year-old girl who hadn't quite lost her babyfat. There was a certain sureness in her posture, a graceful economy in her movements. She reminded Ian of Selma Dougherty, the retired ballet teacher whom he had taught beginning foil.

But Mrs. Dougherty was seventy, and wiry, and this woman couldn't be half that age.

Except for the eyes. They were very old eyes, somehow, although Ian couldn't quite figure out why they seemed that way.

"Jeg hei't Ian Silverstein, gud frøken," he said in formal Bersmål, finding the words coming to him as he spoke, "jeg står till dinab Deres t'jenest." *I am called Ian Silverstein, good lady, and I am at your service.* Strange how that didn't seem either silly or stilted when said in Bersmål, not the way it was in English.

She nodded. "I thank you for accepting our poor hospitality," she answered in the same language, her voice a sweet contralto, rich and warm and musical around the edges: an oboe, not a flute. "Although methinks I can speak thine English quite well enough, Ian Silverstone," she said in English, translating his last name the way Torrie's dad had. Her voice rose and fell as she talked, making the English words sound vaguely Scandinavian.

"Indeed you can," he said, thinking about why he wasn't even thinking of correcting her pronunciation or usage, even of his name.

"Please to speak it, an' it give you comfort." She frowned for a moment. "Ah, that should be: I think I can speak English well enough," she said. "If it's more comfortable for you?"

"Either language is fine, apparently." He nodded. "Thank you for your"—he held out his hands—"help." What a limp word. Help? He had dragged a badly battered Hosea half down a mountain, tearing his hands and blistering his feet, and clearly hurting himself worse than that, so badly that he had been in a coma for how long?

She shook her head. "No, it is we who must thank you. You brought Orfindel to safety, and he's long been dear to mine family."

"Where—who—" Ian didn't know quite where to start. "Where are they?"

"My husband and your companion are down at the ferry, having left you in my hands." She gestured toward a table and chair. "Sit you down, and I'll bring you something to eat; they will join us shortly."

"And how do I speak Bersmål?" he asked in Bersmål, more to himself than anything else.

"Ah. Gift of tongues, it's called," she said in English. "Orfindel has it stronger than anybody I've ever heard of. Stay around him, and some of it shall," she paused, cocking her head, "scrape off? No, rub off: some of it shall rub off." Her smile brightened the room as she raised a finger. "Just be sure you don't lose that accent. It's charming."

She walked over to the iron stove, and pulled open its massive door. A wave of heat washed over Ian's face and torso.

She just reached in and pulled out a pie sitting in a clay pan.

With a muffled cry, Ian lunged toward her to stop her—

Her flesh would blister instantly, and even if she did manage to drop it without shattering the hot pie, splattering her bare legs with the bubbling filling, her hands would be ruined, and he had to—to stop himself after half a step.

There was no need to interfere. She wasn't screaming, writhing in pain. She wasn't even hurt.

The oven was hot enough that even at this distance, the heat flashed warm against his face, and she had reached in and pulled out a pie, and instead of writhing on the floor in agony, she simply balanced it on one hand, while the air above it shimmered like it would over a road on a hot summer afternoon. She took a metal trivet down from a shelf, and set it carefully on the table before putting the pie on it.

Ian realized his mouth was still hanging open, so he shut it.

She glanced over at him and smiled. "Oh. I beg your pardon," she said. "I didn't mean to frighten you." She gestured at a seat. "It's just that Harbard and I are generally alone here, and I've fallen out of practice at doing things the way you young ones do."

"I'm not that young," Ian said, although he wasn't quite sure why. It sounded like the first part of a stupid come-on.

Her eyes twinkled. "That is, I would think, a matter of perspective." With a side glance at Ian, she self-consciously used a hook to remove the cover from another pot. Steam wafted up into the air; the rich smells of stewing meat made Ian's mouth water.

There were distant sounds from outside that Ian couldn't quite place. A deep *thrummmm,* and a couple of loud *whack*s. In a moment, there was another *whack,* followed by hoofbeats and a rush of voices.

"Ah, the ferry is back," she said, wielding what looked like a cross between a triangular-bladed spatula and a hunting knife, dividing the pie into quarters with two quick slashes. "They shall return hungry, or I'll be surprised." She set out plates and metal spoons, and quickly served a quarter of the pie onto each plate. "Shall we go greet them?" she asked, looking up.

"Sure."

She walked to the door, which swung away in front of her, and stepped out into the day, Ian following.

The first thing he noticed was the river. The Gilfi was wide and fast, gray waters rushing away from the far mountains with a constant *whussshh,* a snake cutting across the continent.

The cabin lay just above the flood marks on the riverbank, and below, a stone path wound down the steep walls of the riverbank toward the ferry's dock. It was a simple arrangement, really: a cable had been strung across the river, and the ferry, a barge, was attached to the cable by loops at the front and the back. A loop of cable ran from the near bank to the far bank, coiled around the motive power for the whole thing: a windlass, powered by a single horse walking in endless circles. There were apparently arrangements for heavier loads—in a corral beyond the windlass, another horse pranced about, as though tired of waiting.

There seemed to be something strange about the horse, but Ian's attention was drawn to Harbard lowering a ramp from the ferry, then guiding a horse-drawn wagon down. The drover accepted Harbard's help up to his seat, then flicked the reins, sending the wagon down the road parallel to the river, the one that gradually sloped up the sides of the banks.

The ferry empty, Harbard and Hosea secured it to its dock, then unhitched the horse from the windlass before walking up the long path toward the house, pausing only for a moment when Hosea waved to Frida.

"Well," she said, urging Ian back into the cabin. "Let us eat. Sitsit*sit*," she said. "We don't wait on ceremony here." She ladled thick stew into each of four bowls, and had them and mugs filled with some hot liquid on the table by the time the door swung open ahead of Hosea, followed by Harbard.

While he was half a head shorter than Hosea, Harbard somehow seemed to be too large for the room, as though at any moment he would stretch out in some direction, and unintentionally tear a hole in wall or ceiling or something, like a normal man wearing a tissue-paper shirt.

Harbard removed his cloak and hung it on a peg near the door, under the spear. Blunt fingers tentatively reached out and touched the spear for just a moment, and then fell to his side.

Hosea smiled as he hung his own cloak, then took a seat next to Ian.

"It's good to see you well, Ian," he said with a nod. "In fact, it's good to see anything at all."

Harbard scowled as he dropped into a chair across the table from Ian. He leaned forward, not saying a word, but looking at Ian for the longest time.

It was amazingly hard for Ian to meet that gaze.

It was strange, because there was no physical similarity, but something about the way Harbard held himself reminded Ian of the actor Peter Falk, the one who played Columbo. There was no hesitance in Harbard's voice, but something about the angle of his head, something about the way his eyes didn't quite work together, was the same.

He was trying to decide what that meant when Harbard sat back, shaking his head. "I don't know about this one, Orfindel," he said.

"Hosea, please," Hosea—or was it really Orfindel?—said. "I've been known as that for a time now, and I rather like it better than many of the other names. We all have our favorite, eh, Harbard?"

A grunt was the only reply. Harbard turned back to Ian. "Well, be welcome in my home, my guest," he said, a trifle begrudgingly.

"I thank you."

Harbard glanced over at the steaming mugs on the table. "Tea? Wife, you have freshly squeezed cider set out with dinner, it would appear."

"I like it," Frida said. "And I've mulled it specially; the herbs will help our visitors to rest, and heal."

"Have you tasted the better stuff?"

"No." Her lips were set in a thin line. "Taste it yourself, if you please."

"Fah." Harbard took a large clay jug down from a shelf

on the wall, uncorked it, and tilted it back heavily. "Ahh. Not the best cider, but still a few days from its final turning." He splashed some in a pewter mug he placed in front of Hosea's place, and set another mug in front of Ian.

"None for me, please," Ian said, regretting it instantly when Harbard glared at him. "My apologies," Ian went on, "but I don't drink . . . intoxicants," he said, substituting the English word when the Bersmål escaped him. "I mean no offense."

"None is taken," Frida put in quickly, with a glance at her husband."

Harbard turned his glare on her, then waved it away as he sat himself heavily in his chair. "Well, none taken, none taken." He picked up a still-smoking piece of pie with his hands, unmindful of the way some of the hot yellow-brown filling spilled out, across the backs of his fingers, and bit into it, swallowed heavily, and smiled. "And never let it be said, wife, that your food is unfit." He licked at his fingers.

Frida smiled. "I would hope it to be better than simply not unfit, husband."

"Yes, yes, yes, it's very good." He growled. "I meant no offense, too, just as Ian Silverstone meant none."

"And I take no offense, husband."

"Just the last word, eh, wife?"

"Perhaps."

Ian would have eaten the stew first, but when in Rome . . .

He spooned up a mouthful of the pie, and blew at it for a moment to cool it before putting it in his mouth.

Grmph. It tasted so good that it was almost painful. The crust was just okay—a bit on the crisp side, but with a nice fullness to it—but the filling was somehow sweeter, richer than any apple pie he had ever tasted before.

Hosea smiled at him. "She is known to be good with an apple, eh?"

"Amazing," Ian said around another mouthful.

Harbard brushed the crumbs from his beard, then took up a spoonful of stew. "And this is very good, wife, as well."

"Thank you."

Harbard looked over at Hosea. "How much does this one know?"

Hosea's smile might have been a few degrees cooler. "He knows that his friends are in danger."

Harbard quickly swallowed a mouthful of stew so he could snort derisively. "His friends are dead, if His Warmth gets the idea that they won't work as bait for you. And likely dead anyway."

"I think not."

Ian didn't want to think about that. He cleared his throat. "Why Hosea? Or Orfindel? Would somebody please tell me what this is all about?"

"Hmm." Harbard pursed his lips. "Where to start?"

"Start at the beginning, maybe?" Ian said.

Harbard glared.

"Very well," Hosea said, his index finger idly doodling on the tabletop. "And what would that be?"

"We could start with the Hidden Ways within the Cities," Frida said, "or with the Brisingamen."

Harbard took a final mouthful of stew, set down his spoon, sat back in his chair, and steepled his fingers in front of him. "I'll begin."

Some things are simple (Harbard said), but some things are not. It's a simplicity that a child will grow out of his clothes, will find that which once comforted him and kept him warm to be too small, far too confining.

So it is with a people outgrowing where they have lived.

A long time ago, one of the Elder Races—call them the Dana's Children, or the Tuatha Del Danaan, or simply the Tuatha—found that they had outgrown their little towns and villages, and that they needed larger cities for themselves and their servants to live.

It wasn't just that there were too many of them, for there weren't; the Tuatha were always few in number, and never terribly fecund—

"—unlike some I could name," Frida said, with a decided sniff.

Harbard tilted his leonine head to one side and paused a moment before speaking. "Are you telling this, wife, or am I?"

"Oh, tell it, tell it—but tell it right."

"You'll have your turn," Harbard said. "Be still."

Frida sniffed again.

And they were never terribly fecund nor fertile (Harbard went on). It was that, well, first they had ruled over fields and meadows, and then they had ruled over hamlets and villages long enough, and then they had presided over castles and surrounding towns—now they wanted cities.

But they didn't want just *any* cities built—they wanted them special, distinct, suited to the Tuatha, and growing more and more suited to the Tuatha year by year. The Tuatha have always been, well, discriminating, perhaps. Or choosy.

So they did what others of the Elder Races had always done when they needed something made, something beyond the ability of them and their servants. They sent one of their kind to pay a call to the greatest . . . watchmaker? No. Tinkerer? No. Builder? Builder, call him the Builder. Or the Doomed Builder, for he has never built anything important without great cost to him.

He was hard to find, because like all of the Elder Ones, he had been able to alter his form. Once, taking the form of a giant, he had agreed to build a wall around Asgard, asking as his only pay that Freya be his wife—although the Aesir had combined to cheat him of his pay.

"Loki," Ian said. "I heard that story, long ago, back in elementary school, I think, some class on mythology. Loki turned into a fly and stung his eye, and into a mare in heat and led his horse away."

"Well, so it is said." There was a twinkle in Hosea's eye. "Loki was always the best of the Aesir at changing of shape," he said, "but it was also said that he was always a little slow at it. The stallion . . . caught up with him before he could change back from a mare, and there he was: pregnant. It's said that none of the Aesir saw anything of him until he showed up with a marvelous stallion sometime later. Sleipnir," Hosea said, and smiled. "I'm told Loki never quite walked comfortably again."

Harbard gave out a low growl. "Do you know, Orfindel, why telling a story is like having a woman?"

Hosea raised an eyebrow. "Very well, Harbard: why is telling a story like having a woman?"

"Because," Harbard says, "one can enjoy it so much more if one isn't constantly interrupted."

"My apologies."

In another form (Harbard went on, his mouth twisted for a moment into a frown), at another time—and this was all so long ago, Ian Silverstone, that it's hard to remember which happened first—he and a son had built a maze to contain a monster, but only he had escaped. Flying, that time, not limping.

He didn't always limp, but Asa-Thor once carried him back, injured from the cold North—and therein lies another tale for another time—and it was so cold that one of his toes froze solid, so solid that when Thor reached up to push the naked foot back in the basket, the great toe snapped off in his hand, and Thor threw it skyward, where it remains as a cluster of bright stars. In yet another form—

—but I digress, and if I digress much more, I'll be interrupted yet again.

He had sworn himself never to lay a stone on a stone again, for building had only brought him pain and sorrow, but the Tuatha were insistent, as only Tuatha can be, and finally he agreed, at least in part. He would not forswear himself—it's my belief that he could not forswear himself—but he would and could carve their cities for them, each out of a mountain high in the Medial Mountains, far above the Vanish Plains.

And this time, his price was simple: he was to be left alone. The Tuatha were to see to it: they were to guard him, to protect him, for as long as the Cities stood, so that he would be left alone as long as he wished it.

They agreed, and he got to work. What he had promised to do was far too much for one to do, even one of the Eldest—if he ever could be two places at once, and I think he once could, he had long lost the ability—so he mated with a troll, and produced a race of small creatures, short of stature but deft with their hands, clever in the ways they could flay stone from stone, leaving behind a tunnel, or a room, or a statue.

And they built it. It took many generations of his small-statured servants to rough out the mountains into shape, and many more before the first rooms were cut from the stone, and even more until the work was all done . . . but in those days the Tuatha were patient, and they waited patiently.

And one day it was done. One day the last hinge was installed on its sealed bearings, one day the last course of tile was laid down into niches in the stone. One day the final flue was carved for the kitchen ovens; one day the last wooden door had been fitted carefully into place, to swing open and shut with ease.

The Cities were built; and shiny and new, they were ready for their inhabitants. They were complex and strange cities, mind, with many secret places and passageways, none of them known to the Tuatha.

Which enraged them. Tell me where all the secrets are, one cried. No, tell me! another said. I want to be the one to know.

He nodded. Certainly, he said. After you have fulfilled some of your part of the bargain. Leave me alone and guarded for a short time, perhaps just a few millennia, and I'll tell you everything you want to know. But it is the way of the universe that I seem to be cheated of my payment, and this time, at least this time, I'll have at least a taste of the solitude and privacy I've bought with generations of work.

The Tuatha didn't like this; none of the Elder Races enjoy being thwarted. So the Tuatha banded together, and they hunted down one of Loki's sons, killed him and braided his intestines into an unbreakable rope, then bound the Builder with ropes made from the guts of a god, and left him in a dungeon in what was, then, the chief of their Cities, and they tortured him night and day, demanding that he tell them.

But he never did.

"I doubt that was the only thing they were after," Harbard said. "I think he knew a lot more—"

Frida waved him to silence. "What he knew and what he didn't know, only he could say. I'll take over here."

"And likely be interrupted less than I was, wife."

"Not if you keep up this way, husband."

Well, Ian (Frida went on), the story diverges here, and when it's told around the fires late at night, it often comes out differently, and that depends not only on who it is that does the telling.

Now, some say that the Builder escaped his bonds then, and walked upon Tir Na Nog, the New World, for a time, only to finally succumb to the Sleep of the Gods and merge with, perhaps, the soil, or the trees, or the wind. It has happened to others of the Elder Races. Most of the Sidhe, of a certainty, but not just the Sidhe; it happened to Frigg, for one, and perhaps to Heimdal, I suspect.

It eventually happened to most of the Tuatha; they left their Cities behind for humans. And if you think that the Curse of the Builder had nothing to do with that, then you're more skeptical than I.

I once heard that Asa-Thor himself rescued the Builder, his hammer bringing down one of the Cities in the process, and in thanking him, the Builder blessed Thor and his sons, both human and Aesir. It would explain much—it would help to explain why there are five Cities instead of the seven that there should have been, but save that story for another time. And it would explain the talus pile that stands—or more accurately, sprawls—where one of the cities should have stood. The wrath of Asa-Thor was . . . intense. And it would also help to explain the story of how Loki came to be bound with those same bonds, some time later. That story may be true, or it may not; certainly, nobody ever heard Thor talk about it, and he was a great braggart, but more capable of subtlety than he is usually credited.

Some say that the Builder had not just created hidden passages within the mountains, but that somehow he had tapped into the Hidden Ways built into the structure of existence, making them solid enough that those with the Gifts can find their way among them.

There are some who say that it was but a man who released him from his bonds, and in gratitude the Builder showed him and his family a way to the Newer World. There are some who say he simply died in his bonds, and the Tuatha began to search for his sons, knowing that he would have had to pass on the plans to someone.

Some say that it was the capture of the Builder that finally poisoned the Tuatha, and that he cursed them from his cell, and that is what finally drove them from the Cities, off into the wilderness, leaving behind little of what they once were.

As for me, I think much of it is true. I think he escaped for a time, and was recaptured for a time, and escaped again only to be recaptured again; and while he escaped once again he was, finally, getting weaker with age, and he had not the strength to escape when later captured by humans, and he lay in a dungeon for as long as memory, until he was freed fairly recently, until he fled through a Hidden Way into the Newer World.

That's what I think.

Hosea sat back. "I think you've said more than you know, and both more and less than you should have."

Harbard snorted. "Oh? You'd have us talk of the Brisingamen?"

Hosea looked off into the distance. "You would think he ought to know."

"Then tell him. You, of all, should be the one to tell that part."

"Very well."

The thing you must understand, Ian (Hosea said), is that when she was young, Freya was not only the most beautiful of the Aesir, but the most beautiful that there was. She really was one of the Vanir, actually, before they were largely subsumed by the Aesir. Tyr was born a Vanir, although adopted by Odin, somewhat later—and like her father, Njord, and her brother, Frey, the Vanir were, by and large, better looking than the Aesir, if often not quite as bright.

* * *

Frida chuckled. "Nor were they as arrogant, most of them."

"Hush," Harbard said. "Or I'll leave. I've heard this before."

"Threats become you little, husband."

"Shh."

While (Hosea went on, with a glare at both Harbard and Frida) Odin sacrificed his eye for knowledge, Tyr—

"Tyr was of the Aesir," Harbard said, his jaw tense, his voice louder than it needed to be in the closeness of the cabin.

"Eventually," Hosea said quietly, almost in a whisper. "Eventually. He was adopted by Odin, and Odin was never one to acknowledge a difference between an adopted son and a son of his blood, particularly not when the son was as much of a red-handed killer as Tyr turned out to be, but he was born of the Vanir." Hosea smiled. "I could understand why Odin would want him thought to be of the Aesir; 'Tyr' means victory, and Odin was never one to spurn victory."

"No matter what it cost him," Frida said quietly. "You sometimes do not give Odin his due."

Hosea nodded. "True enough."

Harbard just scowled.

—Tyr, as I was saying (Hosea went on), just sort of lost an arm by being careless around Fenris wolf, and later claimed it was deliberate when Thor laughed at him. You see the difference? The trade of something of value for something of more value, as Odin did, versus simply being scarred?

Well, Tyr wouldn't, or didn't, until he was laughed at.

But I was speaking of Freya, sister of Frey.

The Eddas, the sagas, were full of references to this one or that one wanting her, of a giant stealing Thor's hammer and demanding Freya as his bride for its return, or of the Builder wanting that as the price for the building of Asgard. We know that Loki lusted after her—as did Tyr, although few women escaped that distinction. She was often confused with Frigg, Odin's first wife, and I don't doubt that was because Odin often chose to so confuse her.

There were even some stories that she had come between Thor and Sif, although that's hard to believe. The devotion that Asa-Thor had for his Sif would be difficult to interrupt.

What is easy to believe is that many would have put the universe on a string, and given it to her for a necklace, and that in some senses, one did.

Look in an astronomy text sometime, Ian. Ask an astronomer—*where's all the matter?* As far as the best instruments your science has to offer can tell, there only exists about ten percent of the matter necessary to make the universe cyclical, to—eventually—collapse down into the monobloc whence the universe came, and to start it all over again.

No, if your scientists have found it all, there has been only one cycle of the universe: Ginnungagap does not space the universe's lives apart, but merely is the final heat death, the Ultimate Whimper instead of a slowly paced rhythm of Big Bangs.

But that, of course, could not be true; a thing, be it a flowerpot or a universe, does not simply come into being. It is created by something, in some way. After the end and in the beginning when there was just the One God and the monobloc, for that incredibly long and incredibly short time, the One God pinched off a tenth of it all, and breathed life and change into it, then sent it expanding out, pushing the envelope, and idly squeezed the rest of it into several different pieces, planning to play with it later, perhaps, perhaps as much as he had with the other tenth.

But he never did get around to it, and perhaps nobody knows why.

There are many who have tried to speak to the One God, and even more who claim to have heard an answer, but the answers that they've heard are always in generalities. The One God tells them, they say, to be virtuous or kind; he never says how hot to heat the blade of a sword if you want to put a good temper on it. He urges restraint, but never gives instructions on an appendectomy.

I do think they believe that they talk to him. I think that he's not listening.

But I digress. The point I was trying to make is that all that extra matter was . . . collapsed into several—seven, actually—different pieces, and just left lying about. Eventually, as most things of value do, they came into the hands of the Vestri—

Now, now, now, I'm not being overly critical; I like the dwarves. I have always liked the dwarves. But they were originally fathered by an incompetent upon a troll, and while they're clever with their hands, they tend to keep, to hoard—and for no reason, like a packrat sealing up its middens with crystallized urine. Dvalin's Folk are the worst at that, but they're hardly the only offenders.

It's said that Freya came upon three of the Vestri—call them the Brisings—and that they had taken the seven stones and made them into a necklace we can call the Brisingamen. It was hard to work with the stones, of course, because each of them contains so much matter, but the matter is, well, let's say it's pushed off in another direction—just as Tir Na Nog is off in another direction from the Newer World—held at a distance as long as the stones remain stones, and these three were of the early blood of the Vestri, and still had some of their father's magical adeptness with their hands, even if they had little in the way of intelligence.

Lust they had, though.

Look at it from Freya's point of view: here were three lecherous idiots holding a necklace that was not only beautiful, but contained enough matter to redo the universe. She would do anything for it, and the dwarves demanded that she do just that, that she lie with them for seven days and seven nights.

And so she did.

For some reason, Harbard was glaring at Frida, who looked down, unable to meet his eyes.

Ian shook his head. "You mean that this necklace could be used to—what?"

Hosea looked soberly at Ian. "End the universe; squeeze it all together again; reassemble the monobloc. A magical adept—any of the Elder Races for certain, perhaps even a human—could use it to make himself or herself the One God of the next cycle." He smiled. "And perhaps that may be all to the best; let the God of the next cycle be a poet instead of a watchmaker, eh?"

Harbard scowled. "Foolishness, all of it. The universe will collapse when it's ready; there's no need to hurry it."

Frida tilted her head to one side. "That's what you say; and I say the time will come, but it is not yet . . . but there have long been others with other opinions." She turned back to Ian. "Which is why it was taken from me, and given into safer hands."

Ian was shocked that he wasn't shocked. "Freya?"

She smiled. "Yes, Ian?"

"Really?"

"Ah." Her smile widened. "You don't believe me, young one. Well . . ."

Ian always figured that it must have happened between blinks, because there was no moment where she changed, or where she had changed, but all of a sudden she was *different.*

He could barely breathe for looking at her, and found himself with an erection that was painful. Long, golden hair hung down, caressing porcelain-smooth shoulders in a way that made Ian jealous of it. Her complexion was smooth and creamy, reddened ever-so-slightly at her high cheekbones and at the jawline. Her full, pink lips parted ever so slightly, and the simple shift she wore became a teasing attempt to hide the high, firm breasts beneath it—

"*Stop it,*" Hosea snapped.

Ian must have blinked again, because now her hair was black and glossy as a raven's in complement to her olive skin, almond eyes of a color blue Ian thought he might drown in. Lips as red as blood, pink tongue peeking out, teasingly—

"You *shall* stop it now," Hosea said, placing his fingertips against the tabletop and rising to his feet. "I'll not have you treat the child so, not with the debt I owe him."

Ian must have blinked again, for now she was as he had first seen her: very—but humanly—lovely, of indeterminate age.

She shook her head. "My apologies, Ian. I should not play with your feelings; I would hope I outgrew that many . . . years ago." Her smile warmed him. "At least."

Ian tried to say something but all that came out was a grunt.

Harbard grunted. "Leave it be. We were talking of the Brisingamen," Harbard said. "Tell him."

She pursed her lips for a moment. "Odin," she said, "ordered me to give it to him, which I did, and he gave it into the hands of the Builder, who broke it apart and separated the jewels, hiding each one of them well."

Ian snorted. "Which means that he could reassemble it, or anybody who could make him talk could reassemble it."

"Not quite," Hosea said, his voice sharper than it had been. "Not if he . . . damaged that part of his mind where those memories are, because he had decided that not even he could be trusted with deciding when the universe ought to end. Then, even if he were later caught by . . . the agents of the Armageddonists, call them, and even if they bound him so he could not escape, he would not tell them of the location of the Jewels because he simply would not know, not anymore."

"They were all wrong," Harbard said, his index finger idly drawing through a puddle of mead on the tabletop. "It should have been left with you, Freya. You would have kept it until the time is right, and the time is far from right, yet. The Elder Races grow old and tired, but the younger ones should have their days in the sunlight, eh? Just because I am old, do your bones have to ache—"

There was a pounding on the door.

"You hold that which is needed elsewhere," a deep voice boomed, the sound filling the cabin, rattling the plates and spoons on the table. "Surrender them to me."

"No," Harbard said, finally. "You speak of my guests, stranger, and a willing guest will bide with me as long as I allow it. I would no more permit you to molest a guest of mine than I would permit you to harm my wife." As he spoke, he rose from the table, and walked toward the door. His head was held more erect, and there was a stiffness to his back and a strength in his shoulders that Ian hadn't noticed before. His head didn't bump against the overhead beams, but somehow he seemed to grow larger, more substantial as he stood opposite the door.

The room, which had seemed so warm and comfortable, was now cold. Lamps gave off harsh, actinic light, casting shadows all about. There was no indirect light; it was all either too bright, or black.

Harbard seemed to like it that way as he turned to face the doorway.

"Harbard, Harbard," the voice rumbled, "you would match your will against ours? Old God, you are far too old to be doing that."

Harbard smiled, and his smile was an awful thing to see. "It's been many years since any Tuarin matched strengths with me."

A chill washed over Ian. It was starting to make sense, at least, some of it was—the reason why Harbard's look reminded him of a one-eyed actor, and why his horse seemed to have too many legs.

The mythology books always had Frigg as Odin's wife, not Freya, but they were wrong about other things, as well, it seemed.

"I will match my fire against yours, Harbard," the harsh voice said.

"No," Harbard said, "not today, and not tonight. Remember the stories, old one, remember how I can be killed only at the very end of things."

"The stories lie, carrion god, served only by the dead," the voice rumbled. "For they make Brother Fox out to be allied with the Frost and Fire and with us, and he's never yet been; for they let Uku-Thor live until he faces the Worm, and his bones have long rotted; for they have a place for Heimdal and all the other long-dead gods." There was a long silence. "And they lie, for they do not have us winning, remaking it all in our own images." The rumbling grew louder. "I say again: give Orfindel and his catamite over to me, and you shall be left alone."

"I think not," Harbard said, reaching for the spear mounted above the door. The wood creaked in relief as Harbard took up the weight, but he hardly seemed to notice it. A distant thrumming filled the room, like the vibration of some distant, powerful engine.

"You think not?" the voice asked.

"I think not. I think that Ian Silverstone is no catamite, but a friend and ally of Orfindel, albeit still wet from the womb. I think you do but threaten and bluster, in a place that is of my strength, not yours, and I think that if you do crash through my door into my home, you will not leave again." There was no answer. Harbard hefted the spear once with his right hand. His head twisted on his neck, bringing his left eye into line with the spear, and the muscles in his shoulders stiffened and tensed.

Moving so quickly that his clothes snapped like a cracked whip, Hosea was on his feet, one restraining hand laid on Harbard's biceps. "No." He stepped to the door, fingers running across the wood like a blind man reading Braille. "He wants you to throw it; he's somehow ready for Gungnir."

"You can tell that by feeling at the wood?"

"It's hardly just wood," Hosea said, "as you well should know." Hosea closed his eyes. "It's all one of a piece. It all . . . resonates. I can feel the eagerness out there, the readiness. Whatever it is, whoever it pretends to be, it's hurt, but it's ready now, just as—" he sniffed. "Just as it was ready for me on the side of a mountain, and took on the shape of a bergenisse too quickly, figuring that it would be immune from attack." He turned to Ian. "The sword—what happened when you touched it with your sword?" he demanded, urgently.

"You didn't *watch*?" Harbard snapped.

"I was blinded by the pain, Harbard, and I thank you for your tender concern." Hosea turned back to Ian. "*Tell* me."

Ian clutched at the hilt of his sword. "It—smoked where it touched. The sword, the flesh, I don't know, but it smoked—"

"Ah." Harbard's hand was extended. "Lend your sword to me, Ian Silverstone," he said, quietly. "And I'll return it properly blooded." Ian didn't understand any of this, and he would almost have rather given up his arm than his sword, but at Hosea's nod he drew his sword and offered it to Harbard, hilt first; Harbard accepted it, and started to hand Ian his spear—

Hosea stepped quickly between them, and pushed the spear away just before Ian could touch it. "*No*," he said. "You want to kill the child?"

Harbard shook his head. "No. You should be flattered, Ian Silverstone. For a moment, I forgot that you're but a human, child; it felt, for a moment, like the old days, with one of the Aesir at my side."

"So let it feel again that way, husband," Freya said. "I was born a Vanir, but I have dwelled with you and yours for long enough now. There is one of the Aesir at your side."

Ian couldn't see how she'd had the chance to change, but she was no longer dressed merely in a shift and leggings: silvery armor encased her from throat to toe, her scalp covered by a war-helm, silver wings over the ears. It seemed to be made of impossibly fine scales, for it moved as she moved, its mirror-bright surface casting flashes of reflected lantern light all around the room.

"I shall protect our home, husband," she said, taking the spear from Hosea. Her slim fingers fastened on its shaft delicately, but firmly, and her arms didn't sag as Harbard released it.

The door opened and closed, as though by itself, and Harbard was gone.

It might have been a few moments later; it might have been an hour later. Ian was never quite sure. Freya stood motionless, the spear held out in front of her, waiting, while Hosea listened carefully at the door.

A long time later, Hosea let out a sigh. "It's done. He returns."

Freya was still motionless, waiting.

"No, Freya, it's him; he couldn't hide those footsteps from—"

The door swung open to reveal Harbard. His cloak and trousers looked like they had been more shredded than torn, and as he stepped inside the cabin, he walked with a decided limp. His right eye was covered by a black patch, and it occurred to Ian that the right eye had always been of glass.

"It's done," he said, handing Ian's sword back to him. The blade was clean; it seemed cleaner, shinier somehow than it had been when he had lent it to Harbard. To Odin.

The hilt felt obscenely warm in Ian's hand.

"It was . . . ?" Hosea started.

"A Köld," Harbard said, "and an old, wily one. Fought well. I thought we killed them all ages ago, but it seems not."

Hosea shook his head. "No. None of the Elder Races are all done, or I'd feel it."

"A cold?" Ian put in. "That's—"

"A frost giant, you would call it," Freya said, laying a gentle hand on his arm. She was again in shift and leggings, and her voice was low and gentle once more. "One of the Elder Races," her smile was warming. "Like the Flamme, the fire giants, and the Tuatha—and like us, eh?"

Harbard opened a chest and pulled out some clothing. "I'll bathe myself in the Gilfi, I think. The waters are cold and swift, but I'll not foul my bed with that which it touched. It hit me more than it should have." He grunted. "I haven't had a real fight for more years than I care to count." He looked over to Freya, his mouth tight. "Still, it's good to remember what once we were, eh?"

"Once?" Freya walked to him, a smile on her face. "Once, yes, and still are, when need be." Her slim fingers twisted in his, and she brought their joined hands up to her lips. "And to me you shall always be that which you were, and are." Gently, tenderly, she kissed at his broad hands, at the bloody knuckles the size of walnuts.

Harbard nodded once, and perhaps a trace of a smile touched his face, although Ian wouldn't have wanted to swear either way.

"There will be others," Hosea said. "Now that it's known I walk the ground of Tir Na Nog again, they shall be on our trail."

"Then pack your things," Harbard said, letting Freya's hand go, "for you'll have to leave at first light."

"Yes. I'll pack you food, and I'll make a gift for you, Ian Silverstein," she said, pronouncing his name correctly, not translating it the way Harbard had. "Just a small trinket, but I hope it may serve you in extremity." She licked her lips once. "May your way be safe, and your steps fleet," she said.

"Yes," Harbard said. "May it be so."

CHAPTER THIRTEEN

To the House of Flame

After being marched by the Sons, traveling with the soldiers from the House of Flame was an immediate and distinct improvement in comfort. Torrie and Maggie were loaded into one horse-drawn carriage, Mom and Dad into another—and then, except for being guarded when the procession stopped for rest or relief, they were left alone while the carriage rumbled up the roads, a small detachment of Sons dropping into wolf-shape and loping along behind him.

To be sure, there were horsemen riding at the side of the carriage, and Torrie could always hear the clopping of a horse behind, which put paid to his half-formed idea of cutting through the floor of the carriage and dropping out.

No. It wasn't time; he was beginning to think that the time for that was long gone.

The road led up through the mountains, leaving the Gilfi below and behind. At times it was narrow enough that, looking out the open window, Torrie couldn't see the road itself, and it felt like the carriage was suspended uneasily out over the edge, needing only a wrong breath to tumble down the slope, toward the ribbon of road far below.

"Good day to you, Thorian del Thorian the Younger."

An upside-down head, topped by a thick shock of black hair, an upside-down mouth framed with beard, peered in through the carriage window on Torrie's side. "If I may?"

Torrie tried not to sound sarcastic. "If you may what?"

"Join you?" the stranger said, and at Torrie's nod he reached in, fastened his fingers to the sill over the coach's door, and entered the compartment with a single smooth tumble that let him plop down onto the seat next to Maggie, an expression of almost obscene self-satisfaction on his face.

"Branden del Branden the Youngest," he said, introducing himself, "ordinary of the House of Flame, in service to His Warmth," he said in Bersmål, his accent strange in Torrie's ears. "And you are, of course, Thorian del Thorian."

"Thorian Thorsen," Torrie said.

"I doubt that." Branden dismissed it with a wave. "You're hardly a peasant, even if you affect it with dress."

The strangeness of his accent was itself strange. Torrie had never known there was a language called Bersmål, or that he could speak it, until he had first heard it. It was like the way Uncle Hosea was with languages, and Torrie wondered if he would find himself answering in German if somebody spoke to him in German? Or in Dwerrow, if one of the Vestri spoke in his native language?

Branden sat back, removing his thin leather gloves and dropping them to one side; he reached out a hand toward Torrie, who took it, reflexively grasping Branden's wrist, as Branden grasped his. Branden was perhaps an inch shorter than Torrie, and maybe a bit slimmer across the waist and chest—it was hard to tell, given the way his overlarge shirt ballooned about his chest and arms, but his wrist was thick and muscular, like Torrie's own, and the fingers strong—a fencer's arm and hand.

Branden nodded slightly, as though confirming to himself something he had already been sure of, then reached out a hand toward Maggie. There was an awkward moment as she tried to grip his wrist as Torrie had done, but finally settled on allowing him to take her fingers in his hand. He gently brought her hand up and touched his lips to it. "And you would be . . . ?"

"Maggie," she said. "Maggie del Albert, you would say."

He smiled, and Torrie quickly decided that he didn't like that smile at all. "Not at all. I'd call you the Lovely Maggie, or the Fair Maggie, or the Exceptional Maggie," he said, "and certainly look forward to a chance to so introduce you to others." He gestured at her ragged clothing and unkempt appearance, at once acknowledging and dismissing it, "Once you have the opportunity to . . . refresh yourself." He glanced out the window. "A matter that may well be arranged tonight, if you'd like, although we'll not reach the House of Flame for another couple of days."

"A bath would be nice, but is there any chance we can get some questions answered?" Maggie asked sourly.

Branden affected to look shocked, then recovered. "Ah. The Sons, eh? Well, His Warmth finds them terribly useful for odd duties—as do the other Houses, as well, mind, even the Sky—but they are hardly . . . refined, eh?" He made a lavish gesture that involved touching a finger to his forehead, lips, and chest, then spreading his fingers, palm up. "But yes, certainly, you may ask anything you like, and I shall do my best to answer"—he raised a finger—"if you will do me the favor of joining me for a mild . . . repast."

Torrie's lip curled. "We are at your service." Never mind that he hadn't eaten since God knew when, and that what he had eaten was another moldy couple of apples and limp carrots provided by the Sons.

Branden's mouth twitched. "I would doubt that, Thorian del Thorian the Younger—but may I simply call you Thorian without causing offense?"

Torrie nodded.

"I am grateful." Branden smiled as he stood, and reached up and out of the carriage, fumbling around on the roof for but a moment until he brought his hand back, holding a wooden box by a central handle. He opened it to reveal two compartments, one containing an assortment of greased-paper packages and fist-sized loaves of dark bread, the other glasses and plates and what Torrie would have called silverware if it wasn't the buttery color of gold.

He tried not to frown. There was little point in stealing a dull golden knife, even if it was possible—and given that each glass, each eating prong, spoon, or knife was set into its own place, it was unlikely he'd be able to. The rack served the same function as the outlines on the pegboard that held tools above the workbench at home.

Branden del Branden smiled. "You'll think none the less of me, I hope, if I admit to some Ingarian upbringing and serve us all?"

Torrie spread his hands. "Of course not." If you don't understand what the hell somebody's getting at, it's hard to think less of him.

Packages unwrapped to reveal an assortment of slivered meats and sliced cheeses, some reeking of vinegar or garlic or other spices that Torrie couldn't identify, but that nevertheless made his mouth water.

Branden wielded a set of knives and spoons as foods passed across the cutting board he laid across his lap and onto plates. Ramekins lost their terra cotta covers as sauces and patés were spooned out and sliced to accompany the meats and cheeses. A final series of flourishes put a rosette of something green—it looked like shaved slices of pickles—as a centerpiece on each of the three plates, and Branden set all three plates on the cutting board before carefully laying eating prongs and spoons on the plates.

He lifted the cutting board toward Maggie. "If you would oblige me by the first choice?" he said, offering the choice of the remaining two plates to Torrie when she took one.

Maggie had picked up her eating prong and was reaching it out toward her plate when Torrie held up a hand. "Wait just a moment, and let Branden—let our host start. It's impolite to eat ahead of him."

Branden del Branden gestured toward the remaining plate, now balanced with apparent ease on his knee. "My pleasure, Thorian," he said, spearing a slice of cheese, dipping it in a thick yellow sauce, and conveying it to his mouth without dripping on his beard. "You'll find the artichoke sauce a trifle bland, I'm afraid, but," he said, sampling a slice of meat and a thick red sauce, "the hunter's compote is quite robust." He smiled genially. "If you'd prefer, I could try some from your plates, as well." Branden dabbed at the corner of his mouth with a lacy handkerchief he produced from his sleeve.

Well, what the hell. If Branden was going to poison them, then he probably could, and they were at the dubious mercy of the House of Flame anyway, so there was no point in being overcautious.

Torrie dug in, and after a moment, Maggie followed his example.

The cheeses were ripe and flavorful without being overripe, and the meats had all been smoked to a salty richness. The bread, slathered with creamy butter, was almost impossibly soft inside, in contrast to the hard, rich crunchiness of the crust. The centerpiece that appeared to be shaved pickles turned out to be shaved pickles, their garlicky crunchiness a perfect counterpoint to the ever so slightly bitter notes of liver in the patés.

Hunger was, as Dad often said, the best sauce, but the meaty glaze Torrie dipped the garlic sausage into was a close second.

It only occurred to him a while later that with all the spices he was eating, anybody would be able to follow him by smell for days, at least, until he had sweated it all out of his system.

"You think deep thoughts, Thorian," Branden said.

Torrie shook his head. "Just enjoying the food. And wondering what happens next."

Branden smiled. "Well, tonight we make a somewhat rude camp near the road, and have an opportunity to refresh ourselves." He pursed his lips. "At this moment, in fact, one of my Vestri servants is modifying an outfit of mine for you, Thorian, while another does something similar with a dress that I had bought for my sister, so that it will fit your more . . . slender form, Maggie."

Maggie smiled. "You can start by telling us why . . . why all this? What is it that you want so badly with the Thorsens?"

Branden nodded. "There's no secret about that. Thorian del Thorian was a hereditary—and rather accomplished—member of the House of—of the Society, as they call it. A professional duelist, in the hire of the House of Flame, to represent it in matters of honor where the individuals involved required a level of competence beyond their own—"

"Eh?" She furrowed her brow.

Branden spread his hands. "Well, you can't properly expect an old count to face a young buck who has, say, toyed with his daughter, or a militia captain to directly face one of his own soldiers, can you?"

"Of course not," Maggie said, giving Torrie a what-does-that-mean look.

Torrie shrugged.

"Yet, obviously, there must be some way for honor to be satisfied in the first place, and for a young man to be . . . chivvied back into his proper place when he is serving his city. And then there are matters that are just commerce, and not honor; a gentleman is hardly going to want to dirty his own blade and blood over it. So one hires a professional." He pressed his lips together. "And, of course, when one does, the other side does, most often." He looked at Torrie carefully. "Which was what Thorian del Thorian did, and did well—as had his father before him and his grandfather before him—and did so well that the Thorians had been allowed quarters and free run within the Old City itself, a privilege he used to betray His Warmth by extracting a prisoner from His Warmth's . . . custody."

"Hosea."

"That may be what he asked to be called, but it's not his true name." Branden shook his head. "Orfindel, so he was called. An Old One, and quite possibly even related to the Orfindel of legend, unlikely as that may seem. Certainly, the Old One had enough of the Old knowledge to find a Hidden Way into and out of His Warmth's bank, and to abscond with his person and with that of Thorian."

Branden leaned out the window for a moment, then resumed his seat. "We shall stop for the night shortly. Tomorrow we return to the road, and another long day of travel, and again, and again, until we reach Falias." He touched his eating prong to his cheek. "And then, of course, His Warmth decides what to do about your father."

"Oh?"

Branden held up a finger. "He could have him summarily executed"—he added a second—" or tried by the House of Steel"—a third finger—"or he could do nothing." Branden spread his hands. "Or he could do something else."

Torrie's knuckles were white around his own eating prong. "Summarily executed," he said. "Over my dead body."

Branden smiled. "Interesting choice of words, that."

* * *

Camp that night was as different from the way things had been with the Sons as could be. The three carriages and the accompanying troop of horses stopped at a prepared campsite in a streamside glade, and by the time Torrie and Maggie were released from their carriage, the horses had been led away, downhill and downstream, and multicolored silken tents and flies had been pitched by the quiet Vestri servants on the gently sloping grasses.

It was all calm and peaceful, if you didn't notice the guards.

Herolf, now in his human form, snapped his fingers and gestured to the troop of a dozen gray Sons, who immediately split up and headed for high ground, communicating among themselves with a few high-pitched barks and whiny calls that were repeated every so often, as though they were checking in with each other and their masters—as they probably were.

The third of the carriages rolled to a stop, and Mom and Dad were released from it. Torrie took a step toward them, but a guard dropped a spear point down, leveling it at his chest.

"Please," Branden del Branden said, gesturing the spear point away with a flick of his finger. "I see no harm." He faced Dad. "I offer you parole for the night; your lady to be hostage to your presence, and to your not taking of a weapon to hand."

"And in return?"

Branden shrugged. "In return, Thorian del Thorian, we can see that your arms are freed, and that you have the same chance to bathe and refresh yourself that I will offer your son and his lady, and your . . . wife in any case."

Dad thought about it for a moment. "You have my parole for this night."

"Very well—" Branden snapped his fingers. "Have Thorian del Thorian freed of his bonds, please—and have them restored before first light."

One of the soldiers—from the shoulder tabs, Torrie decided that he was an officer—took a step forward. "Thorian the Traitor? You accept the parole of Thorian the Traitor?"

Enough.

Torrie took a step forward. "Pretty brave words while you hold the sword and we are unarmed."

Behind him, he heard Mom gasp, and Dad grunt.

Standing by himself—none of the humans seemed to want to stand close to him—Herolf smiled, his teeth too sharp, too yellow to be human.

"Ah, one with spine, or at least a simulation of it." The officer smiled thinly, bowed stiffly. "I be Danar del Reginal, minor of the House of Flame, in service as a coadjutant. Lord Branden, might I have your leave to deal with a matter of honor this evening?"

Branden looked like he had swallowed something sour. "To the first touch only," he said. "I'll not see more blood than that shed." He turned to Torrie, all traces of laughter and merriment gone from his face, and particularly from his eyes. "You've not been raised among us, so I ask that you take no offense that I emphasize that this is to one touch only; I will serve as duelmaster, and see to the separation of the parties after that."

Torrie nodded, although his neck felt stiff. "I understand."

Branden's lips pursed. "Well, then, with parole given, and a matter waiting, you had best retire and refresh yourselves." He extended an arm. "Your tent waits; I'll have your lady accompanied to the stream by Vestri."

The inside of the tent was lighted only by a flickering lantern that had been hung on the crosspiece above, just under a hooded vent in the silken fabric. It was floored in a thick rug laid directly on the soft grasses; over in the corner, a pair of bedrolls lay, each secured with a ribbon that had been tied in an overly elaborate knot.

Dad's lips were white. "Why did you do that?"

Torrie could have slapped him. "Because I'm tired of just sitting back and taking it, even though you're not."

Mom looked like he had slapped her. "You don't think—"

"He does." Dad shook his head. "I had to have taught him better."

"Torrie," Mom said, "do you really think your father is a coward?"

"*They* do."

Dad smiled.

Mom shook her head. "And why is that? Perhaps because from the moment he surrendered to save my life and Maggie's he's acted like he is?"

"Yes, all the cowering, and—"

"Which doesn't make any of them less vulnerable to a knife in the neck," Mom said, with a brave grin, "when the time comes." She took his hand and squeezed it.

"If the time comes. I waited too long to free Thorian and Maggie and you," Dad said. "But I saw no good opportunity before."

Mom patted his arm. "It's okay," she said. "We'll make the best of it."

It was the first time they'd had to talk without being overheard in a long time. "Mom? How much of this did you know?"

Her smile was strange. "I had been . . . told much of it, over the years. I don't know how much I believed; I didn't like to think about it." She licked her lips, once.

Dad reached out a hand and squeezed hers, gently. "You think I didn't know, Karin?" he said, quietly. "It's been one of the few . . . ongoing frustrations in what has been a good life with you. A very good life, all things considered."

"Including this." She pulled her hand away. "And you're enjoying this, every moment of it."

"It's what I was raised for, min alskling," he said, quietly.

She opened her mouth and closed it.

Torrie could almost read her mind. Friends have died, and Torrie's killed, and tried to kill more, and you've enjoyed this? How could you?

But there was something about the way Dad was holding himself for the moment, something in his look that said, I can handle this, too, no matter what it is, something of the same look he'd had when he had looked out at the carnage on the front lawn.

It said: I can handle it. It said: this is what I do.

It wasn't a pretty look, even if you had a strong stomach, but there was something to it that reminded Torrie of the way Doc Sherve looked when he squatted in front of a patient and opened his little black bag, or Uncle Hosea did when he picked up a screwdriver and took the cover off a motor, or even Mom, when she sat down with a sheaf of papers in front of her terminal.

"The word for strategy and the one for fencing are the same in Bersmål," Dad said, as though idly, although it wasn't. His lips were pressed together for just a moment. Then he relaxed and shrugged. "Well, an' so be it," he said. "What's done is done; they've maneuvered you well enough."

"Me? They maneuvered me? All they did was—"

"*Thorian.*" He stood there for a moment, silently, then shook his head. "Thorian, Thorian—this isn't Hardwood anymore. You only know about Tir Na Nog from Hosea's stories, and while that might get you by in some minor city in Vandescard, it's not the same thing as having grown up in the Middle Dominion. It is . . . different from what you're used to. Less free, in most ways; more complicated, in most ways. I was born to it, and brought up with it; you were raised differently."

Torrie had never thought of Dad as somebody complicated, or somebody who liked things complicated. It was Mom who spent her days at the computer, trying to make some sense out of the complexity of the stocks and bonds marketplace, and Uncle Hosea who was happiest when fiddling with some obscure mechanism, trying to scry out its intent or flaw. Dad always seemed happiest, say, with his shirt off and a posthole digger in his hand, fixing a fence.

Dad sat down on the burnt-umber carpet, perhaps too heavily. "Take this Danar del Reginal, for example. Do you think there's no reason why he insulted me? Merely the bad manners that would have one taunt a prisoner? A *coadjutant*? No. He was trying to get a response out of me, get me to fight him if possible—and that means he's at least good enough that he expects somebody will learn how my skills are by watching me fight him." He shook his head. "Or yours, for that matter."

"I can take him," Torrie said, hoping he sounded more certain than he felt.

Dad snorted. "Brave words, but how could you possibly know that to be so? And even if you can, is it wise?" He seated himself tailor-fashion on the rug, his hands folded across his middle. "No. You do not win. You lose, and you lose in a specific way. Do you remember when you developed that irritating disengage habit?"

Torrie didn't like the way the conversation was going—and he didn't much like criticism of his play, either—but he nodded. "Nothing wrong with a disengage," he said, idly. "If the wrist is fast enough, and mine is."

"Except that when you disengage your blade, you free his blade too. So early—before he's had time to test your eye and wrist—disengage and let your blade slide out of line outside—"

"I might as well offer him my wrist."

"That's the idea. Don't step forward, just exaggerate what you'd usually do." Dad thought about it for a moment. "That's about right—you're eager, but you're too concerned about the other's point to move closer to it." He clapped a hand to Torrie's shoulder. "He goes for your wrist—tentatively, if he's ever fallen for the trap—and you bring your blade back just a little late. He gets a hit on your arm." He nodded, agreeing with himself. "That should be about right."

Torrie thought about it. "I've never thrown a point." It was common strategy to pretend to develop a habit—say, to stomp before a lunge, or to always riposte after a successful parry—and to wait until your opponent had caught on to that and then catch him expecting the wrong thing. But Torrie had never deliberately taken that to the extreme of losing even a point, and he knew he didn't like it.

But Dad sure sounded like he knew what he was talking about. Torrie looked him in the eye. "I will have a chance to do it as well as I can," he said more than asked. "I will have a chance to fight my best, not simply take a hit."

Dad nodded. "I think that can be arranged. In the right place, at the right time."

Dinner had been light—slivers of smoked fish and pickled vegetables, washed down with cold water, no wine—and an icy bath in the mountain stream was an hour behind him, long enough to loosen his muscles with stretches and sheer force of will.

Torrie had stripped down to a pair of knee-length dueling shorts, borrowed from Branden del Branden, but had declined Branden's offer to have a Vestri servant bind his loins; Torrie settled for wearing his still-damp jockey shorts underneath.

There was a taste of metal in his mouth, and Torrie found himself too conscious of his breathing, of the placement of his feet and what to do with his hands. Part of his mind was just retreating into a shell, the way his scrotum was so tight that his testicles hurt, but part of it had gone all analytical and almost mechanical, as though his body was some sort of distant machine being run by his own remote control, as though he was looking out through remote cameras instead of his own eyes.

So this was what fear felt like. It felt distant. That wasn't too bad. Worse was the way Herolf sat by himself, grinning: for a Son, a grin wasn't a friendly expression. It was the way he freed his teeth for ripping, for rending.

Torches had been planted around a grassy spot against the fall of night, and Vestri servants, down on their hands and knees, had scoured the area for stones and roots, smoothing the turf with their hands as though they were massaging it, leaving it all flat and cool.

His shiny face lit by a flickering torch, Danar del Reginal stood over a flat mahogany case, one hand on his hip, his chin propped up on his other fist, considering. His fingers reached out and stroked the hilt of first one sword and then another, finally selecting a third.

He handed it hilt first to a dwarf, who shambled over, offering it hilt first to Torrie. Torrie couldn't quite figure it, but there was something comforting in the homeliness of the dwarf, in the way he looked up at Torrie beneath his heavy brows.

Torrie wrapped his fingers around the hilt. "I am to use this one?"

The Vestri shook his heavy head. "No, honored one," he said formally. "The coadjutant chose this as a sword to be used in this matter. You may select it, or permit him the choice between it and another two of your choosing, you to choose among the remaining ones."

Torrie handed the sword back to the dwarf, and raised his voice. "I'll let you use this one, Danar del Reginal—I'll use my own. Your dog servants captured it."

Danar del Reginal nodded his head, then held up a hand

when Branden del Branden stepped out of the crowd for a quick whispered word. "You may choose it, of course. But you know there's something . . . elfy about it; I'll want it sniffed for charms, or offered for my use."

Torrie let his laugh be as offensive as he could; Danar del Reginal's jaw clenched. "Very well, have it as you would—but if you choose my sword, I'll choose my father's, or the third sword we brought along; all were made by the same hands. Pick."

Maggie smiled in a way that Torrie thought was intended to be encouraging, and might indeed have been, if she didn't twist her fingers together to make them stop trembling.

Torrie twisted his own fingers together to make them stop trembling.

Danar del Reginal caught the motion, and laughed as he picked up the sword the dwarf had offered Torrie. "As you will."

Torrie kept his face flat and passionless—he hoped—as he squared off against Danar del Reginal.

The night grass chilled his feet, and scratched between his toes, and the wind whipped cold air across his naked chest. When he raised his arms and stretched, it cooled his clammy armpits almost painfully cold.

He would have to watch the footing, he decided. This wasn't like in the fencing studio or in the basement. There, even when Dad had spread some blocks or nails or toys on the floor behind him, Torrie could still count on there being a good, solid surface finally beneath his feet, even if it wasn't the smooth, unslippery surface he was used to.

That was okay with him, too. A fencing strip was supposed to be mopped free of sweat and water between rounds, but sometimes that didn't happen, and Dad had long ago trained Torrie in keeping his feet—and his head—when on slippery or painful ground.

Torrie had always thought Dad had gone too far with that. Too many hours barefoot out on the lawn behind the house, screened by the windbreak of trees while he and Torrie fought freestyle, sometimes leaping over lawn furniture or to the surface of the old oak stump or cedar picnic table. It may have sharpened Torrie's sense of position, he had thought, but it was useless in a real bout—you couldn't circle to the left or to the right on the narrow confines of a fencing strip.

It was worth doing to keep Dad happy, he had long ago decided, but not useful. Fun when he had introduced freestyle to the college fencing set—the strip didn't teach you the value of circling left or right, or of a running attack that threatened to pass rather than try for the immediate touch.

But not useful.

Wrong again, he thought. That was okay; Torrie had been wrong before. Felt kind of like this, in fact.

Danar del Reginal raised his sword and spun it about in an elegant salute, first toward the flares surrounding them, and then to the mountains beyond, and then the sky above, and finally Torrie.

Nice of him to include me, Torrie thought, realizing that joking with himself didn't make him any less scared.

Although there wasn't much to be scared of, not really. A dueling injury was likely to be less painful than the time he had fallen out of the Thompson's apple tree and broken his leg. This was only to the first blood, after all.

He returned Danar del Reginal's salute with one of his own—a fencer's salute, not the broad gesture that Danar del Reginal had performed—and closed with three quick steps, his sword out in front of him along the ideal line, as though reaching for Danar del Reginal's armpit.

The tips of their blades crossed a few times, tentatively.

If Dad was right, that the purpose of the match was to feel Torrie out, to find his limits, the sooner it was over, the better. When Danar del Reginal tentatively extended in sixte, Torrie parried, then disengaged his blade, stepping back, ever so slightly out of line.

Danar del Reginal closed, and lunged for his midsection, and—

Later, it was all clear. He had offered a typical épée target: his wrist. But Danar del Reginal was not trying for a simple blooding; he wasn't going to settle for anything less than running Torrie through.

Most épée points, like most duels, were won with attacks on the arm or leg. It wasn't a matter of gentleness; it was just that the extremities were the most vulnerable to a touch. That was how épée had become popular, originally: a foil fencer, trained to score only on the rough triangle from shoulders to crotch as though the only way to win a duel was with a deadly wound, was too often vulnerable to a quick touch on the wrist or arm, or knee or toe. In a real first-blood duel, an épée-trained fencer had the same advantage over a foil player that a black belt karate fighter had over a boxer.

But a light touch wasn't what Danar del Reginal was after.

Torrie caught the point of Danar del Reginal's blade high on his own blade, almost at the guard, the needle point inches at best from his chest. His wrist spun, maintaining contact as he brought his blade over, around and down, pushing Danar del Reginal's sword far out of line, bringing Torrie's own point into line.

Torrie extended his sword as he stepped forward. To hell with losing by a touch—this bastard meant to kill him. A touch high on the arm would win the bout, and then Torrie would beat the other's blade aside again on the retreat.

But Danar del Reginal's blade never quite got back into line as his full lunge combined with Torrie's forward motion to bring the tip of Torrie's blade past Danar del Reginal's guard; it only stopped when the hilt slammed into Danar del Reginal's chest, and the larger man took a step backward, pulling the hilt from Torrie's now limp grip.

Somebody screamed.

Danar del Reginal looked more shocked than in pain as his now clumsy fingers dropped his sword and reached up to claw at the hilt of Torrie's sword, as though pulling it out would make a difference. His mouth opened, and worked, but the only sounds that came out were horribly burbling gasps, and grunts.

His eyes, lit almost demonically in the flickering firelight, met Torrie's, and held his gaze.

And then they went flat and dead, and Danar del Reginal fell, twisting, landing on his side on the turf, accompanied by a loud flatulence and awful stink that robbed his death of any semblance of dignity.

Branden del Branden stood in front of Torrie, his own blade out to the side, his lips white. "Stop," he said, although Torrie wasn't doing anything at all, just standing there. "Cease," he went on. "Thorian del Thorian has . . . drawn first blood; this matter is ended." He turned and tossed his blade to a Vestri servant, who neatly snagged it out of the air and scurried away with it.

"Well done, young killer," he said with a sneer.

Torrie shook his head. "I didn't mean, I mean he was trying to—"

"Of course," Branden del Branden said, not bothering to conceal his sarcasm, "he was trying to kill you, and the only way you could defend yourself against so obviously inferior a swordsman was to run him through. You couldn't, after all, merely take the touch on his arm and defend yourself if he committed an error of honor, no, no, that would be too difficult."

"You don't understand," Torrie said. "He was trying to kill me. I was just trying . . ." He couldn't go on. Would

Branden del Branden possibly accept that Torrie was trying to lose? No. "I was just trying not to get killed," he said.

Branden del Branden visibly fought for self-control, and found it. "I see," he said, quietly. "Should I ever challenge you, Thorian del Thorian the Younger, I'll be sure that it's to the death and not just to the first blooding." His lip pulled back in a sneer. "I would wish to save you the trouble of having to toy with me, play with me, until you can find a master single stroke to kill me." He turned to Dad and bowed stiffly. "Thorian del Thorian the Elder," he said, "I congratulate you on your son's skills, although I do not congratulate you on the rest of his training." He turned to the guards. "Their parole holds until the dawn. Have him chained again just before."

Herolf, the pack leader, threw back his head and laughed.

CHAPTER FOURTEEN

Silvertop

Frida—no, Freya—was busying herself at the huge cast-iron stove in the early-morning chill when Ian, eyes still full of sleep, staggered toward the door, gathering his cloak about him.

"Is there some sort of problem?" she asked quietly. On their respective sleeping pallets, Harbard and Hosea lay under thin blankets, although Ian wouldn't have wanted to guess whether they were actually sleeping or simply lying back with their eyes closed and resting. Old Ones, it seemed, didn't snore, or toss and turn in the night.

He shook his head. "I just need the outhouse," he said.

She smiled. "It's—"

"I know where it is." He stopped himself for a moment. "You didn't sleep?"

She shook her head. "I can do without, when need be," she said, quietly, looking over at where Hosea and Harbard slept. "And there was much to do this night. I've cut down some of Harbard's clothes for you, and there was the cooking—and no need to stand there listening to an old woman when you need to void yourself, Ian."

He closed the huge door behind him as he stepped out into the gray, pallid light just before the dawn.

There was no hint that anything had happened outside, if you ignored the way the ground was torn up around the cabin. It was quiet, too quiet perhaps, save for the occasional fluttering of feathers when one of the ravens perched on the eaves would rouse for a moment, only to settle down.

"Good morning," he said.

"Thank you," the one on the left said.

Ian almost lost control of his drum-tight bladder. "And good morning to you, Ian Silverstone," it went on, its voice raucous and far too loud in his ears. "I think you slept well. Probably be the last time for a long time. Or forever." It glared down at him—or at least seemed to glare; Ian couldn't read its expression, not really; ravens always seemed to glare balefully—then roused, shook itself all over, and leaped into the air, climbing in an expanding circle as it vanished into the darkness.

The other raven let out a low caw. "Pay little attention to Munin, Ian Silverstone; he always sees the dark side of things. A splendid raven, really, with a deft beak for picking the lice out from my neck, but it has been an old cynic for far too long." It dipped its beak. "I am Hugin, and I bid you well, until we shall meet again." It spread its broad, glossy wings, and leaped into a short, shallow glide before beating its wings and lifting itself up and into the dark sky.

Wonderful, Ian thought. Last night a cold giant was trying to eat me, and today I almost piss in my pants after being greeted by the Tir Na Nog version of Heckle and Jeckle. And they still call me Ian Silverstone, like I'm some sort of nonstick surface.

He made his way to the outhouse, and decided to pretend to himself that his shivering was entirely from the predawn cold.

By the time he had returned, the grays of the distant trees had gone gray-green, Harbard—Ian found it impossible to think of him as Odin—and Hosea were gathered around the table, and Freya had ladled out heaping piles of steaming meat and some sort of fried vegetable cake, and was already pouring steaming tea into mugs.

Ian took the chair Freya offered him, and dug in. The meat—whatever it was, Ian decided not to ask—was rich and, well, meaty, if more than a little tough, although none of the others seemed to notice.

Harbard's half-glassy stare was intact. "Best to eat and be on the way quickly, eh, Orfindel?"

Hosea nodded. "I had best be on my way, yes." He toyed with a spot of spilled tea on the table. "I promised Ian that I would see to his getting home from here."

"Oh?" Harbard's look at Ian was skeptical. "He's earned a steading, certainly, by his carrying of you down the mountain, but you're hardly in a position to award it, and this is not the time."

"No. Not a home here. We need a Hidden Way. Back."

Harbard thought about it for a moment. "No."

"No, you don't know of one, or no, you won't tell me."

"No, you can't go on unaccompanied, Orfindel. You're too old for this, too feeble. You need a champion."

"Be that as it may," Hosea said, his voice level, "I undertook to see him to safety—"

"You didn't promise, and—"

"Wait a minute," Ian put in. "He didn't promise? How would you know?"

Harbard's glare was like a cold wind blowing up Ian's back. "I do not like being interrupted, Ian Silverstone. Do not do it again."

"Husband . . ." Freya frowned. "I would not have you speak so to our guest."

"As you will, as you will." Harbard raised his hands in surrender. "I will let it pass, this time."

"Answer the boy," Freya said quietly. "He's earned that, and more."

"I—"

"Answer the boy."

Harbard scowled. "Oh, very well. One reason I know that he didn't promise is that his promises bind him more securely than you can know, and it wouldn't be a matter of discussion. Another is that he clearly doesn't know whether or not there is a Way open around here, and he'd not promise that which he can't deliver." Harbard shrugged. "But if your guts are of whey and water instead of sinew and muscle, I'll see you to a Hidden Way that would send you back; there is one . . . nearby."

Ian forced a smile. "Why don't you just double Dutch dare me?"

"Eh?"

"Or maybe if you said, 'neener, neener, neener?' I mean, 'if my guts are of whey and water' you'll help me get home? If I'm a chickenshit coward, you'll get me out of this? You must think I was born yesterday," he said.

Harbard grinned. It was the first time that Ian had seen him grin. He was missing an incisor, but otherwise his teeth were straight and white and all there. "It would depend on your point of view, child."

Ian found himself liking Harbard, but not exactly trusting him. There was something about Hosea that inspired faith, something Harbard lacked.

And that's what it came down to. He believed that following Hosea might be dangerous, but that he wouldn't be betrayed. Harbard could easily leave Ian's body in an unmarked grave, and think nothing of it.

"I'll stick with Hosea."

"I am to consider myself flattered, I take it." Hosea eyed him levelly. "You'll ferry us across?" he asked, turning to Harbard.

Harbard nodded. "That could be arranged." He looked pointedly at Freya, who shook her head.

For just a moment, Harbard's face clouded over, and

while Freya met his glare full force, it was only for a moment.

"It's not fair to ask it," she said.

"Then don't ask it, wife," he said. "But if you don't, I shall."

She sniffed. "And your asking would have weight? You have hardly said two words to the boy, you went out and killed the Köld not because of the boy, but because it had the temerity to threaten your home, and you've decided that that gives you the right to ask him—"

"I am who I am."

Hosea smiled. "I think you ought to be careful of saying that, youngster." He stood, and pushed his chair back from the table. "You presume much, perhaps."

Harbard's face clouded over for just a moment, but the moment passed. He raised his hands in surrender. "Have it your way, wife. I shall ask nothing."

Hosea walked to the door, taking his cloak down from the wall.

Freya sat down next to Ian and looked him in the eye. "I do not ask anything," she said, raising a palm to forestall a growl from Harbard. "But I will tell you that should the Brisingamen come again into my hands, I'll protect it better this time than I did last time." Her smile was reassuring, but it wasn't blinding, it didn't cloud his mind or leave him painfully in erection. "I swear it."

Hosea had already shouldered his cloak and slung his quiver, and now hefted his rucksack to his back. "Nothing remains the same," he said.

Freya turned to him, a ghost of a smile playing across her lips. "I'm still who *I* am, Orfindel," she said. "Or Arvindel, or Aurvindel, or Earendel, or Hosea, or whatever your name really is."

"You have been and always will be Freya," he said. "There was a time when I would have gone out and hunted it down for you." Hosea smiled.

"There was a time when you did give it to me."

There. It had been said. Hosea wasn't just Orfindel, an elf, or Old One, or whatever they called themselves. He was the Builder. Ian shivered. Torrie's Uncle Hosea, Ian's traveling companion, the Builder?

The Doomed Builder?

Well, why not? He was having breakfast with Odin and Freya; why shouldn't his traveling companion be the one who had built, well, apparently everything of importance, the father of the dwarves, the—

"And you let it be broken, dispersed," Hosea said, gently, interrupting Ian's train of thought. "Which you wouldn't do now, I suspect; fertility deities are more trustworthy in retirement than otherwise, if less persuasive."

She took a step toward him, then stopped, her arms crossed over her chest. "You think I could not . . . persuade him, or even you? Is this a challenge?" Her lips smiled, but her eyes didn't.

Hosea shrugged. "I don't think it matters. I think you believe that a goal and the method of attaining it are so closely linked that you would no longer try to seduce me or Ian in order to lay your hands on the Brisingamen, because I think you believe that your possession of it would be as cursed as if you had, say, murdered for Otter's Gold."

Harbard's single eye glared, and he stood, a growl deep in his throat.

"What would you say to me, Old God?" Hosea asked. "Would you say that you were younger and angrier then? Would you say that your kind has e'er been responsible in its use of power?" Hosea shook his head, sadly. "I think not. And I think you'll agree."

Harbard nodded slowly.

His sword belted about him, Hosea hefted his bow, still unstrung. "Ian, let us be on our way. Harbard? Would you be kind enough to ferry us across? Now, please?"

"Yes."

Freya handed Ian a bulging leather sack. "A change of clothes for each of you, some food for the road, and a small trinket," she said. "As promised."

Harbard considered the matter for a moment. "And another thing, perhaps," he said. "Your blessing, for the boy."

She shook her head. "My blessing? It's already his." She touched a finger to her lips, and then to his forehead. "As it will always be."

The corral surrounding the windlass was empty, save for the windlass itself, a trough of suspicious-looking water, and a few scraps of hay and dribblings of grain in a large bin next to it. The corral was U-shaped, one arm terminating a few feet into the river, the other running up and over a shorebank ridge, encircling a dark cave opening in the ridge.

Harbard first dropped the bale of hay from his right shoulder, and then the sack of grain from his left—Ian half-expected the seams to split, but they didn't—then stuck two fingers into his mouth, and whistled.

A distant tattoo of hoofbeats sounded, and two horses emerged from the cave at an easy lope that nevertheless ate up the distance quicker than Ian would have thought possible.

Except that one wasn't a horse, not really. A horse didn't have four legs on each side, moving in a rippling cadence that ate up distance faster than any horse could run.

"Sleipnir," Harbard said, as it stopped in front of the fence, a powerful snort sending dust flying as much as its hooves had.

It was a huge beast, easily the size of a Percheron or Clydesdale, and longer. There was nothing elegant or smooth about its mottled gray coat and the long, uncombed mane that reminded Ian more of an old man's beard than a horse's mane.

Nostrils the size of fists flared wide, and it pawed at the ground.

Its eyes were full of intelligence, if not kindness, as they glared down at Ian. It was all he could do to meet its gaze, but he did.

"How . . . does that corral hold it—"

"Him," Hosea gently corrected, pointing a thumb. "Him."

"—him in?"

Harbard's smile was not gentle. "It's not to keep him in; it's to keep others out. So they don't get eaten." He extended a palm with a bloody chunk of meat on it toward the horse. Ropy muscles under silken skin moved quickly, and Sleipner's head shot out like a striking snake, and the chunk was gone, and in a flash, Sleipner had turned and was galloping back toward the cave; he vanished within its mouth. Ian had to bring his hand up to protect himself from the driving dust.

"He stays with me," Harbard said, more quiet and thoughtful than Ian had heard him before, "for much the same reason that Freya does: it's his will, and mine, that he should." He beckoned to the other horse.

"Silvertop," he said.

It was black, black as coal, black as night, black without color or gloss, save for the bright white blaze across its forehead that was picked up in its long, untrimmed mane. It was large, too, but not as huge as Sleipnir, and it had only the normal four legs, although each of its legs seemed thicker, sturdier than it should have.

And there was the same look behind its eyes, of intelligence that had no trace of kindness or warmth in it.

"Silvertop," Hosea murmured, taking a step forward, reaching a hand out for its muzzle. Its nostrils flared as Sleipnir's had, and for a moment Ian thought that it was going to snap at Hosea, but instead it patiently allowed his touch. "It's been a long time." He turned to Harbard. "I had thought him to have died a long time ago. Surt?"

"Freya had thought Surt to have done for him." Harbard nodded. "As did I. Braggi was sure of it. But he showed up here a few years ago, and I saw no need to send him along. Freya's ridden him now and again, when they've both been in the mood."

"And you?"

Harbard shook his head. "No." He produced a wrinkled apple and handed it to Ian. "Offer it to him on the flat of your hand. Keep the fingers extended, mind; he'll not snap at you, but he'll want the apple."

Ian did as he was told, and the horse snuffled over, taking the apple with one quick lunge and bite that left Ian unharmed, if shaken. "It could have nipped at my fingers," he said.

Harbard laughed. "He could have bitten your arm off at the shoulder, if he'd have been of a mind. This is Silvertop, sired by Sleipnir himself on King Olaf's prize mare: half horse, half Aesir, half witch."

That's a lot of halves, Ian thought, but he didn't say it. Harbard wasn't the sort to joke with.

"Silvertop," Hosea asked, "would you accompany us? We are bound for one of the Old Cities, and may have need of your fleetness before all is said and done."

Ian hadn't been on a horse since he was a kid at camp, but the idea of riding rather than walking was appealing. "We take turns?"

Hosea looked back at him as though he hadn't been paying any attention, which was probably true. "Silvertop can carry what's needed, when needed. But we'll not ride him to spare our own feet, but only in extremity." He turned back to the horse. "If that please you, Silvertop."

Ian wasn't surprised when the horse nodded, its mane snapping like a series of whips. He wouldn't have been much surprised if it spoke. It walked off, then spun around, breaking into a light canter, and ran toward the fence, clearing it in a light bound that left Ian certain it could have jumped three times as high and five times as far, then trotted back to stop in front of Harbard, who patted the horse gently on the muzzle.

"Come now," Harbard said. "I still have to hitch Sleipnir to his windlass; the day gets no brighter, and the ferry waits." He looked Ian in the eye. "Fare well, Ian Silverstone. Listen well to Orfindel, for he knows as much—"

"As he can afford to," Hosea said, with a grin, hoisting his rucksack to his shoulder.

CHAPTER FIFTEEN

The Fire Duke

Karin Roelke Thorsen had, she had decided, long since lost her ability to panic. Not that she had ever been the panicky type.

It ran in the family. The time that Dad had sliced two fingers off in the combine, he had calmly walked into the house and picked up the extension phone—with his good hand—on his way to the bathroom, and called Doc Sherve from there, so he wouldn't drip any more blood on Mom's floor than was absolutely necessary.

Mom had once found two strange men, one of them what she still called a Negro, one of them who didn't speak English, hiding in the chicken coop one morning, and had simply invited them in for breakfast. She hadn't panicked; she had quietly woken Dad, and—although Karin wasn't supposed to know; Daddy talked later—while the two men were washing up, she took his old Army .45 downstairs, checked to make sure that it was loaded and a round chambered, and stuck it in the silverware drawer next to where his kitchen chair was. He never did need to pull the gun on Thorian and Hosea, of course; instead he took them on as farmhands.

One night back in high school, Sven Hansen had made

it clear in the back seat of his old Chevy that he wasn't going to settle for some kissing and groping this time, and Karin had stopped trying to pull her wrists out of the grip of his huge, strong hands, but had sat back against the upholstery, and then gently, quietly, explained to him that it stopped here and now or there would be consequences he didn't want to deal with—and it did stop right then and there, and she never did have to find out how hard it would be to bite his penis off; it ended there, and she and Sven even became friends after a fashion, when he married Sandy.

She had handled it. It was the family way.

It was just a matter of handling things. You took a look at what the situation was, you examined your options, and you acted on them. The only time there was any need to shout and scream and prance about was when you'd decided that was the best thing to do, and Karin had never decided that was the best thing to do. There was always another way.

Two years at Macalester had persuaded her that she wanted to stay in Hardwood, where she knew everybody, and not move on to the city the way others had. The town fit her too well; she liked sitting around with Sandy Hansen, talking about anything or nothing, or catalog shopping for needlepoint designs with Minnie Hansen. She liked chatting with old Tom Norvald when she walked over to the post office to mail a package, and on the way back stopping off at the store to pick up a pound of meaty bacon sliced paper-thin, the way only Vicky Teglund would bother.

She wanted the town, but she didn't want to live the marginal sort of life that too many did in town.

And she liked Thorian, and she wanted him.

Even when she had turned up pregnant—*finally*; trying to coordinate her cycle with college vacations and assignations with Thorian had turned out to be trickier than she thought—she had simply explained things to Thorian, told him that she was going to finish her degree while pregnant, then come home to raise the baby, and he could either marry her and let her manage the family money or give her enough of his hidden stash of gold coins to support the two of them; no problem either way.

He married her, of course, as she had always intended that he would.

And Hosea hadn't said anything, but had smiled knowingly, as she had always intended that he would, too.

Assaying costs were high, but a few pounds of homemade gold ingots turned into a large stack of bills, which she turned into stock certificates, which she turned into more stock certificates.

And, soon, when her trading had run up enough profits to justify it, they had bought the old Halvorsen place and settled in to what she found a perfect life. Stock and options trading wasn't hard, provided you weren't too greedy, were willing to work hard at it and admit your mistakes to yourself, and were never unwilling to cut your losses. Karin wasn't greedy; hard work didn't bother her; mistakes happened; and cutting losses was a brutal necessity.

It was fun, finally. All of it. Raising a child was fun; it was like gardening in fast motion. Gardening was fun, as long as you knew you would never miss a meal if your garden failed. Housekeeping was fun, as long as you had two adults to split the chores with, and enough money so that you never needed to scrimp or cut corners. Her mother had always saved soap splinters to mold into a new bar; Karin threw out too-small bars of soap.

She had been afraid that in order to have that kind of life, she would have to leave Hardwood, but the town fit her like a glove.

And then there was Thorian. He was incredibly easy to get along with, amazingly vigorous in bed, even after all these years—and always puzzled and puzzling over life in the latter half of the twentieth century. He was amazing both in what he would and wouldn't, could and couldn't, do. He was honest to the point of bluntness in private, except about his own history; he simply wouldn't discuss it directly, and she had had to give up asking. He would happily spell her for a week of cooking upon request, and would make the bed and do laundry without a fuss, but would not clean a floor no matter what, unless it was a floor in the barn. With the exception of a few times that Torrie had done something really dangerous, like playing in the knife drawer as a toddler, Thorian had never raised a hand to him, but he insisted that Torrie be able to use a sword as though in a real duel, not just for sport.

Well, that was beginning to make sense. Hosea's crazy stories, which always began as though they were a fairy tale, had turned out to be true. Thorian really *was* some sort of champion, and he was in trouble for having freed Hosea (and, at least putatively, for stealing all those golden coins with the strange markings and the unknown face on them), and the trouble had come looking for them.

Yes, she had been scared—the Sons' attack had frightened her more than anything that had ever happened to her, but Thorian had showed up before they could quite cart her off, and even with a knife to his throat, he had handled it.

Her Thorian would handle it.

Karin Thorsen sat back in the coach and smiled over at where he sat diagonally across from her. The guard sitting next to her didn't want them across from each other, and he was wise enough not to sit next to Thorian, because, even bound though he was, Thorian could have taken him if he was within reach.

But with his wrists bound in front of him, and his ankles manacled together and tied to a thick brass staple on the floor of the carriage, he couldn't kick out; the thin wire around his neck was tied to a similar overhead staple. If he attempted to lunge out of his seat, he would throttle himself quickly.

Thorian just smiled encouragingly.

The carriage followed a bend in the road, and again the road disappeared in the window, leaving Karin with the feeling of being suspended in space over a mountain ledge.

But this time, it revealed the City.

Falias looked like it had been carved out of the top of a mountain range by a giant artisan who had simply cut away almost everything that didn't look like City. Spires and turrets rose high, but no higher than the sloping ridgeline would have. The slope had been cut to leave behind terraces of windowed walls, some surrounded by ramparts and balustrades, others with small gently sloped piazzas that served as the roofs for lower levels.

She had expected something austere and gray, but the City was all in green and gold; many of the piazzas were overgrown with huge trees and intricate gardens; other, lower ones were merely squares of green vegetable or golden corn that, despite their terracing and height, reminded her of the fields around Hardwood.

A gate loomed in front of and above them: thick, ancient oaken timbers held together with brass fittings that had long worn a patina of jade green, filling an opening in the mountainside, the battlements above set into the side of the mountain.

Thorian smiled at her. " 'T is something, eh?" he said in Bersmål, then switched to English. "If I see the right opportunity, I'll make a break by myself and come back for you later; do not despair," he said, lifting his bound wrists as though gesturing at something out the window.

"There is to be no talking," the guard said in Bersmål. "You'll have plenty of time to talk to His Warmth, I trust." He was a big man, bigger than Thorian, lightly armored in the black and flame-colored livery of the House, but was armed only with a short truncheon, its hilt wrapped in leather. Whether it was Branden del Branden or Herolf who was really in charge of the party, he knew what he was doing.

Give my Thorian a sword, she thought, and he could take you all on.

No, that wasn't true. Thorian was a man, not an elemental force. He would carve through this bullyboy without slowing down, and could slice his way through another dozen or more, perhaps. But there were more than a dozen of them, some of them with bows.

Karin tried not to draw herself up straight. "Do what you have to," she said.

The guard glared at her. "There is to be no talking," he said.

"Do what you have to," she repeated.

Branden del Branden had dismounted from his carriage, and strode to the gate. A brass plate, incongruously bright and gleaming, was set into the side of the gate; a long hammer lay in an inset in the wall nearby. He took the hammer down, and swung it once, twice, three times tentatively, then struck hard against the brass plate.

Thrummmm. Karin as much felt it as heard it. It was as though it echoed through the whole mountain.

Thrummmm. Again.

Smoke wafted from the battlements above the gate, bringing a smell to Karin that reminded her of french fries, silly as that sounded. She shrugged.

A face appeared on the battlements above, and called down a muttered challenge to Branden del Branden, who responded with a word and a gesture.

The doors opened, swinging silently on hidden hinges, and the procession made its way inside.

It was, for lack of a better word, a courtyard about the

size of a football field, stinking of horse piss and manure, although Karin found those smells reassuring.

It was easy to see why: the mountain-side wall was a high-arched entrance to stables, while a narrow passage, barely wide enough for three men to walk side by side, topped by battlements, led into the city. Soldiers on the battlements above the passageway could make life difficult to impossible for an invading army, even if the battlements contained the only defense.

She doubted that they did; the feel of the arrangement was familiar, although where she had read of it or seen it escaped her at the moment. How did she know that there would be several turns and a broad, sweeping curve in the entry, and that both turns and the curve would contain surprises for an invader?

She shook her head. It didn't matter.

Soldiers in the now familiar black and red-orange livery of the House of Flame waited in the courtyard, although each of these sported a pair of brassards with the flame symbol that Karin knew she had seen somewhere before, but couldn't quite remember when.

A face peeked in the window. "Thorian del Thorian, by my mother's beard!" he more boomed than said, swinging the carriage door open. He was a big, thick man, barrel-chested, his smile a broad white island of teeth in a full, inky beard badly in need of a trim.

"Ho, Ivar del Hival," Thorian said. "How have you been?"

"Oh," Ivar said, "I wouldn't complain." His grin broadened. "It's never safe to complain. I see you are well, albeit a bit thicker in the belly than I remember."

"That may be," Thorian said.

"Although I shouldn't point fingers, when all fingers point back to me." Ivar del Hival patted at his own ample belly. "You're old, but every bit as fast in the wrist, eh?"

Thorian shrugged. "That also may be. We perhaps will

see." He smiled. Karin had never seen him smile quite like that. It was friendly, but there was an undertone of threat to it.

"As I'm sure we shall." He offered a hand to Karin; at Thorian's slight nod, she took it. "You would be the wife of my old friend?" he asked, swinging the door of the carriage open.

She nodded as she accepted his help to the ground. Torrie and Maggie were already out of their carriages; Branden del Branden and a small contingent of soldiers were leading them toward the next gate.

"Karin Thorsen," she said. "And you are his good friend Ivar del Hival?"

His hand was strong, and the fingers ridged with familiar calluses, but his grip was gentle. "I have that honor," he said.

At Thorian's glare, Ivar del Hival finally released her hand. "Ah, he's spoken of me, then?"

Well, no, he hadn't. But there didn't seem to be any point in admitting that, not right here and now. "How could he not?"

Ivar del Hival fingered his beard. "Well, then, I see that you and I shall get along famously," he said, offering her his arm. "May I have the honor of escorting you to His Warmth? He is rather eager to meet you. All of you." He eyed her clothing. "After, that is, we see about getting you washed and dressed; His Warmth dislikes informality."

"You make us sound like guests," she said. "Rather than people who have been kidnapped, and dragged here under threat of death."

Ivar del Hival bit his lower lip for a moment, considering. "Yes, I rather do, don't I?" He tucked her hand into the crook of his elbow and patted at it. "But don't trust anything I say; I'm rather more charming than I am reliable."

"Somehow I doubt that," she said. "I suspect you are

far more reliable than you are charming. And I find you very charming."

Ivar del Hival grinned. "I wouldn't think of arguing with a lady."

Torrie's forehead hurt from the frowning. The passageway into the City had felt strangely familiar to Torrie, although he couldn't place it. Uncle Hosea's stories about the Cities and about the Wars of the Cities had never given any of this detail, so that couldn't be it.

But there was something funny about it, and he wasn't the only one to notice. Mother, on the arm of that fat, bearded guy, noticed it too, but they were being kept too far apart to compare notes.

Deliberately?

Branden del Branden caught Torrie trying to exchange a mouthed word with Mother, and his brow furrowed. "You would be planning something, perhaps?" He rapped a metal-knuckled glove against the wall. "I would doubt that this is the place for it, unless you know some Hidden Way that I don't." He smiled. "If so, I'd take it as a year favor if you'd be kind enough to show it to me, even if in attempting a break."

"No, nothing like that. Besides, there wouldn't be—" Torrie shut himself off. No, there would be no hidden passageway in the main entrance; that would obviate the purpose of it. There was an art to such things: the purpose of, say, the Guest Room wasn't obviated by the secret door between it and Torrie's room; the door could be locked from either side to give privacy. That was the function of what Hosea called a residence room, after all: to give privacy. A lockable way in and out didn't do violence to the spirit of it; it enhanced the nature of the room.

Maggie frowned at him. *What?* she mouthed.

He shook his head. Later. There was something important in all of this.

So far, the passageway had been open on top, leaving them vulnerable to anybody on the battlements more than a dozen feet above, but now it closed down to a tunnel, lit by a series of lanterns feeding off a too-thick silver tube that led inward. Torrie wondered what it would take to make the tube spurt burning oil into the passageway, sucking off oxygen as it fried invaders—but he didn't wonder whether that could be done, just how.

It was all too familiar.

He knew that the next turn would lead into a broad sweeping tunnel, curved sharply enough that he—or an invading army—wouldn't be able to see more than a few yards down it, but not so curved that three men walking abreast would tend to bump into each other.

And it did; and the passageway finally opened on a broad, cobblestone plaza, rimmed by dozens of gnarled potted oaks that looked like they should have been hundreds of years old except that they were barely a dozen feet tall.

Torrie squinted, and he could almost see them as leafy dwarf warriors standing guard forever.

The far end of the plaza forked into stone staircases. One was broad, its lifts deep and risers low, leading up toward another plaza; the other, steep and narrower, led up through the green slope toward the castle above.

That was the one their party took.

The day had begun to heat up, but under the canopy of leaves the air was cool and damp, although a bit musty. Even so, Torrie broke a sweat keeping up with the guards as they climbed up the stairs, stopping momentarily at each landing before turning and taking the next pitch.

Ahead of him, past a trio of guards, Mom and Dad seemed to be keeping up okay, and Maggie was panting only a little.

He smiled at her. "Hold on," he said, in Bersmål, "it all should top out soon."

Ivar del Hival frowned. "Your father seems to have told you rather a lot about the City. Or is it the Cities?"

Torrie shrugged. "Not really; I just estimated how high the keep was, and have kept count of the steps." That sounded lame, but it appeared to satisfy Ivar del Hival, at least for the moment.

It wasn't Dad. It was Hosea. Hosea's sense of style, of building, clearly had been influenced by the design of Falias. The knocking panel he had installed in their house was of the same design as that huge knocking plate at the outer gate here; the curved entry passages were shaped like the curved gates to the holding pens that Uncle Hosea and Dad had built for the Ericsons—pigs would balk at sharp angles, and sometimes try to turn back in a straightaway, but they would follow a curved chute as far as it went.

And a stairway going up the side of a hill would have increasingly short cutbacks until it reached the top, just like the funny-looking stairs that Uncle Hosea had helped Einar Aalberg with down at the silo. It looked funny, sure, but it meant that as you climbed and got tired, you would reach a landing and a built-in resting place with increasingly fewer steps.

It was the same style here.

Just about where he had expected it, the last landing broke on a sharp turn and a mere dozen steps up to a narrow veranda, rimmed by an old stone fence mortared in moss and ivies. An old oak double door stood open, a dark passageway beyond.

"This way to the dungeon, eh?" Torrie asked.

Ivar del Hival grinned, but Branden del Branden pursed his lips together for a moment.

"Would that it were, Thorian del Thorian the Younger," Branden del Branden said, "but it's hardly a crime to be born the son of a traitor, or to kill a man in a duel."

They were met at the door by a trio of Vestri, led by an almost comically skinny man of about fifty, Torrie guessed, his skinniness only exaggerated by the short trousers and black stockings he wore, although the gold-trimmed, knee-length black jacket—coat? It looked more like an overlong, dyed lab coat than anything else—did lend him an air of dignity.

He crooked his right arm in front of him and bowed. "By order of His Warmth, you are welcomed to Falias. I am Jamed del Bruno, klaffvarer to His Warmth," he said.

Maggie's brow wrinkled.

"Klaffvarer," Torrie said. "Keybearer. Butler. Major-domo."

Jamed del Bruno sniffed. "Permit me to show you to the Green Room; His Warmth will see you after luncheon, and there is," he paused to sniff again, "much to do between now and then."

As prisons went, it wasn't bad. The Green Room turned out to be a suite of rooms, high in the southeastern tower of the main keep, built into a thirty-degree slice of that level, sleeping rooms off a radial hallway that opened on a huge room up against the curve of the outside wall.

Low chairs and a funny-shaped couch formed a half circle facing the fireplace on each side of the room, while most of the outside of the wall was a long, curved window that ran from the floor almost to the ceiling. There were taller towers in the City, but they were on the other side; the only thing that Torrie could see rising as high was a distant mountain peak.

"Gorias," Dad said. "House of Stone."

The farmlands below were an earthy quilt of green and brown spread across gently rolling hills, a vast bowl rimmed on the far side by another mountain range, or perhaps part of this one, as though the farmlands of the Middle Dominion had been hollowed out of a mass of mountains, scooped out by God as soda jerk.

Torrie snorted. Not much of a prison. Break the window, slide down a rope, and be gone. Getting into the City might well be difficult; getting out would just be a matter of finding the right place to tie a rope. A bit of rappelling, and be gone.

But be gone *where?*

Dad was at his elbow. "No, that wouldn't work." He rapped a knuckle against the window. It sounded funny. "It's some sort of crystal," he said. "It's stood for more than a thousand years that we know of." He had his belt in his hand, and worked at it for a moment, freeing the buckle. The hidden part of the buckle turned out to be sharp, unsurprisingly; another Uncle Hosea treatment.

Dad reached out the buckle and drew it down the side of the window. Instead of the screaming of metal on glass, it just slid.

"No, not that way out," he said, then sighed, then clapped his hand to Torrie's shoulder. "And not all obstacles are ones you can see," he said, his voice low. "Consider that we'd be traveling with your mother and Maggie, and that neither of them could move as quickly as you and I could, and we could move much less quickly than the Sons His Warmth no doubt has circling the walls, waiting for us." He thought for a moment, then shook his head. "And there are other matters to consider."

Torrie frowned. "The walls may have ears, but I doubt they speak English."

One corner of Dad's mouth turned up. "Oh, and where did you learn Bersmål?"

"Uncle Hosea, obviously," Torrie said. "Wish he had taught me French that way," he said, with a grin. "Would have saved me some trouble in school."

Dad shook his head. "Outside of Tir Na Nog, the gift of tongues isn't one he can bestow so easily," he said. "Or I'd not have had such a difficult time learning English some years ago."

It hit him in a flash. All the talk about Thorian the Traitor was misdirection. Yes, certainly if Dad had betrayed the Guild, the Guild would be looking out for him; yes, if he had stolen money from one of the Houses, the House would want him to answer for it.

But to go to enough trouble to search the Hidden Ways between worlds for him? And for how many years? How could he possibly be that important?

Maybe he wasn't.

But a strange dark man with the gift of tongues could be. A strange man who tended to build things the way the Oldest did, and who probably knew the Hidden Ways in the City better than anybody else.

He could be that important. "It's all about him, isn't it? About him knowing the Hidden Ways?"

Dad's jaw clenched for just a moment. "Sh." He mouthed: *Not another word.*

You mean, Torrie mouthed back, *that they don't know that he's what they're really after?*

No, Dad mouthed back, *I mean that they may not know that* I *know.* He shrugged broadly. *If that's really what they're after.*

Torrie heard the footsteps behind him; it was Jamed del Bruno and another trio of Vestri servants, each bearing a pile of clothing. "I have taken the liberty of sending Mistresses Ingar and Hilge to see to the ladies," he said. "And have brought your clothing myself; your baths and dressers wait. His Warmth has just started his luncheon."

"And we're dessert, eh?" Torrie asked in English, not particularly surprised when Jamed del Bruno started to nod before he caught himself.

"I'm afraid there shall be only time for a quick washing, Sirs; His Warmth is unfond of being kept waiting."

Torrie hated His Warmth at first sight. Not that it mattered.

It wasn't that His Warmth was fat; fat didn't bother Torrie. Grandpa Aarsted's old friend Bob Adams had been fat as a harem guard and twice as gruff, and that hadn't bothered Torrie. It had just been the way Bob was. Torrie's Meat Science teacher, Mr. Bunce, was every bit as thick around the middle as the Fire Duke, and Mr. Bunce was kind and genial enough that all he had to do was whiten his beard a little every winter to go play Santa Claus at the Children's Hospital.

It was mainly the eyes. His Warmth, indeed: they were cold, dark pits in his piggy face, holding no trace of humanity or compassion, just will and intelligence, and probably too much of both.

Torrie wondered what the Fire Duke thought he saw; Torrie thought they all looked pretty impressive. A hurried sponge bath and some quick stitchery from a team of Vestri had left Torrie and Dad clean and in gleaming white shirts, black leather vests, and black cotton trousers. The shirts were tight at the wrist, but ballooned at the shoulders and arms, not restricting movement at all. The vests were of black leather, decorated with silver buckles and ornaments, and fell past the waist, a ridge of leather at the hips helping to hold their swordbelts in place, although they had been asked, politely, to leave their swords in their rooms.

Mom and Maggie each had been arrayed in a gown that kind of reminded Torrie of a sari, except they wrapped differently. Mom's was a blue-black gauzy fabric, wrapped to leave her shoulders bare. It fell almost to the floor on the left side, and was gathered tightly at the right hip by what looked like a giant brooch in the shape of a silver crab, leaving her right leg completely bare to mid-thigh; Maggie's gown, of reddish-purple silk, was wound over one freckled shoulder, then repeatedly wrapped bandeau-style first around her breasts then hips and upper thighs, the sheer fabric leaving her midriff covered by only a single, transparent layer, the effect of the bottom of the outfit about like that of a miniskirt.

Heads had turned as they had been escorted through the corridors, and Torrie didn't think it was because he and Dad looked so spectacular.

"I see," the Fire Duke said, "that you have had the opportunity to refresh yourself."

"For which we are of course grateful, Your Warmth," Dad said.

The Fire Duke had chosen to greet them in what Jamed del Bruno called the throne room, although it appeared to Torrie to be a private study: one of the walls was covered with bookcases, and rolled maps were racked in front of a large easel. All of one wall was covered with a tapestry showing an overmuscled swordsman standing over the body of some vaguely manlike beast, while the third was a hodgepodge of crannies cut into the original stone, some lined with velvet, some covered with almost homelike cabinet doors. Torrie would have bet that all three walls contained some hidden way in and out, and his eyes went immediately to the portion of the carved ceiling hidden in the shadow of the overhead lamps: there would likely be something there, too.

And then there was the floor—under some or all of the squares of wood there would be some sort of trapdoor, or entry to somewhere. It was that kind of style, a very familiar style.

Rising easily for a man of his bulk from a huge wooden chair—Torrie was fairly sure that the leather stretched over the back and seat concealed embedded cushions—the duke stood in front of another of the floor-to-ceiling windows, his feet planted far apart, his hands behind his back.

"Thorian del Thorian," he said. His voice was deeper than Torrie had thought it would be, but it sounded funny, as if there were some harmonics in it, as if the Fire Duke was resonating just above and threateningly below his hearing. "The Elder." He let the words roll thickly off his tongue. His livery lips pursed, then relaxed. "It has been too long since we've met. I thank you and your companions for coming to see me."

Dad smiled, but Torrie could tell he didn't mean it. "Oh, it was nothing, Your Warmth. Your dogs issued such a firm invitation that I couldn't resist."

It was funny. All four of them were prisoners, and all had every reason to be scared, particularly Dad, who clearly better understood more about what they had to be scared of and why, and yet he was standing a little straighter than he usually did, his body more ready than tense, his weight on the balls of his feet like a dancer—it reminded Torrie more of an impersonation of Johnny Carson doing a monologue than anything else. He looked over at Mom; she saw it too.

Whatever was to happen, Dad was ready for it.

The Fire Duke nodded slowly. "They do that. I've asked Herolf and his Sons to keep watch around the walls—I'm expecting some visitors."

"Oh?"

"Your return is such big news, and news comes so rarely to the Middle Dominion. It's really been very boring in your absence. I expect that there will be some answers to a few . . ." he hesitated for a moment "minor challenges I issued of late. And it may well be that we shall have another visitor."

Dad shook his head. "I wouldn't count on it."

"Oh, I would," the Fire Duke said. "A little bird tells me that an old acquaintance of ours is once again upon Tir Na Nog, and I would suspect that he has, somehow, sworn some . . ." the Fire Duke's hand flopped on the end of his hand, like a fish drowning in the air of a riverbank "sort of oath to see to the well-being of you and yours." His shoulders moved up and down fractionally. "But I could be wrong. In the interim, I believe I've . . . advanced you some two hundred twenty-three golden marks, and I trust you'll be willing to work that off. I've taken the liberty of scheduling a few small affairs—"

"Stanar del Brunden?"

The Fire Duke smiled. "Among others. His Solidity and I have some difference I would like resolved in my favor, and I'm afraid that a few first-blood matches with Rodic del Renald haven't been useful. Some to the second blood, perhaps? Or further?"

Dad nodded. "As you wish it."

Torrie took a step forward. "No, wait—"

He never really saw what had happened with the tapestry—he was sure that if it had been pulled aside he would have seen it go somewhere out of the corner of his eye—but suddenly it was gone, and three grim-faced men in House of Flame livery were standing in an alcove behind where it had been, two of them leveling short bows at Torrie, the third having taken aim at one of the others, probably Dad.

"Thorian! Not another inch!" Dad's voice was shrill, but he hadn't moved.

The Fire Duke's hand was held out in front of him, as though dropping it would be a signal for the carnage to start. "There are other options, Thorian del Thorian the Elder," he said, looking at Dad, not at Torrie. "You could challenge me for the money, and let me pick a champion. Of course, if I were to win, you'd owe me twice the money, and I'd be tempted to have your wife work the rest of it off on her back in a Lower City bordello at two bice a throw." His grin was broad. "A long line might form, all things considered."

"I have already agreed to your terms, Your Warmth," Dad said, his voice level. "Overt threats gain little."

"So you have. And so they do. But each gain is important, Thorian del Thorian. It's not a bad idea, every now and then, to remind you how . . . tentative your position can be." Slowly, carefully, the Fire Duke lowered his arm. The bowmen didn't move; it was as though they were clever sculptures, or frozen in time from their eyes to their toes.

The Fire Duke dropped heavily into his chair. "But, as you say, you've agreed to my terms. In that case, you and your party may have the liberty of the City; I've invited Branden del Branden to attend Thorian del Thorian the Younger and his lady, and Ivar del Hival to attend you and yours." His smile was thin. "And I've asked Herolf to look in on you, from time to time."

The smile vanished. "You may leave."

The room outside the Fire Duke's chambers was a long, wide one, the stone floor polished to a high, almost mirrorlike gloss that caught and reflected the long line of lanterns hanging from the high ceiling. At the far end, a raised podium with a suspiciously large throne stood; the space in between was unbroken, save for the figures and reflections of Ivar del Hival and Branden del Branden, who stood, companionably chatting, about halfway down.

Branden del Branden had forsaken his black and flame-colored livery for a less ornate tunic and trousers of a creamy off-white, matched with a similarly colored thin silk scarf—almost a ribbon—tied about his neck, the color scheme broken only by the very ordinary and workmanlike black leather swordbelt fastened tightly about his hips.

Ivar del Hival was all in colors, from the rainbow design of his tunic, which ran from an almost inky violet at the left sleeve through a rich indigo and a sky blue at the shoulder, cascading into a spectrum of forest greens, rich, lemony yellows, and strangely dull oranges, and finally ending in a blood red at the right waist, as though he had been wounded there.

They were a study in contrasts: where Ivar del Hival was large and ursine, Branden del Branden was small and what

Torrie would have called ferretlike, except that suggested a kind of sneakiness or lowness that didn't at all go with Branden del Branden's hauteur.

"There's a small affair tomorrow sundown, on the Ash Plaza," Branden del Branden said, as he led them out onto a terrace, and toward a staircase down to the next piazza. "I am commanded by Lord Sensever del Sensever to invite you," he said.

Over by the wall, three children were playing some ball-bouncing game. It was hard to tell whether they were boys or girls, or a combination; they all had haircuts that reminded Torrie of Prince Valiant, and all three were in short trousers almost covered by cotton shifts.

It was hard for Torrie to make out the words of the song, but it was something about sky covering all.

"I think," Dad said, "that we'll keep to our rooms for the next few days." He made an expansive gesture. "It's been a long tr—"

"I would hope you'd reconsider." Branden del Branden smiled while Ivar del Hival frowned. "He was really most insistent; you're rather the special attraction, the lot of you. Some old friends of yours will be there to see you, and I'd have to insist that the Exquisite Maggie and the Extraordinary Karin grace my arm as I enter. Surely I'm entitled to that as recompense for escorting them to the City." He raised an eyebrow. "There's even a rumor that the duel-master will honor the reception with his presence."

That seemed to shock Dad. "I wasn't aware he was in the City."

"He's aware you are, and whether or not he is here now, it's entirely possible you'll find him there tomorrow. Or, if not, within a few days." Branden del Branden grinned broadly. "Ivar del Hival will conduct you back to your rooms. He and I shall be by to escort you at, say, the thirteenth hour tomorrow evening?"

Dad nodded.

Branden del Branden turned to Torrie. "Of course, Thorian del Thorian the Younger, if you'd care to keep to your rooms, I won't trouble you to accompany—"

"I'll be there," Torrie said.

"Ah."

"Sky covers all," the children sang, as the ball bounced.

Torrie was furious with the silent treatment the other four gave him on the way back across the terraces, down the steps to the tower, and up to their rooms. He tried to start a conversation, but nobody would respond. Mom and Dad shut themselves up in their rooms, and Maggie, pleading a headache, shortly did the same.

"A good afternoon to you, young Thorian del Thorian," Ivar del Hival said. "I'll see you somewhat later; I've family duties to attend to." The big man's bow was perfunctory in a friendly sort of way, and then he spun around and walked off.

Torrie threw himself down on a low couch next to the wide window, and folded his hands across his chest. Damn it, he had to come along. Dad's back—

Torrie stood up and walked to the rack of practice swords on the far wall, selecting a saber that was a little too long and too heavy for his tastes, but would have been serviceable enough if it hadn't had a blunt point, and carefully blunted edges back at least six inches from the point. He stretched a few times, then tried a few simple combinations.

At least this still worked.

It was clearly necessary to get himself ready, physically and mentally. Dad was going to be challenged, and Torrie would have to somehow intercept some of the challenges, because good as he was, Dad wasn't the fencer he had been in his youth. The Fire Duke hadn't had him executed; instead he had pinned him down as his champion, and that meant the death of a thousand cuts instead of just one.

He didn't hear the door open, but when he turned around, Dad was behind him.

"You think you can keep all of the jackals off me?" he said.

Torrie tried to figure out the look on his face. Amused? No. Maybe skeptical, although Dad, as usual, had himself under control. Torrie had never seen his father lose his temper, and doubted anybody else had, either. That wasn't Dad's way.

"Well, somebody has to," Torrie said.

"Oh. You think you can take all comers?"

Dad had stripped down to a pair of shorts, no shoes. Under the mat of hair on his chest, his scars seemed to stand out more whitely than usual, particularly the long one that ran along the outside of his ribs, on the right side. Then there was the one on the outside of his sword arm, almost shoulder-high, and the three on his right thigh that looked like a poor match for the four parallel ones on the left thigh. Both of his knees were dotted with small scars, all half an inch long, or shorter.

Torrie had seen Dad's scars hundreds, thousands of times, but he had never noticed it before, not really: all of Dad's scars were peripheral, along the edge of his body, not central. They were all dueling scars, and all received to peripheral areas, either because nobody here ever attacked a more central part of the body or—more likely—because he had always protected the core of his body, even if that meant taking a cut outside.

"I asked you, Torrie, do you think you can beat all comers?"

"It's possible."

"It's possible," Dad agreed, taking down another practice sword, "but unlikely. You've probably fought more practice bouts in the past few years than I have in my lifetime, but you've only once taken up a sword for real. It's rather different," he said.

"I did well enough."

"Fighting a fool who was out to kill you instead of just draw your blood, yes," Dad said. "Like fighting foil against an épée player. I doubt he'll make that mistake again."

"He's dead."

"No, not that idiot coadjutant. Whoever was behind him. His Warmth, probably. Somebody else, perhaps. The politics of the Cities gets so complicated at times it's best to remember how simple it is, at base."

He gave the sword a few trial slashes through the air, then took an en garde position; Torrie mirrored him.

"And at base?"

"At base, it's just a matter of deciding how large a problem you are going to be. It worked for the Old Cities. Make yourself too much of a problem as a House, and the rest of the Houses come and tear you down, like they did with the Nameless House; make yourself too little of a problem, and they eat you, like they did the Trees." He engaged in high line, tip to tip, and tried a bit of delicate tip play before disengaging and thrusting low line; Torrie parried but didn't press, more interested in what Dad was saying than in another tentative practice bout.

"I made myself too much of a problem, once," Dad said. "For good enough reason, I thought, but that matters little—but let me pay for it. I know the coin; you don't." He engaged in earnest, now, and for a moment Torrie let his wrist do the thinking for him.

He didn't fence the way Ian and the others did, the muscles guided by the mind, conscious of whether he was engaging in quarte or sixte, whether the line was high or low, in or out. It was all a single thing to him, a gestalt. A low lunge forced a blade down to meet yours; a disengage forced him to establish contact or live with it lost and gone. It was all one and the same thing; the wrist did the fencing while the mind floated above, more being than thinking.

Dad let his point sag too low, and had to raise it too

quickly to try to meet Torrie's high-line attack, but Torrie simply disengaged and lunged low for a touch to the thigh, then parried on his retreat.

Dad dropped his point, holding up his free hand to forestall Torrie when Torrie attempted to continue the bout. "That is the sort of thing that I mean. All you scored on me was a wound to my thigh—fine in a first-blood match, but I assure you His Warmth would not surrender an inch of land, much less a point of honor, on a simple wound to the thigh of Thorian del Thorian, Elder or Younger.

"If I'd been able to move fast enough, I could have hit you from anywhere above the midpoint of your chest—one quick thrust through the throat, and it would be all over."

He flipped his practice sword end over end high into the air; it almost touched the high ceiling, then descended until it *thwock*ed into his open palm. "Despite my best efforts, you've trained yourself as a fencer, not a swordsman." His frown was of infinite sadness. "And I'd hoped that would never become important." He clapped a hand to Torrie's shoulder, then backed off. "Come now; if you're going to walk out among cadets, ordinaries, and seniors of the House of Flame, you'd best learn what it really means to take up a sword.

"Have at you."

The shower was a delight, albeit a cold one. A door near the end of the hallway led down another hallway and to another door, which opened on a small dressing area. It was lit by what looked like long, fist-sized holes out through the righthand wall into the day, but the placement made Torrie's brow furrow. That wasn't right—that hole should be parallel to the outside wall, not perpendicular. Two wooden benches stood as the only furniture in the room; Torrie brought one over and stood on it so he could see the hold more closely.

Ah. About a foot in, a mirror was mounted slantwise where the hole took a ninety-degree turn. What appeared to be a straight path was in fact bent once. At least once, Torrie corrected himself. For all he could tell, it could bend back and forth twenty times between there and the outside, as long as each bend had a shiny mirror properly mounted.

He plopped down on the bench and, as the Vestri servant had instructed him, stripped to the skin, leaving his clothes and sword on the bench next to one of the curiously thick, napless towels, taking with him only an ancient long-handled bathing brush and a bar of waxy soap that smelled of grapefruit and honey.

A U-shaped turn led him out and into the shower itself.

It was a niche carved into the outside of the keep, the top open to the sun and view below and to the side by an overgrown concave trellis covered with vines in full flower, the tiny crimson blossoms randomly speckling the expanse of triangular leaves. Water from some distant spring trickled down a carved path from above, splashing into a massive iron pot suspended from the wall on a mount that allowed it to be tilted with a pull on the chain that depended from a ring welded to its side. With the pot full, a constant trickle of water flowed from the V-shaped spout on one side, running down the slanted floor and out a drain down the outside of the shower room.

Torrie quickly lathered himself from toes to head in the thin stream, then pulled on the handle, swiveling the pot on its hinges, dousing himself in the icy water.

His teeth chattered, but he had never felt so clean before.

He had almost finished dressing—he was just fiddling with the hook and eye arrangement that substituted for buttons on his shirt—when Maggie walked in and closed the door behind her. She wore a white, knee-length cotton shift and carried a pile of clothes and about half a dozen towels in her arms. "Bimbur said you would probably be done by now," she said, her tone just a degree short of frosty.

"Bimbur?" Torrie assumed it was one of the dwarves, but he hadn't thought to ask any of them their names. It was just too weird being around them.

"The Neander—the Vestri who came into the rooms to clean up. He said you had gone to the shower, and would likely be done."

Why was Maggie so mad—oh. He had forgotten. Their attempts to appear angry at each other hadn't paid off yet, and might never, but there was no reason not to keep it up. At the very least, it made Maggie a less likely substitute target for somebody trying to get at Torrie.

And, yes, it made sense to keep it up here. While nobody could see them here—the walls and door were thick and solid—it wasn't impossible that somebody was overhearing them. A hole between here and the outside could carry sounds as well as light.

"Well, I can leave," he said, trying to sound angry. "Just give me a moment."

"Thank you," she said icily, her tone belied by her smile. She sat down next to him and put her mouth next to his ear. "I think we'll be allowed to look around, but I don't want to go by myself," she whispered, then turned her head so he could whisper in her ear.

"So what do you want me to do? Drag you along?" he whispered back.

She smiled, and mouthed: *Sure. Just be gentle.*

He had to grin. "And what will you do for me?" he whispered.

Like I said, she mouthed, *just be gentle.* Her fingers toyed with his belt buckle. *The floor is hard.*

Her grin was crooked.

"But . . ."

Amazing what you people keep in your emergency kits. She

produced what looked like a golden coin between two fingers, then bent it in half. "I really don't want to," she said, her smile giving the lie to her words and tone. "*No.*"

Torrie grinned. Well, *most* of the time no means no, he thought.

But not when she brings the subject up with a smirk and a condom, and starts spreading thick towels on the floor.

Wobbling Way wound up and down around the periphery of the city, mostly skirting towers and plazas—sometimes, in fact, running along the retaining wall on the outside of plazas—occasionally dipping into the city, becoming a narrow alley between one building and another, or cutting slantwise across a plaza, the rough adamantine stone of Wobbling Way in stark contrast to the inset polished rectangles of marble and rectangles that made up the floors of the plazas.

As the sun dipped low in the sky, they followed the path down, toward the gate and the broad plaza hidden behind its screen of trees, following the path through a narrow, twisting passage, passing underneath a half dozen raised gates.

"Why are you frowning?"

Torrie shook his head. "I don't get it—why have such an elaborate defense inside the City—"

The path took a sudden right-angled turn, dumping them out in the busy marketplace. Just as the wind seemed to have carried smells away from them, some trick of acoustics had kept the clamor from them until just now.

Over by a stall built up against the outside walls, peasants hawked their produce. A bubble-cheeked apple seller paused in his singsong praise of his own works to pick up a fist-sized, ruby-red fruit and polish it on his surprisingly clean canvas apron; next to him, a chicken seller had just finished stringing up a freshly plucked bird and was eyeing the stock in his wooden cages; beyond him, a miller carefully scooped a measure of sorrel flour into a small sack, then tied off the mouth of the sack with a quick twisting of string.

Vestri and humans, most in variants of House of Flame livery, mixed as they moved among the rows of stalls.

Across the plaza, away from the cacophony and motion of the market, a row of stone tables had been set up next to where the stone path led, and a quartet of young women sat on stone stools around one, toying with the contents of several plates that were in the process of being replenished by a procession of Vestri servants who came and went through another passage beyond them.

Torrie nodded a greeting.

"Good afternoon to you," one said in Bersmål, her voice lower and melodic. Red highlights in her brown hair were echoed and accented by coppery threads in the short dress that left her long legs bare to her sandaled feet. Torrie would have guessed her, like the other three, to be in her late teens, but he wouldn't have wanted to bet a lot.

Torrie clasped his hands at the waist and bent slightly, the way Uncle Hosea tended to do when he didn't stop himself. "A good afternoon to you, as well," he said. "I am—"

"Thorian del Thorian," another said, interrupting. Her hair was so light blond as to be almost white, but her skin was sun-darkened almost nut brown.

"The Younger," said a third.

"Son of the very famous Thorian del Thorian," said the second, "the—"

"Beli*ana*! Your manners!"

"—the Elder, I was going to say," the blonde said, her face studiously sober. "What *is* your complaint, Geryn?"

Geryn frowned. She, too, was blonde, but the coloring of both her hair and skin was more moderate than Beliana's. "Well." She touched a well-manicured fingernail to her forehead. "I would guess my complaint is with myself, for having let you lure me into a pointless accusation." She picked up a tiny crystal-stemmed glass, and sipped delicately at a thick honey-colored liquid.

The corner of Beliana's lips lifted only slightly. "I don't know what you could possibly be talking about." She held Geryn's gaze for a moment, until the other frowned and dropped her eyes. She turned to Torrie. "You and your party are all the talk of the City, Thorian del Thorian. This would be, I take it, Maggie, called the Exquisite? We are Emberly, Geryn, Dortaya, and Beliana," she said, indicating each with a fingernail that finally came to rest on her own chin. "All ordinaries of the House of Flame, or we would not be so hard at work on such a fine day."

Torrie repressed a smile. "I am pleased to meet you," he said.

"As well you should be," Emberly put in. "Although without our beaus present, you will be pleased to meet us and then on your way," she said, with a sniff. "Unless, of course, you intend to abandon the Exquisite Maggie and pay court to one of us?"

Geryn's nose twitched. "I doubt Deverin del Ordein would take that well, dear Emberly."

"I am always thoroughly interested, of course, in your doubts about Deverin, beloved Geryn," Emberly said. "Please do tell me more."

Would you all like something to drink? Torrie asked silently. *How about some nice saucers of milk?*

Dortaya cleared her throat as she stood. "It has been very nice meeting you, Thorian del Thorian," she said. "Maggie will join us here, and we'll see that she's returned to the Green Rooms at an appropriate time."

Maggie looked questioningly at Torrie, who shrugged. It didn't look dangerous, unless you could get cut with a sharp comment. "That would be fine with me."

Emberly sniffed. "Your opinion, Thorian del Thorian, has not been asked. On your way, if you please; this is becoming unseemly. Unless, dear Maggie, you plan to spurn our company this fine day?"

"I wouldn't think of it." Maggie took a step forward. "I'd be very . . . happy to join you."

"Sit-sit-sit," Geryn said, raising her hand and gesturing with her fingers at a distant Vestri servant. "How do you take your jasmine tea?"

Torrie frowned. "I'm not entirely sure—"

"*I* am entirely sure she shall be quite safe with us." Emberly sniffed, rising to take Maggie's arm.

Beliana flicked her fingers. "We shall see you tomorrow night, at Lord Sensever's reception, no doubt." But her attention was all on Maggie as she led Maggie to the chair that she, Beliana, had just vacated. "If you please. The servants will be along momentarily with another chair, and it would honor me if you would replace me here."

There were four pointed stares at Torrie, followed by a fifth one from Maggie.

He turned, shrugged, and walked away.

Karin Thorsen leaned against the railing as she looked down on the marketplace below, watching her son walk off. "They seem to be playing their parts well," she said.

If anybody had asked her, the dramatics of Torrie and Maggie not getting along were being played to an inattentive audience, but nobody was asking her. That was okay. Karin trusted Thorian.

"It's good practice, if nothing else," Thorian said, thoughtfully, touching her lightly first at the elbow, then resting his hand on her hip. "And I wouldn't be surprised if you're right that nobody's noticing," he said, responding to what she had thought, not said. "Or if you're wrong and somebody is."

What was it that made them able to almost read each other's minds, she wondered idly. Was there something in her body language that had told him what she was thinking? Or in her voice? And how had she known that his touch on her arm near the elbow meant for her to be careful and that the touch at her hip was intended to be reassuring?

You live with a man long enough, her mother had once said, and sometimes you won't know where he starts and you end. If you're lucky.

Maybe that was it.

He let his hand drop. "But we are faced by failure no matter which way I turn," he said. "We can't stay and let ourselves be used to bait Hosea—"

"Orfindel," she said. "I've heard the name."

"—and I can't try to escape by myself, not with you and Thorian as hostages. He is held in place by their grip on you and Maggie, and perhaps on me, as well."

"I'm not exactly helpless, you know," she said.

"But you're not capable of making your way across Tir Na Nog by yourself, either. I might be able to find my way home; you could not," he said, with the sort of finality that Karin had no desire to dispute.

"You make it sound hopeless," she said, letting her smile give the lie to her words.

"There are always possibilities." His fingers entwined in hers. "There are always possibilities, min alskling," he said, bringing their fingers to his lips. "If I have the skill and we have the patience."

"Skill? Patience?"

He raised a palm. "Just . . . just let me handle it. It's a man's affair. Strategy, politics, honor are—"

She bristled at that. "I'm not one of these local women, good for nothing except clothes and"—she waved her hands—"whatever else they do."

He smiled. "That's always true," he said. "But neither are these local women useless. Talented as they are at clothes and 'whatever.' "

She tilted her head to one side.

He pursed his lips for a moment. "You see young Maggie there, sitting and taking tea with those flitterbrained young women? Silly, flighty little things who simply sit out in the fresh air, sipping flavored teas, while real work goes on about them?"

She nodded.

"Well, they are perhaps not as flighty as they look. My guess would be that they are all wardens' daughters; most wardens like to keep a daughter in residence in the City, and not just so she can compete for the best husband, either. Notice where they sit: from that spot they can watch the trades at most of the stalls in the market, and when one of them gets up to look around, she seems to cover the rest of the ground." He grinned. "And it'll happen, from time to time, that some freefarmer seeks to deprive the Dominion of its portion. The taxes are complicated, and records are difficult to keep."

"And they stop him?"

His lips pursed. "Perhaps it's just a coincidence that those farmers who do well in the market but claim difficulty at tax time are those who the local warden—usually an ordinary of the house, but sometimes a cadet—pays a visit on." He shrugged. "I don't believe in coincidence, myself, particularly since it works the same way in the town and village markets as it does here. Oh, I'm sure that neighboring farmers often work out private trades late at night that are never registered, never taxed. But I am also sure that little escapes the attention of these supposedly inattentive girls."

Below, one of the young women had taken out a small, inlaid wooden box, and opened it. Inside was an assortment of small things that Karin couldn't quite make out.

"The game is called Whimsy," Thorian said. "I could never quite get the spirit of it, but the object is to determine which squares each of your opponents holds based on sometimes inadequate information."

Karin's brow wrinkled. "That sounds like . . . poker?"

Thorian shrugged, dismissing it. "Perhaps." Money games didn't interest him. Chess, yes—he and Bob Aarsted had spent many nights over coffee and an old battered chessboard that had probably come over from the old country—but he had turned down the occasional offers to join the biweekly poker game over at Sven's for so many years that Sven had finally stopped asking.

Karin nodded. Chess, but not poker; strategy, but not money. It helped to explain why he had never as much as asked about her stock trades.

"So, let me guess," she said, "you all want a girl who is good with figures."

He smiled as he placed his hands at her waist. "Among other things."

Her hands snaked around him, but then she caught herself. She wasn't used to Thorian distracting her, but he had. She held her body stiff. "You didn't tell me what you are planning on doing."

"It's—" he thought about it for a moment. "It's not difficult. I plan on staying alive, and talking at length about what I've been doing for the past years, about how close Hosea has become to our family, and demonstrating how good I've become with a sword." He patted the hilt of his sword. "I'm going to defeat every man that any other house puts up against me, and make it look easy, and all the while I'm going to let everybody know that, eventually, I will be the key to Orfindel. I'm going to give His Warmth everything he wants," he said, his jaw tight, his lips barely parted, "until the other Houses decide that that's too dangerous, that His Warmth has become too great a threat."

Karin frowned. "But what will they do then?"

He pulled her too him. "Sometimes," he whispered, softly, gently, "you ask too many questions. Hold on, my Karin. There is no hurry."

CHAPTER SIXTEEN

Escape

Hosea called for a break late the second afternoon, as he had on the first day.

Ian was grateful, but Silvertop tossed his massive head, snorted, and trotted off through the thick brush, downslope toward where a slender silvery stream twisted and shimmered in the daylight. Not much of a stream, perhaps, but it was slender snowmelt streams feeding into larger ones that eventually built into the Gilfi; a mountain, no matter how huge, is just a pile of little rocks.

The horse crashed through the brush.

Well, if Silvertop didn't want to rest, screw him. Ian was tired. After they walked a million miles yesterday—okay, okay, but it *felt* like a million miles—before stopping when it got too dark to continue, his night's sleep had been fitful moments of slumber, repeatedly punctuated by moments of wakefulness when an insect or a bird chirped, or when the wind made the leaves rustle, or when he had just plain woken up for no reason. A lot of insects and birds had chirped, the wind often made the leaves rustle, and Ian had woken dozens of time in the night.

Walking had gotten the stiffness out of his muscles, but by noon he had been tired; it had only gotten worse from there. So Ian plopped himself down on an upthrust curve of root of an old oak, not bothering to take off his rucksack—it made a decent rest against the roughness of the bark—while Hosea simply squatted, spiderlike, rummaging through his pack, producing the waterbag, which he tasted, then dumped on the road.

Granted, the water didn't taste as fresh as it had yesterday, but there was no point in wasting it.

"Hey—" Ian started, then caught himself. Oh.

Hosea smiled, his teeth too white in his dark face. "Yes, I'd rather have some fresh stream water than what's left of the water from the well." He eyed the slope ahead. "And given that there are cedars upstream from here, this water is likely to keep well."

"I think I read that in my Boy Scout manual," Ian said.

"Oh? You were a scout?"

Ian shook his head. "Just for a while. The old bas—my father put an end to it." He shrugged. Ian had said something to Mr. McLintock, the scoutmaster, about life at home; and when McLintock had made some gentle inquiries of Ben Silverstein, dear old Dad had immediately pulled Ian out of Scouts, muttering veiled threats of lawsuit that were enough to frighten the scoutmaster off.

Not that there was anything anybody could do about it, mind. You had to show bruises, and a lot of them, to get the authorities interested in child abuse, and most of the shit Dad piled on Ian's head was just words, just drunken, screamed words.

Nothing illegal about that.

Hosea nodded. "Surely enough."

Ian pulled off a boot and rubbed at his foot. It helped to restore the circulation, and besides, a bit of air would do his socks and feet some good, although if there was anybody with a nose downwind from them, they'd know about it for miles and miles. Speaking of which . . .

"I thought you said there would be a lot of things looking for you, now that you're back . . . here." Wherever here was.

Hosea took a piece of jerky out of his pack and took a bite, considering. "Well, there are," he said. "I do look a little different—and, thankfully, smell a little different—than I used to. More like a nightelf than anything else, although I'd have to be one with heavily mixed blood to stand the daylight." He considered the back of his hand as though he had never looked at it before. "But Odin and Freya recognized me immediately, as any of the Elder Ones would." He raised his head and smiled. "So it would be best if we were to avoid any of the Elder, eh? At least until we get there."

"There? And where is there?" he asked, again, feeling like a kid asking *Are we there yet?*

Hosea pointed. "Still that way," he said, patiently. "A few days' journey, if we're fast on our feet and not much delayed; one less day's travel than when you asked yesterday. Falias, where our friends have been taken."

Ian grunted. "And there won't be lookouts on the road for you?" he asked. He had thought of the question yesterday, but by the time Hosea had called for a break, Ian had been more involved in being tired than in being curious.

Hosea nodded. "I would suspect so. But we're not taking the main road, or a particularly good one, for that matter. It's likely to be less well watched, particularly since the final leg up to the City is—"

"Hidden?" Ian gave it the extra emphasis.

Hosea frowned. "No. Just hidden. But perhaps unmarked, even to this day."

"So that's the plan? We walk in the back route of this Falias city and walk out with the Thorsens and Maggie?"

Hosea was silent for a long moment. "Tell me, Ian: what are the codes a Trident submarine captain uses to launch his missiles?"

Ian spread his hands. "I don't know."

"Very well. Now: imagine I'm applying red-hot pincers to your genitals—and I ask you again: what are those codes? Tell me!"

"Okay, okay." Ian's mouth twisted. "What I don't know, I can't spill. Even under torture."

"Or worse."

"What's worse than torture?"

"It is my hope that you never find out." Hosea looked at him thoughtfully for a long moment. "Never." He straightened himself and settled his pack more securely on his back. "Let us be on our way. I want to make that ridge by nightfall."

Some idiot was shaking him in the dark, waking him out of the weirdest fucking dream he had ever had.

Ian reached for the switch on his bedside lamp, but instead of the cold, round little knob, his fingers found wet grass.

Not a dream, he decided, wondering why he had never tried to get out this way before. If it was a dream, he could wake up—

"Wake up, Ian Silverstein," Hosea hissed. "We have some difficulties."

Ian sat up, tossing his blankets aside, reflexively reaching for the hilt of his sword. When had he developed that reflex? It wasn't the first thing a fencer did in the morning, or when he woke in the night.

He must have been sweating in his sleep, because the night air felt too chilly; he wrapped his cloak tightly about him as he rose to his feet in the dark.

It was too dark; he could barely see his hand in front of his face, and while he could make out a vague bulk in front of him, he only knew that it was Hosea because Hosea had spoken, not because he could see anything. Clouds had rolled in, and that turned the night from a bright starlit one into the inside of a coal pit.

Try to find the road, sure.

Off in the distance, a dog howled. Or not a dog—it was a long, attenuated cry, that sounded more like a canine yodel than anything. "The Sons?"

"Mmm." Hosea listened silently, while another long howl rang out. "One of them has cut our trail, he says, and he's reporting where, waiting for instructions and a response before he comes looking for us."

"How's his night vision? I can't see anything," Ian said.

The cold dark felt threatening. Eyes and fangs could be out there, waiting for him, just feet away, and there was nothing he could do about it. Draw his sword and hope to flail around?

"The Sons have very good night vision, although on a night this black, they'll have to move more slowly than they're accustomed to, if they don't have a scent trail to follow. Silvertop? *Silvertop.*"

Ian could hear the horse crashing through the brush, and the changing wind brought Silvertop's peculiar, harsh horsy smell to his nostrils, but he couldn't see even a white horse on such a black night.

"How about Silvertop, and you?" Ian asked.

"Silvertop can't see without light. There was a time when I"—a pause—"and I can't see without light, either."

Then what the fuck do we do? "Then if we're going to run, we'd better make a torch or something."

Hosea grunted. "In the light, I'd find a birch and strip it of bark for a torch, as perhaps I should have. Or taken some ticking and doused it with lantern oil, which I don't have, because I don't have a lantern, because I'd not wanted to make a light at night, because—" He sighed.

Ian wasn't sure whether or not he was more scared or more irritated. Werewolves—Sons tracking them in a darkness that didn't seem to bother them any, but had Ian,

Hosea, and Silvertop stopped dead in their tracks . . . "So what do we do? Wait for them?"

"There's little choice." Ian could hear Hosea fumbling with the straps of his rucksack. "I know I had one of these in here . . . ah." Then there were sounds that he couldn't make out, and a muttering or two.

Light flared bright from the palm of his hand, too bright, pushing the darkness away to the edges of the small clearing. Hosea's long, bony face, lit almost demonically from below, gleamed, the hollows of his cheeks and the shadow cast by his bony nose seemed too black. "And there was light," Hosea said, with a grin. The silver Roosevelt dime in the palm of his hand glowed white, so white Ian reflexively shuddered at the heat.

But there wasn't any heat. This close, a white-hot piece of metal not only would have burned through Hosea's palm but the heat of it would have washed across Ian's face in a fiery wave.

Hosea held the coin sideways between his middle and ring finger, his arm thrust out ahead of him, the palm of his hand acting like a reflector.

In the bright light Silvertop pawed the ground and snorted hard, the pawing sending detritus swirling up into the air, and the snort splattering Ian's face with awful moist horse-gunk.

Ian wiped his face on his cloak. "So why didn't you do this in the first place?"

Hosea's mouth twisted. "Perhaps because I didn't wish to advertise to any magical adept within a hundred . . . miles that I'm here. Would that reason satisfy you? Or perhaps would you understand that one who has once flown easily gets no pleasure from crawling painfully?"

"So now we make a run for it, eh?"

"No." Hosea had already donned his own cloak, and he produced a handful of leather thongs, which he used to bind the top of his quiver closed and his unstrung bow to the straps of his rucksack, leaving his hands free. A few quick turns of leather tied his sword into its scabbard; he tossed Ian a thong, and Ian did the same.

"A matter of extremity." Hosea laid his free hand on Silvertop's neck. "I know you can outrun them, old friend—"

Ian stifled an objection. A horse couldn't outrun a pack of wolves, but then again, Silvertop was no ordinary horse any more than the Sons were ordinary wolves.

"—but we need for you to do so without throwing us from your broad back. Can you try?

"One snort for yes, two for no?"

Ian wouldn't have believed that a horse could glare, but it did, as Silvertop's massive head bobbed slowly up and down. It snorted again, and tossed its head, tendrils from its long, ragged mane cracking like whips.

"Come, Ian Silverstein," Hosea said, dropping to one knee and cupping his hand in front of him. The glowing dime lit only his chest and face, and the broad black side of the horse. "Silvertop will not tolerate a saddle on his back or a bit in his mouth, but he will allow you to hold onto his mane, and hold on as tightly as you can, with your hands and your legs."

I'm a fucking city kid, and I don't ride horses, much less huge horses, much less huge magical horses, much less huge, magical, immortal horses, Ian thought, but he put his boot in Hosea's hand and sprang to Silvertop's broad back. It felt like sitting on a hairy statue. The horse's hair was coarser and harder than Ian had thought from looking at it, and the muscles underneath its skin were rock-hard, unmoving. He could have pounded on its back and done nothing more than broken his hand.

Hosea slipped to the horse's back behind him, and slipped one steel bar of an arm around Ian's waist. His other arm he thrust forward, the glowing dime lighting the path back to the road, albeit only dimly.

It was enough for Silvertop. The horse set off at a slow, gentle walk, and Ian wound his hands in the horse's mane, the none-too-clean strands ungiving in his grip.

"For the love of all, Ian Silverstein, hold on," Hosea said. "Careful of your eyes, now."

Branches whipped at Ian's face; he ducked his head and closed his eyes to protect them until they reached the road, and the rustling and snapping of brush became the clop clop clop of Silvertop's massive feet as the horse set off in a fast walk. The rhythm of it was simple to move with, and for a moment Ian thought that this would be easy.

Clop clop clop clop became clop-clop-clop-clop and then clopclopclopclop, and it was only a little more difficult to anticipate the rhythm, to shift from side to side in concert with the horse.

Silvertop broke into a canter—clop-*wham*, clop-*wham*—and broke Hosea's grip on Ian, and the grip of Ian's legs on the horse's broad back.

Ian pitched forward, hard, sliding across Silvertop's withers upside down, holding onto the mane for dear life. His shoulders bore his weight, and he thought for a moment that his arms would rip right out of their sockets as he jounced around, one kick from Silvertop's right foreleg catching him on the boot before the horse could stop.

It was all he could do not to scream.

Hosea was still on his back, his leg-grip unbroken. "Hurry, Ian Silverstein, hurry."

"This—this isn't going to work," Ian said. "We have to try something else—"

He was interrupted by a wolf's howl, and not as far off as it had been, and Ian cursed himself for an idiot as he accepted Hosea's free hand, and levered himself once more to Silvertop's back.

"Okay, Silvertop," Ian said, "let's go for it."

This time Silvertop set off in a canter right away, which should have thrown Ian off again, but somehow he was able to hold on, even though his butt bounced hard against the horse's back with every buck and rear, harder and harder as the horse's speed increased.

And then a strange thing happened: clop-*wham* clop-*wham* became a steady stream of *clop*ita-*clop*ita-*clop*ita, and as the hard wind whipped tears even from his closed eyes, the back of the horse seemed to stabilize. Beneath his thighs and bruised buttocks Ian could feel the hard muscles under the thick hide, but it all was happening so fast, so rhythmically, that it was smooth, more like riding a steel locomotive than a horse.

He opened one eye, and past his wind-whipped tears the dark road twisted through the night, illuminated by a glowing dime held on an outstretched hand.

He closed his eyes tightly, and prayed for the night to end.

CHAPTER SEVENTEEN

Hunters

It's possible to hold still for as long as you have to, but not day after day: Arnie Selmo was allowed five minutes to stretch—and snack, if necessary—every hour on the hour. Orphie took his five minutes on the half-hours.

As the second hand swept up toward the twelve, Arnie sat back in the lawn chair, the BAR across the arms of the chair, a hot cup of coffee competing with a roast beef sandwich to warm his insides. A bit later in the morning, when Davy Hansen and the idiot Cotton kid were to relieve him and Orphie, he would supplement the coffee with a short pull from the silver flask in his breast pocket, but for now, the coffee and sandwich would have to do.

You make do the best you can with what you have. His family always had.

His grandfather Hansen had been living in Northfield, Minnesota, the year that the James and Younger gangs rode in to terrify the squareheads and rob their banks, and Grandpa Hansen had helped bury some of the bastards, one of whom he had shot with his old squirrel gun.

In the back.

From behind a tree.

Twice.

Whenever he would tell the story, Grandpa Hansen would finish with a snort. "Didn't ask him to ride into my town," he would say.

You made do with what you had.

Like the BAR, and the Garand in the oilcloth on the ground next to him. In one sense, Arnie would have preferred to have the Garand as his main artillery, with the BAR in reserve or over with Orphie, but that really didn't make sense.

He had the steadier hand, and the BAR was a real, full auto weapon—Orphie's Class III license made it legal, although Arnie couldn't have cared a fig about the legality—and it could empty its twenty-round magazine in about the time it would take to fart. And not only was the BAR loaded with the Thorsen silver-tipped hand loads, but Arnie now had a half dozen mags full of the same hand loads in the ammo bag a few feet in front of the lawn chair.

Werewolves might be able to shrug off lead and copper, but Torrie had left behind a couple of bodies that showed what silver would do for them.

Good boy.

Just a matter of applying the right tool to the job. Like in the old days. Given enough support from the fucking tanks—which were usually somewhere else when you needed them—they could have held the Chinks back. But for tanks to knock back infantry, what you needed was canister, not the AT they had.

But that was half the planet away, and a lifetime ago. Best to keep to the here and now, and here and now the BAR was the right choice for his main weapon.

Of course, if Arnie hadn't set the lawn chair up against something as solid as the base of the huge elm tree it was now resting against, the recoil would knock him out of the chair. But he had, and that was that.

He settled comfortably into a light reverie. That was the

secret of hunting: pick your spot, and wait. Deer would easily outrun a walking hunter, and they could hide in brush so thin you'd believe it couldn't conceal a woodpecker's pecker. A woodchuck could disappear without a trace down his hole at the slightest movement. Even a rabbit could leap from one improbable hiding place to another before you could react.

So the trick was not to be there.

If you sat in your blind and didn't move, didn't twitch, didn't belch or fart, you weren't there. The brush piled around Arnie's seat at the base of the old elm wasn't a perfect blind, but Arnie wasn't wearing hunter's orange, either, just an old brown wool coat over khaki workshirt and workpants.

He sat there, not there, thinking of everything and nothing until he heard a sound behind him, a rustle of branches.

"Arnie?"

"Yeah," he said, pulling the clip and ejecting the round from the BAR before rising. He put the round back into the clip and reinserted it into the weapon, then rubbed at the small of his back. It hurt, but the walk out to the car would stretch it out some, make him feel better.

He pulled the flask from his pocket and took a long pull, letting the whiskey warm him from throat to middle. Just enough to get him going.

Davy Larsen was decked out in his old army fatigues today, as usual, and as usual topped by his olive drab army jacket. He dropped his own lunch bucket next to the lawn chair, accepted the BAR with a nod and without comment—good boy—racked a round into the chamber with a practiced motion, and seated himself in the chair without a word, already just this side of invisible and absolutely motionless before Arnie was well on his way down the path.

Enough for today, Arnie decided. Time for some sleep,

and maybe cook himself a little dinner before he was back on shift.

He made his way back down the path toward where Orphie's old Chevy Nova was parked just off the road, exchanged a quick nod with the idiot Cotton kid, who was already heading back toward the stand, then pulled open the passenger door, seated himself and waited.

In about ten minutes, Orphie staggered down the path, favoring his right leg. He opened the driver's side door and plopped down on his seat.

"Shit, boy," Orphie said, accepting Arnie's flask and taking a pull, "this don't get easier."

Arnie shrugged, the way he shrugged every day. "Doesn't need to. We just need to hang in there."

Orphie rubbed at his stubbled chin, then reached down and turned the keys, swearing under his breath when the engine coughed three times before turning over. "Tomorrow, you think?" he asked, as he did every day.

Arnie shook his head. "I don't know. I don't much care. One in three chances it happens on our watch. As long as it happens at all, I don't care."

Orphie chuckled as he backed up down the road, one hand thrown over the back of the bench seat to steady him. "Odds are against us getting it."

Arnie shook his head. "Doesn't matter, as long as it happens." He took another swig of his whiskey. "I want those dogs." They killed Ole Honistead, and while Arnie and Ole hadn't always gotten along, but damn it, Ole was a neighbor, and you didn't go kill Arnie's neighbors.

He took another swig. "Let's get home. I need to wash up, and then get some sleep."

It was good to have some reason to live again.

CHAPTER EIGHTEEN

Hidden Ways

There were things about life in Falias that Torrie hadn't had a lot of trouble getting used to, he decided, as he returned from a solitary shower to his room, the thick, napless towel wrapped around his waist his only garment.

Having servants set out his clothes wasn't going to be a hard adjustment.

He picked up the white tunic and pulled it over his head.

Most of their gear had been left in Torrie's room, a comfortable enough cell, although it was lit only by a pair of lanterns, one set just above head-high in the wall.

He quickly finished dressing, except for the short cape and the swordbelt, and there was no rush about either, so Torrie sat down hard on the thin mattress—the bed was little more than a sheet wrapped around a blanket, supported by a weaving of leather straps on a wooden frame—and started to go through the gear, figuring that there wouldn't be anything of use.

The pistol was long gone, of course, and so was the Gerber hunting knife—why let him keep his sword if they were going to deny him a knife? Ah, of course: a sword was many things, but a concealed weapon wasn't among them.

But why leave him the Swiss Army knife? Well, it didn't look to Torrie like much of a weapon, but . . .

He shrugged. Not his problem. At least, they had left him some of his survival kit. Enough for a getaway, if they could make one, and maybe enough to help set up for one. He would have to do something; somebody had to.

He took out the physician's kit and eyed the little bottles of Demerol, morphine, and Vistaril. Sure, he could use those to knock somebody out, but that would take minutes at least—assuming that narcotics worked at all in Tir Na Nog, an assumption he didn't want to test.

Best to be ready, just in case. He opened a condom and dumped a few matches in it, adding a few fingerfuls of the dry straw from his mattress ticking, then inflated it just barely, so that the air cushion would protect the latex from the straw ends, then tied the top.

Amazingly useful things, condoms.

A bureau was built into the stone wall; ancient, heavy oaken drawers slid silently into and out of recesses on hidden supports. Torrie tried a few until he found one with spare sheets, took out a sheet and spread it out on the bed.

He set the still-sealed food and the fire-starting kit in the middle, opened a pair of socks and slipped one around the condom, then added another pair and the shirts and trousers, then topped the pile with the Mylar sheeting and the monocular and the Swiss Army knife, binding it all with line from the fishing kit into a square bundle that he could carry.

It left some things out. Like the Paratool. Of all the combination tools—the Leatherman, the Gerber MultiPlier, SOG's ToolClip and MicroToolClip—it was Uncle Hosea's favorite. He could open it one-handed, and the needlenose pliers had almost perfect registration.

The tool selection was the best: not only did it have the two knives and bottle/can opener, but no fewer than four screwdrivers, a serrated saw blade, and a file strong enough to take the rough edge off a piece of sheet metal and smooth enough to even out a small bump in unfinished wood. Perhaps best of all, the various blades were removable with a pair of nut drivers, and that had given Uncle Hosea the chance to replace the small knife—the large one came to a fine enough point—and the largest screwdriver with a couple of long, bent pieces of stiff wire, useful in resetting hidden lockwork or opening hidden catches.

Torrie held the closed Paratool in his hand. Closed, it was about the size of a roll of quarters, except flatter, easier to conceal.

Conceal. He smiled.

Now, back at home, a bureau with drawers like this concealed the hidden panel between Torrie's room and the Guest Room. You could pull the bureau away from the wall—it would stick for just a moment—and even stick a piece of wire into the small gap between pine panels that covered the hidden way, but you'd never open the panel, because the catch wouldn't give unless the weight of the bureau, sitting on the small projection at the junction of wall and floor, was holding the panel down.

Torrie took another look at the built-in bureau. The wall was rough, more hewn than finished, pitted naturally, as though a thousand stone-eating worms had idly chewed through it. There was a tiny pit on the wall, near the juncture of the top drawer and the wall, although it had long since been clogged up with dust or some other—

Nah. A chill ran down his back.

Torrie opened the pick, locked it into place, and pushed it into the pit, pushing away whatever it was that had blocked it, feeling the end of the bent piece of wire fitting into a hidden catch, just the way it had hundreds of times at home.

A twist, a pull, and a whole section of wall swung out on silent, hidden hinges.

Holy shit.

A puff of stale air brought smells of ancient mustiness to his nostrils, as a dark corridor loomed in front of him.

Torrie shook his head. This wasn't just in the style of Uncle Hosea, this was *him*. The hole was at the same height as the one at home, and the hidden lockwork not only worked the same way, but felt the same way—it had that same worked-smooth-without-being-oily slickness that everything Uncle Hosea made seemed to have.

He knelt at the entrance. The floor inside was covered with dust, but only lightly, and the dust was smooth and unmarked. It felt like it had been unused for a long time.

Footsteps sounded outside in the corridor; he pulled the Paratool out, and quickly pushed the secret door shut, then folded the Paratool and tossed it on the bed like it was too hot to handle.

There was a knock on his door.

"Torrie?" Maggie's face peered in.

"Come on in," he said, beckoning.

God, she looked good. Vestri servants had twisted her short hair back and up, fastening it into place with a hundred small pins topped by tiny pearls. Her dress, made from something silken and sky blue, and edged in silver and black, was cut low in front and fell full to the floor, sweeping the floor as she moved.

"Where were you?"

She smiled. "Tea and Whimsy with the girls again," she said.

"You seem to have made some friends quickly."

A shrug. "Well, they're racing each other trying to figure out where I belong in local society. The winner gets either to ride my coattails partway up the next rung if I turn out to be above them, to shame the others by being the first to drop me if I'm below, or to be my lifelong friend if it's neither."

"Is it really that . . . much?"

"Well, yes and no." Maggie's mouth twitched. "I mean,

technically speaking, Emberly and Geryn are senior to Dortaya, all three are ordinary families, which should make them junior to Beliana—her father is a major, but he married a common girl and has to handle his money himself, so it depends—" she let herself trail off. "It's complicated."

"You've picked up a lot in a couple of afternoons," he said, impressed. Most of the stories Torrie had been told had been about politics and honor, not about money and status. That was—

"Oh, I'm awful bright for a girl."

"I didn't mean it that way."

" 'Course not. I just like having you on the defensive." Maggie's smile broadened. "Branden del Branden stopped by to pay his respects."

"Oh?"

"Yes. He'll be looking for us this evening, he said."

"I'd expect so. He and Ivar del Hival are supposed to escort us over." Dad clearly didn't want any part of this reception, but Torrie was looking forward to it. A chance to get out, to learn more about what was going on. He found that he was jealous of Maggie; she seemed to make friends easily—

But, then again, she wasn't Thorian del Thorian the Younger. There were reasons why he hadn't been approached.

She cocked her head. "You look like you're thinking deep thoughts."

He shrugged. "Not very." He forced a smile. "You look great, by the way."

She smiled. "Better than that road-dirty wretch they dragged in here?" She came into his arms and held him tight.

Well, why not? She smelled of summer and sunshine, with no trace of anything under the dress, and her breath was warm in his ear.

"Would you get your hands off my ass for a moment?" she whispered. "We might be overheard."

Torrie shook his head. "I doubt it," he said, quietly. "The secret passage hasn't been used for a long time."

She made a face. "Secret passage?"

He held up a finger for silence, then walked to the door, pausing silently. Nothing.

Well, if he was going to be indiscreet . . .

He opened the Paratool, extended the bent wire, and pulled open the secret door.

Maggie's mouth opened and closed, then opened and closed again. "Who—where does it lead?"

Torrie shrugged as he shut the door. "Somewhere. Anywhere." No. He knew more than that. "Probably everywhere. This place is going to be honeycombed with secret passages and hideaways, and many of them—not all—are going to interconnect."

Not all; Uncle Hosea would have built a few equivalents of the safe room under the northwestern corner of their living room, a safe place for secreting people or stuff that didn't lead anywhere else, but that wasn't what this felt like.

It was a way out, although how and where it led was something that he couldn't figure. There was surely another door before it joined up with the main passage, just as at home the "priest's hole" that led from the main bathroom to the crawlway under the porch was hidden at the crawlway end behind a false wall.

"How do you know?"

He shook his head. "I should have figured it out a long time ago. Somebody who thinks like Uncle Hosea built this," he said, lying.

He knew that it wasn't anything of the sort: this screamed of Uncle Hosea.

When he was a kid, he had always felt deep in his gut that his parents and Uncle Hosea had been around forever, but that was the way kids always felt about grownups. He had grown out of that feeling with Mom and Dad, but had more suppressed it than lost it about Uncle Hosea. "It's like he did in the house, except more so—that lockwork is the same . . ." He let his voice trail off. You Just Didn't Talk About Private Family Business.

But Fuck It. Maggie was in this as deep as Mom and Dad and Torrie were, and damned if she didn't have the right to know. "It's the same as the lockwork behind the bureau in my room, that opens a door to the back of the closet in the Guest Room." He shook his head. "It even feels the same."

How long could metal stand against metal without adhering?

Apparently forever, if Uncle Hosea had treated it properly—metals annealed to the surface? Some coating? Magic?—because Torrie was sure that that door hadn't been opened for at least decades, probably longer.

"It's all his style," Torrie went on. "He put knocking plates in the doorframes of our house like the one out front here, just smaller. The lockwork is the same, and the whole style of it is the same." Torrie pursed his lips. "Somewhere there'll be a hidden abditory—"

"Abditory?"

"—hiding place with something of some value in it, and beneath that will be something of even more value," like the way that one of the hidden gun safes at home was a cover for what remained of the strange old gold coins with the lettering on them that Torrie would bet his right hand he could read now. "It'll all be done perfectly, to last forever, because that's the way Uncle Hosea makes things when he can." His head was spinning. They had a way out—

No. Uncle Hosea was too clever for that.

Branden del Branden had already hinted that some of the Hidden Ways around the City were known, at least to the nobility, and Uncle Hosea would have counted on that. Finding one, or even several entrances to some hidden passages wouldn't be the key to all of them.

But that didn't explain much of it. If finding these passageways and abditories was so important, why didn't the locals just batter their way through walls looking for hidden paths?

Torrie picked up the Paratool again, this time opening the knife blade. It wasn't the original knife blade; Uncle Hosea had replaced it with some high-tech steel, tough enough to cut through cable.

He scraped it against the wall; it left behind no mark at all.

Well, that explained that. The locals didn't smash their way through the walls because they couldn't, because the Cities had been built of some sort of super-stone, which also explained why an ancient stone city, battered by weather and war over millennia, looked so unworn.

It was beyond Torrie; he already knew not nearly enough, and too much.

"Dad?" he said, sticking his head out the doorway. "Do you and Mom have a minute?"

Dad's face was pensive as he emerged from the secret passage, and clicked the hidden doorway slowly shut, dousing the lantern with a gentle puff.

"It won't work," he said, finally. "I would have to lead them myself—the cues for the Hidden Way back home aren't something I could explain." He ran a hand down the front of his silken tunic, smoothing it over and over, as though he was afraid that a wrinkle would show where he had been.

"But it does connect?" Mom's hair was twisted back into a knot, fastened with a trio of long white pins that could have been made of ivory, or bone. Her dress was cut low in front and in back, and seemed to cling too tightly to her torso, until it flared at the hips into a full skirt.

He nodded, slowly, carefully, gently, as though afraid a sudden movement would hurt. "Easily. Hosea was kept in a cell in the base of this tower. It was that cell that he showed me the way out of; a rock that must be pressed a certain way for a certain time."

Torrie frowned. "Then why couldn't he escape himself?"

"He was bound. His . . . bonds were special, intended for someone else, but capable of binding a god, or at least one of his . . . ancestry." Dad shook his head. "Better no more is said. The threat looms—"

"What do you mean?"

"I mean," Dad said, his voice low and flat, almost without passion, as though he were reporting something he didn't care about or couldn't let himself care about, "that if I had taken a move toward escape, Branden del Branden and Herolf would have bound me with the guts of my own son, something I could no more free myself from than Uncle Fox could, long ago."

Maggie tilted her head to one side. "Are you saying that Hosea is Loki? The villain of the whole Norse saga? Really?"

Dad shook his head. "Hardly." His lips pursed for a moment. "He is older than Aesir, or the Vanir, and enough proof that the Tuatha and Tuarin were both older than them and ancestors to them. Loki . . . I used to think that the Fire Duke was Loki, somehow having captured or killed Anegir del Denegir, and taken his place, but no."

"You're sure of that?"

"Very," Dad said. "When we made our escape, we did it via a secret entrance to His Warmth's office, and bound him with . . . that which had long bound Hosea, hiding him in a secret abditory." He smiled. "A large abditory. One of the Aesir or Vanir couldn't have escaped, so bound.

But he moves well for one of his fat; he escaped quickly enough to raise the alarm that had us fleeing down Ways Orfindel only half remembered." He took his wife's hand in his larger one, and brought it to his lips for a moment. "Not that I regret that, you understand."

"So what do we do?"

"Nothing, for the time being. We can't all try to escape, as His Warmth has put his own guards and telltales in the passages he knows, and they would be searched quickly were we to be shown missing. And I can't go and leave you behind," he said. "So we wait. For the time being."

"But—"

Torrie was interrupted by a loud knocking on the outer door of their suite.

"That will be Branden del Branden and Ivar del Hival, to escort us to the reception," Dad said, adjusting his sword belt.

Ash Plaza: a circular piazza half the size of a football field, floored in ancient marble, reddened in the light of the setting sun, rimmed on the mountain side with tall ashes, their leaves rustling dryly in the wind in counterpoint to the scratchings of the quartet of musicians sitting on the lip of the curiously silent fountain in the center of the court. The drummer, his instrument an elongated copper tube topped with a well-darkened membrane, kept up a complex beat over the droning of a remarkably mellow bagpipe, the tune alternately taken up by what looked like a fat-bellied lute and some sort of flute with a lipped mouthpiece that sounded more like a particularly mellow trumpet than anything else.

The marble had been polished to a high, even gloss: upside-down, fiery reflections of well-dressed lords and ladies turned in time at the entrance of Torrie's party; and then, as though practicing the steps of a dance, most turned back.

One pair didn't: a tall, slim man, his blue and silver tunic topped by a curiously plain gray silk cape, offered his arm to a plumpish woman, and walked deliberately up to where Dad had halted, Ivar del Hival at one side, Mom at another, Torrie and Maggie behind them.

Branden del Branden bowed at their arrival. "Lord Sensever del Sensever," he said. "Emissary of the House of Wind to the court of His Warmth, and the Fascinating Lady Cirsta. I have the privilege to introduce the Exquisite Maggie and the Extraordinary Karin. You know Thorian del Thorian the Elder; may I have the honor of introducing Thorian del Thorian the Younger, an . . . accomplished duelist in his own right?" His smile was wolfish.

"Thorian," Lord Sensever said, ignoring Branden del Branden and the rest, "it's been a long time." His voice was perhaps half an octave higher than Torrie had expected, and his vowels had curious flatness. He patted at the hilt of his sword. "I see you are back at your old post, eh?" His face was long and bony, pleasant in a homely sort of way, particularly when he smiled. Torrie found himself warming instantly to the tall lord while at the same time disliking the fat dowager on his arm.

Dad nodded. "His Warmth has been kind enough to allow me to work off my debt."

Lady Cirsta's lips pursed. "A great favor, I'm sure."

Sensever patted her on the arm. "Lady, I—"

"It is not your hereditary fief that is being challenged, milord, but my brother's."

Sensever nodded. "That is true, but be that as it may . . ."

". . . and there's not a lick of justice in that claim, milord . . ."

"Rather beside the point, milady." Sensever's voice was studiously calm. "But yes, yes, that would appear to be the case."

Dad's face was a mask. "That is something that remains to be seen."

"Quite possibly it shall," Sensever said, quietly.

"Enough of this nonsense." Ivar del Hival scowled. "Challenge has neither been given nor accepted; it's unseemly to—"

"Anticipate that it shall?" Lady Cirsta's nostrils flared. "Simply because His Warmth has only intimated that should His Force not surrender Kerniat, challenge will be issued, with Thorian del Thorian issuing challenge to all who dispute His Warmth's ownership? With each bout to the death?"

"Enough." Sensever laid a hand on her arm, seemingly gently, but Torrie didn't fail to notice that when she tried to pull away, neither the hand nor the arm moved. "Lady wife, Thorian del Thorian is the champion, not the one who issues the challenge."

"If it is issued," Ivar del Hival said quietly. "That hasn't happened yet."

"And it may not," Sensever said. "And should it be, it would be understood, at least in the House of Wind, where offense is given, and how offense is taken." He shook his head for a moment as though to clear it, then: "And for now, please be welcome. As I recall, you've been known to be fond of a properly prepared terrine, and I've had four different ones set out."

Dad smiled. "Thank you, Lord Sensever."

Sensever was turning away when Ivar del Hival cleared his throat. "Now, wait a moment. You sound like you know who has been selected to stand for the House of Wind—is there any reason we shouldn't know?"

"None that I know of," Sensever said, quietly. "It will, of course, be me." He turned and left, his wife in tow.

Dad's lips were white. "We shall perhaps see about that." He offered his arm to Mom. "If you please?" and walked off with her toward the tables and the crowd.

Branden del Branden bowed—"I shall certainly see you later," he said—and followed them.

"What was all that about?" Maggie asked before Torrie could.

"Ah, it was foolishness. Leave it be, leave it be." Ivar del Hival hitched angrily at his swordbelt, and led them toward the nearest serving table. On a white linen background, seven round plates were arranged in a staggered line, each holding small pieces of bread with something on it. Torrie was fairly sure that the first was cheeses, and the third was some sort of paté, but the rest escaped him.

Oh, well, it was unlikely to be poisoned, and the meal a trio of Vestri servants had delivered to his room was too many hours in the past for him to be picky. He picked up a slice of bread with something dark and oily on it, bit into it tentatively at first, then wolfed it down. It was smoky and rich, like good jerky, but tender as fish, with a slightly oily taste that would have been unpleasant if it had been any stronger, but as it was made the taste richer and meatier.

Maggie took a bite, nodded. "You can pick out my food all the time."

Others were giving Torrie and her glances out of the corners of their eyes, but nobody approached.

"You were going to explain this foolishness?" Maggie asked Ivar del Hival.

"Only if you insist," he said, tearing off a hunk of bread. He looked at her expression and his glare softened to a smile. "Which I see that you do."

"She always has before," Torrie said, stepping back to avoid Maggie's elbow in his ribs.

"Very well. His Warmth," Ivar del Hival said, his voice lowered from its usual bellow, but not by much, "is playing games. He's . . . suggested he's going to issue a challenge to the House of Wind for a fief that's not only clearly properly of Wind but has no connection to the House of Fire."

He shrugged. "He would ordinarily have enough trouble finding a champion even for a contest to the first blood—except, perhaps, among the House of Steel, but then the prices would be prohibitive, and the chances of going beyond the first blood nil—but Thorian's agreed to serve him unconditionally, and His Warmth has suggested the battle will be to the death." He shook his massive head. "Not a wise move, perhaps, but His Warmth hasn't asked my opinion."

Torrie frowned. He had the feeling he could trust Ivar del Hival, as long as it didn't involve telling him anything that might compromise his loyalties to the House of Flame. "So what does all that mean?"

"It means that your father will have to fight any challengers to the death, and either die defending a spurious claim—assuming he steeps himself in the herbs and rituals, which he won't—or win an affair while definitely in the wrong, shaming himself. And not likely for the last time." His broad smile seemed forced. "Not quite like being a lawyer in your world, is it?"

Torrie started. "How would you know about that?"

Ivar del Hival's lips were a thin line in his bushy beard. "That would be telling, wouldn't it?"

"You were explaining why this isn't a wise move for the duke," Maggie said.

Ivar del Hival snorted as he reached for her hand and brought it to his lips. "By Baldur's balls, Maggie, you *are* a find: a woman who doesn't think she understands politics, or at least pretends she doesn't think so. Will you marry an old widower? No, no, don't answer me now: merely say you'll think about it, and I'll be satisfied."

His voice was light, but Torrie caught the undercurrent. Despite her spending time with the local tea-and-taxes set, he probably had a better idea than Maggie what her status was here: problematic. Mom was the wife of Thorian del Thorian, and that probably would keep her reasonably safe; Maggie's relationship to Torrie wasn't as well established. Torrie didn't have his father's reputation or status, and the one man who had issued him a challenge, thereby acknowledging him as an acceptable recipient, was dead. That might mean that Torrie's lady was somebody not to be trifled with; it also might mean that she would soon be available, were Torrie to make a habit of death duels. But with Ivar del Hival proposing to her, even if partly in jest, she was clearly under his protection, as well.

He caught Ivar del Hival's smile, and gave a slight nod, rewarded by an ever-so-slight pursing of the lips and as small a nod as Torrie had ever seen.

Maggie's brow wrinkled in a puzzlement that Torrie pegged as just this side of confused. She had figured out some of what was going on, but not all of it. Torrie would have to tell her the story of Ingmark and the Three Virgins sometime, or better yet, have Uncle Hosea tell it.

If he ever saw Uncle Hosea again.

"You still haven't explained it to me," Maggie said, stubborn.

Ivar del Hival frowned. "Very well, if I must—"

"Please," Maggie said. "It would be a kindness, if you would."

Why don't you just bat your eyelashes and be done with it? Torrie didn't say.

"If," Ivar del Hival said, "you'll promise to consider my proposal? And if you, my dear young Thorian del Thorian, promise to take no offense at my impertinence in proposing to your lady?"

Torrie nodded. Officially, of course, to make a move on Maggie was something he could take offense at, but he knew—and Ivar del Hival knew that he knew—that this proposal was a friendly act. "None taken, Ivar del Hival," Torrie said.

"And yes, Ivar," Maggie said, "I promise to consider it. If—"

"If I explain, I know." His smile evaporated. "Well. Try it this way: it is one thing for my old friend Thorian to cut hired champions to little pieces—that's his profession, and theirs, and they are paid in gold and respect for what they do, and for the risks they take. While they try to be on a side they believe to be right—their rituals make it more likely that their wrists will fail them if they fight for something they believe to be wrong—they are often willing to, well, push the border of fairness a touch, in favor of those who hire them.

"But it's another to cross swords with a respected nobleman like Lord Sensever del Sensever, a man of high regard and ancient lineage, in a fight where one like Thorian knows he is wrong. It's . . . humiliating, perhaps. Marginally dishonorable, possibly. Distinctly uncomfortable, for certain, and generally not done." He sighed and shook his head. "And for His Warmth to have a champion who not only is willing to do that but is as good with a sword as Thorian del Thorian, well, that's dangerous to everybody, and no good can come of it. It gives His Warmth the means to challenge for, well, anything, and shows him willing to use that means. The only merciful thing about it is that His Warmth is issuing this challenge over a small matter, suggesting—just perhaps—that he will use this . . . indiscriminate champion only with restraint. Perhaps." He shook himself for a moment, and then his broad smile was back in place, threatening to split his ugly face in two. "Now, now," he said, his voice back at a comfortable bellow, "you have agreed to consider my proposal, have you not?—oh, yes, yes, please join us," he said, beckoning. One bravo, leather cap set jauntily atop a head that seemed slightly too small for his body—or maybe it was just that the cap was too large—strode up and introduced himself as Verniem del Eleric, then beckoned his companion to join him.

Behind him, Torrie recognized Beliana from the day before, accompanied by another young man perhaps in his middle twenties, tall, lean, and weighted down with far too heavy and large a cape for his skinny body. Beliana nodded a meaningless smile toward Maggie, and then caught two of her other friends' eyes and beckoned them and their young men over with a quick twitch of her head. Torrie had trouble remembering their names: Geryn, and Emberly, perhaps?

"Ivar," Verniem del Eleric said, his mouth wreathed in mustache, his voice too smooth, "you are betrothed once again, perhaps?"

"I might well be." Ivar del Hival nodded slowly.

"Ah. I'd not have thought it of you," he said. "The old goat still may have a butt left, perhaps, eh?"

Ivar del Hival rested his hand on the hilt of his sword. "The old blade may still have a slice or two, yes. If you'd care to try it, that could be arranged?"

"No, no," Verniem del Eleric said, raising his hands in mock surrender, "I mean no offense, nor am I likely to take any from either of you." He turned to Torrie. "There are those—foolish, foolish ones, I say—who would say old Ivar del Hival is too antiquated to keep his sword tip steady, but I'm not one of them. I say that he simply misleads many with his meandering manner, that's what I say, and loudly."

"Loudly, indeed," Torrie said. "And with an excess of alliteration, perhaps." There was a mocking tone in the other's voice that he didn't like.

"Loudly is the way I like it." Ivar del Hival grunted. "I want it shouted from the rooftops, from every stair and plaza in the City, that I still am dangerous, even at my advanced age. It saves the wear and tear on my clothing, not to mention my tender body."

Verniem del Eleric was looking at Torrie strangely. "And what of you, Thorian del Thorian the Younger? What would you say?"

Torrie thought about it for a moment. "I say that accidents happen, that's what I say."

"How so?"

"Well, it might be that Ivar del Hival has caught the Lovely Maggie in a weak moment, and will find himself married before the sun rises; or it might be that somebody could misinterpret his friendliness as weakness, and find himself bleeding from his arm, with his sword down around his ankles; or it might be that somebody would interpret an agreement as a challenge, when one would neither look for nor run away from any such." He looked Verniem del Eleric in the eye. "So I say that accidents happen, and I for one would like to avoid one, like I had with Danar del Reginal." The story—Branden del Branden's version of the story—had already spread through the City, but that wouldn't necessarily be the end of it. "Which was unfortunate for him more than me, but unfortunate for the both of us, nevertheless."

Torrie closed his eyes, remembering that awful moment when his sword had gone through Danar del Reginal's misplaced defenses and into his body, feeling the life drain out through the other as he collapsed, leaving behind no trace of dignity, nothing but a bad smell that was quickly shattered in the breeze and a pile of flesh and bone for the Vestri to bury.

His eyes stung as he opened them. Yes, Danar del Reginal had been trying to kill him, and he should be glad the idiot was dead, but he wasn't.

Verniem del Eleric pushed the silence away with a clearing of his throat, and clasped Torrie's arm in a friendly way. "Yes, accidents happen," he said, swagger and bravado replaced by a quiet sincerity, "and such ought to be avoided, particularly on a lovely night like tonight."

That broke the ice; dozens of young nobles and their ladies crowded around, waiting for introductions. Torrie tried to file away all the names, but he knew that he would forget some, or many.

Until a familiar face almost shoved itself in front of his. Older, yes, but—

"Reginal del Reginal," he said, with an elaborate bow, as though to take any precaution to avoid offense, that was in itself an offense. "Ordinary of the House of Flame, older brother to Danar del Reginal, who I believe you met, once, briefly." His face was flushed, and his voice slightly slurred. Not staggering drunk, but drunk enough. There were companions tugging at his arms, but Torrie's universe had narrowed to that ruddy, sweaty face out of a nightmare, a tick in its neck.

There was a tightness at Torrie's scalp and it felt for a moment like he was outside his body watching it all, once again.

The world was not a place where everything was clear, but here it was. Forces in Falias were lining up to challenge Dad to numerous duels to the death. Eventually, somebody would either be better than Dad or get lucky, and that was not to be tolerated.

There was a way out. It would be tricky, but not impossible.

"Briefly," Torrie said. "He tried to kill me in a duel that was only to be to the first blood, and ran himself into my sword. That seems foolish, but—"

"In the pigsty in which you were bred and borne, shitbreath, do they often speak ill of the dead?"

"—but I believe he was pressured into it by someone he must have respected," Torrie went on gently, "as I intend no offense to his memory or his family, just as I'd brook none with mine. Do you of Falias often interrupt, Reginal del Reginal? Or do you give one a chance to finish his words before deciding whether or not to take offense?" Torrie spread his hands. "As I meant none." He raised his voice. "Has offense been given here? Who is senior? Who will rule?"

He hadn't noticed Ivar del Hival leave, but he must have, as Dad and Ivar del Hival were pushing their way through the quickly forming crowd toward them, Mom trailing. Maggie's mouth hung open.

Verniem del Eleric's face was as somber as Branden del Branden's had been. "I am an ordinary of the House, of ancient lines," he said. "And I'll declare myself senior, and see if another wishes to take up the burden."

The whole plaza had gone silent, no sound save for the whistling of wind, softly rattling the leaves of the trees that rimmed it.

Verniem del Eleric sighed. "So be it. I rule that offense has been given. Your terms, Thorian del Thorian the Younger?"

"Here, now. To the first blood only," he said, and as he said it, people pushed back from the two of them, Ivar del Hival pulling on Maggie's arm, until, almost instantly, Torrie, Verniem del Eleric, and Reginal del Reginal were alone in a rough circle five or so meters in diameter.

"Seconds? A judge?" Verniem del Eleric asked, quietly. "Where shall we procure them?"

"You to stand as judge; we need no seconds."

"Now, you say," Reginal del Reginal said, tossing his cape aside. "And now it shall be."

His sword was already half drawn. The codes would have required that he wait for his opponent to be ready, but the trap Torrie had laid for him had infuriated the larger man.

The damn fool.

Torrie spun his cape in the direction of Reginal del Reginal, drawing his own sword. By the time Reginal had completed a lunge that would have done credit to a sober man, Torrie had stepped to one side and brought his sword up to parry a high-line attack, engaging and binding the other's blade, coming corps-à-corps with the bigger man.

A quick twist, a push, and Torrie swung his wrist and arm, hard, in a broad circle.

Reginal del Reginal's sword was tumbling end-over-end, sprained fingers yet to trigger a scream, and Torrie pushed away and slashed once, his sword whistling through the air.

He brought his blade up. "Stop," he shouted. "I have drawn first blood, and claim victory."

"You can if you wish," Reginal del Reginal said, "if you're peasant enough not to let me reclaim my sword." He sneered, and spread his arms wide, exposing his chest. "Try your coward's thrust, pig."

Torrie forced his voice calm. "I said that I *have* drawn it, not that I will. Look at the edge of your right hand." He pointed with his blade. "You'll find it cut, and your blood on the tip of my blade, Reginal del Reginal." Torrie pulled a handkerchief from his pocket and slid it down the length of his blade, never taking his eyes off Reginal del Reginal. "I could have decorated my sword from point to hilt with your heart's blood, mind you, but I do not willingly kill in a duel to the first blood, and I did not." He snorted. "Be happy you fought me to the first blood and not my father to the death, eh? He would have killed you, and all without any offense being given."

Torrie lifted the point of his sword and raised his voice. "There's been some talk of some brave fools who want to face my father, thinking that he's slowed down. I have reason to know that they're wrong, that his wrist and eye are as strong as they've ever been, and that years of practice have seasoned his mind beyond what you all remember.

"But perhaps I bluff.

"Perhaps he has slowed, just a trifle, and perhaps the best of you has a chance of not lying in a pool of your own blood and urine and feces at the end of a bout with him." Torrie sheathed his sword with a decided snap. "Then try him." And, unspoken, because an overt, direct challenge would have to be met: *And then you try me.*

It might work, or it might seem to work for a time, and that would be enough. Torrie was good with a blade, yes, but he wasn't invincible, and only an invincible swordsman could survive unending challenges.

But, so far, his gamble had worked: not only had he beaten both of the sons of Reginal, but he had killed the first with one stroke, and disarmed the second with another. Never mind that the first victory came only because Danar del Reginal had gone for a one-touch kill and left himself exposed; ignore that Reginal del Reginal had been played for the drunken idiot that he was: Torrie had pulled it off, and by morning the word would be around the castle that Thorian del Thorian the Younger was, if anything, even more deadly than his legendary father.

Useful.

He could tell by their faces that Mom, Dad, and Maggie didn't get it, but now wasn't the time to explain things to them. Torrie spun on the balls of his feet and stalked off. Only when he passed through the archway and reached the balustrade on the walkway toward the tower did he let himself start shaking, and he didn't stop until long after he was safely ensconced in their rooms.

He had fallen asleep when she came in.

In a dream, Maggie had slipped from her clothing in one smooth motion, her slim body glistening in the lantern light as she knelt down beside the bed to put her mouth on his, her kisses moving down his chest—

"What the fuck was that about?" she asked, shaking him awake.

Damn, damn, damn.

He was muzzy with sleep. "Mom and Dad with you?"

"Yes, but—"

"Get them."

Torrie was already on his feet, reaching for the emergency pack.

Dad had his shirt and boots off, getting ready for sleep.

"Quick," Torrie whispered. "Get dressed, and get yourself gone."

He had worked it out in a second. Yes, there would be telltales in the known passageways, and there were guards outside their door, and probably a Son or two hidden away in the Secret Ways between here and home.

But they were waiting for Thorian del Thorian the Senior, a citified duelist, not a man who had learned how to hunt—how to walk silently, how to listen, how to be invisible and unseen—from the likes of John Bjerke and Uncle Hosea. The Sons were sloppy, used to besting ordinary humans with their superior strength and quick bursts of speed—but a man could outrun anything, given enough of a head start.

And besides . . . perhaps there was a deal to be made here, a deal that could better be made as a fait accompli than otherwise.

A deal that would be kept? he asked himself.

Are you fucking kidding? he answered.

His father had long taken on something approaching Hosea's sense of honor, of a promise being like, well, like the creation of a natural law. Probably the only thing that would let Dad run now was his promise to Grandpa to take care of Mom.

For Torrie, though, it was different. A promise made to somebody who had had Maggie and Mom dragged off into the night, leaving neighbors behind dead or crippled . . . that wasn't just a breakable kind of promise; it was disposable, like a used Kleenex.

"Hurry," Torrie said. "I'll handle things here. I'll delay their discovery that you're gone as long as I can, and then hold off telling them about the hidden entrance here as long as I can do that. Get home; I'll escape and join you when I can."

Dad shook his head. "No. You're my son; I can no more leave you than I could—"

"No. You don't get it, do you?" Torrie reached out and grabbed him by the shoulders. "You're needed to find the way home; I can't negotiate the Hidden Ways." There was something strange about them, something that defied mapping. "And the Fire Duke needs a champion, a good one, one who doesn't care what the subject of the conflict is. It's clear he's irritated all the other Cities with his subtle and not-so-subtle threats; it's time for him to put up or shut up, and for that, he needs a champion.

"I'm it, at least for the time being. You saw the crowd; I can probably trade that off against him not chasing after you—as long as you're gone, as long as he knows that he can't simply bring you back."

Yes, yes, His Warmth would have Torrie locked up, but Torrie had been raised by Uncle Hosea. Every inch of the keep shouted his handiwork; Torrie, of all people, would be able to find his way free.

Get home? That would take some doing, and perhaps he never would.

So be it; he was Thorian del Thorian, son of Thorian the duelist and Karin Roelke Thorsen, and the blood of heroes ran in his veins from both sides of his family.

Let the others escape. He would find his own way.

Dad shook his head. "You'll never find your way by yourself, any more than your mother or Maggie could. It has to be all of us or none."

No.

They were counting on the women to anchor the men in place.

But Dad was the key; he was His Warmth's ticket to power. So remove the ticket, and remove the problem.

"We can't all escape," Torrie said. "You know that. It

would be noticed by morning at the latest, and you're the one who told me you need more of a head start than that. He has to need me to champion his challenge, or I don't have anything to bargain with. Which is why—" Torrie found his voice rising in pitch and volume, and forced himself to lower it. Mom and Dad were never moved by hysteria. "This is our one chance, Dad," he said, quietly, calmly. "If it doesn't work, if they capture you, do you think we'll be left free to try again?"

Dad thought about it for a moment.

"You promised Grandpa you'd take care of Mom," Torrie said. "What are your promises worth, Thorian del Thorian the Senior? You would keep one to that fat murderer rather than to my grandfather?"

"Your grandfather would have . . . No. Let it be as you will." Dad nodded slowly, then turned to Mom and Maggie. "We'll leave now. Dress in the pullovers from the emergency kit; they'll help you vanish in the dark." He closed his eyes for a moment. "I'll need most of a day's head start to have a chance. The Ways are long—"

"Not 'while the evil days come not,' " Maggie said with a smile.

"Eh?"

Torrie caught the reference. "Sure enough. You okay, Maggie?"

She shrugged. "I've been better. But I guess there's only so much scared I can get. Can't wet a river." The tiny quaver in her voice was the only sign of fear.

Torrie smiled. "Good girl."

"Good girl?" She started to flare, but fell silent when he offered her his sword, hilt first.

He grinned. "Just an obligatory bit of macho bullshit, and a reminder—the most the locals will think of you is that you're good with tea and arithmetic, not a sword. If they catch up with you, they'll be looking at Dad as the problem, not you. I want you to have this," Torrie said.

"I'll take the spare one, the one that Dad brought for Uncle Hosea.

"The blade was made by Uncle Hosea," he said. "There's some silver in it, I'm sure, and he tempered the edge in his own blood; it'll kill a Son. Don't try to get fancy, and don't try to learn how to use the edge, not now; just keep it out in front of you and stick them with it."

Dad already had his own sword belted on; he frowned. "I think—"

"No, Dad," Torrie said, "you don't. I've fenced with Maggie; you haven't. She's better than you think she is, and the Sons won't be expecting anything out of her. You can use every advantage you have."

Dad nodded, tightly. "As you will."

Mom shook her head. "I can't—"

"You can't waste time now, Mom." He drew himself up straight. "I'll handle things. I'm not your little Torrie anymore, eh? I kind of grew up when you weren't looking."

She shook her head. "It's not like that."

"You can tell me what it is like later."

There was something wrong about all this, but this part of it felt right: he hugged Mom tight for a moment, then released her. She turned her back as she unself-consciously shrugged out of her dress, accepting Dad's offer of the stretch pants and trousers.

Maggie came into his arms. "Torrie, I—"

"Shh," he said. "Some other time." Maybe. "Just do what Dad says, and everything should be fine."

Her lips were soft on his, her tongue warm in his mouth until he pushed her away.

Dad had the lantern lit but rigged the baffles to let only a narrow beam of light out. Their three faces seemed somehow paler than they ought to be as Torrie closed the hidden passage door behind them, then turned and reset the lockwork. There might be a way to do that from the other side, there likely was a way to do that from the other side, but he didn't know it.

He folded the Paratool and tossed it back on the bed, leaving it out in the open. Naked is sometimes the best disguise.

There was something wrong with all this, but they ought to be safe. That was enough for now.

He lay down on his bed and tried to sleep.

The trick would be to wake before the servants showed up, and cover for the rest.

CHAPTER NINETEEN

Falias

Dawn broke dry and clear, and Silvertop slowed to a walk as the road twisted up through the mountains.

The silver dime was again just a dime, and Ian was just riding on the back of the horse, and if his buttocks hadn't been battered to what he was sure was black and blue, and if his shoulders and neck didn't feel like the bones and tendons were cooking over a slow fire, and if—

He wished he could think of last night as just a dream.

Behind them, the road disappeared into the timberline, perhaps half a mile down the slope. Or maybe further. It was hard to tell.

The road had become strange. It was flat and uncracked, although covered in spots with dirt and plants, as though it was the bones of the world peeking up through the brown and green flesh.

Ian shuddered at the image and tried to dismiss it from his mind, but it persisted.

For no reason that Ian could see, Hosea cleared his throat and asked Silvertop to stop.

"We go from here by ourselves," Hosea said, lowering himself to the road before helping Ian down.

God, he hurt. It took more for Ian to straighten his back than he thought he had in him.

Silvertop took a prancing step, and another of his snorts sent dirt and dust flying into the air.

"I thank you, old friend," Hosea said, his long fingers stroking the horse's muzzle gently, clearly out of affection rather than need. It would probably take a pickax to hurt Silvertop, and Ian wouldn't have wanted to bet that a pickax would do the job.

Upslope from him, the dark gray stones peeked out, like the tip of a jagged dagger pointing at the sky. "Tyr's Knife, it was once called," Hosea said. "And here is where we part ways, Silvertop."

The horse simply turned and galloped away, its massive hooves thundering on the road, clods of dirt and bits of grass and brush flying every which way.

Aesir horses, it seemed, weren't much for saying good-bye.

Hosea stretched mightily, then started loosening the thongs that held his gear on him; Ian did the same.

"So what now?"

"Now we rest for an hour or so." Hosea seated himself on the road surface, tailor-fashion, then spread his cloak out next to him and lay flat on his back. He made a palm-up gesture at Ian to do the same, which, after a hesitation, he did. *I mean, what am I expecting? A truck or an Aesir horse is going to come along and run me over?*

"And then?"

"And then we climb, and then make our way across a difficult saddle, and come in the back way, and hope that we're on time." He sat up. "There is one more thing, friend Ian," he said, slowly. "The sword you hold was made by me, and its edge cured and tempered in my blood; in your world, I could impart no other virtue to it than this: there is nothing that it can't kill."

"You want me to use it to defend you?" Ian shrugged. "I thought that's what I signed up for."

"No. That's not it at all. If all fails, if you believe I am about to be captured, I want, I need—" Hosea swallowed. "I need for you to use it to kill me." Hosea shook his head. "Promises come easier to your kind than to mine, so I'll not ask you to promise. I'll tell you that you'd find it more difficult to do than you think, but I swear to you that it must be done." Hosea leaned back on his cloak, wide eyes staring at the sky. "And perhaps it's about time that it be done, eh?"

CHAPTER TWENTY

Breakfast and a Challenge

Off in the distance, dishes clattered loudly enough that Torrie would have feared breakage, if they were his dishes.

Damn. He had wanted to wake before this, but—

Buts never bought you anything. He tossed aside his blankets and stood, then wrapped a linen towel around his waist and came out of his room to confront a Vestri setting out breakfast in front of the picture window.

As before, it reminded him more of a Neanderthal than anything he would have called a dwarf, but Torrie had never visualized a Neanderthal clean-shaven except for a ring of beard rimming its thick jawline, or with carefully clipped hair neatly combed and slicked back, or decked out in comfortable-looking taupe trousers and jacket with the crimson orange trim of the House of Flame.

"What do you think you're doing?" Torrie asked.

"Setting out breakfast, Honored One," the Vestri said, his voice slurred, as Vestri always spoke Bersmål. Something about the palate, perhaps? "As I have been instructed to," the Vestri went on, "by Jamed del Bruno. I am Broglin, at your service. Do the Honored Ones wish to be served in their rooms, or here in the parlor?"

Dad needed more time than this. "I'll—I'll see," Torrie said, walking back to his room. He leaned his head in. "Maggie, do you wish to break your fast now," he said in Bersmål, "or would you care to sleep some more?" he asked the rumpled bed, and then hummed low in his throat, hoping that Broglin would think it her mumbled response.

"Very well, as you wish," he said in Bersmål. "I shall wait, as well."

He smiled at the Vestri, who watched him without comment, his thick face blank, as Torrie crossed the hall to his parents' room and knocked a knuckle against their door, opening it as though he had heard something.

"Father, I—oh, very well. I'll see you later."

He turned to the Vestri. "They are all somewhat . . . indisposed this morning. Too much of your fine Ingarian wine, I suspect."

Broglin nodded his massive head, as though understanding. "I am sure that is so, Honored One. I am familiar with a concoction of herbs, milk, brandy, and plover eggs that seems to work well in such matters; shall I prepare some?"

Torrie nodded. "That would perhaps be a good idea, for when they awake. I would guess that would be late this afternoon, and would have them sleep until then."

"I will return with it then, Honored One," the Vestri said, shuffling toward the door. Torrie stepped aside to let him pass.

So far, so good.

There was a knock on the door; Broglin opened it to reveal Branden del Branden, looking all too fresh and clean in white linen shorts and tunic, his cape-of-station only a token one also of white linen, barely larger than a dish-towel, thrown casually over one shoulder, his heavy low boots and plain swordbelt a jarring contrast.

"Good morning, Thorian del Thorian the Younger," he

said. "His Warmth would have company as he breaks his fast this hour; he's sent me by to offer your father the honor of joining him, should he be up and about."

Torrie could hear his own heart pound. Damn, damn, damn—caught already. And without a way to delay for even another—

"I grovel," Broglin said, bending his head at the neck. "I abase myself in shame," he said. "Disgracefully, I have already fed Thorian del Thorian the Elder, his woman and girlchild; they have returned to their beds, a cure for the drinker's malaise making them sleep, albeit fitfully. I prostrate myself, I—"

"Silence, Vestri," Branden del Branden said, not unkindly. "Enough. I guess I'll have to disappoint His Warmth, though I don't care to do that. I can't imagine he'd want a drugged Thorian del Thorian for company."

Never look a gift horse in the mouth, Torrie thought.

Pulse still pounding like a trip-hammer, Torrie arched an eyebrow. "Did he ask for Thorian del Thorian the Elder, or just Thorian del Thorian?"

Branden del Branden smiled. "The latter, I'm amused to admit. I assumed, but—"

"But nothing. I just happen to be Thorian del Thorian." Torrie tossed his towel aside, quickly donning the clothes that the Vestri was already handing him. He hopped on one foot, then another, as he pulled on a pair of tan linen trousers, then shrugged into a loose white tunic that fell to his thighs. He plopped down on a chair to pull on his boots, but Broglin was already kneeling in front of him with a pair of socks. The Vestri's blunt fingers were surprisingly adept as he quickly slid the socks and boots on Torrie, blousing the trousers with gentle tugs of his fingers.

Torrie stood, accepting his swordbelt and buckling it around his waist. "I'll be pleased to join His Warmth at table; I missed the serving here. I . . . need to handle something, then I shall join you."

"Eh? I'm to bring—"

"I need to go to the place where even dukes walk."

It took a moment. "Ah. The garderobe is—"

"I know where it is," Torrie said, stepping forward. The hall was narrow enough that Branden del Branden had no choice but to back up.

Torrie turned to shut the door behind him; the Vestri was already there. "Be thou well, friend of the Father of Vestri, he who was Father of the Folk, until we meet again," the dwarf said in a low, guttural language that Torrie had never heard before.

"Until again we meet, friend of this friend," Torrie responded in the same language, "well be thou."

Branden del Branden was impressed. "You speak Vestri, too, eh? How did that come to be?"

One thing that was clear was that Branden del Branden didn't speak Vestri.

"You should have attended Hardwood High," Torrie said.

"Apparently." He dismissed the idea with a shrug. "Still, what benefit is there of learning Vestri, when they can be taught Bersmål?"

"I couldn't say," Torrie said, precisely.

On pleasant days, Branden del Branden explained, His Warmth breakfasted on a small veranda outside his private office.

It was a warm and clear day; high above and to the east, a flock of birds was making its way north to south, broad wings beating slowly, lazily, as though to rush neither themselves nor the day. Further to the east, cottony puffs of clouds hid the distant peaks, casting dark shadows on the greens and browns of the valley below. It was clear enough that Torrie could even make out the distant shape of a peasant and his oxen working their fields, and they must have been a good ten miles away.

"A good morning to you, Thorian del Thorian," His Warmth rumbled, his face showing no surprise at Torrie's presence. "Join me, if it pleases you," he said, waving Torrie to the seat opposite his bulk, another flick of his wrist urging Branden del Branden to the seat next to him. His overtunic had been constructed of leather straps, loosely woven and edged in gold, revealing a glistening white shirt beneath. It looked uncomfortable, but Torrie doubted that it was; the Fire Duke would hardly put himself to any trouble.

It couldn't even be very functional, given the spaces between the leather straps. Torrie wondered what would happen if he simply drew his sword and lunged, but His Warmth shifted slightly in his chair—as though preparing or prepared for that? No, but still he would have thought about it.

Torrie sat.

The table had been set for five, but there was enough food for ten gluttons. The centerpiece was a small pyramid consisting of ten of what Torrie would have called Rock Cornish game hens—small chickens, each with its skin roasted to a perfect brown. The platter was rimmed with a dark rainbow of sliced meats and cheeses, from a dark, almost black, paté through brown meats and darkly yellow cheeses, occasionally interlaced with slices of red onion so thin as to be almost transparent.

Near a squat teapot, another platter held the smoked fishes. Torrie was certain that the orange stuff was smoked salmon, but he wouldn't have wanted to bet on the identity of the thin, almost translucent slices of some white fish, and wouldn't have even bet that it was a fish if the centerpiece of the gray platter wasn't a trio of fish heads standing on end, sliced so cleanly and artfully that it looked like they were leaping out of the platter, itself the color of a lake on a stormy day.

His Warmth gestured, and Jamed del Bruno emerged

from a dark entrance, a crystal carafe on a silver salver balanced squarely on the palm of his hand. Jamed del Bruno, his long, bony face impassive as a surgeon's, filled Torrie's goblet with a quick, practiced splash of the darkly purple liquid that left the goblet full, but didn't so much as spill a drop on the tablecloth. He bowed stiffly, and repeated the performance with Branden del Branden.

"A fairly modest wine, from Wind Naravia, but enough of an earthy tone to do justice to a Stone Moranian, I think," the Fire Duke said, lowering his own goblet so that Jamed del Bruno could refill it. He took another polite sip. "Please."

Torrie sipped. Not bad, although Torrie was no wine expert. There was a dark sweetness, like that of berries, but other than that, all he could say was that it was cold and tasted good.

"A naive little Naravian," Torrie said, "but I'm amused by its presumption."

His Warmth smiled. "Ah. A not uncommon reaction this morning, to a variety of things. I'm sorry your father is unwell. Actually, he was the guest I had in mind when issuing the invitation—welcome as you are, of course."

Torrie shrugged. "Sorry." He found a large prong on the table that he hoped was intended for the purpose, and helped himself to a chicken, tearing off a tiny drumstick rather than using the two-pronged fork and tiny, scalpel-like knife beside his plate.

Now *that* was good. Gamier than he was used to, but with a decided flavor to it.

Like all of this.

He should have been scared—anybody with half a brain and a quarter of an adrenal gland ought to be scared—but his heart wasn't racing, and his palms didn't sweat. He had been much more scared the first time he had tried to slip his hand into Heidi Bjerke's bra than he was sitting across the table from the Fire Duke.

The Fire Duke was frowning at him.

Torrie swallowed. "As long as you're burdened with me, Your Warmth, is there anything in particular you'd like to talk about?"

Branden del Branden cocked his head to one side. "I would think you'd want to be less informal with His Warmth."

"I have no objection to a small taste of informality. A small taste." His dark eyes had never left Torrie's. The Fire Duke's lips pressed together. "Word of your . . . escapade of last evening has reached me. I wonder if you're aware of what you have taken on."

Torrie patted the hilt of his sword. "I'm competent enough. Better, perhaps, than you would think."

"Oh." The Fire Duke could have meant anything or nothing. He quickly lowered his goblet. "I see that my other two guests are here."

The old man and Herolf made an odd couple as Jamed del Bruno ushered them onto the patio. Herolf: tall and hirsute, his hair his only clothing, his teeth a trifle too pointed as he smiled; a mane of hair still wet from a morning bath, or perhaps a swim. He flopped down into a chair and reached out long-fingered hands for a chicken, tearing into it with his sharp teeth and a low growl. "Good chicken," he said, his mouth full, "but I prefer it with some blood still in it."

The other stood, waiting. He was an old man, gray-bearded and gray-haired, his shoulders perhaps a trifle too straight, his white linens loose on his bony frame. He was slim but not terribly so, and he moved as though every step was painful, but from a pain that would have to be ignored.

His face was bony and angular at the cheekbone and the back of his jaw, his beard short and pointed, his nose thin and aquiline. While his left eye stared out from beneath heavy gray brows, his right eye was covered with a patch of the same fabric as his white linen tunic, secured with a thin leather strap that ran back through his dull gray hair.

If there was a color other than black, white, or gray on his person, Torrie decided it would have to be his underwear.

The old man hooked his thumb in his swordbelt, but there was nothing of bravado or threat in the motion; it was more like he was trying to support himself on himself. Too stubborn to lean on something or somebody else; too proud or polite to sit until invited. There was something familiar about him, although Torrie couldn't have sworn what it was.

"Thorian del Thorian," the Fire Duke said, "I have the honor to present Thorian del Orvald, the duelmaster."

"Thorian del Thorian the Younger," the old man said, nodding. "Son of Thorian del Thorian, so I understand."

"I would have introduced you last night, Thorian del Thorian," Branden del Branden said, "but your party left the reception long before the duelmaster was to arrive."

"No matter," Thorian del Orvald said. "I was tired from my journey, and I'm a patient man." He served himself a few slices of smoked fish, a quick plop of some mustard-yellow sauce he spooned from a ramekin, and added an already peeled orange. "I had thought we would be seeing your father this morning."

"He's in bed, recovering from an excess of the local wine last night."

"Pity. He was not so careless in his habits in the old days." The old man declined Jamed del Bruno's offer of wine with a wave of his hand. "Stream water, if you please." Jamed del Bruno inclined his head, returned in a moment with a crystal water pitcher, and repeated the fill-with-a-splash that had impressed Torrie the first time.

Thorian del Orvald picked up his bone-and-silver eating prong and carefully cut off a tiny piece of smoked fish, conveying it to his dry lips carefully. He chewed and swallowed even more carefully, as though everything he did in life was so significant and important that each detail must command his full attention.

"I take it you know my father from before," Torrie said.

Herolf laughed. Torrie didn't like the laugh, but then again he didn't much like Herolf. Not that there was a lot to do about it.

Then again: "Herolf," he asked, "are you subject to challenge? Or are you dogs beneath it?"

Herolf smiled, if that rictus could be called a smile. There was a low growl in his throat.

Torrie slid his chair back from the table. The move was obvious: at Herolf's first twitch, Torrie would backhand his wine goblet toward Herolf, kick out against Branden del Branden's chair both to put Branden del Branden off balance and to slide his own chair away from the table, and use the distraction as an opportunity to get his sword in his hand. Herolf hadn't paid attention to the sword before Torrie's duel; he didn't know who made it. Torrie was willing to bet that any sword Uncle Hosea had made would be able to kill a Son, or maybe more than a Son.

"Be still, Herolf," the Fire Duke said, shortly, sharply. "Your incessant growling is disturbing the tranquillity of my breakfast."

Yeah, doggie, down when your master speaks.

He turned to Torrie. "Still, I understand the . . . temptation of Herolf's. And his disappointment. He was looking forward to witnessing a reunion of sorts this morning, as was I." The Fire Duke sipped at his wine, then used his eating prong to convey a palm-sized piece of smoked fish to his cavernous mouth. Two quick chews and it was gone. "Understandable, no?"

Torrie shrugged. "So my father used to work for this duelists' guild—"

"He was a member of our body," Thorian del Orvald

said, quietly, "sworn with blood, fire, and semen to be faithful to the body, which he betrayed."

"Uncle Hosea was held in a pit here—for how many years? Bound and tortured for how long?"

The Fire Duke shook his head. "Apparently not long enough. There is much I would have known."

And would still know. Torrie didn't let even a trace of a smile show on his face, and he wasn't sure whether it should have been a smile or a look of horror. This wasn't about Dad, it wasn't about him at all. That was a sideshow. Maggie and Mom had been bait for Torrie and Dad; Torrie and Dad were bait for Uncle Hosea. This wasn't about getting the Fire Duke a willing champion, or about playing politics with the other Houses. It was about getting hold of Uncle Hosea and a handle with which to control him.

So it wouldn't work.

The Fire Duke wouldn't call off his dogs in return for a promise of Torrie's services; that wasn't what he was after. Torrie was like . . . like the film canisters filled with cotton, then doused in doe urine, that they used to bring deer into range: just bait for the real game.

There was only one thing for the bait to do: disappear. With Dad and Mom gone and Torrie dead, there would be nothing to draw Uncle Hosea here.

Disappearing was, of course, easier to desire than to do.

Short of taking a running start and diving headfirst over the balcony, smashing himself on the pavement far below before anybody could stop him, Torrie didn't have any idea of how he could remove himself as bait.

And, besides, killing himself probably wouldn't work. The Fire Duke could probably keep the secret for a long time, certainly long enough to trap Uncle Hosea.

Jamed del Bruno had returned, a thin piece of parchment pinned to his salver with a smooth stone. "Adjutant Eldren del Eldren has a report for you, Your Warmth."

The Fire Duke folded his hands across his ample belly. "I would take it that you've already read it."

"Yes, Your Warmth; it was unsealed."

"Not that that would have stopped you. Very well: its import?"

"Thorian del Thorian the Senior, his wife, and his son's companion, known as the Exquisite Maggie, have escaped their rooms by a secret way."

Torrie would have said something, but Thorian del Orvald's hand was on his arm. "Be still, be still. There's nothing you can do at this point, and little point in flailing about to no purpose."

Branden del Branden muttered an oath as he crumpled his napkin and tossed it to one side.

The Fire Duke smiled. "Ah. I knew there was a secret way from that suite; perhaps now they can be prevailed upon to disclose it, when the Sons drag them back." His smile was as wolfish as Herolf's. "There are three possible Ways that might connect with the tower; I took the liberty of having Herolf hide a pair of Sons in a known abditory in each of them." His smile broadened. "Known to me, that is."

"Yes, Your Warmth," Jamed del Bruno said. "That is the other part of the message. Eldren del Eldren reports that two of the pairs have seen nothing, and await orders, and the third . . ."

"Well, yes, out with it!"

"The third pair lies dead on the floor of the tunnel." Jamed del Bruno examined the letter again. "Ah, yes: 'There is rather a lot of blood about, Your Warmth, but all of it appears to be theirs. The dead Sons', that is.' "

Thorian del Orvald's face held just the hint of a smile. "I would have thought my son could take on a pair of them, given the tools; I am surprised he was able to come upon them by stealth."

"Stealth?" Herolf practically hissed.

"Oh, yes," Thorian del Orvald said. "Stealth. They would surely have raised an alarm otherwise." He sat back in his chair, picked up his knife and prong, and resumed his meal.

Torrie kept a grin to himself. Trust these people to underestimate Mom and Maggie, as the Sons probably had. Mom was an old country girl, and while these days she bought her meat at the butcher's, she was just as capable of neatly slitting a pig's throat as Grandma had been. And Maggie was not in Torrie's or Ian's league as a fencer—she hadn't been at it as long—but her form was good, and he could imagine the surprise on the face of one of the hairy bastards as she neatly slipped the point past outstretched claws or sharp teeth to plunge into—

Waitaminute. *My son?* Torrie turned to the old man.

Thorian del Orvald nodded. "I'm your grandfather, young Thorian," he said gently, almost affectionately. "Your grandmother would like to meet you sometime. She lives in a village some days' walk from here; I join her when and as I can." He examined the food on his plate carefully, then pronged a small piece of meat and conveyed it to his mouth, chewing thoroughly before swallowing. "Of course, it would seem unlikely you will have the chance, all things considered." He daubed a napkin against the corners of his mouth. "Your Warmth, I take it you would like to have Thorian del Thorian the Younger challenged for offense given?"

"Please."

"The offense?"

The Fire Duke pursed his lips. "Oh, let's call it a conspiracy to elude my justice, in his aiding his father's escape."

"Very well." Thorian del Orvald turned to Torrie. "Do you deny involvement in such a conspiracy?" His voice was casual, but there was a ring of formality in his tone.

"And what if I don't?"

"Then His Warmth will sentence you, appropriately." His lips pursed to a thin line. "I would not advise you to put yourself so in his hands."

"My other choice? If I deny involvement?"

"Then His Warmth will provide a challenger to accuse you in the amphitheater, for you or your champion to prove him true or false with your body and arm."

"How about if I admit doing it, but say it's no crime?"

Thorian del Orvald shrugged. "As you will, and call it a denial or an admission, as you will. The results are exactly the same."

It didn't matter. Torrie and Maggie had faked not liking each other, but nothing useful had come of that, just as nothing useful would come of denying his involvement with the escape. Much better to have Mom, Dad, and Maggie gone than to try to persuade the Fire Duke that he didn't care about them.

So Torrie forced a smile. "Then I'll admit it, and say it's no crime to help my father, my mother, and my companion escape from His Warmth's perversion of justice."

He didn't get a rise from anybody for that.

Thorian del Orvald turned to the Fire Duke. "I assume it's to the death?"

Thorian del Orvald either didn't know, or didn't get it. Torrie was the bait; the Fire Duke wouldn't order him killed openly—not if he wanted to use Torrie to lure Uncle Hosea into range.

"Quite." The Fire Duke nodded. "Repeatedly, if necessary—"

What?

"—the first bout, say, this evening?" He turned back to Torrie. "What appears to be the problem, Thorian del Thorian? Does the food not agree with you?"

"It agrees with me just fine, Your Warmth," Torrie said. "Who are you sending up against me?" He gripped the hilt of his sword and rose, slowly. "Perhaps your good self?"

At his movement, two archers appeared on the battlements above, arrows nocked and fully drawn.

It didn't matter how fast Torrie was. Even if Herolf or Branden del Branden couldn't stop him—and he was none too sure of that—he wouldn't reach the Fire Duke with the tip of his blade before being shot, and probably by more than the two bowmen he could see. The entrance to the Fire Duke's private office was dark, and there were probably more there.

But he might have tried if Thorian del Orvald, moving far more quickly than a man his age had any business moving, hadn't pushed back from the table and taken a position blocking him. "No, Thorian del Thorian the Younger, you'll not face His Warmth here; you'll face his champion in the amphitheater, tomorrow. And then another, if necessary." His eyes didn't leave Torrie's as he spoke to the Fire Duke. "Your Warmth, who would you like as your champion?"

The Fire Duke waved it away. "Any senior duelist will do, Thorian del Orvald."

"Stanar del Brunden is certainly available; I'll see if he's willing."

"You may tell him that twice his usual fee, as well as augmentation to an already fine reputation, will await him if he wins; another duel will await Thorian del Thorian the Younger otherwise." The Fire Duke turned to Herolf. "On another matter: there is a map in my office, and—"

"I remember the way from last time," Herolf said, with a growl. "I'll want another half dozen Sons with me."

"Make it a dozen. Bring back trophies, only. I'll not need to see them again."

Herolf grinned. "You don't mind if we play with them a little first? The women might be amusing, and none of my bitches are in heat at the moment."

The Fire Duke *tsk*ed. "Didn't the bitch who bore you tell you not to play with your food?" He waved it away.

"As you wish." The Fire Duke gestured to Jamed del Bruno, a flip of his thick hand. "Make it so: admit a dozen Sons to the Gold Suite. Blindfolds for all—I don't need to share the secret of the entrance with them, as of yet." He waved Torrie to a seat. "Sit, sit, sit, Thorian del Thorian the Younger. There's no need to rush your breakfast."

Torrie sat down, hoping that he showed no trace of panic on his face.

None of this made sense. If the Fire Duke had decided to try and have Mom, Dad, and Maggie killed, then Torrie wasn't expendable, but yet he had set Torrie up to be killed. But the whole family was bait for Uncle Hosea, unless Torrie was dead wrong.

It didn't make sense.

Well, to hell with it. As soon as they got him back to his room—assuming that they let him back to his room—it was time to get out the Paratool, open the secret door, and get the hell out of town.

In the meantime, best to simulate a lot of interest in the upcoming duel.

Torrie reached out a hand and picked up his eating prong; he speared a piece of smoked fish and conveyed it to his mouth. He chewed and swallowed without tasting, and then picked up his wine glass, proud that the surface didn't quiver.

"No need to rush at all, Your Warmth," Torrie said, keeping his voice low and level. "I trust I'll be allowed some time to work out today?" He worked his shoulders beneath his tunic. "I'm a bit out of practice."

The Fire Duke nodded. "Of course. Would you care to name a second?"

"I'll want three, if that's not too much trouble."

"It's two more than traditional, but no trouble at all, I assure you."

"I choose Ivar del Hival, Branden del Branden, and my grandfather."

Branden del Branden's eyes went wide, while Thorian del Orvald nodded, slightly. Approving? It was hard to tell.

The Fire Duke made a face. "The duelmaster is normally exempt from such things, but—have it your way."

The guards took up positions outside the door to his room. "Food will be brought at your desire, Thorian del Thorian," the senior said. "In the interim, we wish you a good rest."

The door shut, followed by the thunk of a crossbar being dropped into place.

His Paratool was still on the bed. Time to leave.

It couldn't be easy, but at least he would have a chance—

No.

Where the hole in the wall was supposed to be was a pinprick glint of metal. Torrie tried to push the plug away with the Paratool, but it didn't move.

He sat down on the bed and began to shake.

A long time later, Torrie raised his head from his hands.

So fucking be it. He would handle it.

He was Torrie Thorsen, dammit, son of Karin and Thorian Thorsen, grandson of Tom and Eva Roelke, and apparently of Thorian del Orvald and some grandmotherly type he would never meet. He was a son of Hardwood, North Dakota, neighbor of the likes of Arnie and Ephie Selmo, and if Ephie could carry herself with grace, dignity, and good humor while cancer ate her vitals out, piece by piece, her last days, and if Arnie could dash off into the night to help a neighbor, by God Torrie could stand up and take what was coming.

His sword lay on the bed beside him. Uncle Hosea had made it himself, and with his hand gripping it, it became an extension of his arm.

And it wasn't just the sword, either. Dad and Uncle Hosea had made him into a weapon the likes of which these people maybe had yet to see.

So I'll give them a show. He banged on the door with his fist. "Open," he said, imperiously.

There was a click as the bar was slid back; the door opened just a crack. "Yes, Thorian del Thorian the Younger?"

"I've been promised some time in a dueling studio," he said. "I need to prepare for this evening. Lead me there."

The guard nodded. "As you wish."

CHAPTER TWENTY-ONE

Tunnels

His lungs burning with a distant fire, his fingers almost numb from the pain, Ian Silverstein pulled himself up to the rocky ledge and stretched out on its stone surface like a lizard in the sun.

He could hear Hosea's labored breathing in counterpoint to his own gasping, but it would have taken more than he had to lift his head and see to the older man.

Crossing the rocky saddle from Tyr's Knife to the back face of the mountain that was Falias had been hard enough; climbing straight up had been worse.

The stone should have been faulted in a hundred thousand places where heat and cold cycles had created tiny cavities for water to do its work, with more heat and cold cycles to enlarge them until plant life had gotten enough of a hold to take over from there, but cracks in the stone were few and far between, and even then, even when filled with mosses and tiny ivies, were far more regular than they should have been.

But they were enough for Hosea, climbing ahead of Ian, to lodge a spike every now and then, and they and the spikes were enough support for Ian as he used the climbing rope where his fingers and toes couldn't find enough purchase. The whole thing felt strange, more like the climbing wall Midwest Sports had set up behind their three-story brick building than any real rock face Ian was familiar with, and Hosea had scooted up it, moving back and forth across the face as he did, as though he had the map of a reliable route in his head.

As he probably did.

Ian finally forced himself to raise his head. A couple of feet from him, Hosea lay on the hot stones. His formerly white tunic was filthy, and sweatstained at the armpits, the stains surrounded by a halo of salt. The fingers of his outstretched hand were cracked at the nails, and bleeding from a hundred cuts, but somehow or other he managed to get a long, thin arm underneath him, and lever himself to a sitting position, his back against the stone, and open his rucksack, producing a water skin. He reached out gentle fingers and helped Ian to a sitting position before uncorking the water skin.

The water was too hot, and there was some funny taste of cedar and perhaps of mouse in it, but it was the best thing Ian had ever had to drink.

The saddle from Tyr's Knife was below and to the east, somewhere; below, the valley spread out, like a green and brown and golden banquet, just out of reach. Ian could almost feel the cool breezes as he baked on the hot rock, and he could have sworn that the hot wind brought scents of flowers and sunbaked grasses to his painful nostrils.

Two ravens wheeled through the sky high above. They could have been just any two birds, but Ian wouldn't have been surprised if they turned out to be Hugin and Munin.

Hosea leaned his head against the rock. His face was paler than it had been, and dusty where it wasn't caked with accumulated dirt and sweat. He looked like death warmed over, if just barely warmed over.

Ian handed him back the water skin, and Hosea, his long, thin fingers trembling, managed to bring it up and to his mouth and tilt it back, his strangely smooth throat working spasmodically as he swallowed. It seemed to restore some of his strength: his breathing became less ragged, and his stare less glassy.

"How are you?" Hosea croaked out.

Ian was too tired to shrug. *Half a dozen stitches, a tetanus immunization, two thick steaks, an apple pie, and three or four days of bed rest and I'll be okay.* "A few days bed rest," he got out with difficulty, "and I'll be fine." He didn't ask how much further they had to go; he didn't want to know, and in any case, he wasn't ready for it.

"Don't have enough time for that," Hosea said. "Ever since I . . . started the glow, it's accelerated things. We made good time, but they will be ready for us, or at least, readier than they ought to be."

He closed his eyes for a moment, and sagged back against the rock. His breathing slowed, and the ragged pulse in his neck did, as well. When he opened his eyes, his gaze was steady, not glassy. "That's the best that can be done for me, but let's see to you," he said, his voice more slurred than it usually was, but not as weak as it had been.

"Why not try the same thing with me? I don't mind a bit of magic."

Hosea shook his head. "It's nothing of the sort. Just a little buddha's trick."

"You mean 'Buddhist'."

"Whatever." Hosea was already fumbling in his pack. "Just a matter of moving the pain and discomfort to a single point on my body, then pushing it outside. Think of it as self-hypnosis, if you'd like, but it lets me draw on the body's reserves almost directly."

"Think you could . . . teach it to me?"

Hosea nodded. "Almost certainly. Given, perhaps, ten years."

"And if I promise to work really hard?" Ian grinned.

"Twenty years, then. Maybe fifty. Ah." He extracted a small leather drawstring sack from Ian's rucksack, and pushed its mouth open, and pulled out what looked like . . .

Like a long turd. "What is that?"

Hosea sniffed at it. "An apple sausage, apparently," Hosea said. "A gift from Freya. There are perhaps two dozen of them." He crawled over and, drawing his knife, cut off a small piece. "Eat."

No chicken soup. Ian didn't need an apple sausage; he needed rest and medicine. "Hosea, this isn't going to—"

"Eat."

It was all brown and horrible looking, but when Ian took a tentative sniff, it smelled exactly like one of Freya's hot apple pies, fresh from the oven. If he hadn't known it was cold, he would have expected it to be filled with hot apples, melting in the sugar and cinnamon as they baked, the edges of the almost liquid pieces crisp but tender.

He took the piece in his mouth, and if anything, it tasted better than it smelled. The sweetness and pungency of the apple was there, supported by waves of sweetness and cinnamon that made his mouth water, but with a tart tang underneath that both made him want to keep the taste in his mouth forever and also made him chew quickly, and swallow.

He took another bite, and then another, and then opened his eyes to see Hosea offering him the stubby end of the apple sausage.

Ian had done some generous things in his life, but nothing more so than when he opened his mouth and said, "You have some of it."

Hosea shook his head and dropped the last piece into Ian's hand. "It won't work on me."

"Work?" It wouldn't taste that good? It wouldn't—

Waitaminute.

He didn't hurt anymore. He wasn't slumped painfully on a stone ledge, barely able to move, his shoulders burning as though somebody had stuck hot wires in them, his head pounding, his fingers bleeding . . .

His fingers weren't even bleeding. The cuts had scabbed over thoroughly, so thoroughly that when he rubbed a dirty, cracked nail against one of the longer ones, it hurt in the gentle, reassuring way that pushing on a scab that was about to fall off hurt, not with the tender, deep aching he would have gotten from touching a fresh wound.

He took the last piece in his mouth and chewed it slowly before swallowing.

Ian got his feet underneath him with no difficulty at all, then helped Hosea to his feet. "Is there something I should know?" His voice wasn't the ragged croak it had been.

If anything, it was stronger than usual.

He felt like he could wrestle his weight in Sons, although that was probably wrong by a factor of about ten.

Hosea smiled. "Many things, Ian Silverstein. For now, leave it that Idunn's orchard grows in several places, tended by a select few of the Eldest, and shared only rarely." He tilted his head to one side. "I would have thought you more observant. The morning after you dragged me down to Harbard's Landing, you didn't notice how quickly you recovered?"

Ian shrugged. "I always have healed fast, but this—" he stopped himself. "Later, perhaps—you said we're in a hurry." He looked up the slope. Maybe twenty feet overhead, an overhang blocked Ian's view. "Let's get to climbing."

"That won't be necessary." Hosea shook his head.

"Oh?"

Hosea's fingers stroked the rock face for a moment, searching. Then: a press, a click, and a ragged door opened into darkness. "This way," he said.

Ian followed him, with one backwards glance to the sky. Both ravens had banked out of their circle and headed south, their huge wings flapping slowly.

Well, Harbard would know what had happened to them so far. Of course, it was what was going to happen next that was important.

Ian wasn't at all sure he was going to like it.

Ian had never had much of a sense of direction, but he was sure they had worked their way far inwards from the entrance to the ductwork where he and Hosea crouched. The entrance tunnel had terminated in a sideways T; one shaft, footholds carved into its surface, led up. Whispering so quietly that he had to put his lips to Ian's ear, Hosea had admonished him never to take that one, as the way gradually led to what Hosea called a mousetrap.

The other shaft, sides polished smooth, became a slide that twisted down and in, and dumped them off in a small circular room, lit by reflected light from somewhere up above. Hosea had reached up to the ceiling and manipulated a carving; the ceiling swung down and became a set of stairs that led up to another tunnel, to a crawlway that narrowed until Ian had to take off his pack and push it ahead of him as he crawled on his belly, getting stuck for a moment on a rise in the floor, feeling the weight of the whole City pressing down on him, suppressing the waves of panic, forcing himself to breathe out, out, out, until his chest narrowed enough that his toes could find purchase to push him through; climbing, and crawling, and sliding, and creeping, feeling like a rat in the walls of a god's house, until a hidden door dumped him out onto what felt like an honest-to-God airshaft, to follow Hosea along on hands and knees, toward where light splashed onto the floor of the airshaft.

Hosea held a long finger in front of his lips as he crouched in front of a latticework. Directly beneath him was what looked like an empty opera box, overlooking a sandy arena.

A gentle breeze blew in through the latticework, bringing him vague smells of distant perfumes, and something peaty that he couldn't quite identify, while the sounds of an excited crowd babbling to itself filled his ears.

And below, on the floor of the arena, Torrie, stripped to shorts and sandals, accompanied by three men, faced off against a pair of swordsmen.

Hosea looked at Ian. *Now it comes*, he said, his mouth moving silently. *Do you trust me? Can you trust me?*

With what, dammit? he mouthed back. *You've deliberately not told me what this is all about, and you're not telling me anything* now.

True enough, Ian Silverstone, Hosea said. *But can you trust me now, to follow my lead, to do as you're told, knowing that the risk is great, but the rewards real?*

And if I can't trust you?

Hosea held out the leather bag that contained the rest of the apple sausages Freya had prepared.

Do you trust her?

Hosea dumped out a pile of apple sausages, setting them carefully aside, then pulled out the sole remaining contents of the package: a small object, wrapped in silken cloth. Hosea placed it in Ian's hand.

His fingers trembling, Ian unwrapped it.

It was a small wooden carving, that was all. But it was of a fencer in sixte, his face covered by a mesh mask.

Hosea fitted a miniature sword into the fencer's hand. No, not sword—it was a foil, the blade a slim sliver of flexible steel. And the fencer—he was too skinny, really, although that was masked in part by the fullness of his fencing tunic and the short trous—

Ohgod. It's me.

Do you trust her? Hosea mouthed. *Do you accept that Freya wishes you well, and has told you to be yourself, to be what you are—*

There's a lot you aren't telling me, Ian said.

I'll tell you this, Hosea said. *There's to be confrontation here, and you are the last, best chance of winning it. Not Torrie, not me. You.*

You're not worth much, are you? his father said in the back of Ian's head. *The old man doesn't know shit, or he wouldn't be relying on you. Probably doesn't. Probably going to sacrifice you in some sort of squeeze play. Probably all you're worth.*

Do it now, Ian thought, then said: "Do it now." There was no point in whispering, not anymore.

And by God that felt good.

Hosea gestured toward the latticework. "I'll be with you in but a moment."

A couple of faces below had turned up, staring wide-eyed at the grillwork; Ian set his back against the side of the duct, and kicked out hard once, twice, three times.

The metal grillwork squealed in protest, then snapped, and fell away.

Thousands of eyes were on Ian Silverstein as he dropped lightly to the floor of the box below.

CHAPTER TWENTY-TWO

The Duelist

Torrie had just finished his stretches when the other three showed up.

The wheel-shaped fencing studio was high in one of the towers—it was a slice right through the tower, entered and exited by the central spiral staircase. Underneath the thin rattan matting that covered the floor, there were almost certainly secret entrances to one or more of the sets of tunnels that honeycombed the City, but they were under the matting and Torrie wasn't, and the occasional visits from the guards posted on the floors above and below were more than enough to prevent any extended searching.

Sunlight streamed in through the barred windows on the sunny side, while the windows opposite had been shuttered, perhaps to keep the wind from blowing too hard. He could have opened them, but he didn't. That would be the last thing Torrie would need, to work up a sweat and then get his muscles all stiff and slow from a cold wind.

He reracked the practice sword he had been using, and dropped to the mat for another series of stretches, trying to keep himself patient. There was nothing he could do for Mom, Dad, and Maggie here and now, and if he didn't win tonight, there would be nothing he could do for anybody.

So he pasted a calm expression on his face.

His workout had been just enough to loosen his muscles and warm them, not long enough to tire himself. That was the trick of a prematch workout, after all, whether the reward was a mass-produced trophy or getting to breathe for another day: make it long enough to warm you, but not long enough to tire you.

This was different, though. A tournament was a series of bouts, each one of which would last only minutes, with plenty of time if you won to consider your next bout, and maybe to check out your next opponent; if you lost, even more time to watch the others, look for a telltale habit or weakness.

There would be none of that today, which was why Torrie had asked Thorian del Orvald to be one of his seconds.

His three seconds arrived in company: Thorian del Orvald, moving painfully but precisely, dressed in gray and black, his eyepatch still the same white linen it had been this morning; Ivar del Hival, a big bear of a man, his large chest and larger belly encased in a brown and green tunic, buckled tightly at the waist with his swordbelt; and Branden del Branden, trim form and freshly trimmed beard, a light tan overtunic covering an almost impossibly white, blousy shirt.

Torrie stood. "Thank you all for coming."

Thorian del Orvald smiled precisely as he leaned against a rattan-shrouded pillar, trying to look casual, rather than in pain. "What is it that you wish of me, Thorian del Thorian the Younger?"

"Well, for one thing," Torrie said, "I'd like you to call me Torrie, like my grand—like my other grandfather does. Like everybody else does."

Again, a precise smile that spoke of amusement, if only a little, and of self-control, as much as would be required.

"Agreed, certainly, Torrie. And this, perhaps, is why you chose me?" The smile didn't quite broaden as much as it seemed to become more sincere.

"No." Torrie shook his head. "I'd like your help. I won't have the chance to"—there wasn't a Bersmål word for "scout"—"to analyze the techniques of Stanar del Brunden. Does he have any preferences, habits, mistakes I might take advantage of?"

The duelmaster shook his head. "No, nothing of the sort. Oh," he said, with a precise flick of his hand, "perhaps he thinks a trifle more strategically than tactically, but he's no more likely to be brought down by a simple feint-high-and-outside-then-lunge-low-and-inside than he is by a Carpacian Attack." He stroked his beard with two fingers. "He's absolutely mechanical in a first-blood bout—I've never seen him go for a body touch when an arm or leg touch was available—and opportunistic in moderated affairs." The bony shoulders moved up and down, once. "I've not seen him in a death battle; such things are, despite your circumstances, rare. There are young peasant boys who have played with sticks and think themselves swordsmen trying to challenge themselves into what they admiringly call the House of Steel all the time, but it's been more than a dozen years since one was good enough or obnoxious enough to put a guildsman to the trouble of actually killing him."

Ivar del Hival whistled through his teeth. "I've sparred with Stanar del Brunden, as I have with most guildsmen who have passed through here—"

The guildmaster smiled. "And rarely scored from them."

Ivar del Hival grunted. "I'm an ordinary of the House of Flame, with two peasant villages to supervise, and little enough time to try to find myself a new wife, much less spend endless hours sparring, as I used to with your son."

"Unfortunate. As it might be unfortunate for you to involve yourself in this matter." Thorian del Orvald touched a fingertip to an earlobe, then to the corner of his good eye. It could have been accidental, or it could have meant that Ivar del Hival should be concerned about being overheard or even seen.

"Pfah. I'm not worried. And if we be overheard, let them hear that I'm unworried." Ivar del Hival turned to Torrie. "His Warmth's feelings about it don't need to concern either His Warmth or me. My family has been loyal to the House of Fire as long as fire has burned; I can still second an old friend's son, and am honored to have been asked." His bow was formal; Torrie returned it with one equally formal, equally stiff.

"What I don't understand," Branden del Branden said, "is why me?"

Torrie blinked. Branden del Branden's face was perhaps a shade paler than it had been, and there was a bead of perspiration on his face, just above his mustache.

He was scared. He was trying to act somewhere between irritated and insouciant, but he was scared.

Why would he be scared? Unless—

Torrie shrugged. "Because I thought we might become friends, before the bout with Danar del Reginal, and because I did nothing to . . . betray that beginning friendship." Torrie took up a practice sword, and gave it a few tentative swings. "I was supposed to be killed—"

"Yes, yes, you've said that before, and—"

"And before," Torrie said, working it out aloud, knowing where it was leading, "I thought it was His Warmth. But how would the Fire Duke know that his dogs were going to capture not one Thorian del Thorian, but two? When would Danar del Reginal receive his commands from the Fire Duke? No; that doesn't make sense." He tossed the practice sword to Ivar del Hival, and accepted the sword that Uncle Hosea had made, the needle point nevertheless strong, the sharp edge cured in Uncle Hosea's own blood.

It wasn't Torrie's own sword—he had placed that in Maggie's hands, hoping that it would serve her well—but it would do.

Torrie raised it in salute. "I've been thinking about it, and trying to decide who would have a reason, and what that reason might be." He dropped the point of his sword. "Maggie is rather pretty, isn't she? And somewhat exotic, by local standards—the short hair, the slightly upturned nose, the sharpness of her chin and her wit—"

Branden del Branden's lips were almost white. "And what might you be suggesting?"

"I am suggesting," Torrie said, "that it would not be the first time that a man has killed for a lovely face, or suggested to a friend that he do so, playing down the sort of training that I could have gotten in the Newer World." Torrie sliced his blade through the air, tentatively, not looking Branden del Branden in the face. "Me dying would leave Maggie without a protector, and while her status is uncertain, her attractiveness is not. Her rank could be discussed later, with His Warmth; but in the interim, the only man interested in defending her honor or person would be my father, and he would be too busy, eh? If it turned out that her rank was insufficient, she could be dropped like a peasant girl; but if it was sufficient, if she was of high rank, well, then, an up-and-coming ordinary of the House of Flame could well find his stature increased by such a marriage."

"Be careful what you say, Thorian del Thorian," Branden del Branden said.

"Exquisitely, Branden del Branden," Torrie said. "Entirely. I wouldn't want to accuse somebody of something so dishonorable . . . unless I were sure, that is." He smiled. "I'm not even sure it was dishonorable. Danar del Reginal seemed eager enough to provoke me, and Maggie and I were trying to make it appear that we didn't get along, and that might persuade a decent man that she needed rescuing—"

"Ah." Thorian del Orvald nodded. "It seems you do have at least a vague sense of strategy, young Thorian del Thorian. With the Exquisite Maggie appearing to be of less value to you, she was less of a lever as a hostage." The duelmaster raised his eyebrow. "And what had you planned to make your mother seem less valuable?"

"I hadn't worked that out."

"Pity."

Branden del Branden had regained the self-control that had slipped for just a moment. "And so, you wished to have me as your second so that you could taunt me with vague accusations? And that is it?"

"No," Torrie said. "I wanted you as one of my seconds so we could make peace between the two of us." *I've few enough friends here, and the reason you're mad at me is because you have wronged me, and I want that over.*

One way or another.

"And if not?" Branden del Branden asked.

"If not," Torrie said, his sword in his hand, his feet placed properly, at right angles to each other, "there are four of us here. Pick your second, and pick up your sword, if you'll not accept my hand in friendship."

Branden del Branden was silent for a long time.

Torrie sheathed his sword with a snap, and held out his hand. "Take your pick, Branden del Branden."

Branden del Branden closed with a step and a half that could have been a lunge, and his hand closed on Torrie's forearm while Torrie's closed on his. His grip was strong, and his nod seemed genuine.

"You should be able to beat Stanar del Brunden," he said, releasing Torrie. "I've seen both of you fence—your wrist is definitely faster; I've seen its equal only rarely." He picked up a practice sword.

Thorian del Orvald raised an eyebrow. "An ordinary of the House of Flame paying more attention to a duelist than does the duelmaster? Will the wonders of this day never cease?"

"Please, Thorian del Orvald." Branden del Branden made a complicated gesture, part bow, part salute, part dismissal. "You are the duelmaster for the whole guild, and have little time to pay attention to your individual duelists. Stanar del Brunden is the favored duelist of His Solidity, and His Solidity often has disputes with His Warmth; for an ordinary of the House of Flame to pay attention to his strengths and weaknesses is unsurprising, if that ordinary has a lick of ambition."

"Ambition." Ivar del Hival grunted. "More than a lick, I'd wager," he said.

Branden del Branden picked up a practice sword. "His opening moves are often like this . . ."

Underneath some flowery essence, sprayed about with a heavy hand, the amphitheater smelled of death, Torrie thought, then decided he was being too dramatic.

Then again: he was about to fight a professional duelist to the death; perhaps he should allow himself a bit of drama.

But it didn't feel dramatic. It just felt scary, but underneath the fear, there was a feeling that Torrie recognized, a sensation of competency he felt whenever he walked onto a fencing strip; whenever he climbed up to a deer stand; whenever he put his foot in the stirrup, his hand on the saddlehorn, and lifted himself to Jessie's back: a sensation of this I can do; the doing of this doesn't just belong to me, but is part of me.

He smiled. He had once said something like that to Uncle Hosea before they went for a ride, and of course that was the time that Jessie had been startled by a woodchuck and threw him.

Torrie had stripped down to shorts and shoes; he gave a few tentative stretches before bending over to check his laces, not paying any attention to where Stanar del Brunden and his seconds waited, halfway across the amphitheater.

Keep it the same, he told himself. Yes, instead of cotton, the laces of his boots were of layered leather, stitched together by clever Vestri hands, but he fastened them with the same bow-and-knot. Yes, the match would end with blood on the floor, but it would depend on his eye and wrist, on the springiness of his thighs, and most importantly on his mind. Fencing was a sport of the mind, played out with the body. The mind had to be clear and unencumbered, calm as the surface of a quiet pond, ready to have the body react before it even knew what it was doing.

Thorian del Orvald eyed the edge of Torrie's sword with a practiced eye. "A fine weapon," he said, slipping a guard over the tip and bending it into a wide U—the old man was stronger than he looked.

He let it straighten and sighted down the blade again. "A fine one, indeed." He clapped a hand to Torrie's shoulder. "Fight well, young Thorian del Thorian; you seem to be a fine young man yourself, well-tempered and well-mannered; I would hope to have the chance to get to know you."

Torrie's mouth was dry; he couldn't quite force the smile he knew he should. "Thank you, Grandfather."

"Don't worry about him, about me, about anything," Ivar del Hival scowled, as he towered above Torrie. "Just keep your head about you, and take his."

Branden del Branden's jaw was set. "I've given you all that I can. Do well, friend," he said.

Torrie moved a few steps away from them, more aware of a strong urge to piss than anything else.

He raised his sword in salute—

* * *

There was the squealing of metal above, and something fell to the floor of the amphitheater. Somebody—Ian, by God!—crawled out of a hole in the wall above the box opposite His Warmth, and dropped first to the floor of the box, then to the floor of the amphitheater itself, taking up the shock easily with his long legs.

"Hey, Torrie," he called out in English, "the cavalry's here." He was dressed like a rich peasant—trousers bloused in his black boots, a plain bulky overshirt of dull taupe belted tightly at his waist, but it was belted with a swordbelt like Torrie's own.

Slapping at his trousers, Ian turned toward the large box, where His Warmth was already on his feet.

"My name is Ian Silverstein," he said in Bersmål, not translating his last name. He looked more comical than dignified as he stood with his skinny arms folded across his chest, "although most of you seem to want to call me Ian Silverstone. I am champion for Thorian Thorsen."

There were shouts and calls from the crowd.

The Fire Duke seemed amused as he spread his fingers on the brass rail surrounding his box and leaned forward. "I had not known he requested one, or required one, Ian Silverstone," he said, loudly. "Nor had I heard that you had prayed for admittance to the City."

Ian shrugged. "There's some hidden ways in and out of the City. I used one," he said, casually. "And if you'll just let my friend go, we can simply use it to leave."

The Fire Duke pursed his lips. "You don't seem as deferential as I am accustomed to, and I do not recall owing any favors to the House of Silverstone, if such a house there be. Why should I grant your request?"

Ian hesitated for a moment—

"Because that's been your whole purpose here, Your Warmth," Uncle Hosea said, lowering himself carefully from the ventilation duct to the floor of the box opposite the Fire Duke. "Because the prize you've long sought is here in me, and because that will be an additional stake in my friend Ian Silverstone's championing. For if he loses, I will put myself, and all that I know, in your hands, in return for the release of young Thorian del Thorian." There was a spot of blood at the corner of his right eye; he wiped it away with the back of his hand.

"And why is he so important that you would risk that, Old One?" the Fire Duke asked, mockingly.

"Because I swore I would, on the day he was born. Because on the day of his birth, his grandfather, who took me in when his father and I were hungry, made me swear I would protect him as much and as well as I could until the day he released me from that oath." He looked down, fondly, at Torrie. "Never you mind that I've seldom had that chance to help raise a young one from birth to adulthood; that's a joy I've rarely been granted. And never you mind that I find myself unaccustomedly fond of him; that's a feeling you'll not share. You'll not understand any of that, Your Warmth, but you'll understand the oath, and that by my own oath I bind myself to share with you all that I know, should your champion defeat Ian Silverstein here and now."

There. It had been said. Torrie had been right: somehow or other, this was all about Uncle Hosea, not him. And somehow or other, the Fire Duke had known that Uncle Hosea was nearby, and had forced this in order to make him reveal himself.

But Ian? Ian as champion? No. Ian was a better foil fencer than Torrie, but in freestyle or a real bout, Ian wouldn't stand a chance against an experienced épée player, much less the likes of Stanar del Brunden.

It wasn't right. It had to be Torrie, not Ian. Torrie was the one trained from birth for this moment, not Ian. Ian was just, well, just another guy. Torrie was—

"No," Torrie said. "I'll do it. I'll take it on."

Uncle Hosea looked down on him with sad eyes. A long finger came up to the outside corner of his left eye, and brushed away a dark tear.

A drop of blood. How had Uncle Hosea cut himself near the eye, and what did it mean?

"Do you trust me, young Thorian?" he asked, his voice slurred around the edges as always. "Will you trust me enough to stand aside here and now and let another defend you and me, knowing that runs contrary to everything you have been raised and trained for? Can you? Will you?"

Ian stepped in front of him. "And how about me, Torrie? Am I a trusted friend, or just your sidekick?" He quirked a smile. "Maybe next time it'll be your turn. I have it on . . . on good authority that this one's for me, for Ian Silverstein, the loser. The guy who's just a foil fencer, and not good for much of anything except to be the foil for your sharp wit."

Torrie opened his mouth to protest; Ian silenced him with an upraised palm.

"Some other time, perhaps," Ian said. He raised his voice. "Do you accept me as your champion?" he asked, loudly. And, *sotto voce*: "Don't fuck up on me, Torrie. I've come through too much, too far for that."

You have to trust your family, your neighbors, your friends. Nobody in Hardwood had ever exactly said that; it wasn't something that needed saying. It was like breathing: it was something you just had to do.

Torrie unbuckled his sword and dropped it to one side. "I do." He glared up at the Fire Duke. "I accept Ian as my champion in this matter."

The Fire Duke might as well not have heard him. He looked across at Uncle Hosea. "And you bind yourself to my command should my champion defeat this Ian Silverstone, this champion of yours."

Uncle Hosea nodded. "I do."

The Fire Duke seemed somehow more solid and less fat

as he dropped his cape to one side. "Then your terms are accepted, and I shall champion my own House." Moving far more easily than a man with his bulk should have been able to, he vaulted the railing and dropped easily to the sand of the amphitheater.

He raised his sword. "Have at you, Ian Silverstone."

And in his mind, Ian heard a voice whisper, *Make it easy on me, loser, and I shall make your end swift.*

CHAPTER TWENTY-THREE

The Fencer

Ian barely had time to draw his sword before the Fire Duke was upon him.

Don't fight. Lie back; let it happen, whispered in his head.

Shit.

Ian backpedaled, barely parrying the Fire Duke's tentative attack.

Let me make it quick and easy for you. Don't draw it out. You'll only embarrass yourself.

It wasn't a noble of the Middle Dominion Ian was facing, but one of the Old Ones, a Tuatha, or a Tuarin, or whatever the hell it was. The Old Ones were all shapeshifters to various degrees; this one had taken on the shape of the Duke of the House of Fire for—

There wasn't time to think about why; Ian's sword parried the Fire Duke's high-line attack as though of its own volition, and as the Fire Duke was about to launch his next attack Ian tried a stop-thrust, which the Fire Duke parried easily. He moved too easily, as though he was a muscular athlete dressed in a balloon suit, and not the fat man that he surely was.

Don't raise your hand to me, boy, sounded in his head.

The voice could have been Benjamin Silverstein's.

No, no, no, that didn't make any sense. It wasn't the old bastard, not here; the Fire Duke had reached into Ian's head and found the voice and words from the nightmare Ian had lived.

Just put down your sword, and let it be over. No more of that silly Robin Hood shit for you.

It was just foil fencing, after all, about as useful for real combat as knitting. It didn't teach you to—

Pain lanced through his arm as the Fire Duke's blade went past Ian's defenses, his point barely scoring, but his sword parried again. The rhythms and patterns of it had been trained into his mind and muscles; they weren't just something he did, they were a part of him. He didn't have to think in order to fence, not on the level of conscious thought.

Do it that way, and make it easier on me, and I shall make it easier on you, you little worm. It will all be the same in the end.

The Fire Duke was right. Ian had no chance. This was a job for a duelist, and Ian was a foil fencer. After all they had been through together, Hosea had suckered him, pushed him to the center of the amphitheater like a chess player pushing a pawn to the center of the board, to be snatched up, perhaps forcing the other player to expose himself, perhaps to protect a more valuable piece, perhaps for some sort of subtle exchange.

And Ian was just a fencer, just a pawn, just—

No. By God, no. Freya had told him that what he was was of value, and he believed in her.

And by God, maybe I can believe in myself.

He wasn't just a foil fencer; he was the best foil fencer that he could make himself, and that was something not only worth doing, but worth being, and if there was a message in Freya's statue, that was it.

He could analyze it all day long, how the Fire Duke was

fencing like a duelist, avoiding exposing himself anywhere, because his entire body was a target; not pressing an attack unless he had the other's blade beat fully aside, because in a real duel, it didn't matter if you beat the other on the attack if his blow landed on a more important part of the anatomy than yours did.

It was why épée players had almost always been able to beat foil players in real duels, because foil fencing was an art form and a sport, and épée a simulation of a duel. Yes, foil fencing had started out as a simulation of dueling, but not of a real duel, usually ended at the first blood or by disabling the opponent with a series of minor cuts.

To actually wound an opponent in a way that would score a point in foil would require a hit that would, if real, be at least life threatening, and more likely just plain deadly.

And none of it mattered anyway, because an ordinary blade can no more end the life of an Old One than a cotton ball could kill you, boy.

None of it mattered. Ian wasn't an épée player, and he wasn't a duelist, and when he saw an opening that would let the tip of his sword touch the Fire Duke just under the armpit—

—it didn't matter that lunging for that touch left Ian exposed from toe to head, whether the Fire Duke parried or not—

—he went for it, the tip of his sword whistling through the air.

It sank perhaps half an inch into the Fire Duke's fat before the Fire Duke's sword pierced Ian's side, just above the waist.

Nothing had ever hurt so badly.

Ian staggered back, his free hand clapped over the wound, as though to hold himself together. His jaws were clamped together, but a sound halfway between a scream and a groan forced itself out through his lips.

Half-blind in pain, he beat seconde, but all his blade encountered was air.

He forced himself to breathe. It didn't matter how much it hurt. He needed oxygen, he needed to see, he needed to move, and without air in his lungs he was dead. Ian sucked air in with a ragged gasp.

Why wasn't he dead?

He forced his eyes to focus.

The Fire Duke stood ten feet away, the white of his blouse stained with blood every bit as red as that on the tip of his blade, his mouth open, his eyes wide in his piggy face. Dots of sweat speckled his cheeks and lip, and a trace of white spittle was at the corner of his mouth.

Every movement agony, Ian brought his sword up and took a step toward the Fire Duke.

It's not an ordinary blade, Duke, he thought, knowing the other was still reading his mind when the Fire Duke paled ever further. *Orfindel made it himself.*

Even if he didn't know it, he made it for me.

For me.

Because he's right. It's not a sacrifice; I'm the right man to take you on, asshole. I'm not just Torrie's friend; I'm what's needed here and now.

That's the secret, you see, Fire Duke, or Tuarin, or Tuatha, or Fire Giant, or whatever you really are. It's simple: fencing is just that silly Robin Hood shit to my father, and this is all just a game to you. And I'm by no means the best that there is at it, and I only picked it up as a way of rebelling against that bastard of an old man, because he despised it, and I only stayed with it because it fed me.

But, by God, you old bastard, while I'm not the best fencer that there ever was, I've worked hard to make myself the best one that I can be, and that's what's called for here.

You could beat any real swordsman, because you're faster, because you know how they fight, and you can read their minds, and because they don't know how to leave themselves wide open the way a foil player does.

Yeah. You can nibble away at them until they give up or until your little cuts bleed them to death.

But you can't do that to me.

I'm a foil fencer, and I don't give a damn whether your point gets to me as long as my blade gets to you first, because I'm not trained to go for a cheap little shot to the toe or the knee or the arm.

Because I'm a foil fencer, fucker, and when I've got the advantage, I go for the kill every damn time.

I can take every cut you give me, I can take everything you can hand out, and I can give you one more, until—

Ian closed with a running attack that no épée fencer would have ever considered, and lunged in full extension, his form perfect, no attempt to parry, the point of his sword traveling the ideal line, past where the Fire Duke's blade waited to drink his blood, his muscles and body moving faster than thought would have taken him, and the tip of his blade slid through the Fire Duke's flesh and into his heart as though it was traveling through butter.

And if but a fraction of a second after that the Fire Duke's sharp sword cut through Ian's own belly, and turned the world into red pain that refused to go away, what of it?

He had touched first, after all.

The point was his.

Ian was lying on the hot sand, the pain . . . distant? Vague? No, not that. It was there, but it was like it was happening to somebody else, somebody who Ian cared about, but not him, not anymore.

"Be still, Ian Silverstein," Hosea's gently slurred voice said. "I've done what I can for the moment. You'll heal fully, I promise you."

"But—"

Ian opened his eyes. It was hard to focus; the form lying on the sand next to him, its dead eyes staring up at the carved ceiling, seemed too close somehow, but—

"You won." Hosea's dark face loomed above him. "The Fire Duke was a fire giant; he long ago took on the form of His Warmth." Gentle fingers touched at his forehead, and urged his eyelids shut. "Sleep now. We will talk later."

No. He had to—

To what? He was done, now, for the time being.

Hosea leaned close and whispered, his breath warm in Ian's ear. "Your father wouldn't have been proud of you, Ian," he whispered, so quietly that nobody else could possibly have heard it, "but that's just because he's a fool."

Hot tears streamed down Ian's face, although he couldn't have said why. It didn't hurt so much, not anymore.

CHAPTER TWENTY-FOUR

Profession

Branden del Branden had seated himself behind the Fire Duke's massive desk, Lord Sensever having taken up a position to its side. It seemed only fair to Torrie, all things considered, that a noble of Falias should be holding down the seat until Venidir del Anegir could arrive from the Old Keep to take his rightful place as Fire Duke. While there were majors of the House of Flame senior to Branden del Branden—rather a lot of them—none seemed eager to even temporarily occupy the seat that had been held by the imposter.

For how long? Torrie dismissed it. It probably wasn't important.

Ivar del Hival, impatient, paced back and forth, when he wasn't pretending to examine something in one of the nooks and crannies that decorated the wall. Thorian del Orvald, on the other hand, sat quietly in a chair over in the corner, his single eye watching all.

"How is Ian Silverstone?" Branden del Branden asked. "I've instructed Jamed del Bruno to see he is given the best of care; Lord Sensever has been kind enough to have his Vestri chirurgeon looking in on him."

Sensever was idly drawing with his finger on the smooth

surface of the desk. "It seems fair, all things considered; I owe him and you rather a lot, speaking for His Solidity." His smile at Torrie was warm without being effusive. "If nothing else, I suspect that the new Fire Duke won't want to press the late His Warmth's claim to Kerniat."

"But Ian?"

"He will be as well as he can be." Sensever smiled gently. "Bimdel was sucking the poison from wounds in my father's time."

Torrie looked over at Uncle Hosea, who nodded. The nod said all that needed to be: Ian would be fine.

Torrie flopped down in a chair next to where Uncle Hosea sat. The City had become more of a comfortable place than he had thought.

He would miss it.

"We don't have much time," he said to Uncle Hosea. "I need to get into the Secret Ways, and home. I'll need you to guide me."

"I'll come with you, Thorian del Thorian," Ivar del Hival said, his voice a basso rumble. "Just in case an extra sword, an extra hand is needed."

Torrie nodded. That was reason enough, and if there was trouble, it would be good to have another sword handy. With any luck, of course, Dad, Mom, and Maggie had managed to stay ahead of the Sons, and the odds of Torrie being able to catch up in time to do any good were just this side of nil if they hadn't, but . . .

Hosea shook his head. "I can't tell you where they are. I don't know."

Torrie flared. "Don't give me that, Uncle Hosea. You built this City; everything about it shouts of your construction. You know where every Secret Way, every hiding place is—"

Uncle Hosea shook his head. "Not any longer. I—it's odd that it would be me who fails of faith, but fail I did. I"—he shook his head—"I no longer remember much of it." He smiled sadly, and tapped a finger at his temple. "It could be said that I should have had more faith in Ian, but the risk was too great. I . . . took a tool and excised the knowledge, and other knowledge that the fire giant wanted. If he won, he would have little." He gestured feebly. "As is true for you, I am sorry to say."

Lord Sensever's lips pressed together. "Which makes you rather less of a prize, Orfindel, and rather less in demand, eh?"

"Clever." Thorian del Orvald raised a gnarled finger to his brow. The duelmaster could appreciate a sly strategy. "My congratulations, Orfindel, or whatever your name is."

Torrie shuddered. He had known Uncle Hosea was different, but to take a probe and stick it in his own—enh.

The slur in Uncle Hosea's voice was worse than it usually was, and—"This isn't the first time you've done that, is it?"

Uncle Hosea shook his head. "No. Nor the second." He raised a hand. "Leave it be, Thorian; leave it be."

The massive door opened. Jamed del Bruno, saturnine and somber in black and beige, a trio of Vestri servants in his wake, entered bearing a platinum platter amply laden with ripe cheeses and fist-sized loaves of bread, all warm and yeasty-smelling. The three Vestri, their blunt fingers working far more delicately than they appeared capable of, quickly opened up the tops of the tiny loaves with three slashes of a knife followed by a deft tug, and filled the openings with cheeses, topping it with a sprinkling of some green herb before serving small plates of it about.

"I felt a small repast was in order," Jamed del Bruno said, "despite the hour." He walked to the side of the room, and pushed aside the tapestry to reveal what appeared to be a blank wall. "His late Warmth kept his most prized wines and brandies here," he said, pushing at a couple of spots a hand's breadth apart.

Torrie nodded. He would push in both places, where the thin wall was just flexible enough to give a trifle, then wait for the count of three while the internal mechanism momentarily brought the locks into the right alignment, then bang on the wall between the two spots.

Jamed del Bruno did just that. There may have been the ghost of a smile on his face as the ragged door opened on silent hinges, revealing a cupboard-sized repository, filled with dusty bottles lying on their sides. Jamed del Bruno carefully selected one, then eased the cork out with practiced thumbs, filling the wide-necked wineglasses with a black-red splash as quickly as one of the Vestri could bring them.

The three Vestri served out bread and wine; it took a moment for Torrie to realize that the Vestri serving him was Broglin.

"I apologize, Broglin," he said in Vestri, accepting the plate with one hand and the glass with the other. "And I thank you for your help before."

The dwarf hesitated for a moment, then shrugged. "It was as it should be, Thorian del Thorian," he said in the same language. "Although there is much you have to learn of subtlety. Need everyone here know that I would serve you no matter the cost?"

Torrie flushed. "Why would anybody know Vestri?" he asked.

"Because knowledge is good," Thorian del Orvald said in Vestri. He grunted. "One would have thought your father would have taught you that."

"Because it is worthwhile to know the language of those one supervises," Jamed del Bruno said, also in Vestri.

"Because it is even more worthwhile to know the language of those one rules," Lord Sensever said in the same language, with a grin. "Being a member of the ruling class does require some work, you know."

Uncle Hosea shrugged. "It would be nice to know what

all of you are speaking of, but I guess that would be too much to ask."

No. Uncle Hosea not understanding a language, particularly this language? Had he cut out so much of his brain?

Torrie kept his face straight. "Nothing of importance, Uncle Hosea." He waved it all away. "But I have to find the Hidden Way back. They didn't have enough of a head start on the Sons; they'll need help, and every minute . . ."

"Is but a minute," Broglin said in Vestri, "as always it shall be."

Jamed del Bruno nodded. "You might as well tell them; if not, I shall." There was silence for a moment. "Very well," Jamed del Bruno said. "I can show you the Hidden Way His Late Warmth sent the Sons on, and their tracks shall not be difficult to follow, at least for the first while." He frowned. "There was an accident, of sorts. It seems that a powerful purgative was inserted into the last meal fed the Sons before they left. It will slow them down until they work it out of their system." He poured more wine. "I always felt that a contest was more interesting when the prey had a chance to escape."

"Then we have to hurry; even if they make it—"

Uncle Hosea raised a hand. "Torrie, Torrie, you have too little faith. They shall be fine; trust your neighbors. Trust your mother and your woman, as well as your father." He considered it for a moment. "Still, if you will show us the way back, Jamed del Bruno, I think it appropriate that young Thorian, Ian Silverstone, and I return there, if only for a while."

The door swung open yet again, and Ian Silverstein walked in, a rucksack slung across his back. He was wearing the red-orange-trimmed black tunic and trousers of an officer of the House of Flame, but the boots were the ones he had been wearing, and the sword at his waist was the one Uncle Hosea had given him.

Perhaps his face was a trifle pale, and possibly his step

was not as firm as it should have been, but he held himself straight—perhaps too straight, but not like a man in pain, afraid that any move would tear him apart.

Torrie smiled. "I take it the Vestri are better healers than we've been told."

Ian shook his head. "Nah," he said in English, "tell you later. You might even believe me." He tapped at his belly. "Feels like it's about to fall apart, but it's not hurting, and I'm told the . . . bandage will hold things together long enough."

He dropped the rucksack down on the desk in front of Branden del Branden. "I've also been told that the House of Flame is officially beholden to me," he said.

Branden del Branden chuckled. "That would seem to be the case, although I'd not care to make any major decisions right now; the new His Warmth will shortly be on his way from the Sky, and he's likely to hold me responsible for anything . . . excessive."

Ian raised an eyebrow. "Just enough gold to carry, and directions home?"

Torrie cleared his throat. "We were just talking about that. Everybody thinks Mom, Dad, and Maggie had enough of a head start, and—"

Ian shrugged. "I'd trust your Dad to handle things, Torrie." A cloud could have passed across his face for a moment. *And, if not, it's all over by now, and there's not a damn thing we can do about it*, he might as well have said. "But I still have some things to do there."

Torrie forced his hand to unclench. Ian had the right of it. "So you want to go home, eh? Back to school?"

"Well, no." Ian frowned. "We'll talk about it some time."

Thorian del Orvald eyed him carefully. "There are other possibilities. What the outsiders call the House of Steel is perhaps beholden to someone who exposed the usurper who commanded our services."

Sensever nodded. "Exposed? That's a weak way of putting it. But he's quite right. Speaking for His Force, there would likely be a place in the House of Wind for one who has served us so well, if unintentionally. The late Fire Duke was a creature of ambition, and some of his ambitions seem to have involved my House."

Ian shook his head. "Maybe some other time. Right now, I'll settle for the gold—and directions."

Branden del Branden pursed his lips judiciously. "Gold would be no problem, particularly if we didn't have to bother the bursar major, but rather had access to His Late Warmth's private safe." His mouth twisted. "I've known the bursar major for some years now, and suspect she still has her first obol tucked safely away between her weathered dugs." He grunted.

Hosea rose from his chair. "I remember that much, long though it has been." He knelt near the corner of the rug and pulled it back. The floorboards under it were a dark wood, with a deep luster. Hosea pushed near the joint of two floorboards, and when it gave slightly, pushed at another board beyond it. A section of floor swung up, revealing the mouths of four canvas bags. Hosea rose as the three Vestri pulled the bags out, clever blunt fingers untying complicated knots in the leather thongs that held the bags closed.

Ruddy gold shone. "I think that ought to be more than sufficient," Hosea said.

Branden del Branden smiled. "I think you ought to take what of it you and a Vestri servant can carry, Ian Silverstone. We owe you at least that much."

Ivar del Hival stroked at his beard. "I think a Vestri might seem out of place where Ian Silverstone is going; I'll help him carry his booty."

"Sit," Uncle Hosea said, "if it please you, Ian Silverstone. There's much we have to talk about."

Ian's forehead wrinkled. "Let's talk in private, please."

He jerked his head toward the veranda beyond. "Just you, me, and Torrie."

High, above, a black bird circled; Torrie had thought at first it was an eagle, and then from the shape of the head, a crow, but it was probably neither; the head was sloped too much for it to be an eagle, and it was far too large to be a crow.

Ian rested himself on his forearms, leaning on the railing at the edge of the balcony. "So you didn't trust me, eh?" he said, quietly. "Asshole."

Torrie flared. "Don't you talk to him like that—"

"You too, Thorian del Thorian," Ian said. "You don't know what's involved, you don't know how important this all is." He turned to Uncle Hosea. "You should have let us all die, if necessary; you know what the stakes are. A human Fire Duke could well have been after a map of the Hidden Ways, but you know full well that the fire giant was after the Brisingamen jewels."

Torrie shook his head. He had no difficulty believing that objects in Tir Na Nog could be invested with great power, but how could they really be *that* important? The Brisingamen was something out of the stories Uncle Hosea used to tell, a necklace of great power, but this much? Ending the universe was just too big an idea to deal with.

Leave it be for now.

"Ian, Ian," Uncle Hosea said, slowly, tired, his voice slurred, "I could no more break my word to Thorian's grandfather than I could to anybody else."

"Then you shouldn't have promised him, you—"

"There are many things I should and shouldn't have done." Uncle Hosea licked his lips once, twice, three times. "But leave that for today. What would you have me do now?"

"You purged from your mind the entrances, and the locations of the jewels—but could you find your way through the Hidden Ways back to Hardwood?"

Uncle Hosea thought about it for a moment. "Likely. It's not like I was able to hack precisely. Likely you'll be able to follow the trail of the Sons; there'll be a freshness to it that—" He waved it away. "So you wish to go home, Ian Silverstein."

"For a time, Orfindel," Ian said, fitting the words to his feelings, finding that they felt good. "But only for a time. I want to take that gold and set up a trust fund to pay for some legal fees." Ian smiled. Let somebody who wanted to be a lawyer chase down bastards like Benjamin Silverstein. He never wanted the career anyway. That was just a way of getting even, and while that work was important, he could let others do it, now.

I reject you, you miserable excuse for a father. I'll let others even the score for me, by proxy. I've got my own life to live.

"Just some business to settle. Your mom can launder some money for me, I take it, maybe set up a trust fund," he said to Torrie.

Torrie shrugged. "I've really never been much interested in the money side of things," he said. "I guess I got that from my father."

"She has done similar things before," Hosea said. "You do not plan to spend the money yourself?"

"Hey, I don't remember taking a vow of poverty." Ian smiled. "Oh, sure; I'll keep some, and enjoy spending it. On some camping gear, yeah. And I'd like to lie on a beach on a Caribbean island for a couple of weeks, maybe. And then if I have to pay Torrie's dad for some freestyle lessons, I'll pay." He felt at his side, at where the false Fire Duke's sword had cut into him. "I need to be better at that." Grinning made him feel positively giddy. "If lessons aren't available from Thorian del Thorian the Elder, perhaps Thorian del Orvald can be persuaded. Foil fencing has its limitations."

Torrie grinned, too. "But it's got its uses, too, apparently. And then we go looking for the Brisingamen jewels, eh?"

"We." Ian nodded. "Yeah. We." This had been his turn to take center stage, to make all the difference. Next time might be Torrie's.

Or it might not be either of theirs.

But fuck it. I'm Ian Silverstein, companion to Orfindel, friend of Odin and Freya, slayer of some unknown fire giant; I may just be up to what's necessary.

"And what do we do with the jewels when we find them all?" Torrie asked. "I mean, like, if they're so important, who do we trust?"

Ian snorted. "Well, we don't trust some conspiracy of fire giants and bergenisses, that's for a start. I have an idea in mind, but I'm not sure you'll like it." He turned to Hosea. "I wouldn't be the first one to trust her with the jewels, would I?"

Hosea shook his head. "No, you wouldn't be the first. But leave that for another day."

Ian nodded. Yes, it was enough for a day. "Well, then, shall we rejoin the others?" Ian led the other two back inside.

Little had changed, except that Ivar del Hival was gone and that another Vestri had arrived bearing familiar-looking rucksacks.

Lord Sensever poured an inky wine into a long-stemmed tulip glass, then raised it to his nose, giving it a quick sniff before he tasted it. "Quite nice, indeed. Jamed del Bruno has gone with Ivar del Hival; they should return shortly, and you'll be sent on your way." Raised eyebrows invited the others to share the wine; Ian shook his head, as did Hosea, but Torrie nodded.

"Sure. I'll take some." He was already back in his chair, his swordbelt off and looped over the back of the chair, leaving the hilt within reach, his feet propped up on the edge of the Fire Duke's desk. One thing Torrie knew how to do was relax; Ian had always envied him that, and probably always would.

Branden del Branden accepted a glass, and eyed Ian over its rim. "You are, of course, welcome to stay. I'm sure the new His Warmth would like to meet all of you—"

"But not certain enough that he'd let us go?"

Branden del Branden shook his head. "I could argue either that you're too insignificant to be that worried about or that you're too important to trifle with. Either way, I doubt he would want to detain you." He looked carefully at Hosea. "At least, the two of you. I'd rather not think about what he would wish to do about Orfindel, so I won't."

"Good idea." Torrie's smile wasn't entirely friendly.

Ian tugged his own rucksack open. His clothes had been washed and neatly folded and packed away. He wondered idly what they had used to clean his shirt and trousers, but didn't figure that asking Sensever or Branden del Branden or Thorian del Orvald would make any sense.

Branden del Branden set his wineglass down to finish loading the last of four small bags with gold coins.

Ian would have made some comment about stinginess, but he hefted one of the little bags, surprised to find that such a small thing weighed easily twenty-five, thirty pounds, and decided it would get heavier before it got lighter. He turned to Torrie. "We split it?"

"Nah." Torrie leaned back, his head pillowed on his hands. "I've got money; Mom and Dad have seen to that." Torrie's broad face almost split in a grin. "Might let you pick up a couple of airline tickets, though, if you don't mind some company on a beach."

"A couple? Maggie?"

Torrie nodded. "I did promise her a vacation, and I don't think this counted. Do you?"

Ian pursed his lips. "No. No, I don't." He hefted the sack again. "What *is* gold going for these days?"

Torrie shrugged. "Three hundred an ounce? Maybe more? I've never been much interested; my mom could probably tell you."

Hosea nodded. "Most likely she could. To the penny."

Hmm . . . about twenty-five pounds per bag, and there were four bags. Something like half a million dollars. Four bags, but—oh, that was right. Ivar del Hival wanted to come along.

"You've got something special in mind?"

Ian nodded. "Tell you about it sometime."

It wasn't an immense amount of money, but it didn't have to be enough to finance everything. Just some seed money, for the right lawyer starting off on a new specialty.

Call it making the bastards pay . . .

Branden del Branden loaded each of the bags into a rucksack; Ian tied his shut and hefted it to his shoulder.

It was funny, really; with about forty pounds of gold and gear on his back, Ian felt lighter, somehow. He couldn't help grinning, and he probably would have laughed if his belly didn't feel so tender. His gut didn't hurt, but it felt like it was made of tissue paper.

"Well, let's get Jamed del Bruno back here and get us on our way," he said.

Branden del Branden seemed to relax, although Ian hadn't noticed him being tense. Branden turned to Torrie. "I do have a request of you."

Torrie cocked his head to one side. "Well?"

"You'll convey to the Exquisite Maggie that she always has at least one admirer here, one who would assure that her status would be . . . sufficient."

Sensever took another sip of wine. "Oh, I doubt that would be necessary. Her association with this whole affair would guarantee much interest in her, even if the young ladies of this House were not already gossiping about how facile her mind is, and how quick with learning not only graces and niceties but more practical skills for a noblewoman." He raised his glass to Torrie. "A charming young lady."

Torrie nodded. "I'll tell her that," he said, to both of them. "I'm . . . fairly fond of her myself."

Branden del Branden waved it away. "The lady can always choose."

Ian hid a smile behind his hand. Seemed that somebody was taken with Maggie.

A thought struck him. He hadn't seen anything but his clothes . . .

He set his rucksack down and opened it up again, pawing through it with increasing panic until he found the leather bag Freya had given him, and pulled it out.

The apple sausages were still inside, as was the wrapped figurine, the miniature sword once again safely tucked away.

The others were looking at him looking at it. Feeling vaguely embarrassed, he wrapped it up and tucked it away again. "A gift from a friend."

"Lady friend?" Torrie asked.

Ian grinned. "Always." He hefted his pack to his back. "Shall we get going?"

"We have to wait for Jamed del Bruno and—"

"My good self," Ivar del Hival boomed from the doorway. "And I am quite ready." He was out of his garish City livery, dressed in a white shirt and brown trousers that would have looked ordinary enough on the streets of Hardwood or anywhere else, if it wasn't for their slightly unusual cut and the fact that the front of the trousers was secured by an open row of buttons instead of a zipper concealed by a flap.

And the sword belt, of course, but Ian had gotten used to that, and to the sword belted around his own waist. He would probably want to talk Ivar del Hival into having his ponytail bobbed, and his bushy beard trimmed a bit, but he looked more like a fifty-year-old hippie type, albeit an unusually muscular one.

Torrie levered himself to his feet, and grunted his way into his rucksack before belting his sword about him. "Branden del Branden," he said, "I thank you for your hospitality, and hope to avail myself of it again." He turned to Lord Sensever. "And I thank you for your kind wishes for me and my family."

"Yes. Do be sure to send them to your father, and your mother, and the Exquisite Maggie."

Torrie nodded. "Of course."

Thorian del Orvald rose to his feet and steadied himself with one hand on the edge of the desk. "I'll walk you to the hidden exit, Grandson," he said. "If you do not mind the company."

Grandson? Ian raised an eyebrow.

Later, Torrie mouthed, then turned back to Thorian del Orvald. "My pleasure, sir. Perhaps when we return, you'll find occasion to introduce me to my father's mother?"

"Yes, your grandmother would like that." Thorian del Orvald smiled. "I'll attempt to find such," he said. "I hope that it won't be terribly long." He cleared his throat, and seemed to have some difficulty speaking.

The pack wasn't getting any lighter on Ian's back. "Hey, Torrie, enough of the good-byes. Let's make like a tree and hit the road."

Hosea grinned. "I like that."

They were two floors down and several corridors away when Torrie stopped, suddenly, his mouth open, his eyes on something far away. "Holy shit." He shrugged out of his rucksack and dropped it to the ground next to Jamed del Bruno. "I'll be right back," he said, taking off in a sprint, running back the way they had come.

Ian looked to Hosea, who stared back, blankly. "I do not know, either, Ian Silverstein," Hosea said.

Ivar del Hival lowered his own rucksack to the floor. "You'd best see to the lad, the two of you," he said. "I'll wait for you," he said, helping Ian and Hosea off with theirs.

Torrie had a head start on them, and he had run faster than Ian cared to and Hosea could. By the time Ian, Hosea and Thorian del Orvald in tow, arrived back at the study, Torrie was already on his knees on the floor, beside the hidden safe that was still mostly filled with gold.

Torrie was pulling out handfuls of golden coins and more scattering them than piling them on the floor, while Branden del Branden, Lord Sensever, and Thorian del Orvald watched, only Thorian del Orvald letting his curiosity show on his lined face.

Torrie's face was sweat-sheened as he looked up at Hosea. "It's just like the gun safe at home, Uncle Hosea," Torrie said. He scooped out a last coin and then reached his hand into the safe. "Can't feel it, but . . ." He looked up at Branden del Branden. "Can you get me a light? A lantern of some sort? A candle?"

Branden del Branden was trying too hard to look impassive as he nodded and rose and walked out, returning in a few moments with a lit lantern that he handed to Torrie.

Torrie set it down next to the hole and peered in. "Damn. I can't see well enough. What I really need is a flashlight, or maybe . . ." He reached into his pouch and took out a tool that opened up into something that looked like a needlenose pliers, except that it had swing-out tools in each of its handles. "The Paratool," Torrie said, grinning as he swung a bent piece of wire out of one handle. "Don't leave home without it." He reached the tool into the safe and felt about. "I can't see it, but it should be here somewhere," he said, his brow wrinkling in effort. "It should have felt strange. Why would the Fire Duke keep so much gold in such a useless place? A few coins, perhaps, if he liked to take it out and handle it, but what use is the Duke of the House of Fire going to have for a lot of gold? That's what he has a bursar for: to keep it, to spend it, and besides, preoccupation with money is a woman's thing here, beneath the notice of men."

"The one you knew as the Fire Duke," Hosea said, "wasn't really of this City—"

"No, but he was pretending to be," Torrie said. "Why pretend about everything except this? If he—ah, got it. Hang on a sec," he said, slowly, carefully lifting up.

He pulled out a piece of metal about the size and shape of a dinner plate, smooth on top, an ungainly-looking set of lockwork protruding from the bottom. Torrie carefully removed it from the lockpick of the Paratool, and set it down on the floor next to him, bottom-side up. Ian couldn't make much sense of the lockwork, except for the six bolts, now retracted, equally spaced around its edges. Extended, those would have done one hell of a job holding it in place.

Ian found that his heart was thumping. If the real safe was under this safe, that meant that all that gold was just a decoy. Which argued that the gold was phony—but he knew it wasn't phony; this was from the same source that Torrie's Dad and Hosea had stolen the gold they had taken with them when they had fled, the gold that Torrie's Mom had laundered and invested.

Which meant that whatever was inside this safe-within-a-safe was valuable enough that hundreds of pounds of gold was by comparison cheap enough to be used as a decoy, which meant that what was in this safe was at the very least far too valuable to be messing with without having thought it all through.

"Torrie, it's—" Ian caught himself. It was too late for that, as Torrie reached back into the safe, his arm going in all the way to the shoulder.

He straightened, bringing with him a small leather bag. Trembling fingers pulled the mouth open.

The room was somehow darker than before.

The round, irregular red gem that lay in the palm of Torrie's hands not only glowed as though from a deep crimson fire but seemed to soak up light and heat, not just from the lantern on the floor next to it but from the entire room itself. In its ruddy light, Torrie's face was streaked with dirt and sweat. It seemed to take more effort than it should have for him to close his fingers around the gem, chasing the darkness and the strange crimson light away, bringing ordinary daylight and lantern light back to the study.

Hosea was on his knees next to Torrie. "It's *the* ruby, cut from the broken necklace of the Brisings, blessed and cursed," he said, shaking his head. "He had already found one, it seems, and was searching for the rest."

Sensever nodded soberly. "That was the part that bothered me. His Late Warmth was better at holding his form than any of the fire giants I've ever heard of. All of the Elder Races can do some of that, but I would not have thought a mere fire giant capable of such an extended masquerade. To take on a form for an hour, or a meal, or a day, perhaps—but years? It seems he had a source of power close to hand." He reached out his hand. "I'd best take charge of it."

Branden del Branden was already on his feet. "I think it had best stay here, in the House of Fire. It is a flame gem, after all."

Thorian del Orvald stood, as well. "The duelmaster is bound to the Dominion as a whole," he said, his hand on the hilt of his sword, his face turned ever so slightly to the side, turning his blind eye away. He wasn't moving like a sick old man. "I'd best take it, in the name of the Sky."

No. None of them could be trusted with it.

Torrie rose to his feet, the jewel in his left hand, his right hand on the hilt of his sword. "You think you can take it away from me?" he said.

Thorian del Orvald nodded. "Yes, Grandson, I think I can. And I am sure that somebody in the City could. You don't want to hold that gem, young Thorian. It's far too dangerous."

Fuck you, Torrie, Ian thought. It was all far too dangerous, and it was Torrie's fault, for dashing back here to pull the jewel out of the safe, without even pausing to discuss it, to think through the consequences.

Hell, blame it on his father and mother, and his neighbors. Torrie had been raised too gently, surrounded by people he could trust. He didn't understand the way the world really worked sometimes, that you couldn't always trust even the ones that you should have had every reason to believe meant well by you.

Ian knew that. Benjamin Silverstein had beaten that into him.

Sure, Torrie was friends with this Branden del Branden, and Lord Sensever looked kindly upon him, and Thorian del Orvald was his own grandfather, but this gem was part of the Brisingamen, and each one of them would find a reason why it was too valuable for Torrie to have, each would find a reason why he or the interests he represented would be the best guardian of it.

Damn it, Torrie.

They would either have to give it over or fight their way out, and the two of them had no chance of fighting their way out of the City.

Unless . . .

Moving quickly while trying not to seem jerky, he stepped around behind Branden del Branden for the doorway that led out to the veranda.

"Torrie!" Ian called out from the doorway. "*Here.* Guard me."

Torrie barely hesitated; then he tossed the gem underhand toward Ian, then leaped toward the doorway to block the others, drawing his sword as he did, his back to Ian.

"Whatever you're going to do, do it fast," he said. "Our situation sucks."

Tell me about it, Ian didn't say. Recriminations could wait for later, if there was a later. "Give me a minute."

Ian stepped back out on the veranda. The gem was warm in his hands, too warm for just having been held by Torrie for a few minutes, and while it didn't feel heavy as he held it there, it seemed to be heavier when he tried to move it, as though whoever had pushed its mass and inertia far away hadn't quite synchronized the two.

He scanned the blue skies. A richer, deeper blue than he was used to, the puffy clouds so white and pure they dazzled the eye.

And high above, a black bird circled.

A crow, perhaps?

No. Ian smiled.

A raven.

It was all logical, really. The gem needed to be kept by somebody who understood what the Brisingamen meant, who could be trusted to keep it, and perhaps the rest of the Brisingamen, until the time was right to end this cycle of the universe.

Not yet, Ian thought. I've got a lot to do before then, and I'm not the only one.

"Hugin," he shouted. "Hear me, come to me. Munin, come here, come to me, Ian Silverstein."

He had seen the bird circling high above before, but it hadn't quite registered on his consciousness. Still, they had told him they would see him again, and it would make sense for Harbard to want one of them to keep an eye on developments in the City.

The black bird high above continued in its wheeling flight over the city, and Ian's heart fell.

"Ian," Torrie said from behind him, "it's not going to hold for long in here."

"Shut up," Ian said, desperately trying to think of another choice. Swallow it? No; they'd just have to cut his belly open to get it, and there was no reason to think they wouldn't.

Run with it? Where?

The raven banked into first a dive, then a full stoop, its wings back.

It dropped like a stone from the sky, then spread its broad, oily wings wide, wider, as it dived down, toward the small veranda where Ian stood.

Yes. "Bring this to *her*, from me," he shouted.

Ian threw the gem high into the sky.

It tumbled through the clear air, catching the rays of the sun and holding them for a moment, then flared brighter and brighter, a small sun all by itself, difficult to watch, impossible to turn away from.

The raven's talons fastened about it with an audible click.

"And thank her for the apples," Ian said. "And for the carving, always for the carving." And he added in a whisper, sure that the bird wouldn't hear: "Thank her for telling me that I'm . . . worthwhile as I am."

"If you weren't such a fool, you wouldn't have needed a retired fertility goddess to tell you all of that, Ian Silverstone," it said, its harsh voice already receding in the distance. "But I'll tell her. Be well, Ian Silverstone," it said, its broad wings beating the air as it climbed high into the sky, already heading south.

"Thank you," he said, doubting that the raven could hear him.

Was it Hugin or Munin? Would it be thought or memory that would bring this piece of the Brisingamen back to Freya, to be guarded as she had promised, until the end of time? Torrie was an idiot if he thought he could trust everybody. But Ian wasn't about to be the other kind of idiot, the fool who would never trust anybody.

The answer to the folly on the left is not the folly on the right.

Ian smiled, as he turned to face the shocked faces.

It had worked.

Thorian del Orvald was the first to settle back into his chair, a thin smile on his lined face. He touched a crooked finger to his brow, as though in a parody of a salute.

Lord Sensever cleared his throat a few times, but then subsided, while Branden del Branden settled back behind the Fire Duke's desk, his expression working until he settled on a look of attempted calm dignity that almost made Ian laugh.

"So much for that," he said.

Ian nodded. "Yeah."

He slipped a hand around Torrie's shoulders, and another around Hosea's waist, and they walked back into the study. "Time to go home. For now."

He turned and looked out through the doorway into the blue sky.

Far away, almost vanished in the distance already, the black bird was lazily flapping its wings homeward.

"We'll be back."

EPILOGUE

Neighbors

When it finally happened, it all happened fast, the way Arnie Selmo had always known it would.

That was the way of it. Hunting or war, you spend most of your time waiting. He didn't complain; there was a time when he had waited for a couple of days in a half-frozen, stinking foxhole. This wasn't bad, not by comparison.

He had been lying in the lawn chair, its back resting against the base of the tree, the BAR across his lap. Orphie was in his own blind, maybe twenty yards away, snoring, as he had been since about the first hour of their shift.

Dammit. Orphie was too old for this. Arnie was too old for this, and he was ten years younger than Orphie.

Well, what to do? He couldn't ditch Orphie; that would hurt the old fellow too badly. And while Arnie thought that there really ought to be two men on each watch, maybe one would do. Shit, even two might not be enough, but it was all he figured he could get from Doc Sherve and his crowd.

One thing for sure: less than one on duty wouldn't do.

Arnie would have to make damn sure that he didn't fall asleep, but ever since Staff Sergeant Pernell had found Arnie asleep on guard duty one dark night in Uijongbu, and kicked the everloving shit out of him, Arnie had been unable to go to sleep with a rifle in his hands, so that was that.

But shit, boy, you'd better wake up quick if the—

There was a scrabbling over by the burial cairn, and a pair of hands, one holding a bloody sword, clawed at the edge of the hole, finally finding a grip. A dirty face emerged from the hole—Torrie's girlfriend, it was, followed by the rest of her, followed by an impossibly filthy Karin Thorsen, followed, at last, by Thorian Thorsen.

He looked the worst of all of them: shreds of what had been a shirt hung loosely from his torso, and he was bleeding from a hundred dirty cuts, although, like the girl, he had still managed to keep a bloody sword in one hand.

And while he was scrabbling on the ground, more crawling than running, a long gray snout pushed its way up through the hole.

It was a magnificent beast in its own way, but Arnie had already risen from his lawn chair, his BAR held high in his hands. Like a man decades younger, he dove forward for the open, breaking his fall with the butt of the rifle, landing him right next to the ammo bag.

He brought the BAR down, his eye focused not on the sights, but on the wolf that was bounding for Thorsen.

A single shot barked out, and the wolf dropped like a puppet whose strings had been cut.

Arnie grunted. Maybe Orphie wasn't so useless after all.

One after another, two more wolves sprang from the hole. Arnie lightly stroked the trigger of the BAR—

—*Remember*, he could hear old Homer Abernathy snarling, *it's like you're stroking a tit, not like you're jerking off*—

—and stitched a gorgeous three-shot burst through first one, then the other. The first wolf dropped where he was, but Arnie had caught the second in midleap, and the beast rolled to a stop with its gaping mouth, showing yellowed fangs the size of Arnie's thumbs, barely inches away from the girl's foot.

She surprised him by reaching out and stabbing at it with the sword she still clutched, although she didn't surprise him by scooting back on her butt as she did. Arnie didn't blame her, mind.

More shots rang out, followed by the distinctive *spung* of a Garand going empty, followed quicker than Arnie expected by the zipperlike sound of another stripper clip's worth of cartridges going in.

The harsh smell of gunpowder mixed with the reek of the wolves fouling themselves, but Arnie Selmo laughed. Son of a bitch, the old guy was better than Arnie had expected.

"*Reload*," Orphie shouted, still hidden in his own blind. "I've got it."

Arnie thought about it. He still ought to have four shots left, but there was no point in not reloading. While Arnie was fumbling with the catch of the ammo bag, three more wolves emerged from the hole.

Orphie got two of them; Arnie barely got the BAR back in action in time to nail one.

It seemed quiet in the clearing, as Arnie made his way toward where the wolf-bodies lay, the BAR cradled in his arms, his finger off the trigger.

Pretty beasts, now that they were dead, although . . .

He pointed his chin at the largest of them, one that had only a single wound in its side.

Orphie, now risen to his full height in the waist-high brush, nodded and raised his Garand to his shoulder, firing once, rewarded by the loud report of the Garand and a small gout of flesh and blood from the wolf's side. It was dead.

Maybe they all were dead, and maybe they were all there were.

And maybe not.

Arnie Selmo kept the muzzle pointed high, but he kept his finger near the trigger of the BAR as he stepped between the places where the two dirty women and one dirty man lay on the ground, panting. "I've got it, Orphie," he said. "You might want to get these folks some water, and then some food. Sandwiches still in the cooler."

He didn't look at them as he spoke; he kept his eyes on the hole in the ground. Just in case.

Thorsen grunted out something, probably a thank you.

"Welcome home, neighbor," Arnie Selmo said.

Author's Note

Anybody with a decent road atlas can follow the directions in Chapter One and find that I've placed the fictional town of Hardwood, North Dakota, pretty much squarely on top of the very real town of Northwood, North Dakota, where I lived for several years, some thirty years ago, when my father was one of the two town doctors. In fact, I shuffled the town around some to put the fictional Thorsen house very near to where my boyhood friend Jeff Thompson's house was.

Anybody with a Northwood phone book, or any phone book from that part of North Dakota, will discover many people with names like Selmo and Bjerke and Thompson and Larsen and such. Those names are common in that part of the world; any similarities between the Selmos and Bjerkes and Thompsons and Larsens and so forth of any real towns in North Dakota (or anywhere else) and those of my fictional town are entirely coincidental and unintentional—with the exception of the late John Honistead, the retired town cop of fictional Hardwood, who actually was a handyman in Northwood and was, to the best of my memory, the first friend of mine who ever died.

I figure old John wouldn't mind.